PRAISE FOR *THESE TOXIC THINGS*

"Rachel Howzell Hall continues to shatter the boundaries of crime fiction through the sheer force of her indomitable talent. *These Toxic Things* is a master class in tension and suspense. You think you are ready for it. But. You. Are. Not."

—S. A. Cosby, author of *Blacktop Wasteland*

"*These Toxic Things* is taut and terrifying, packed with page-turning suspense and breathtaking reveals. But what I loved most is the mother-daughter relationship at the heart of this gripping thriller. Plan on reading it twice: once because you won't be able to stop, and the second time to savor the razor's edge balance of plot and poetry that only Rachel Howzell Hall can pull off."

—Jess Lourey, Amazon Charts bestselling author of *Unspeakable Things*

"The brilliant Rachel Howzell Hall becomes the queen of mind games with this twisty and thought-provoking cat-and-mouse thriller. Where memories are weaponized, keepsakes are deadly, and the past gets ugly when you disturb it. As original, compelling, and sinister as a story can be, with a message that will haunt you long after you race through the pages."

—Hank Phillippi Ryan, *USA Today* bestselling author of *Her Perfect Life*

PRAISE FOR *AND NOW SHE'S GONE*

"It's a feat to keep high humor and crushing sorrow in plausible equilibrium in a mystery novel, and few writers are as adept at it as Rachel Howzell Hall."

—*Washington Post*

"One of the best books of the year . . . whip-smart and emotionally deep, *And Now She's Gone* is a deceptively straightforward mystery, blending a fledgling PI's first 'woman is missing' case with underlying stories about racial identity, domestic abuse, and rank evil."

—*Los Angeles Times*

"Smart, razor-sharp . . . Full of wry, dark humor, this nuanced tale of two extraordinary women is un-put-downable."

—*Publishers Weekly* (starred review)

"Smart, packed with dialogue that sings on the page, Hall's novel turns the tables on our expectations at every turn, bringing us closer to truth than if it were forced on us in school."

—Walter Mosley

"A fierce PI running from her own dark past chases a missing woman around buzzy LA. Breathlessly suspenseful, as glamorous as the city itself, *And Now She's Gone* should be at the top of your must-read list."

—Michele Campbell, bestselling author of *A Stranger on the Beach*

"One of crime fiction's leading writers at her very best. The final twist will make you want to immediately turn back to page one and read it all over again. *And Now She's Gone* is a perfect blend of PI novel and psychological suspense that will have readers wanting more."

—Kellye Garrett, Anthony, Agatha, and Lefty Award–winning author of *Hollywood Homicide* and *Hollywood Ending*

"Sharp, witty, and perfectly paced, *And Now She's Gone* is one hell of a read!"

—Wendy Walker, bestselling author of *The Night Before*

"Hall once again proves to be an accomplished maestro who has composed a symphony of increasing tension and near-unbearable suspense. Rachel brilliantly reveals the bone and soul of our shared humanity and the struggle to contain the nightmares of human faults and failings. I am a fan, pure and simple."

—Stephen Mack Jones, award-winning author of the August Snow thrillers

"Heartfelt and gripping . . . I'm a perennial member of the Rachel Howzell Hall fan club, and her latest is a winning display of her wit and compassion and mastery of suspense."

—Steph Cha, award-winning author of *Your House Will Pay*

"An entertainingly twisty plot, a rich and layered sense of place, and most of all a main character who pops off the page. Gray Sykes is hugely engaging and deeply complex, a descendant of Philip Marlowe and Easy Rawlings who is also definitely, absolutely her own woman."

—Lou Berney, award-winning author of *November Road*

"A deeply human protagonist, an intricate and twisty plot, and sentences that make me swoon with jealousy . . . Rachel Howzell Hall will flip every expectation you have—this is a magic trick of a book."

—Rob Hart, author of *The Warehouse*

"*And Now She's Gone* has all the mystery of a classic whodunnit, with an undeniably fresh and clever voice. Hall exemplifies the best of the modern PI novel."

—Alafair Burke, *New York Times* bestselling author

PRAISE FOR RACHELL HOWZELL HALL

"A fresh voice in crime fiction."

—Lee Child

"Devilishly clever . . . Hall's writing sizzles and pops."

—Meg Gardiner

"Hall slips from funny to darkly frightening with elegant ease."

—*Publishers Weekly*

PRAISE FOR *THEY ALL FALL DOWN*

"A riotous and wild ride."

—Attica Locke

"Dramatic, thrilling, and even compulsive."

—James Patterson

"An intense, feverish novel with riveting plot twists."

—Sara Paretsky

"Hall is beyond able and ready to take her place among the ranks of contemporary crime fiction's best and brightest."

—*Strand Magazine*

THESE TOXIC THINGS

ALSO BY
RACHEL HOWZELL HALL

And Now She's Gone
They All Fall Down
City of Saviors
Trail of Echoes
Skies of Ash
Land of Shadows

THESE
TOXIC
THINGS

RACHEL
HOWZELL HALL

THOMAS & MERCER

Text copyright © 2021 by Rachel Howzell Hall
All rights reserved.

Published by Thomas & Mercer, Seattle

www.apub.com

Amazon, the Amazon logo, and Thomas & Mercer are trademarks of Amazon.com, Inc., or its affiliates.

ISBN-13: 9781542027472 (hardcover)
ISBN-10: 1542027470 (hardcover)

ISBN-13: 9781542027496 (paperback)
ISBN-10: 1542027497 (paperback)

Cover design by Anna Laytham

Interior illustrations by M.S. Corley

Printed in the United States of America

First edition

To Maya the Beautiful

Every sweet hath its sour; every evil its good.

—*Ralph Waldo Emerson*

OUTLOOK GOOD

Tuesday, November 19
A Place for Children
Simi Valley, CA
10:43 p.m.

At that time of night, there was peace. No burbles from the water cooler. No ringing telephones or whooshing copiers. Just her hands scratching against paper envelopes. Just her sweet soprano harmonizing with Ariana Grande's.

At twenty-three years old, and the most junior on the team, Allison Cagle stuffed envelopes as part of her job. Didn't matter that she didn't have a car. Didn't matter that Jessica, her work best friend and regular ride home, had just called three minutes ago—little Conner had a fever and Jessica needed to drive him to the emergency room. (*Watch your back! Don't wanna stress out over you two!*) Didn't matter that Allison had no idea how the hell she was getting home now. None of that mattered because the annual awards luncheon was tomorrow afternoon and three hundred envelopes—containing drink tickets, table numbers, and for fifty VIPs, parking validations—needed stuffing.

With smoky-blue eyes and a sleek SoulCycle body, Allison hadn't anticipated this much office work. Filing, collating, and stuffing killed her manicure. She preferred driving around Ventura and Los Angeles Counties, picking up in-kind donations from stores and bakeries. The Lakers, once. She'd expected more wooing donors and taking minutes at important meetings as she brushed blonde tendrils from her heart-shaped face. Flirty work, all in the name of charity and for kids caught between the foster care system and juvenile detention.

"Not stuffing fucking envelopes alone in a building at ten o'clock at night," she muttered as she pulled a can of pepper spray from her purse and slipped on her raincoat.

Busy in the afternoons, Cochran Street was now clear of all traffic. Streetlamps threw weak light on wet roads, wet sidewalks, and the leaves of the magnolia trees. Rain—the annoying, gnat-like kind—swirled around her. Way out here in Simi Valley, forty-one miles north of Los Angeles, the brush fires had nearly burned down the Ronald Reagan Presidential Library. The flames had leveled too much brush, and now the streets chugged with mud.

Allison tapped the Uber app on her phone.

One car on the map. Ten minutes away.

She tapped "Confirm," then turned back toward the sherbet-colored building.

A car horn tooted. The headlights of a gray Prius sped toward the curbside. The passenger-side window rolled down, and the driver shouted, "Are you Allie?"

This wasn't the red Toyota Camry that was supposed to pick her up.

Gripping the can of pepper spray hidden in her pocket, Allison bent to peer into the car. "Do I know you?"

There was a US Army Special Forces patch on the front of the driver's black mesh baseball cap. "Jess feels awful for flaking on you."

Muscles tense, Allison blinked at the driver. In the rain, standing this far away, she couldn't see the person clearly. Fair skin, the cap, and Elvis Costello eyeglass frames. Not the stereotypical Green Beret, with a square jaw and steely eyes.

Allison said, "Umm . . ."

The driver tapped their head, all *Silly me*. "Sorry. I'm Dale, Jessica's cousin. She asked me to come pick you up since I live in this direction. It's about to pour buckets, and she didn't want you standing out here alone, waiting for a car."

Allison remembered that Jessica's cousin—*Dale?*—had been a decorated ranger. Smart. Christian. A hero. "She told me about you," Allison said now. "Welcome home."

Jellybean-size raindrops exploded from the sky. In the roar of rain, another car horn blared, this one from a white Ford F-150 driving from the opposite direction. Skinheads. Jessica had warned her. *Watch your back!*

The Ford slowed as the driver eyed her.

Allison had suffered through previous run-ins with stupid rednecks. At the mall, she'd made the mistake of wearing a Rihanna T-shirt, and those freaking white-trash losers had followed her to the Uber stop, lobbing "nigger lover" at her head. Sucked 'cause she didn't even *listen* to Rihanna—the T-shirt had just looked so freaking cool at Urban Outfitters. Anyway, seeing a truck filled with loser-dudes probably high on meth on a stormy night made everything inside her diarrhea-loose.

"You getting in or . . . ? I mean, you can wait for your Uber," Dale said, shrugging.

The Ford U-turned and headed back their way.

Dale watched the truck's reflection in the rearview mirror. "Friends of yours?"

Allison said, "Hell no."

"Then you need to make a decision. I'm not interested in meeting those guys. Are you?"

And so Allison decided.

It was warm in the Prius, and it smelled like cinnamon buns and coffee.

"You don't mind dropping me?" Allison asked. "An Uber's four minutes away."

"Of course not. Cancel it." As the Prius pulled away from the curb, Dale's eyes flitted from the slippery road to the reflection of the Ford in the rearview mirror. "These assholes."

The Ford's horn honked again, and the truck sped up until its chrome grille was just a kiss from the hybrid's rear bumper.

Dale swerved to the right.

Allison's heart jolted in her chest, and she closed her eyes and grabbed the door handle.

The Ford veered around the Prius.

Splat!

Yellow egg yolk mixed with the rain and slid down the Toyota's windshield.

The truck sped east into the night.

Knuckles tight around the steering wheel, Dale exhaled. "I wanna say that I can't believe those guys, but that wouldn't be true."

"Ha. Right?" Allison said.

Dale increased the windshield wipers' speed to clean the egg off the glass.

Her lungs flexible again, Allison took a deep breath, then found her phone in her purse. She opened her Messages app and texted Jessica.

TY for sending your cuz!

Right on time!

Rain & skinheads.

"How long have you worked with Jess?" Dale asked.

"About six months." Now, in the car's quiet—and with her pulse no longer thundering in her ears—Allison could focus. She tried to

6

remember any conversation she'd had with Jessica about her cousin coming home. *Sale at Topshop . . . the best acai bowl in the Valley . . .* Ah! Dale was . . . was . . . *shit.*

"You're welcome," Dale said.

Allison started to say, "For what?" but sensed that would be the wrong word choice. Instead, she said, "Yes—thanks so much for picking me up. You came in the nick of time."

"You shouldn't rely on other people to take you places. Because when you do, dangerous situations like this happen."

"You're totally right. I'm saving up for a car—" She cocked her head—Allison hadn't told Dale her address, and yet they were now close to the Sage Creek Apartments off Yosemite Avenue. "You know where I live?"

An ice pick of fear drove through her head.

Dale tossed her a smile. "Jess told me—that's how she knew that I could take you home. I live about a mile west of you, on Christine Avenue."

"Ah. Makes sense." Her insides burned. Good intentions or not, Allison didn't appreciate Jessica sharing her personal information with a stranger, courageous war heroes included.

Dale must've sensed her anger. "Forgive Jess—she just wanted to help."

Allison's phone vibrated.

A simple message from Jessica.

??

"You and I met once," Dale said.

Really? When? Allison typed back.

Dale picking me up

Ellipses bubbled on the phone's screen.

"The carnival at Mayfair Park last month," Dale said. "You worked at one of the donation tables."

According to Jessica, their boss had stationed Allison at the annual-giving table because she was pretty. Men gave more if pretty women asked them. And now, Allison could almost remember seeing Dale wearing the Rangers baseball cap and the glasses . . .

"Do you remember me?" Dale asked. "You told me to smile, that I was at a carnival and needed to relax."

"To be honest? No. That was a busy—"

Allison's phone buzzed. As she read Jessica's response, the cloth seat beneath her warmed. Her bladder had released every liquid she'd drunk since dinnertime.

Desi is still in Iraq.

Skyped w/her yesterday

WHO R U IN THE CAR WITH??

With a shaky hand, Allison brushed her nose, touching the emerald stud in her left nostril. Her sister Lauren had boosted the gem from one of those cart vendors in the Galleria. Emeralds were her birthstone, and this stud was the most expensive, precious thing she owned.

And now, she had another decision to make.

Pull the can of pepper spray from her coat pocket or text Jessica for help.

Can't do both.

Fingers numb, she tapped HEL—

Dale grabbed the phone and tossed it out the driver's-side window.

"Relax, Allie. Better me than the skinheads, right?"

1.

I give him a woman's smile, the smile that has beheaded more important men than the one seated across from me at this high-gloss conference table. "Old lover" amalgamated with "bemused friend" brewed with "scorned woman." A cyanide smile.

I'm only twenty-four years old and I've already perfected this smile. As the only child of Coretta and Orson Lambert, I've watched my mother closely, learning her ways and parroting them earlier than most daughters mimic their mothers. She taught me this smile just like she taught me how to moisturize to keep my chestnut skin supple and how to clean up after myself. And she also taught me how to spot slights like this . . .

Interesting that Chris and I aren't meeting in his corner office. Interesting that he chose *this* conference room with its three glass walls. *I have to be transparent, baby. That's why . . .*

I move my shaky hands off that table, and ghosts of my damp fingers shimmer on the surface and then disappear. Like I was never here. My underarms prickle, and the hot air of anger and embarrassment warms my upper lip.

"Mickie . . . so does that mean . . . ?" Christopher Fenton—a golden boy with his symmetrical face and vintage Vans hoodie and black specs that don't enlarge one goddamned thing—smiles at me from across the table. It is a man's smile, the smile that unwinds across a man's face before he's maimed by a woman's razor-sharp nails and knife-edged words. He (unsuccessfully) sneaks a peek at the digital clock on the conference room wall, then says, "You get the gist? The scope of this one? Please let me know if I'm not being clear or . . ."

If I were a stronger, braver woman, his time of death would be 2:33.

In six weeks, I will include this resolution—to become stronger and braver—on my list.

Right now, though . . .

I underline the address I'd written in my binder.

111 Marlton Road

I tap the name beside the address—*Nadia*—and say, "I get the gist *and* the scope. And you're being absolutely clear. No problem."

Christopher's gaze makes me melt, and so I look out the large-paned window at his back.

Crows flock against the blues and oranges of the dying Los Angeles daylight. They're searching for their last meal of worms, flies, take-out Mexican food, and anything else Southern California crows eat.

"You just seem . . ." Chris pulls both strings of his hoodie. "*Muted. You're usually . . . bubbly.* Do you need time to think about it? I want you to be comfortable . . ."

"*Oh?*" I offer him another cyanide smile. "I'm as comfortable as I can be." I sit on my weak left hand and use my right hand to scribble *Start.* "When do I begin?"

He folds his hands before him on the table. "She—as in our client, Nadia Denham—said to come in tomorrow morning around eleven. But you can drive by her shop before then to get a sense of things. You know, the prep work before the prep work. She's old, which means she'll have a lot to say, and you listen well, and I'm *still* amazed at the bank you created for the 102-year-old Avery twins, who couldn't stop talking . . ."

I write *Nov. 21* next to *Start* as tears burn my eyes. I will them away by remembering that I could have any man I want, that I deserve a love greater than Chris Fenton's, that he's talking to me like I'm just another employee of the Memory Bank, and ohmigod, how jacked up is *that*. Thinking about these things pisses me off, and I close my binder with a pop.

Chris grabs his cell phone, the one I found after he'd lost it in a bin of apples at the grocery store. "Ms. Denham paid for the Mega-Memory Package."

"Awesome." I blow my bangs from my eyes and push away from the table.

Five thousand dollars for a specially curated, next-generation digital scrapbook that will recall those special places she's visited as well as souvenirs, pictures, and objets d'art that she's acquired. As a digital archaeologist, I transform a client's memories into Memories™. Pictures, letters—all scanned, photographed, captioned, and narrated—then uploaded into a voice-controlled box with an eight-inch screen and speakers.

A client request: *Memory Bank, tell me about Great-Great-Great-Grandmother's voyage to America.* I would've already composed that memory, and my colleague Willow—whose smoky British voice would make the technical-specs manual to build a toilet sound absolutely enthralling—would've voiced my narrative of Nana's immigration to the States.

But the feature that makes me twirl? Augmented reality. There's a small projector atop the bank device that casts a hologram, similar to the stars-and-moon projector in a kid's room but three-dimensional. *And!* With my hands over the bank's sensors, I can turn the projection this way and that. Pinch my fingers to zoom in and spread both hands to zoom out. *And!* You can email a picture of the artifact by simply asking. *Hey, Memory Bank, send the picture of the butterfly hand mirror to Aunt Shelby.*

We're now testing my idea: ROAD TRIP! GPS coordinates are attached to each item, and the ROAD TRIP! app directs you to the artifacts' origins. Visit Nana's homestead in Mobile, where she wore those curated baby shoes, then drive over to the jewelry store where Pop-Pop purchased her curated engagement ring. At each destination, ROAD TRIP! superimposes those shoes and that ring over the real-world location—the house, the jeweler's—similar to the cat ears over your picture in Snapchat or the first-down line on televised football games.

Christopher never thought my ideas, including ROAD TRIP!, were stupid or outlandish. "Let's go for it!"—that's what he's always said. A good listener and a great motivator: two qualities I loved about him.

"Mickie, are we okay?" Christopher asks now as he points from his chest to mine. "I know—me asking that question is like a lumberjack who just cut down a tree."

His words are fog.

I squint at him. "Chris, how am I supposed to feel right now?"

He blinks at me, then slaps his forehead as his skin creaks into a flush. "Crap. You didn't think I asked you to come in today to . . . ?"

Apologize for being an asshole?

Take back wanting to break up with you?

Say, "I'm stupid. I should've chosen you over The People, but now I do; I choose you."

Yes. I'd thought he'd asked me to come in today to say all those things. I'd even composed a memory about our reconciliation—*you realized just how much you loved me*—and had planned to upload this thought into my bank along with a picture of his make-up gift. That's not gonna happen.

Imani was right—I *am* simple for a Black girl. *Make it make sense,* she told me last night right before the male strippers hit the stage at the Right Track. We were front row during this, the second of two bachelorette parties for our friend Sasha. *Chris is living his best life and you're sittin' here, waiting for him like a left-behind ratty sock at a ghetto laundromat,* Imani said. *Abandon the sunken place, Mickie,* she added before giving me a roll of twenty-dollar bills to stuff into Chocolate Romeo's G-string.

"I'm *so* sorry." Chris now holds his hands prayer-style at his lips. "We just hadn't seen each other since . . . since you moved out, and it's not . . . it's not like we're *totally* broken up." He pauses. "Are we?"

I cock an eyebrow. "I don't know, Christopher. It's been a month. *Are* we?"

His Adam's apple bobs in his throat.

I want to cut it out—then nurse him back to health.

I am conflicted.

Christopher aims those blue eyes at me, and says, "We'll figure it out, okay?" He holds out his right pinkie for me to shake.

I hook my pinkie around his. Then he tosses a wave to Marti, his administrative assistant, who's standing on the other side of the glass wall, now motioning to her watch. He gives her a "one moment" finger, then grabs a bottled vanilla latte from the credenza for me and a cranberry Snapple for him. "You start on your mom's bank yet? The big five-oh next year, right?"

I nod, enthusiastic now. "May thirteenth, yeah. And I'm gonna add ROAD TRIP!, too. So all around LA, up to UC Santa Cruz, then New Mexico . . . I've uploaded a bunch of her baby and elementary-school pictures, pictures with her sister, Angela—"

"Is she the one who was killed?"

"Yeah. I took pictures of the hospital where Mom was born. Took pictures of the flute she played in high school. I found a teacher who wrote one of her college recommendations—"

"You're including *people* in her bank?"

"Angie is important. She's a big part of Mom's past."

"I mean . . . like . . . *other* people."

"I know we're not supposed to, but Mrs. Anderson was the one who—"

"But what if there's something about Mrs. Anderson that—"

"I know, but—"

"And your mom sees her and remembers that Mrs. Anderson, that bitch—"

"But what if my mother absolutely melts in a *good* way and—"

"Fine." He smiles, but the nerves above his eyebrows twitch. "Let me know if you need anything or wanna try something new, okay?"

He opens the door, and the clamor of the open-space work environment floods over us. Memory-making is loud work, from clicking keyboards and the digital voice read-back of recorded remembrances to the chatter of writers, programmers, and graphic artists talking about the last seasons of *The Walking Dead* or the next iteration of *Star Wars*.

Chris, the executive vice president in charge of content development, cofounded Memory Bank with his best friend, Orin, and invested thousands into the venture. I joined the company in August after leaving my job as a junior editor at Bowen & Miller LLP. The decision may have seemed impulsive to my parents, but deciding to quit had been simple: work at an exciting new tech firm as a digital archaeologist alongside the man I'd fallen hard for *or* remain junior editor of corporate communications at my father's accounting firm.

Not a lot of "hmm" went into my decision.

And they didn't know what impulsive meant until I moved in with a guy I'd dated for three months.

Umbrella up, I dash through the parking lot, but wind and rain slow my steps. The scent of tar—from last-minute street repairs on Wilshire Boulevard, from the million-year-old La Brea Tar Pits across the street—lingers on wet air. The building that houses the Memory

Bank hides behind the curtain of this late-fall storm. For a moment, I've lost my way.

I can barely see the world around me.

Eventually, I make it to level P4, and I lunge into the driver's seat of my "legacy" car. Mom's ancient Mercedes-Benz, another high-end hand-me-down, is quiet. Clean, too.

"It *was* the right choice," I say aloud. "It *was*. It *is*." Corporate communications didn't excite me. Memory-making and storytelling do—I majored in narrative studies at USC. Creating content, shaping stories, learning how a story shapes popular culture? It's like they created that major just for me.

"And Chris and I *will* figure it out," I tell my best friend, Sasha, over the phone as I back out of my parking space. "He still loves me. He just said it. Kind of. We pinkie-shook on it."

Sasha grunts and her fingernails click against a keyboard as we talk.

"Am I on speaker?"

More clicking and keyboard tapping.

I swipe at a teardrop rolling down my cheek. "I actually picked up the phone, tapped your number, and *called* you, but you're not listening to me. I'll let you go."

"Just got last-minute contract changes for this Black College Expo event." *Tap-tap-tap.* "Anyway, you shoulda hooked up with Chocolate Romeo." *Click-click-click.*

"Ew. Then I'd be smelling like Drakkar Noir and regret right now." *Tap-tap-tap.* "As opposed to . . ."

I snorted. "Tom Ford and regret."

At Chris's request (*his!*), I had moved out of my cottage (okay, apartment over a garage) behind my parents' house in Baldwin Vista to his twelfth-floor condo on Miracle Mile ten miles away.

Mom and Dad don't like Chris.

"Because you're not a priority to him," Dad told me.

"Because in a relationship," Mom said, taking the scenic route, "there can only be one flower and one gardener. You, Michaela Lambert, are the flower. Not *that* fucker."

Fortunately, I can work remotely, and since our breakup I've taken advantage of this option, curling up in my parents' well-lit breakfast nook to write. I stay away not only to avoid seeing Chris but also to avoid looks from coworkers who knew Chris and I were together. They saw me wear the sweater he'd worn to work two days before. They saw the flowers he'd have delivered to my office. I'd become accustomed to walking into a room filled with people who fell into sudden silence, their words still heavy gas against the ceiling.

"You can always quit," Mom suggested.

Yeah. I could. Maybe I'll quit after this last client. Maybe I'll start my own firm. That's something to consider. For now, though, I have a client to think about.

Nadia Denham. An elegant name that evokes lovers and dances, spiced teas in fragile cups, and secrets, lots of secrets.

Old ladies keep the best secrets.

How many secrets should a woman keep to be thought of as interesting?

I'm an only child with loving and attentive parents. I attended all-girl schools and grew up in a *benevolent dictatorship*. I voiced my opinions on dinner, vacations, study time, and wardrobe—and my opinions had weight in my family. Living with Chris for two months had been the only time I'd lived away from Mom and Dad. There aren't many areas of my life that they don't know about, and I've willingly shared more than the average amount with my mother.

That means I'm a late-blooming secret keeper.

The number of men I've slept with—that's a secret, although that number is too low to be provocative. Although . . . one of those men had been married. Not that he'd *worn* his wedding band. I just happened to notice the tan line around his ring finger and then confronted him.

Another secret: I deleted text messages on Imani's phone from her toxic ex-girlfriend after their breakup because I didn't want them to reconcile. Imani was passed out on my couch, her ex kept texting, Imani's phone was right there, and her thumb was *right there*, too, and one thing had led to another.

I crashed my father's Audi into a trash truck but told him that the truck had backed into me. That's a secret. And a lie.

But will these secrets shock my future grandchildren? Will they gasp? Will their eyes bulge? Will they say, "Nana, you were such a slut / liar / agent of chaos"?

I wonder about this as I drive. Every now and then, I pass a landmark designated as important to my clients. I turtle past the cream-colored Bryson Apartments. Sure, the Bryson may have been featured in Raymond Chandler's *The Lady in the Lake*, but Mrs. Pulaski stored her curated cigarette-girl uniform there in a closet inside her eighth-floor apartment.

The storm has passed, and the city glints, clean and slick from rainwater and the teardrops of a million motorists. My heart hurts less. Sitting in LA traffic in the rain allows enough time for most things to heal.

Minutes before five o'clock, I reach 111 Marlton Road, home to Beautiful Things. A block west of Crenshaw Boulevard, my client is located somewhere within the Santa Barbara Plaza. According to the big sign at the driveway entrance, this dying parcel of land will be resurrected and transformed by the Weller Group.

Almost thirty years have passed since the 1992 uprisings, and developers point to the new Kaiser Permanente medical offices as the plaza's most successful improvement. But the rest of the mostly empty parking lot grows weeds. A few beat-up campers line the lot's edges. There's a shuttered nightclub that catered to the over-fifty crowd (Link's Lounge), a coffee shop (Anna's Place), a locksmith (Kim's Keys), and a hair salon (Sistas Scissors Styling Salon). The Baldwin Hills Mall—the first shopping mall built in the United States—sits across the street. It, too, is rumored to be about to undergo another makeover.

During my mother's childhood here, the plaza bustled with grocery stores, fish markets, and small Black-owned businesses that did your taxes, developed your film, and repaired your vacuum cleaner. She and her little sister, Angie, slurped Icees at Newberry's, gobbled grilled cheese sandwiches at Woolworth's, and chomped salted cashews and Rocky Road from the basement candy store in Broadway department store.

The plaza will be a stop on Mom's ROAD TRIP! I'll have to find a new spot to eat grilled cheese sandwiches, though, since those dime stores no longer exist.

My relationship with this plaza is less sentimental. After college graduation, I bought a television from Sears over there. Every few months, I guzzle margaritas on Taco Tuesdays at Mexicano right there. I buy things from a few boutiques anytime I'm close. Whatever.

Actively driven cars also sit in this damn-near-abandoned place, and so I pull into a space with no cars around. I've scraped other vehicles since that crash into the trash truck.

An old redheaded white woman wearing oversize BluBlockers, a blue fedora, and a matching blue trench coat shuffles away from Beautiful Things.

My phone chimes with a text from Mom. Home tonight?

I type YES.

At last night's bachelorette party, I spent almost $200 on that chocolate-box assortment of banana-thonged strippers. Imani—out $500—invited a stripper named Tiger into our hired Suburban, and the temporary couple insisted that we stop for chicken and waffles. I didn't eat because I stayed in the parking lot to pat Sasha's back while she vomited tequila sunrises and strip-club hot wings into a Target bag.

Tonight, I want to stay home. I want to hang out with my parents. I want to watch *Wheel of Fortune*. I want to leave my phone in my apartment and disengage from other millennials. I want to fall asleep on Mom's shoulder. Have Dad slip a blanket over me on the couch as I snooze.

The air smells of movie popcorn and greasy Mexican food—there's a movie theater and Taco Bell across the street. My stomach bubbles and creaks. I've forgotten to eat again.

"A few pictures." I pull my hair into a ponytail. A sketch or two and then I'm out.

Gravel crunches beneath my heeled boots. I purposely selected Mom's designer shoes and her red wool skirt along with my low-cut faux-cashmere sweater to wear to my meeting with Chris. I also liberated one of Mom's lesser-used Givenchy satchels to carry my stuff. I'd done all this to look good and together and *not* broken.

I open my book and sketch the ornate gold scrolls and flecked gold letters on the store's vintage wood-and-slate sandwich-board sign.

Heavy cranberry-colored curtains block views into the emporium.

What type of person owns a shop like this?

Someone fascinated with stuffed parakeets and Three Stooges salt and pepper shakers?

One of my clients collected David Hasselhoff memorabilia. Another client collected the teeth of her six snaggle-toothed children.

Were there baby teeth and Hasselhoff-branded extension cords in Beautiful Things?

I will save that adventure for tomorrow.

Back to the car I go.

"Hey!"

A scowling sixtyish Black woman with a short, curly Afro and bright-coral lipstick is stomping toward me. She holds a gigantic Styrofoam cup in one hand, and a giant purse hangs from her free arm.

Is this Nadia?

The woman launches the cup at me. It's filled with soda and bangs off my hip and splashes my clothes, neck, face, and feet.

I shriek, "What the—"

"We're sick of y'all coming 'round here," the woman snarls, pointing at me. "Tell that son of a bitch Weller—"

"Who?" I glare at her, then at Mom's now-sticky boots and sopping wool skirt.

"Your boss," the woman spits. "We ain't selling, so stop taking pictures—"

"I don't work for Weller, you shriveled *bitch*."

"Don't lie to me, girl. I'm too old for this."

"I don't know *who* you are, and I could give a damn about what you're too old for." I shove my hand into my bag for a tissue. My anger fizzes like the soda puddles at my feet.

She crosses her arms. "Then what do you want if you ain't working for Weller?"

"I'm working on a project for Nadia Denham over at—" Frustration flares in my gut. "The *hell* is wrong with you?"

"Answer my question."

"I *told* you. I'm working with Nadia Denham."

Her mouth hangs open, and her eyes peck at my wet . . . everything. "Weller's been sending people over here to threaten us and—"

"Who? *What?*" My eyes fill with hot tears.

Wobbly-lipped, the woman digs into her own purse. "Child, I am *so* sorry." She finds napkins and dabs them at my hips, at my neck . . . Her hands are everywhere.

My patience rips and I swat at her hands. "Stop. I got it. I got—"

She offers me the damp napkins, then holds her cheek. "I don't know what's gotten into me." She takes a deep breath in and slowly exhales. "I'm Anna, and that's my diner right over there." She points at the coffee shop next to Beautiful Things. "Let me make it right, okay? How about lunch and breakfast on the house anytime you're over here?"

The napkins leave lint on the skirt, and I'll be sticky until I shower. And being mad at somebody's ratchet grandma won't change any of this. "Sure," I say. "I'll be around for a couple of weeks anyway. I'm Mickie."

Her eyebrows knit.

"Short for Michaela."

A smile breaks over Anna's face, and her small gold hoop earrings wink with parking-lot lights. "What's this thing you're doing for Nadia?"

I've brushed off embers of anger, but panic is taking its place. Mom will be pissed that I messed up yet another pair of her shoes (wet paint the last time) and her skirt (permanent marker the last time) and her butter-soft leather satchel (exploded containers of Greek yogurt, twice).

But the soda-thrower is waiting to hear my story. So I tell Anna about the Memory Bank and that I'm making one for my mother's fiftieth birthday. With my phone, I show her pictures of the device and video of the Icee hologram that will go in Mom's bank. "Cool, huh?"

Anna tries to smile, but her expression says, *This is witchcraft and sorcery!*

I still offer her a business card and tell her that memory banks make great gifts and that I may be starting my own company and would love to do one for her. I nod back at Beautiful Things. "Looks like Nadia's a collector."

Anna clicks her tongue. "I love her, but that store is *weird*. She sells a few regular things, like postcards and keychains, but most of that stuff is strange stuff. Like earthworms in frames and bats in gold cages. And Nadia—she's weird, too. One of them artsy-fartsy types. Doesn't talk much to anybody if she ain't in her shop."

"Is it just her working there?"

Anna stoops to swipe at lint on my skirt. "Riley, she's the manager. I call her 'Little Boss Lady' because she takes over when Nadia needs her to. And that's been a lot lately because Nadia's getting up there."

The woman taps at her earring. "She got a best friend, though. I think her name is Esther. I see her a few times a month. She makes sure that Nadia has groceries, fresh flowers, and company. Nadia ain't alone, and that makes me feel better. Nothing worse than being by yourself when you can't remember your life." Anna plucks the now-empty soda cup from the gravel. "You like peach cobbler?"

Joy dances on my taste buds, and I smile for the first time today. "I *love* peach cobbler."

Anna taps my wrist. "I'll make one special just for you. Really, I'm so sorry for my actions. Them Weller assholes—they're driving me crazy."

I've read newspaper articles about backroom meetings between developers and city officials. Those breathless accounts revealed politicians ignoring zoning regulations and engaging in pay-to-play shenanigans. Breaking the law to win contracts for a thirty-story condo tower that would ultimately gut this plaza and people's houses.

"I hear they wanna make this area New Las Vegas," I say.

Anna's face darkens. "They told us to either upgrade our businesses or be prepared to be bought out. But has anybody given us any money to upgrade?"

"Of course not," I say. "So you thought I was taking pictures for comps and all that."

"Yep. Me and Mr. Kim, the locksmith? We been here since '77. Nadia been here since '80. We survived the riots and the recession, and now some white man is trying to take what's ours? What we fought to keep? That's not right."

"It's not," I say. "Keep fighting. Miracles happen." I toss a worried look at the sky as raindrops speckle car windshields.

"I gotta lock up," Anna says. "I only came out here to throw soda on you."

I claw at my sticky, itchy neck. "Check that off the list, then."

She tells me to pop in anytime—she cooks everything. Grits, bacon, grilled cheese sandwiches, and gumbo on Friday.

Ooh, gumbo!

Ooh, grilled cheese sandwiches! Anna's Place can replace Woolworth's.

After I promise to stop by, Anna shuffles back to the diner. I walk back to my car. My feet stick to the boots' uppers and I smell like Dr Pepper.

An old wood-paneled station wagon rumbles into the lot. The old woman wearing the BluBlockers, fedora, and trench coat climbs out of the driver's seat. She carries a grocery bag in one hand and a bouquet of pink roses in the other. She stops in her step, then cants her head.

I don't move—it feels . . . *wrong* for me to be standing here. But standing here in this seedy parking lot with RVs and weeds is *not* wrong.

She hears something that I can't and snaps her head to the west. She waits . . . then she looks over to me and nods.

I nod, but I'm cold, and the longer I remain, the colder—and more scared—I become.

She keeps her gaze trained on me as I slip into the driver's seat.

Satisfied that I'm now tucked away, she tromps over to Beautiful Things. Soon, the store's downstairs lights turn off, and a moment later, the upstairs lights burn bright.

2.

The old woman in the fedora . . .

Was that Nadia's best friend?

Strange how she stared at me like that.

It is almost six o'clock as I drive up twisty Mantova Drive to our house. This high, I can see all Los Angeles, from the mountains to downtown. An expanse of open park sweeps behind my neighborhood, and it always feels like I'm somewhere else in the world. The nights are very dark up here. As a child, I was scared to live on the perimeters of Kenneth Hahn Park—monsters lurked in that wild land.

On one trail a few years ago, joggers found a dead girl shoved inside a duffel bag. Last October, hikers found an altar of sacrificed chickens and dogs near the hummingbird garden.

As I drive up the road, a silver Ram truck rolls down toward me.

I open my window. "As I live and breathe."

Dad's big brother, Bryan, grins at me. His mischievous brown eyes shine. His face has slimmed in the last month—less fast food, less Los Angeles Police Department–branded stress. More whole grains, more CrossFit, and more free time during his half retirement. "You settled back in now?"

I make sad-puppy eyes. "My pride remains in one of those boxes I haven't unpacked yet."

He thumbs at the house. "They're happy you're home."

I poke out my bottom lip. "Will I ever find someone to love like you love Uncle Griffin?"

Uncle Bryan smirks. "And how long did *that* take?"

"Your line is: 'Mickie, love is just around the corner. He's looking for you just like you're looking for him.' Okay, now you try."

Unblinking, he says, "Mickie, love is like a corpse flower. It may take seven years for it to bloom, but then, when it does—"

"It stinks up your life?" I give him a raspberry. "Since you're here, I have another business proposal for you. Remember how we talked about helping families of victims heal?"

He sucks his teeth. "No one can afford those fancy scrapbooks—"

I hold up a finger. "First of all, they aren't fancy scrapbooks. They're augmented-reality, high-tech memory banks. And second, I considered what you told me the last time, and now I'm thinking about a contract with the *city* instead of approaching individual families."

"Look at you, taking a moment to analyze." He nods, thinking about it now. "Let me get back to you on that."

"This could be your key to full retirement," I say. "It's one-of-a-kind technology. We're partnering with travel companies to book trips to places mentioned in the banks. Like . . . *Memory Bank, what are the cheapest vacation packages to see the leaves change in Vermont?* Et voilà, you're gazing at maple leaves from the patio of a renovated-sawmill B and B."

"So more ways to spend money."

"More *meaningful* ways to spend money."

He laughs, then points at me. "You be careful. Folks are wildin' out lately."

I salute him. "There's Mace in my glove box. Give Uncle Griffin a kiss for me."

He rolls up the window and rolls down the hill to his house, just three minutes away.

Spilled-milk clouds race across the black sky. The white stucco of our two-story house is dark from the rain, and the chocolate-blond window- and doorframes look bloodred. Newspapers wrapped in plastic sit in the driveway. A ladder leans against the side of the house. Dad has vowed to put up Christmas lights earlier this year.

I ease into the driveway until I reach the garage, a.k.a. Mickie's mansion. I smell garlic and grilled meat. My stomach growls in anticipation of food and drink I haven't ordered through a speaker. Home cooking is the best and worst part of moving back. Fried potatoes. Macaroni and cheese. Marbled rib eyes. Cookies. Mom's wine. Dad's bourbon.

I am a decent chef, even if I forget to eat most times. My best culinary moments, though, in my kitchen—or Chris's kitchen—have never felt as warm as Coretta and Orson Lambert's kitchen. Could be the souvenir magnets from Puerto Rico, Hawaii, and all our vacation destinations on my parents' fridge. Could be the ream of my handwritten Christmas lists from the last fifteen years beneath the magnet of my tenth-grade high school picture.

Anyway, my parents' food and booze *almost* make up for their whispered conversations and forced smiles.

"*—who do you think . . . ?*"

"*—can't talk to you about this anymore . . .*"

"*—ruin everything . . .*"

"Maybe they're swingers," Sasha suggested once.

"Or Satanists," Chris had guessed. "Like in *Rosemary's Baby*, and you're the baby and therefore the daughter of the devil."

Maybe Chris and Sasha are onto something, because right now Mom, wine opener in hand, stands over Dad, who's seated in the breakfast nook. She's using big hand gestures and waving around a piece of paper as she speaks. He's nodding, then shaking his head. Meanwhile, flames dance beneath a skillet on the range top's front burner. A bottle of Bordeaux and two wineglasses sit on the counter, unattended.

27

The security system's sensor bings, and I let the service-porch door slam behind me.

Mom spins around and shouts, "Damn it, Mickie." She holds a hand over her heart.

"Oops. Sorry." I see myself in the near-fifty-year-old woman. The big brown eyes, the chipmunk cheeks, the judgy way her left eyebrow cocks even when she's not being judgy.

I kiss Dad's forehead. "Don't rob that bank and you won't be scared."

"Too late," he says. "Explosives are already on the vault door." He glances at Mom.

She folds the letter in half and turns back to the stove.

"If you're not robbing a bank," I say, "why are you whispering?" I pluck a wineglass from the cabinet and bring all the glasses and the bottle to the breakfast nook.

"We're not whispering," he says. "We're planning a vacation."

I snort. "That's a lie, but I'll allow it. Just saw Uncle Bryan. Everything okay?"

Dad peels off the bottle's foil and wedges the wine opener into the cork. "He's bored and wanted company. Griff is still seeing patients. Everybody has the flu this year."

"What's in the letter?" I ask.

Mom says, "Umm . . ." But that "umm" isn't about the letter. She's scrutinizing my feet, and that left eyebrow is as high as Saturn. "What the *hell*?" Eyes bulging, her gaze lifts to her skirt. "You fall into a land-fill?" The vein in her neck is seconds from rupturing. "Instead of busting off in my house, trying to mind *my* business, *you* need to—"

I hold up my hands. "Mom, let me explain. It really wasn't my fault this time." And I tell her about that diner owner's suspicion that I worked for a greedy big-city developer, and how awful the woman felt afterward, and how she planned to make it up to me.

Mom crosses her arms. "How is peach cobbler supposed to get my shit dry-cleaned?"

"Cori," Dad says, "I'll pay for the damn dry cleaning. Relax, dude."

He and I exchange looks once she surrenders and turns back to the brussels sprouts. He was just as chill after I spilled coffee on the French-cuffed dress shirt I'd plucked from his side of the closet. Dad said, "You looked better in it than I ever did," then told me to keep the shirt.

And now I mouth, "Thank you" to my father.

He nods and pulls the cork from the bottle. Unlike Mom, he doesn't let the wine breathe. He immediately pours rich-red French wine into three glasses. "You sitting down to eat with us, or you plan to nervous-hover like that all night?"

I take a few sips. "Eating with you, but I'm sticky, as you can see. Quick shower and I'll be right back."

"And after that," Mom says, "you can deactivate your account to my closet."

Never. I hug her because I've given her sticky hugs since forever. "I luh you."

She knocks on my forehead. "I luh you, too."

Rotting crab apples litter the grassy walkway that leads to my apartment above the garage. It's a smaller version of my parents' Spanish-style, offering more white stucco and brown wood frames. One bedroom, but I don't need more than that. Moving boxes and shopping bags crowd the carpet. Some are still taped shut in case Chris calls to say that he misses me and wants me to move back.

I thought today's call *was* that call. Since I was wrong, I will unpack another box. Guess that's my equivalent of pouring one out for things that no longer are. Sometimes, I empty more than one box, usually when I'm looking for a skirt or pair of shoes among the flotsam and jetsam of my shattered love affair.

Shattered love affair.

Sounds far more dramatic than how we ended.

I open my front door, and like the security system in the main house, the sensor alerts and says, "Front. Door." The system doesn't *beep-beep-beep*, though, since I didn't arm it before leaving this morning. I flip the light switch to illuminate the staircase that leads up to my living room. But my eyes are drawn to the foyer's tile floor. Someone slipped a piece of grimy yellow folded paper through the gap between the door and threshold. *Huh.* I pluck it from the ground and open the note:

YOUR SO PRETTY

Dad may sometimes have issues with "your" and "you're," but this handwriting—narrow, left-slanted—is not his. Did the gardener leave this earlier and I just noticed it? Possibly. Maybe our mailman?

I notice that my hands are shaking. I'm being watched without the pleasure of knowing who's watching me. In college, a stalker left notes on my car. After two weeks, he turned his attention to another girl. After she rebuffed him, he attacked her in a parking structure on campus.

A hum and a rumble make my pulse jump. I look up from the note.

The thermostat and hot-water heater. I'm used to them by now. I'm also used to the loose window screen in my bedroom rattling at this moment. But there's a new noise tonight. Barely there scratching. In the walls? On the roof? In my head?

On the bottom of the note, I scribble the date and time I found this message in my foyer, then slip it into my sketch pad. Just in case. I'll tell Mom and Dad, and we'll either fire the gardener or file a complaint with the postmaster. I will *not* be terrorized in my own home.

After showering, I pull on Dad's USC sweatshirt and a pair of his unworn boxer shorts. I pull my hair out of the ponytail holder, and the tension on my scalp ebbs.

Heart heavy, I wander to my living room television stand. There sits my own memory bank, dust collecting on its screen. I haven't asked for a memory in weeks.

I click off the floor lamp. "Memory bank, tell me about the road trip to Santa Barbara."

The screen brightens with a selfie of Christopher and me standing on the pier.

Willow's smoky voice fills the room: *It was a clear-sky day as you and Chris drove up the coast. Your first stop was the pier.*

The small projector atop the bank glows, and soon that selfie hovers in the air. Bobby Caldwell's "What You Won't Do for Love" plays because that afternoon, the Yacht Rock station spun that disc three times in two hours.

A new projection replaces the selfie: a giant ice tower of shrimp, oysters, and crab legs.

You drank Bloody Marys and ate your weight in seafood.

From Caldwell to the caw of seagulls and the clank of far-off buoys.

Another selfie: Christopher kissing my cheek.

It was your first getaway together.

A last photograph of the setting sun with Christopher standing in shadow, looking out to the Pacific Ocean. The roar of waves crashing against the shore.

That night, he told you that he had fallen in love with you.

Christopher broke up with me a week after we'd successfully tested ROAD TRIP!

Downstairs, someone knocks on my door.

I run down and squint through the peephole. It's Dad.

"You're crying." He follows me up the stairs. His eyebrows crumple as he spots the projection of Christopher. "What's wrong?"

I swipe at my cheeks and then swipe at the sensors to close the projection. "Allergies."

He points at his sweatshirt. "I've been looking for that."

I turn on the floor lamp, then pull a ceramic smoking frog from the box. The amphibian wears a taco-shaped hat with MEXICO painted along its brim, and this tacky memento is now a hologram in my bank as the first gift Chris gave me.

"Oh," Dad says, smiling. "He's cute."

"Yeah. I decided to unpack the 'We're in Love, Let's Go on Field Trips' souvenir box."

There's a hot-pink leather bag from Miami shaped like a bikini top and a hella-misspelled WHAT HAPPENS IN BEGAS STAYS IN VEGAN bumper sticker.

Dad nudges another box with the toe of his sneaker. "Need help?"

"I got it, thanks." I cock my judgy eyebrow. "Didn't look like you and Mom were discussing a vacation."

"We were discussing the pros and cons of a cruise and buying travel insurance."

"Is something wrong? Is there a reason why we *wouldn't* go?"

"*We?* You're gonna join us?"

"Sure. Is this trip anytime soon, or is it our birthday gift?"

Dad points to his chest. "It's *my* birthday gift to your mother."

I pick at a thumbnail. "I have something planned, just so you know."

"Yeah? What?" He plops onto the couch.

I grab a stuffed manatee from the box and fling it across the room. "Secret. Can't say."

Dad grabs an aquarium snow globe and shakes it. "Don't wanna get her the same thing."

"That won't happen." I pull out a pyramid-shaped flashlight from Las Vegas. "Want this?"

"Keep it—that's your memory."

I shake my head, thrust it at him with my eyes averted. Soon, the weight of the light leaves my hand.

Dad clicks on the flashlight. "Your mom wants to go during Thanksgiving break."

"Sasha's wedding is next week. Thanksgiving Day, remember?"

Dad remembers, and Mom sure as hell remembers. She just doesn't care. She's gone on and on about how crazy it is to make people attend an out-of-town wedding on Thanksgiving.

"Not that her rants matter," Dad says, reading my mind. "I can't go on a long vacation right now anyway."

An accountant's work is crazy at the end of the year.

I grin. "Hooray! Since I'm not at the firm anymore, I don't have to care about calendar year versus fiscal year."

"They're still trying to fill your spot. Everybody misses you. *I* miss you."

I make a show of pulling out a pink feather boa that I purchased after Elton John's Vegas concert. "I love my new job. Chris doesn't change that. I *do* miss hanging out with you. I *don't* miss writing about charity drives, corporate compliance training, and staff changes. And being micromanaged by Phoebe. Ohmigod, I couldn't stand that woman. It's a *newsletter*, Phoebe, not fucking . . . *Vanity Fair*, calm down." I fling my head back and pose with the boa.

Dad throws a couch cushion at me. "I guess newsletters are dull compared to—"

"Everything else? The math nerds worshipped me. I liked that a lot." I blow at a loose pink feather to keep it in the air.

Dad watches me blow at that feather, then rests his hand on my shoulder. "Time to eat. Maybe play some happy memories on that gizmo over there."

I find the Vegas-branded Magic 8 Ball in the box. "I'll take Mom's skirt to the cleaners tomorrow. And I'll be fine, Father. Right, Magic 8 Ball?" I shake the toy and read the prediction.

Outlook not so good.

Oh. My chest tightens as Dad pulls himself from the couch.

"I'm hearing scratches," I tell him. "Like, either in the walls or on the roof."

"We live an inch away from an urban forest."

"You want mice building a castle in the eaves? Also, can you do something about the window screen frame in my bedroom? The racket is keeping me from my beauty sleep."

He holds up both hands. "Okay, I'll check and make sure no one's built another encampment back there. And I'll make sure no mouse droppings are near the vents and I'll fix the screen. Anything else, Mrs. Helmsley?"

"Ha. *You* wanted me to move back."

His head drops and he fake-frowns. "Yeah. What the hell was I thinking?"

"Dad!"

He winks at me. "Come down to dinner—you've pissed off your mother enough tonight, and I can't protect you again." He plods down the stairs.

After he leaves, I sink against the couch as my nerves pop against my skin. Crap—forgot to show him the strange note.

The scratching starts again.

I freeze as goose bumps march across my arms and back.

Furious scratching, like he's digging for his life, like something is chasing—

I shout, "Stop it, stupid mouse."

That scratching is joined by a metallic *knick-knick-knick-knick-knick*. The loose screen.

There's a loud *pop*. Something just snapped in the wind. A branch, a wire . . .

I swallow against my heart rising in my throat. A city girl freaking out over mice, window screens, scraping branches, and wind. True danger is not an inch away.

The scratching stops.

The bogeyman must have caught the mouse and gobbled him up.

I pop down the stairs to make sure the door is locked. I nudge the security chain into its slide, but something I see makes me stop in my step.

Another sheet of folded paper on the tile floor.

Like the earlier note, this paper is also yellow and just as grimy. Narrow, left-slanted handwriting sits in the center of the sheet.

YOU LOOK LIKE HER

3.

Mom can't stop gaping at the notes in my hand.

"I keep telling you," I say, almost shrieking now. "I haven't met anyone new online. No one's come up to me or followed me. Nothing. I would've noticed—"

The service-porch door opens. Dad and Uncle Bryan join Mom and me in the kitchen. "We don't see anyone back there." Uncle Bryan nestles his gun back into his shoulder holster.

Mom grabs her phone from the counter. "I'm gonna check the doorbell camera."

She thumbprints her way into the security app. We crowd around her, breathless as we watch the mailman, the water delivery guy, and the take-out-menus and landscaping guys come. No one breaks from his path. No one lingers.

"He must've entered from the park," Uncle Bryan says.

I wag a finger at my parents. "I *told* you that I was seeing more people back there. And what did you say? 'It's just your imagination.'"

Mom squints. "I said, 'I can't make people stop coming to the park.'"

"And I said, 'Keep your windows closed at night,'" Dad adds. "And arm the security system we're paying for."

Mom places her arm around my shoulders. "I know you're grown, but mind staying up here with us tonight?"

"Good idea." I text Imani and Sasha. **OMG Another stalker!**

No! Imani texts.

U OK??? Sasha texts.

I'm totally freaked out!

Did U see him? Imani asks.

No he slipped a note beneath my door.

I know your dad ready to shoot somebody!! Sasha texts.

Dad? Imani adds. Cori about to whup somebody's ass

Ha yeah sleeping in the big house tonight

Call us in the morning, Sasha texts.

Trembling, I stand in the open doorway of my old room. It's still painted Tiffany blue, and the shelves still host my trophies and ribbons for soccer, honor roll, and writing competitions. The Backstreet Boys posters are gone, though. So is the pink plastic blow-up chair. The glow-in-the-dark stars on the ceiling that my babysitter Tracy helped me put up one summer—those are gone, too.

I want to cry. Not only have I returned home after my shattered love affair, but I'm now sleeping in my little twin bed. And I'm sleeping in my little twin bed because a stranger has entered our gates. What in the actual hell? And just like I did as a kid, I now listen to the murmurs of my parents down the hall as I fall asleep. And I hear—rather, I *think* I hear—Mom say, ". . . *kill* him if he comes near her . . . not again."

Like warm milk and lavender baths, Mom's declaration soothes me as I drift . . . drift . . .

Kill him . . . *who?*

Not again . . . *what?*

When was the first time?

At eleven o'clock on a rainy Thursday morning, there aren't many cars in the parking lot. The creepy old woman's station wagon is here along with a black Honda hatchback and a silver Hyundai sedan. The sandwich board at Beautiful Things sits in the breezeway outside the store.

I am a bit scratchy from startling awake with every rumble of the furnace or drop of ice into the fridge's ice bucket. I grab my satchel, heavy now with my laptop, sketchbook, white archival gloves, and chargers. Umbrella up, I scan the parking lot for a stalker, but I glimpse only soggy RVs and an abandoned shopping cart. I'm alone . . . hopefully.

I hurry toward the shops. Mom's old Gucci loafers are a better sartorial choice on the gravel than yesterday's high-heeled boots.

The door to Anna's Place is open. Sam Cooke's voice rides on aromas of fried meat and vanilla-scented pancake batter.

As I cross the threshold into Beautiful Things, a bell over the store's front door tinkles. I stow my wet umbrella in the courtesy holder, then tuck strands of damp hair behind my ears.

Animal skulls in glass domes sit next to tarnished candelabra. Silver flasks and yellowing globes are arranged beside totems and pocketbooks. Brass platters. Stuffed ravens. Cuff bracelets. Framed maps. Jukeboxes. Tea service collections.

The kind of brass bell that a traveler taps at a hotel rests near the antique turquoise cash register. I tap the bell, and the peal is as pure as it is loud. An open foam carton full of half-eaten chicken wings and waffles sits on the stool.

"One moment," a woman's contralto calls out from a back room.

A text from Uncle Bryan buzzes my phone. U OK?

I send a thumbs-up just like I sent Imani and Sasha earlier.

Any more notes? he asks.

Nope. Thanks for coming last night!

I press "Record" on my fancy digital voice recorder, now hidden in my pocket.

California is a dual-consent state, and yes, *technically*, I break the law anytime I record someone without their knowledge. However, I'm also a single woman visiting shops and homes alone who's now on the receiving end of anonymous, creepy notes. If something were ever to happen to me, my last recorded moments would be automatically stored in the Memory Bank's cloud.

Over by the jukebox near the entrance is a table dedicated to cloth-covered journals. A sucker for those, I pick up a cracked blue journal protected in plastic. I lift the cover. "*. . . says I have a gift—my voice is beyond measure, but I lack judgment and I am not properly trained . . .*"

"That is a mid-nineteenth-century travel journal of a noted mezzo-soprano from the New York Opera Company." This woman's voice belongs to a wrinkled face as pale as a fish's belly. Sharp blue eyes watch me from behind wire-rimmed glasses. She wears a long blue pinafore and a white turtleneck. A ruby teardrop pendant hangs from a gold chain around her neck. She rakes her fingers through her short silver hair and smiles at me with crooked yellow teeth.

"Nineteenth century—awesome." I return the book to its slot. "Is Nadia Denham in?"

The woman cants her head. "And you are . . . ?"

"Michaela Lambert, digital archaeologist from the Memory Bank. Nadia hired—"

"That's right!" The woman claps and grins. "*I'm* Nadia. Well, hello, Michaela Lambert." She holds out her arms. "Welcome to Beautiful Things."

I do a slow turn, and say, "You truly have a lot of memories."

Good-natured, she flaps her hand. "I don't need to remember any of *these* things. What I want to remember is back in the office. First, though, let me give you the grand tour."

She pivots and heads toward a collection of framed maps hanging beneath a row of Jesus-themed wall clocks. She touches one chart—a brown octopus labeled "Russia" is surrounded by green China, yellow Turkey, and other lands denoted by Japanese calligraphy.

"One of my prizes," Nadia says. "An anti-Russian satirical map. Made in 1906 during the Russo-Japanese War." She runs her finger along the caption. "The store's very first collectible. I didn't acquire it. The original owner of the shop found it back in the late seventies."

I bring out a pen and the sketch pad from my bag.

Nadia blinks at my tools. "Have I said something interesting?"

"Maybe. I'm taking notes for context. So . . . the original owner . . ."

Nadia stares at the pad, then shrugs. "Sarah Park, a very nice South Korean woman. She opened the store in 1977. But she . . . well . . . something happened back in her home country. A sick mother. Oh, I can't remember the details now, but Sarah's spirit surrounds this place. In some ways, she never left. In every way, she's still here. And—oh, look! You'll like this."

Over at a bookcase, she pulls out a book with a faded red cover and a gold torchbearer on its front. On the spine: *Anna Karenina*, Leo Tolstoy.

"First Modern Library Edition," Nadia says. "Considered by some the greatest piece of literature ever." She offers it to me, then watches as I gently flip through the pages of the story about a Russian socialite's torrid love affair. "Have you read *Anna Karenina*?"

Excitement swirls through me like dust. "Oh my goodness, yes! I took Russian lit in college. I love how authentic the relationships were, the depiction of class, his writing . . . I lost my copy about two years ago and . . ." I gape at her. "How did you come across this? It must be worth—"

"Eight hundred dollars. Up until a year ago, I'd take a monthlong trip across the country. I'd visit flea markets, estate sales, stores like mine . . . And I'd shop, and I'd find things no one else wanted, and I'd ship it all back.

"This book was in a dead man's garage sale bin somewhere in New Hampshire. I think he was a professor, but he didn't leave much money, so his family . . . Well, here it is. And now, it's yours. From me to you. To replace your lost copy."

I shake my head and hold the book out for her to take. "I can't."

She smiles her butter-teeth smile. "Why not?"

"I can't accept gifts worth more than seventy-five dollars. Tax reasons."

"Bah," she says, then flaps her hands at me. "The shine in your eyes, it's obvious there's love there. This book deserves that kind of love. You have a dollar?"

I pull a five-dollar bill from my wallet.

"Sold." Nadia plucks the money from my fingers and stuffs it into her pocket.

I slip the book into my bag. "Who does the collecting across the country now?"

"The store manager." Nadia beckons me as she shuffles over to the collection of board games in aging boxes. "Her name is Riley and she's a little firecracker. She's the one who thought we needed to sell postcards and whatnot. She'll be in later today or tomorrow."

I pick up a Parcheesi box. "Does she know that I'm working on . . . ?"

"My memory bank?" Nadia nods. "She's not thrilled about it." She holds up Operation and smiles. "Everyone's favorite. It's not the project *per se*. She's not thrilled about the reason *behind* the project."

"Which is, if you don't mind me asking?"

She says nothing for several seconds. Then a sad smile spreads across her thin lips. "Let's talk about why you're here."

We move past the Native American jewelry and embroidered pillows and into an office that resembles 1940s industrial America with its sleek, clean lines, chocolate wood, and gunmetal. The file cabinets and desk drawers boast brass pulls and label frames. Large magnification mirrors are screwed above tables. Filled, stacked boxes tower over filled, stacked baskets, but the battered butterscotch leather couch is clutter-free. One box window brightens the space more than the ceiling fan light above us.

A large map of the United States hangs on the wall above the desk. Multicolored pushpins crowd both the East and West Coasts. A few pins stick Louisiana and New Mexico.

Nadia plops into the banker's desk chair. "Some of the pins match my special memories—memories that I'm starting to forget. It is really . . . serendipitous. I was flipping through the magazine that comes with the Sunday *Times*, and there it was! This . . . *contraption* that banks your memories and then projects it into space, and well, it sounded like something out of *Star Trek*. And I absolutely loved *Star Trek*." She wiggles her fingers.

"That ad was my idea," I say. "My boss didn't think people still read newspapers."

"Old people do."

"Our future customers."

"Smart girl," she says, finger on her nose. "You deserve a raise *and* a promotion. Anyway, I'd been trying to organize this special collection for years and failing miserably. And then, the way I was doing it." She sticks out her tongue. "A complete mess. I could never find the right words . . . Then I'd forget words. Saying them. Writing them . . ."

Nadia removes her glasses, rubs her eyes. "You see, Michaela . . . First, I kept forgetting where I parked the car. Harmless. *Everyone* forgets that once or twice. But then I'd keep asking Riley, 'What time are you coming in?' And I'd get lost driving to the Rose Bowl every weekend even though I'd gone to that flea market forever. A few times, I had no idea where I was. I even got lost in my own store once and . . ."

She slips her glasses on again, then fumbles with the white MedicAlert bracelet on her wrist. A tattoo of a heart and a pair of dice flashes beneath that bracelet. "A month ago, I was diagnosed with Alzheimer's."

I press my hand against my chest. "I'm so sorry."

"As you can imagine, for someone like me—someone who collects and sells antiques and memorabilia—that diagnosis was absolutely devastating. The idea that one day I wouldn't remember the stories behind . . ." She points to the pins on the map.

"Is that the project?" I ask. "Cataloging memories from those places on the map?"

"Yes." She rolls her chair over to a project table near the window.

Random things cover the long wood surface. A music box, a hairpin, a pipe . . . Torn sheets of notebook paper sit beneath each item.

"These twelve things mean the most to me," Nadia says. "I want to remember them as long as I'm walking aboveground. And I want the people who love me to have this, too, once I've left this world."

She touches a silver cigarette lighter. "As you can see, I'd started cataloging each piece with bullets on these slips of paper. They're very detailed, my notes, but not well written. I've put down as much as I can remember about each item, so you'll have to . . . fill in the gaps."

"No problem."

"And now, with the memory bank, there will be a picture. You can add little factoids about that part of the country where I acquired it, yes?"

I take a quick picture of the collection. "That's how it works. And the tech guys will add GPS coordinates to map it. We'll load an app on your phone for that. But before all the techy stuff, I'll do the research, write the story using your bullets, upload the pictures, whatever you'd like. And if I'm stuck or need more context, I'll just pop up front and ask."

Nadia's hand trembles as she picks up a toy mouse. "Seems like a lot of trouble. Just so people like me can remember."

"Well, it's a great service," I say, "and it's emerging technology, which—I don't know if Chris Fenton mentioned, we'll continue to update the techy stuff since you're one of our early adopters. As for the writing, you're paying for me to be here, and I love a good story."

She laughs, and it sounds like the bell at the cash register.

"What hours do you want me to keep?"

"After today, come during opening. Riley's usually up front. I've been upstairs in my apartment nowadays or back here, remembering . . ." Her shoulders sag. "How long will it take?"

"Maybe a month for the writing since Thanksgiving is next week. And then another two weeks for the tech stuff. We should have your completed box by the beginning of the year."

She pushes her tongue against her cheek. "I can hang on that long. Can I give you the order of things?"

"Sure," I say, "but it won't matter. You can call up things in any order—"

"This is so exciting!" She clasps her hands to her chest. "This means so much to me, Michaela. I know this isn't personal to you, but . . . someone thought of this, for people like me, with my condition . . . So meaningful."

"I'm glad we can help. We have over five hundred clients, and I'd say that more than a third struggle with memory disorders. I'm pushing us to partner with hospitals and retirement villages and nursing homes, occupational therapy . . ."

"Wonderful." She slips her arm through mine, a difficult thing to do since she's five inches taller than me. "Can you start this evening? I want to put everything in order. Maybe write another snippet or two. Add a few more items."

"Of course. So is your store's entire collection in the one space out front?" I ask.

Her eyes brighten. "No. There's a bunch more stuff in the basement. Every so often, I rotate a few things from down there to up here. Come, let me show you."

Outside the office, we turn left and head to a closed door. Nadia opens the door, and cold, sour air snakes past us. She taps a wall switch and descends a flight of stairs.

"Riley doesn't come down much," she says. "That's because nothing truly interesting exists down here. Mostly things that used to be."

Old boxes and steamer trunks covered in yellow plastic, creaky floorboards, and bare brick walls. An exercise bike and a high cabinet filled with yellowed apothecary bottles. White powder shimmers across an otherwise clean floor.

"It's a bit spooky," I admit. "No cobwebs at least."

"Just a dead body or two." She chuckles. "Oh, and rats. Be mindful of the rat poison. As you can see, I've sprinkled it everywhere. Got a little carried away, eh?"

"I'd take bodies over spiders and rats," I say. "Will I need to come down for anything?"

Nadia taps her chin as she thinks. "No, but don't hold me to that."

I follow her back up the staircase.

In the store, a white couple with a towheaded toddler marvels at a butterfly collection.

Nadia shouts over to them: "Hello, lovely family. I'll be with you in a moment."

The father waves. "Thanks."

Nadia leans close to me and whispers, "More of them are moving into the neighborhood. I know that I, too, am white, but I've been here since the seventies. I *care* about this community. I'm not trying to change things. I'm not forcing Anna to make ridiculous things with quinoa like that Weller asshole wants. Did you know that since Tucker and Penelope over there eat quinoa, the poor Peruvians who harvest it for their own sustenance can no longer afford it?"

I groan. Must they gentrify ancient grains, too?

"Usually, I'm very 'live and let live' but . . ." She glares at the young couple. "They're destroying everything. And they have a champion now. Peter Weller's trying to force me out. He's sending his goons to threaten me, but they don't know me. I don't scare *at all*."

Darkness passes across her face and she finds her smile again. "Five o'clock good?"

"Five is great. I have a few errands to run anyway."

She squeezes my shoulder, then shuffles over to the family. Before she reaches the trio, she glances out the window. What she spots makes her stop in her step. She stands there, unblinking, seeing something—or someone—I can't see.

Several seconds pass before her gaze returns to the family. "Isn't your son just the *cutest*?" She taps the toddler's head. "So *cute*. I could just . . . *eat him up*."

4.

Crackles of nervous energy fuel my trip to the parking lot. I move as fast as the small rivers sweeping cups, fast-food wrappers, and plastic bags to the sewers and storm drains. The wind batters my umbrella, and somehow, raindrops are falling sideways.

I think of the notes at my door again. Am I being watched? By whom? For how long?

The next showing of a film I want to see—a Black couple on the run after killing a cop—starts at two o'clock. I can drop Mom's skirt at the dry cleaner and search for Sasha's wedding gift afterward. And since I live eight minutes away, I can also drive home to work on Mom's memory bank while she's at school.

In the car, I upload my first conversation with Nadia into the cloud, and then I text Chris an update on my progress.

Met Nadia

Will start officially later today

My phone rings.
Mr. Why Text When You Can Talk is calling.
I say, "Hey. You didn't have to call."

"I can never pass up an opportunity to talk to you," Chris says.

"You were right. Ms. Denham is interesting. She has Alzheimer's, which sucks, and I think I'll enjoy curating her collection . . . but . . . I think this will probably be my last one." I chew on my tongue, not sure why I said this.

Chris breathes through the phone and says nothing.

Sweat stings my upper lip, and I slide my tongue over it to moisten my now-dry mouth. "I should go—"

"You say this like it's your final decision. Is it?"

I press my hand against my forehead. My brain is cherry slush. Now it's my turn to say nothing, but only because I don't know the answer.

"You're the best memory-maker I have," he says. "And yeah, you're more than that to me." He pauses, sighs, says, "We shouldn't have this conversation over the phone, Mick."

My emotions are the cups and wrappers floating all over the parking lot.

I end the call without a goodbye and toss the phone on the passenger seat.

Our house is tucked into a copse of California sycamores with gnarled limbs that twist up and out. Most of the leaves are rust colored, and now they make the world around me smell fresh and earthy. No other vehicles are parked in the driveway. No one is prowling the street, clutching a notepad of yellow paper filled with creepy notes . . .

Hopefully, Dad has called the fence makers.

Heart pounding, can of Mace in hand, I open the front door of my apartment.

No new note in the foyer.

I return to the big house. The scent of Mom's perfume hangs in the air, and I wish the memory bank were 4D because I'd include bursts of her cologne with her artifacts. The foyer's thermostat senses my presence, and the vents whoosh with warm air. I slide into the breakfast nook as rain lashes at the windows, pull my laptop from my bag, and fire up the content-management system as thunder booms and a crack of lightning washes the sky electric purple.

I stare at the deluge and then write the passage I was thinking about during my drive.

It was summer 2010. You were excited to visit Carlsbad Caverns in New Mexico. We flew there and rented a white Jeep. Little did we know there'd been a rabies outbreak and the park had closed. On the drive back to Trinity Hotel, you cried because we couldn't go inside the caves.

Built in 1892, the Trinity used to house a First National Bank. On this trip, we stayed in the room that had been the office of Pat Garrett, the sheriff who shot and killed Billy the Kid. Derek, the owner of the Trinity, asked the chef to cook an off-the-menu glazed rib eye for you. He comped the bottle of Cabernet Sauvignon. All this to make up for the sick bats.

Pictures that will project throughout this narration: Mom behind the wheel of our rented Jeep. The **WELCOME TO NEW MEXICO** highway sign. A family portrait by the **CLOSED** notice at the entrance to the national park. Pictures of wine bottles and sad, drunk Mom. Tech will add sound effects. Cave echoes. Bat squeaks and squawks. Wine poured into a glass.

I slip the can of Mace back into my pocket, and then snap photos of the bat magnet that still lives on the refrigerator door. In the family room, I snap photos of the Carlsbad Caverns snow globe on the fireplace mantel.

Memories also live in my parents' room. On sick days, I'd lie in their bed with bowls of soup from the can, ginger ale in big tumblers, and sleeves of saltine crackers. I'd watch *I Love Lucy* DVDs between naps. On healthy days, I'd play with all my naked Barbies in that same bed, and on stormy nights, I'd snuggle between my parents for protection from the lightning and thunder.

Most days throughout my childhood, Mom and Dad locked their bedroom door. That's because Dad, son of a cop, brother of a cop, kept a gun in the house.

I saw him holding it back in 2005. A little before four in the morning, Dad heard someone scratching at the service-porch lock. Wood cracking—that's what had awakened me. Dad was already in the kitchen, gun steady, waiting for the burglar to cross our threshold.

Mom held me close in one arm and called 9-1-1 with her free hand.

Shaking, I hid my face in her red fleece robe and prayed to God that we'd live.

Dad, gun out, shouted, "Give me a reason, nigga; give me a reason."

The burglar changed his mind and ran.

Since I'm no longer a child, there should be no reason why my parents' bedroom door is locked, other than, you know . . . *sex*. But since they're too old for that (ha), up the stairs I go.

A few feet from their bedroom door, I stop in my step.

The doorknob in the kitchen . . . Is it wiggling? And what's that creaking?

I pull the can of Mace from my pocket.

Nothing creaks or groans without pressure.

Has the note-leaver returned?

Mace in hand, I tiptoe back down the stairs and crouch-creep to the kitchen. My pulse booms in my ears as I slowly . . . slowly . . . ease my head above the windowsill and . . .

No shadows lurk near the door. No hunched figure skulks in the yard.

No one is here.

Anxiety bops in my belly, readying me for the worst. My skin crawls because there's creaking. What is that creaking?

Just our neighbors' wobbly gutters.

And that pounding? Just heavy rain whipping the windowpanes.

I slink back up the stairs and down the hallway—*just the water heater, just loose gutters*—while battling the scream waiting in my throat.

I reach my parents' closed bedroom door. As I turn the knob, thunder cracks against the sky. I hop, and a yelp flutters from me like a trapped bird.

Deep breath . . . and out . . . deep breath . . . and out . . .

I hold my stomach and reach for the knob again.

No give.

The door is locked.

Damn it.

Why is the freaking door locked?

5.

Are they hiding baby pandas in the laundry hamper? Thirty kilos of coke in the false bottom of their waste can? Do they realize that they're still locking the door out of habit, even though I'm grown and they no longer have to?

Sure, every family has secrets. Imani's uncle (by marriage) had an affair with her cousin (the daughter of his wife's brother). Christopher's father wasn't on a long summer trip during the summer of 1999—he was in jail for selling drugs to his patients. In my family, Uncle Bryan kept his sexuality a secret until after he'd graduated from the police academy. I'm sure there are other family secrets: an affair, a drinking problem, or the real reasons behind a job change.

My parents have always been up front with me. Lately, though . . . This locked door, those tight lips, and shared glances. What aren't they telling me? Is Mom sick? Are we broke?

The rain has stopped, and before I climb back into my car to drive to the movie theater, I draw in that clean air. Woody sycamore. Medicinal eucalyptus. Moss, sage, and chaparral from the park behind us. God's aromatherapy.

The movie theater is nearly empty. I'm one of four people at the showing. My phone rings. "Michaela? It's Nadia from Beautiful Things."

Her voice sounds like sunlight. "I'm so excited. May I add two more things? This is it, cross my heart."

I smile. "Of course. Just put everything on the table, and we'll go over it at five."

I'm so excited that Nadia's so excited. What wonderfully weird artifacts await? A ladybug pillbox? A cricket in a glass?

Halfway through the movie, my cell phone vibrates again.

I reminded Dad about the gate

Mom taking care of business.

Someone's supposed to come out for a quote

Since I'm sitting in the back of the theater, the light from my phone's screen doesn't bother anyone other than me. I send back, I'm not overreacting am I?

No! You'll always be our baby!! Someone messes with you they mess with me!

U DA BEST MOM EVER any clue about who could've left the note tho?

Ellipses bubble on-screen, then stop, then bubble again. No. Love u Text messages make my phone dance, but those texts aren't from my parents, so I choose to watch the movie and cry on cue until the credits end. Then I trudge through the parking lot over to the mall. After a dip into my favorite boutique, I leave the mall with leggings and a cranberry-colored sweatshirt.

Over at Santa Barbara Plaza, an ambulance pulls out of the parking lot. A better view sits beyond that, though. The colors of the hillsides are richer, truer, deeper after storms. Lights from houses glow in the dusk but can't distract from the golds and reds of the trees. Clouds roll above my head and puff from my mouth.

I drive back to the plaza.

A fire truck and three police patrol cars are parked at the curbs closest to the shops. Cops talk to other cops. Cops talk to firefighters. Clumps of onlookers crowd the walkway outside Beautiful Things, and yellow tape stretches from the sandwich board to the store's doorknob. No one is rushing, even though night is coming.

I park my car and find Anna in the crowd. She's hugging a woman wearing a hairstylist's apron.

What's happened?

Anna holds out her arms. "Mickie! There you are! This is just *awful*."

We hug. I ask, "What's going on?" I can barely hear myself over the bursts of static and chatter from police radios.

"Nadia . . ." Anna's face quivers. "She passed this afternoon."

"What?"

"The paramedics got here about an hour and a half ago. Her MedicAlert bracelet went off. I heard the sirens, so I ran out to see them rushing to the store. I went in behind them, telling them everything I knew, and . . . and . . . There was a plastic bag over her head and a . . . a yellow cord tied . . ." Anna covers her mouth as she weeps.

"She . . . *Suicide?*"

Anna nods. "She . . . she . . . was ha-having memory problems."

Nausea bubbles in my stomach. "She told me—Alzheimer's . . . That's why she hired me to . . . Doesn't make sense. She was happy, excited to get . . . I just *talked* to her and she wasn't . . . Oh no. No . . ." I can't catch my breath. I want to vomit.

"He got the nerve." Anna has stopped her crying to scowl at a tall white guy strolling from the parking lot. "Who the hell called *him*?"

"Him" is fortyish. Lean. Almost handsome. All-the-way cocky. A Walmart version of Tom Cruise wearing a blue pin-striped suit and brown shoes. He looks like the kid back in third grade who took every-one's toys—not to play with them but just because he could.

If she held a drink in her hand, Anna would certainly have thrown it at him.

I ask, "Who's that?"

"That's the man I thought you worked for," Anna says.

"The one who wants to tear down the plaza and build hotels and condos?"

She nods, her hands clenching into fists.

I would throw a drink at him, too.

"How's everybody doing?" Weller asks no one specifically. His smile is a little too gleeful for the occasion.

His head swivels in our direction. "Anna! I just heard about Nadia. Awful."

"You look heartbroken."

Weller's face reddens, but he pushes away angry embarrassment. His smile returns as he gives me the up-and-down. He holds his hand out for me to shake. "Peter Weller. And you are?"

"My niece, and she's none of your business." Anna yanks me closer to her. "She ain't got nothing to say to you."

"Anna, you're upset," Weller says, "and that's understandable. But now, maybe we can move forward. Let's honor Nadia with progress. Let's do something special for her. Like . . . we can name something after her in the new plaza. How's that sound?"

"You drove her to this," Anna spits. "You threatened her. Made her—"

"I did no such thing." Weller's face turns to stone, but he tucks his chin in, shamed.

"We're not gonna stand here and listen to your lies. C'mon, sweetie." Anna pulls me until we're inside the diner.

I settle on a bloodred vinyl stool at the counter and watch her fill two cups with coffee. She slides one cup over to me, then snatches a napkin from the holder. As she weeps, I stare at my reflection in the stainless-steel backsplash above the coffeepot.

The crackles of police radios outside mix with stranger-chatter and my new friend's weeping. Three men wearing blue sports coats linger in the breezeway. Their belts shine with gold badges.

"Detectives are here," I report.

Anna blows her nose, washes her hands, then pulls a plate of sweet potato pie from the carousel, placing the wedge before me.

I slide my fork through the glistening orange custard until the tines crunch through the golden crust. "What's gonna happen to the store?"

She pours more coffee into her cup. "Riley will keep it going. She's *always* been there, but lately she's had to do more . . ." She closes her eyes, then shakes her head. "Poor Nadia."

"Nadia told me that Riley's coming back from a shopping trip either today or tomorrow."

"Guess I gotta tell her."

We say nothing else, and I finish my dessert. "It was a pleasure, Anna. The pie was delicious. I was looking forward to getting to know you and hanging out here. Can I bring my mom over for grilled cheese and Cokes?"

Anna smiles. "You and your family are always welcome here, Miss Mickie." She comes from around the counter and hugs me. She's soft and firm like her sweet potato pie.

Before I leave, she presents me with a plastic fork and a take-out container of pie.

I finish my second dessert during my eight-minute drive home.

As I turn onto Mantova Drive, my phone vibrates.

I don't know this number.

I thumbprint my way into my messages.

Stop now or

Payback is gonna come

6.

Stop *what*? And "payback"? What the hell?

Panic blooms in my heart, as big as the puffy white clouds bumbling across the sky.

Could this be the note-leaver switching from nice to nasty?

One hand grips the steering wheel as the other holds my cell phone. At a red traffic signal, my thumbs fly across the phone's keyboard as I type, **Wrong number.** Wrong number. Wrong woman. Wrong everything. I don't do drama like that.

Home now, I pull into the driveway. No construction truck from a fencing company is parked at the curb. Why isn't there a man wearing khakis and carrying a clipboard following my father around our yard? The curtains in the den are open. Dad sits on the couch, game controller in hand, his favorite video game on the television screen. In the living room, Mom plays "Clair de Lune" on the piano. Debussy is her go-to composer after a hard day.

Have they forgotten about me? Have they forgotten the notes?

Since I don't plan to stop at the main house, I text these questions to my mother.

No we haven't forgotten, she texts back.

We're not the only people in LA wanting a fence

I open the door to my car.

Silence.

No more Debussy.

I glance over my shoulder.

Mom is looking at me from the breakfast nook's window. She looks like a small, tired child wearing her mother's sorority sweatshirt. Like me ten years ago.

I toss her a wave and hold up my shopping bag from the boutique at the mall.

She rolls her eyes and blows me a kiss.

I store that kiss in my soul's medicine cabinet. Like before, it will heal any future hurts.

During my drive to dinner in Beverly Hills, I texted Christopher that our newest client had died. I'm going to dinner now I'll call you later.

He immediately started to blow up my phone.

I ignored his call cuz *bitch, don't kill my vibe.*

Sasha's cousin Rick, a server at a Michelin-starred restaurant, had invited us to dinner on him, a gesture of gratitude for helping him land an interview at my father's accounting firm. Just as Rick lifted the dome from my platter of smoked oysters, Christopher's face and name brightened my cell phone's screen again.

"Do not answer that," Sasha demanded. "He's gonna ruin our free dinner."

"But he's ruining dinner with all these freaking texts."

"Turn it off," Sasha said.

"Turn off . . . the *phone*?" I gaped at her.

She gaped at me.

We both doubled over with laughter.

But I am only a woman, and I answered.

I am now pacing La Cienega Boulevard instead of gobbling tapas with Sasha.

"We should think about this from the family's perspective," Chris is now saying.

"That . . . Nana is *dead*? That Memaw killed herself? That Mom felt so scared of what was coming that she decided *this* was the best solution? Is *that* the perspective you're talking about?"

"Or . . ." Chris says. "Wow. Mom paid five thousand dollars on this awesome device for this thoughtful service. She must really want it."

"But what if the memory bank reminds them of . . . you know?"

"What if it doesn't?" Chris counters. "Until we hear otherwise, we continue our work. That's the direction I've received."

"From?"

"That shouldn't matter to you and what you need to do. Breathe, Mick. Focus."

"There's police tape blocking the doors," I say, not breathing, not focusing.

"You said it was a suicide," Chris points out. "The tape will come down."

The violet sky buzzes with helicopters. Cars—from Hondas to Bentleys—zoom through intersections, veering from one lane to the next.

I tell him that I *like* when he plays devil's advocate, but this time, it isn't that simple.

"It *is* that simple," Chris says. "And you can do it. And when the store reopens, you'll pick up where you left off."

"I uploaded the recording of our time together," I say. "Besides that, I haven't done much else."

Chris doesn't respond.

I say, "Hello?"

"What have you been doing all this time?"

A solar flare erupts from my throat. "*Excuse* me?"

"I don't mean . . ." His blush blooms through the phone. "I'm not asking in a micromanager way. I mean . . ."

"I *told* you that I was supposed to go back later."

"That's right. You're right. My bad."

Then I tell him that I toured the shop with Nadia. I tell him that she showed me the artifacts that she wanted to curate and said to come back at five that evening. But then, when I returned to the store, the poor lady was dead.

Back at my table in the restaurant, Sasha tugs at her gold satin dress and plucks an anchovy-stuffed olive from my plate.

"I'm sure," Christopher is saying, "that Ms. Denham's family would love to have the bank, especially considering these tragic circumstances." He cares, but he also doesn't wanna return the money. "And think about this: a bunch of her family and friends will see the bank on the fireplace or piano, and they'll go, 'Wow. What's that?' This is free advertising, Mick."

Yep. Money. Moving more units.

"Fine," I say. "I'll go back to the store in the morning, and if it's open, I'll start."

By the time I return to my table, the oysters and olives have disappeared from my plate and the smoke from my liquid nitrogen–laced pisco sour has evaporated.

"Dude, really?" I say to Sasha, eyebrows high.

"You're the fool for leaving this here plate of delicious food," she says.

She's right. I *am* the fool. For leaving my plate. For believing Christopher wanted more from me than work. For wanting more than work from him. Fuzzy-headed and fuzzy-hearted, I sink into my chair.

When it comes to guys, I don't know *what* I want. My phone vibrates, and I try not to look at who's texting, but I can't help myself. Because maybe it's Christopher again.

No I got the right number

I know what you're doing

DO NOT fuck with me

This stranger: she is not part of the plan.

The obnoxious blonde in the valley? Yes.

The waitress in the South Bay? Soon.

But the Black girl speeding south in an old Benz . . . She is a pop-up. A detour.

At the red light, the black German sedan slows to a stop. In the car's cabin, the young woman's hands move through the air and her head waggles. She's talking on the phone or singing a dramatic song. She's not looking in her rearview mirror. She doesn't notice that she's been followed all evening—from the house in the hills to the restaurant in Beverly Hills to . . . *Where next?*

Item number one on tonight's original to-do list: cleaning. With bleach. With ammonia. And then: burning clothes. Then, finally: destroying that knife. Not . . . *this.*

Although clouds have swallowed the skies above, the streets still glow with neon signs. VERSAILLES COMIDA CUBANO. SHELL GASOLINE. KAISER PERMANENTE.

Maybe things will change. Course-correct. Maybe this new girl will disappear and no longer be around to kill. This will all depend on how brave—or stupid—she is. How . . . *unaware* she remains of her surroundings and who she invites into her life.

Like right now.

If she doesn't disappear, and if she remains this gullible, then taking her will be easy.

She'll be a bonus. A finale. It will take a moment. Watching her, trailing her, maybe even striking up a conversation about traffic, the president, holiday plans, climate change . . .

New plan: Find out her favorite places to eat. Learn her schedule. Discover if there's a lover. One nugget of information: she lives in an apartment behind a bigger house—

"Shit!"

The Benz suddenly brakes. The brakes of cars in every lane, including this one, squeal.

A homeless man has shuffled into the middle of La Cienega Boulevard. He yells curses at the young woman as he weaves his way to the curb.

The Benz moves on, closer now to the looming hills. The car slides into the left lane. The young woman's hands flit again. Her head moves, and in the rearview mirror, her eyes look ahead and shine with dashboard light. No furtive glances in the mirror at the car behind her.

Not paying attention.

The Benz turns onto shadowy residential streets with windows aglow with lamplight and televisions. The sedan makes a right to ascend Mantova Drive.

No need to learn anything else tonight. It's decided. She will be the third in the new collection. The world will have one less memory-maker.

And then, a much-deserved and hard-earned retirement. That means waking up late, catching up on TV shows, maybe even learning Portuguese.

Tonight is not the night.

Maybe tomorrow or Saturday. Weekends were made for fun.

YOU MAY
RELY ON IT

7.

You up?

I don't answer Christopher's text. Instead, I lean over in bed to peek past my curtains. Outside, wisps of fog curl around the sharp edges of sunlight. Inside, my bedroom remains lost in shadow. At seven o'clock on a Friday morning, the answer to Christopher's text message should be "already in the car." But after a day of looking over my shoulder and receiving nasty text messages from a stranger . . . after guzzling craft cocktails to loosen my shoulders . . .

. . . after drunk-texting my ex-boyfriend a picture of my nipple and summoning him to my apartment because the cocktails didn't banish *all* my stress—and him actually *showing up* with his own drunken grin . . .

. . . after begging him and him begging me and the two of us slamming into each other like we had slammed back hundreds of dollars of top-shelf booze, Christopher slunk out of my apartment before the newspaper landed in the driveway and the lights in my parents' bedroom popped on . . . Soft black skies . . . No chirping birds . . . That single bright star over my left shoulder . . . One last kiss . . . *Melting, I'm melting* . . .

. . . after falling back asleep and waking up alone . . . and freaking out as my phone vibrated with messages but then realizing Christopher— not a random psycho—had sent them . . .

Being with you is mind-blowing

Just had my breakfast meeting with investors from CT

Were your ears burning?

I talked re u A LOT and how u came up w ROAD TRIP!

It has been an anxious two days, so I don't regret being with Christopher. Right *now*. I'll check back around noon. By then, the fog of sex will have cleared, and the soreness and sourness of our encounter will have fully bloomed.

An overnight rain has left the grass and driveway wet. But Mom's boots are dry, and I grab them as I head to the door wearing her loafers. Skin clear, shoulders loose, pep in my step.

The house smells of fresh-brewed coffee and Dad's favorite veggie breakfast patties. He dares to spread blackberry jam on his toast while wearing a white dress shirt.

"You're a brave man." I sling my arms around his neck and kiss his cheek.

Mom, wearing a classic wrap dress I have yet to steal, throws an eyebrow at me. "G'morning, Michaela. Sleep well?"

Blushing, I sneak a peek at my father (who is now trying to dab jam from his cuff). I hold out Mom's boots and say, "Yes. Uh-huh. Look what I have."

She knows about Christopher's late-night visit. Of course she does.

"Being careful, Mouse?" Mom asks me now, ignoring the boots.

"She went to dinner in Beverly Hills, Cori," Dad says. "Not brunch in Syria."

Mom rolls her eyes at him, then squints at me. *You know* exactly *what I mean.*

I nod. "Yes, I am, Mother."

"Did you receive any more notes?" Dad asked. "Did you catch someone following you?"

My throat tightens, and I pray that Dad remains clueless.

"I got two text messages," I tell them.

They both shriek, *"What?"*

My hands shake as I show my parents the Payback and Do not fuck with me messages.

Confused, their eyebrows scrunch.

"I know," I say. "Strange, right?"

Dad nods. His eyes meet Mom's.

She stares back at him, blank-faced. "We should let Bryan know."

Dad tells me to send him screenshots of the texts and he'll talk to his brother later today.

We all push out cleansing breaths, then resume our morning routines.

Mom waves a hand at her boots. "Bedroom closet, please."

"Is the door unlocked? Can I go in there now?" I set the boots next to the breakfast nook.

"Once you stop taking my clothes," she says, "I'll start unlocking my bedroom door. Speaking of my clothes. My skirt at the dry cleaner's . . . ?"

"Should be ready after three." I take screenshots of the weird texts and send them to Dad.

His phone chimes from the nook's table. He grabs the device, then texts his brother.

A weight that I hadn't realized was still pressing on my lungs has now lifted.

Three slick brochures sit on the breakfast table. I pick up the middle pamphlet. "Ooh. The Mediterranean. We haven't done this one yet."

Mom slides a fried egg onto a slice of bread. "There's a boat next week—"

"We can't do next week—Sasha's wedding." I accept the bacon-and-egg sandwich she's offering me and scoot into the breakfast nook. "And anyway, I must finish this project."

"Thought you said the lady died," Dad says, his mouth full.

"She did, but she paid. Her family will want something, especially now. And I'm planning it out. See, there's this large map of the country in her office, and it's filled with pushpins, and so I'm gonna use the map as the main projection and artifacts will pop over those pins, and it looks better in my head than how I'm describing it, but trust me: it will be *awesome*."

Mom breaks another egg into the skillet. "Have someone else do it. I'm sure Christopher won't give you grief since you're . . . *friends* again."

Did she hear me talk about my vision just now?

Still, I square my shoulders as though I have *no idea* what she thinks happened on her property late last night . . . and early this morning. As stress abatement.

"This is a job, Mother, not a tennis lesson or a gift certificate to some fancy spa. I can't just . . . *give* it away." My ears burn because I certainly gave *something* away late last night . . . and early this morning . . . for wellness. "Also," I continue, "we cannot skip the wedding. I'm *in* the wedding. If she doesn't change her mind at the last minute, of course."

"What does *that* mean?" Dad asks.

"Eh. She's hot. She's cold. She's Sasha," I say.

Mom sighs as she grabs a bottle of vanilla latte from the fridge and sets it before me.

"Who gets married on Thanksgiving?" Dad wonders.

Mom flips a second egg in the pan. "I forgot about the wedding." She tries to smile back at me, but the edges are as soft as her egg.

I twist off the latte's cap with a *pop* and guzzle half the bottle. "I'm late. I'll eat my breakfast in the car. What about the fence people? Are they coming out?"

Dad says, "Tomorrow morning."

Mom slips the egg onto another slice of bread. "I bought a pair of Vans last night—"

"Ooh," I say, sliding out of the nook. "The blue ones?"

She points at me. "You will *not* wear them until February. Eat your breakfast, Michaela."

"Eat my breakfast? Not until February?" I find aluminum foil in the cupboard to wrap my sandwich. "The world may end by February."

Which means I'll be wearing those sneakers by Christmas.

Over at Anna's Place, the aroma of bacon and eggs wafts from the grill. The jukebox is playing Aretha Franklin's "Chain of Fools," and Anna's leaning across the counter, in deep conversation with a man wearing a puce Kangol cap.

The yellow tape that blocked the entrance to Beautiful Things is gone. Not even a scrap of plastic is left on the stucco. The store's cranberry curtains are open, and the brass bell above the door rings as I enter. Light shines upon the glass cabinets, salt and pepper shakers, and tea sets. Bright. Cheery. Whimsical. Like nothing tragic happened here yesterday.

I shout, "Hello?" I move deeper into the store, passing stuffed ravens and belt buckles and spinning away from glass cases of glistening beetles. Nausea wobbles in my stomach—from the dead things, from not eating before surrounding myself in dead things, from a vague sense of dread.

In the back office, artifacts cover the project table. There are a few items that weren't there yesterday. Nadia must have added them before she . . .

My skin turns into gooseflesh as I remember the shopkeeper telling me about her map of Russia and the journal kept by the opera singer . . .

I slip off the trench coat, drape it across the couch, then pull my writing tools, laptop, and digital recorder from my bag. My phone chimes with a text. I hesitate, freaked out by what I might see.

It's Sasha.

Please tell me u didn't sleep with him??!!

I type, OK I won't tell u but I was STRESSED OUT!

Didn't want to be ALONE!

And DON'T say I should've slept in my parents house again!

I turn to the project table. Since Nadia wanted me to go in order, I select the "1" note.

"You can't be back here."

A midthirties redhead wearing a butter-yellow T-shirt and cargo pants stands in the doorway. Her hands are balled into fists, and her hot blue eyes drill into me.

I smile and hold out my hand. "I'm Mickie Lambert from the Memory Bank. Nadia asked me to work with her on a project. Are you the store manager?"

The woman blinks and leaves me hanging. "Nadia's dead." She sniffs the air and frowns. "Did you bring food in here? You can't eat in this office."

"Sorry. Just my breakfast sandwich." That I forgot to eat. I drop my ignored, unshaken hand and say, "Yes. I know Nadia passed. I was with her briefly yesterday, and I'm so sorry—"

"Don't." She squeezes the bridge of her nose. "I can't . . . I mean . . . I've gotten through the morning without . . ."

She swallows, then clenches and unclenches her hands. "Nadia wouldn't want me moping all day. She'd want me connecting people to coin collections and Snoopy pot holders and . . ." She points at the project table. "What's all that?"

"Items Nadia wanted me to curate. Sorry, I didn't get your name?"

"Riley. I manage the store. *Curate?* Seems pointless and trivial to curate things, especially now that she's gone. *Curate?* Like you're some type of . . . museum worker?"

"Digital archaeologist."

Riley snickers. "Seriously?"

"I dig, but not in dirt. So . . . yeah."

The excitement that comes with describing my job rises in me like sweet foam. "I'm actually more interested in the memories that these things evoke. It's not this"—I point to a wooden music box on the table—"that she cared about. She cared about the place she found it, or the person who gave it to her. Nadia gave me bullets of information about each item, and I'm going to write a brief story, something interesting about the item or place or circumstances through which Nadia came to possess that memento. Then we'll create these projections—holograms, if you will—and let me show you." I reach for my phone to present the demo.

She flicks her hand. Not interested. "Will you write about people?"

"Names will be mentioned, but unless Nadia specifically requested it, I won't be doing any deep dives into anyone's background."

Riley nods. "Again, she's dead. There's no one to do this for."

"She paid. We cashed the check. I gotta do it. You can have it, or Anna at the diner may want it since they were friends." I pause, then add, "This will be *incredible*; you'll see."

Riley grunts. "Seems like a waste of money." She picks up a card that sits beneath a gold hair clip. "How long is this gonna take?"

"My part won't take longer than six weeks. After that, the tech guys—"

She grunts again and shakes her head as though my words are gnats.

Out in the store, the bell over the entrance rings. Footsteps tap through the shop.

Riley shouts over her shoulder, "I'll be out in a minute." To me, she says, "So there's a set list of things to *curate*? No need to wander around the rest of the store?"

"No need." I wave my hands at the table. "And I'm only focusing on these things here."

"What if I want to add a few things? Items that Nadia absolutely would've loved to include but may have forgotten because of . . ." She motions to her head.

"Well . . ." I gaze at the fourteen stacks of notes on the project table. "I can probably add two more if you absolutely need to include them."

Riley smiles. Her blue eyes twinkle like the sea, and the freckles around her face dance. "You know, maybe there's a partnership in this. Maybe this bank thing is something we can offer to our customers. Make us . . . relevant. Hip. Tech-forward, you know?"

I clap my hands and point at her. "Exactly! We're already—"

"Okay." She turns to leave but stops and peers back at me. "I have things in here that people would kill to have. So don't even *think* about taking anything. This place may look like a mess to you, but everything is numbered and tracked."

My nerves bristle—she's calling me a thief—but I force a smile. "Of course."

Riley blushes. "I know I'm being harsh, but there's already too much drama right now. And I'm just trying to think of ways to keep the guy who's buying up land around here away from the store, and maybe Nadia will want to . . ." The light dies in her Pacific-blue eyes, and the freckles flatten across her nose. "If you need me, I'll be out front," she says as her smile washes back out to sea.

Because she remembers—Nadia is dead.

"Oh." Riley stops in her step. "If someone comes asking you about Nadia or me or the store, let me know. Okay?"

Someone?

Who?

And asking about . . . *what*?

Artifact 1: Hand-engraved music box plays "You Are My Sunshine." Hand crank. Made from teakwood and finished with wood stain. Acquired on September 3, 1979.

Location of Acquisition: Taos, New Mexico, is located in the Sangre de Cristo Mountains, the southernmost subrange of the Rockies. It is home to the Taos Pueblo, the only living Native American community designated as both a UNESCO World Heritage Site and a National Historic Landmark. Taos Pueblo, inhabited for over a thousand years, is known for its fine art, great cuisine, music, and natural beauty.

Last Owner: Katrinka McLaren.

Memory: You met Katrinka in the parking lot of Joe's Diner. Hungry and cold, Katrinka had been hitchhiking for days across the great state of Texas and had recently reached New Mexico. Over coffee and blueberry pie, she shared bits of her past.

You told her, "Stop thinking dreadful things about yourself."

"Look at me," Katrinka said. "I look awful cuz I live awful."

She looked forty years old even though she was twenty-three. Chewed-down nails, bad skin, rotting teeth, and a smell. You thought she had lovely hair.

That evening, a storm moved into town. This was no weather for hitchhiking. You paid for Katrinka's room at the Sagebrush Inn off Highway 64. Back then, the stays were only fifteen dollars a night, and you could afford that.

The young woman had no idea where she was headed next. "West," she said. "Away from the troubles of the world."

You had a vague notion that Katrinka was running away from something, or someone.

But she said, "Nope. Ain't nobody lookin' for me. If I dropped off the face of the earth tomorrow, no one would know or care."

Katrinka had no money but insisted on giving you *something*. So she gifted you a music box that plays "You Are My Sunshine."

Every September 3, the day you met the young runaway, you turn the crank on the music box and sing this favorite childhood song.

8.

The Memory Bank pays for subscriptions to all the best information depositories. At the tap of a button or keyword, I can search LexisNexis, the *Los Angeles Times*, the *New York Times* (including its historical archives), and EBSCO Information Services. I follow links on the Smithsonian Library's web page as well as in the Gale Biography and Genealogy Master Index.

I don't need any of that right now.

No, I need my laptop to work. I need that "one minute, please" cursor to stop spinning. I need to upload the picture of the music box as well as a clip of "You Are My Sunshine." Since this is my first music box, I wonder whether the Memory Bank has to request permission to use this . . .

I text my inquiry to Elise in Legal, then pluck Nadia's first keepsake from the table.

A simple blond-wood box. So adorable. Couldn't have cost more than twenty dollars.

I always fall in love with the first item that I bank. A client's silver cocktail shaker used to make Hemingways—I now make that cocktail using a similar shaker for friends on boozy afternoons. A broken, tarnished pocket watch from a survivor of the Holocaust. An *Archie* comic book bought from a Brooklyn corner newsstand. A Holy Bible autographed by Johnny Cash.

Is it because that first artifact signifies the beginning of a new adventure?

Is it because that first piece is usually loved the most by my client?

Don't know.

But I love this music box.

My phone vibrates.

The sound makes my spine stiffen. Is it Elise in Legal, or is it the *Payback* texter?

I stare at my device, a cobra now instead of a minicomputer, and my stomach churns.

Once the phone stops vibrating, I grab it.

Just Elise in Legal.

My underarms prickle. I wish it were happy hour and that I hadn't caught the eye of someone with a grudge and my phone number.

As I wait for my computer to work, I grab my pencil and sketchbook to draw the box. Researchers say that sketching helps extend the memory. That these throwaway scribblings "reduce the burden we experience" as we're trying to remember something or solve a problem.

I wind the music box's hand crank. Mom sang this song to me as a kid and I'd cry because her voice was so beautiful to me. And those words . . . Thinking about them now and remembering Mom and me cuddling . . . Agitation slips from my skin like silk.

The motel in New Mexico where Nadia and Katrinka stayed—the Sagebrush Inn—still sits off Highway 64. Rooms go for $127 a night and offer complimentary breakfast. A few suites boast fireplaces and wooden-beam ceilings. One day I will take a lover there and listen to local bands play while we eat repochetas and sip Sagebrush Signature Margaritas.

The office is quiet. No more churning laptop. It's ready to work again.

I type the first letters of Katrinka McLaren's name into a search engine, but I stop myself. No pictures or "where are they now" updates in memory banks except when requested—and Nadia didn't request.

I upload the pictures of the music box into the content-management system and polish the narrative as the cursor spins and spins . . .

Memory one successfully saved!

I can't resist my curiosity and enter Katrinka McLaren's name into Google. I expect search results to include skin-flick credits like *Desert Desserts* or *Hot Babes in Taos-Land*. There are two results: a Black woman with an easy smile and a small Afro, and a white woman with kohl-lined eyes and frosted blonde hair. In her notes, Nadia mentioned blonde hair, and anyway the Black woman has a Twitter account and earned a BA from Florida State in 1992. Too young to be hitchhiking across New Mexico in 1975. The picture of the blonde fits the era: black eyeliner, blue eye shadow.

The hyperlink beneath that picture leads to a website called the Charley Project.

In a new window, I open the website again and click on the FAQ page.

. . . *a clearinghouse of information for missing persons* . . .

I click around to see thousands of cold cases—men, women, and children of every race from all across America who've disappeared under mysterious circumstances. The website's administrator has listed demographic information as well as details surrounding their disappearances. Phone numbers to the relevant investigating agencies are included with each listing.

I bookmark this site, then tab back over to Katrinka McLaren's page.

There are three thumbnail pictures of her. The second picture—apple cheeks and a sleek ponytail—looks like a driver's license or passport photo. The third is a candid shot at a sand dune, where she's sitting behind the steering wheel of a dune buggy. Her middle name is Lara.

She's five feet seven and 130 pounds and has a tattoo of Tinker Bell on her left thigh. On August 15, 1975, she was reported missing from Houston, Texas.

Missing?

In September 1975, she met Nadia and told her that no one would miss her if she were gone. According to Nadia's recollection, Katrinka had been depressed, but coffee and pie at Joe's and a motel room at the Sagebrush Inn were the respite the young woman needed.

At the bottom of Katrinka's web page: RESOLVED in thick red letters.

I exhale, relieved to know that she wasn't forgotten and that her case wasn't shoved into a box in back of a storage room at a police station—

Oh no.

> Katrinka McLaren's remains were found in the Carson National Forest outside of Taos, New Mexico. She was identified in March 2004. Her death is considered a homicide and remains under investigation.

Katrinka McLaren is dead.

9.

I slump in the banker's chair. "Damn it, Mick."

This is common. Memories from older people who have died often include other now-dead people. This dead woman, though . . . She's different. Katrinka McLaren was murdered after being rescued by my client in that parking lot. This is why Christopher demands that his digital archaeologists avoid looking for people. *"Where are they now?"* he asks during every new-employee orientation. *"Who cares? Just keep them out of the banks."*

I stand from the chair to stretch. My spine clicks. A peek out the window shows a blue sky alive with light and a monarch butterfly fluttering in the breezeway. It is closer to lunch than it is to breakfast, and maybe I'll order a grilled cheese sandwich over at Anna's Place.

Up in the store, Riley stands at the postcard carousel. Two men wearing suits and ties tower over her as they write in small notepads. The Black man spots me standing by the back counter. His partner's head lifts to see me, too.

Their wolflike attention makes my pulse pop. Muscle memory tugs me back from that flare-up as my body remembers . . . cops. Having grown up in a law-enforcement family, I know these two men are police detectives. Those suits. Those hard, inquisitive eyes. And yeah, the gold shields on their hips.

Smiling, I walk toward the trio. "Didn't mean to interrupt. Riley, I'm going to lunch next door. Want me to bring you something back?"

Riley's eyes are bloodshot. She mumbles, "No." She doesn't introduce me to the men.

So I keep walking, and my ears burn as I open the door and the bell tinkles.

Anna's Place smells of frying hamburgers and the seaside. Gumbo Friday! Her customers have more white hair than black and will take all afternoon to finish their turkey sandwiches and bowls of gumbo.

I sit at the counter and flip through the box holding the jukebox's song choices. One quarter later, the Brothers Johnson sing "Strawberry Letter 23."

"Good seeing you again," Anna says. "What you gonna have?"

"Grilled cheese on white and tomato soup." As she cooks, I tell her about the detectives questioning Riley over at the shop.

"Guess they gotta check it all out," Anna says, slipping a plate before me. "Nadia dying like that makes sense to *us*, but to Johnny Law?"

American cheese ooey-gooeys from the diagonally cut bread and wraps around my thumb. My stomach growls in anticipation since I didn't eat my bacon-and-egg sandwich.

Anna wipes down the counter and says, "I heard Nadia left a note."

Breathless, I whisper, "What did it say?"

She shrugs. "But if you find out, let me know. Any information will get you *two* free slices of pie." She cackles and cracks the rag against the counter.

"Wonder when they'll have her funeral."

"And who's gonna pay for it?"

I lift my eyebrows. "She doesn't have family?"

"There's a son, but I haven't seen him since maybe back in the summer. He's in and out, that boy. Guess I'll put in money for the service if I need to. She was so generous." She leans over the counter, whispering, "You don't think it's weird?"

"*What's* weird exactly?"

"Nadia wore one of them MedicAlert bracelets. But it wasn't that heart monitor that went off at first. One of the paramedics told me that she intentionally pressed the button."

I shiver. "Ohmigod, she changed her *mind*?"

Anna clucks her tongue, and her gaze moves to the windows.

"There go the detectives," I say.

The two men stalk away from Beautiful Things and pause to talk at the black Crown Victoria parked at the curb. The Black detective shakes his head as the other man reads from his notepad. Then they climb into the car.

"Wonder what they're looking for," I say.

Her gaze settles on me. "They asked me about you."

"What did they . . . ?" My mouth pops open and then slams shut.

"Do I know you; do I know where you live; do you really work for that company?"

My mouth moves to interrupt, but I still can't form words.

"I told them that you had nothing to do with Nadia being dead. I'm sure they're gonna talk to you, though, so be ready."

I'm a person of interest? A *suspect*? For freaking . . . *murder*?

"Hopefully," Anna says, "they'll stop looking at you and look at her MedicAlert bracelet."

With a shaky hand, I slide a french fry through a pool of ketchup on my plate.

"Stop worrying," the old woman tells me. "You ain't done nothing wrong. The cops would never arrest an innocent . . ." She stops right there, and our eyes meet. Because of course they would. She reaches across the counter to squeeze my wrist. "I still say you didn't do it. I'm a good judge of character, and it's obvious you didn't do it. Now eat your food, child."

I chomp a few fries and nibble at my grilled cheese sandwich. "When did you first notice that Nadia's memory was going?" I try to sound normal, but hysteria swirls through my tone.

"Let's see . . ." Anna gazes at the ceiling. "She got mad at me a few months ago. I went over to the shop to ask if she wanted me to make her something for dinner, and she almost bit my head off. She looked depraved, her whole face changed. All lizard-like. 'You're not supposed to be in here. This is my shop.' That's what she shouted at me."

"Okay, that's weird. What did *you* say?"

"My cousin had Alzheimer's," Anna explains, "so I know how to act, okay? So I apologized to her, and I asked, real sweet and patient-like, 'When can I come in?'"

"And?"

"And she was smiling all crazy, and she said, 'I don't let Blacks in my store.'"

My eyebrows scrunch. "That . . . is unexpected."

Anna flicks the rag at me. "Child, that was the disease talking. She was probably a bigot a long time ago. The Nadia I knew treated everybody with kindness. I mean, she'd been living and working in one of the blackest parts of the city for forty years. She just had one of those spells. I sure as hell stopped popping in, though, after that day. She didn't look like the Nadia I'd known all this time. Didn't sound like her, either. This version scared me to death."

I sit back on the stool. "Poor lady."

"Yeah. Poor Nadia." Anna stares out the window again. The Crown Victoria is now gone. "Wonder what them detectives asked Riley."

Back at Beautiful Things, Riley meets me at the door. Her bloodshot eyes are damn near swollen. Her neck and wrists are bright red—she's been scratching and crying. Alarm cycles through my body. Without thinking, I grasp her arm. "What's wrong? What happened?"

She bristles and pulls away from me. "I need to close the store early."

"Did the detectives—"

"Upset me a little? Yeah." She tries to smile and fails, her face stiff and waxen. "I started to leave, but I remembered that your computer and materials are still back there."

"What did the detectives say? Anna mentioned that Nadia left a note—"

"What?" She frowns at me, then shakes her head. "Can you just—"

Panicky, I take a step, closing in on her again. "Wanna talk? Go grab a drink and—"

"Stop," she says. "Just . . . go. *Please?*"

Cheeks burning, I hurry to the office.

"I'm so sorry," she shouts at my back. "You keep trying to gain some traction, but things just keep happening . . ."

I shove my laptop, pens, and sketchbook into my bag and hustle back out to the store. Did the detectives question her about me? Did they tell her that I'm a person of interest?

Riley perches on the stool behind the register now. "I probably should've closed the store today anyway," she says, chin resting on her knees. "But I thought I'd be able to handle it."

I sling my bag over my shoulder. "It's okay, Riley. Yesterday was rough for me, and I didn't even *know* Nadia. Take care of yourself. She would want you to. I'm sure of that."

"Thanks, Mickie. And the detectives just wanted to know how Nadia had been acting over the last few days. You know, if she'd been depressed, that sort of thing. I told them that she was being harassed. That's what I meant this morning, about people asking about the store."

Acid burns up my throat from grilled cheese and anxiety.

Riley claws at her neck, then snarls with frustration. "Tomorrow will be—*has to be*—better. Right?"

10.

With Friday afternoon open, I pick up Mom's skirt from the dry cleaner and then make a quick stop at home. Holding my breath, I check the security app's video feed history: no strangers wandered onto our porch. In real time, I scan up the block . . . down the block . . . and across the street to my neighbors' yards.

Mr. Nealy is raking fallen leaves from his wet lawn.

Mrs. Birdie is carrying grocery bags from the trunk of her car to the inside of her house.

No strangers are lurking on the sidewalks or looking at me from their cars.

Life is normal right now. I feel it in the rhythmic thump of my heart. That feeling is galvanized by Mrs. Birdie leaving her front door open like that. Also, the day has passed without a crazy-ass text message telling me to watch my back.

I hurry into my house, lay the skirt across the couch, then beat it back to the car. A minute later, I'm driving west to meet Sasha and Imani at Red O for late lunch or early happy hour. Tourists crowd the Santa Monica Pier. Waves from the Pacific boom against the sand but cannot soften the shrieks and rumbles made by people and their things.

Yes. Life is normal today.

Sasha, demure in bright-red denim, shows me the latest dick pic in this week's collection, then points to my Bloody Mary. "You gonna eat all those olives?"

"What's up with you taking all of my olives?" I slip the green globe off the toothpick and roll it around my mouth.

Sasha chuckles. "That what you do last night with Christopher's—"

Imani slaps the tabletop. "I do not wanna hear that man's name during this pre–happy hour celebration. Understand?" She raises her perfect eyebrows, not nearly as stunning as the magenta eye shadow against her sable skin.

Sasha sucks her teeth. "How are we supposed to give advice if I can't say dude's name?"

"Yeah," I say. "Also? We didn't trip when you asked us to pray for you and Emily's situation. Sasha didn't like her pasty, basic ass, and neither did I. There. I said it."

"Who the hell leaves nasty toenail clippings in the shower drain?" Sasha asks, lip curled.

I shudder. "What's-her-face with the cute butterfly tat? That's who *we* want for you."

Imani slips on her sunglasses. "And *we* want someone else for *you*, Mick. Chris was cool at first, but then, then he started flaking on you unless he was gettin' some that night."

"Last night, *I* wanted some," I say. "And he's good at giving it away. I needed strong arms after my day of domestic suspense."

"*Fine,*" Imani says. "Like I was saying . . . I don't think that old white lady died by suicide one hundred percent. The MedicAlert bracelet, she pressed it, and that's a deliberate act."

"But the bag around her head is just as deliberate," I counter.

"It could've been both," Sasha says. "Kinda like how you told us she thought the diner lady was a trespasser. Maybe she forgot that she wanted to die, but by then, it was too late."

I say, "Hmm," because that's a possibility: Nadia awakened from the fugue only to discover she'd done the worst and couldn't undo it.

Sasha returns to swiping through her photo album of penises. "A shame I'm gonna have to give these up next week."

I glance at Imani, then say, "I think you should've given them up when Tyler proposed to you back in March."

Sasha waggles her phone. "There are life lessons found in each of these dicks." She swipes through the album and finds a tremendously engorged pink . . . *life lesson.* "With him, I learned that Geminis are batshit crazy. Stay far, far away."

Another look passes between Imani and me, and Imani asks, "So we're still walking down the aisle wearing gold satin on Thanksgiving in Temecula?"

Sasha scowls at Imani and me. "Why y'all keep asking me that question?"

"Cuz you're still collecting dick pics," Imani says.

"Make it make sense," I say, "and we'll leave you alone."

"Tyler is my rock," Sasha says, tapping her heart. "He is Black royalty."

"His dad runs a barbecue joint," I say.

Sasha holds up four fingers. "*Multiple* barbecue joints passed down from generation to generation, *and* he has a reality show."

"Move over, Shirley Chisholm and W.E.B. Du Bois," Imani snarks.

I squeeze Sasha's hand. "We're teasing you, love."

The bride-to-be's smile brightens, and she points to Imani. "You're still leading my glam squad next week? I want that Hollywood magic, that thing you do for them Real Housewives."

Imani lifts her cocktail. "Affirmative."

Sasha points to me. "You still gonna let Chris attend?"

"No," Imani says, "she's not. They aren't together. Don't wish that on us."

"Ohmigod." Sasha's eyes are big and now glued to her phone.

I chuckle. "Another man sent you—"

"I know this girl." With a shaky hand, Sasha holds out the phone for us to see a headline from a local news station. "They're saying she's dead."

◆　◆　◆

Police find woman's body stuffed in a suitcase.

"Allison," Sasha says, her voice tight. "We used to do conventions together last year."

"The pretty blonde one?" I ask. "Looks like Amanda what's-her-face from *Mean Girls*?"

Sasha whispers, "Yeah."

The article is short—it's a developing story—but Allison Cagle had been missing since Tuesday night. She lived in Simi Valley.

Sasha's lips move as she reads the story again. Her thumb keeps flicking up her phone's screen—she wants to learn more—but that's it. There are no other details. Deflated, she sits back in her chair, stares at our empty cocktail glasses, motionless, tight.

"Wow," Imani says. "I'm so sorry, girl."

Sasha makes a sound in her throat and reaches for her glass of sparkling water.

I don't know what to say.

Death has a way of stealing everything. And it comes in threes. There was Nadia. Now there's Allison. Who's next?

So much for normal.

Though the sun is dropping in the sky and we've lorded over this table for hours now, we can't leave Sasha, not with her frozen like this. Imani and I order more appetizers, and we eat and drink and wait until our friend recovers from the disorientation that only death brings.

It's eight o'clock by the time storm clouds herd over Los Angeles and my car slides up Mantova Drive. It is nine o'clock by the time I pry myself off Mom and Dad's family room couch and the first drops of rain dot the path between their house and my apartment. My mind tumbles among the murder of Sasha's friend, the cause of Christopher's attentions, the truth behind Nadia's death, and the person who left notes at my door.

Dad walks me the few yards back to my apartment.

No messages left in my foyer.

He checks the bedroom, closets, and bathroom. Nothing strange, no one strange.

"You gonna be okay back here?" he asks.

I say, "Yep," and wrap my arms around his middle. "Thank you. G'night."

After he leaves, I stand in the middle of my living room. The apartment is quiet—no scratching, no creaking, no *knick-knick-knicking*. Outside, the wind rustles the leaves of the sycamores. On the TV stand, my memory bank is cycling through those pictures of Christopher and me in Santa Barbara.

Enough.

"Memory bank," I say, "tell me about New Orleans."

Pictures of Imani, Sasha, and me fill the device's screen. *You celebrated that day . . . sexy wide receiver of the Saints . . . fried alligator tail . . . said what the hell and you lifted your T-shirt.*

That night, the guy on the Zulu krewe float threw me *all* his coconuts.

The device projects a hologram of Imani, Sasha, and me with shot glasses between us. Wilted, stained, goofy, happy. The sounds of people milling and a brass band playing . . .

"Memory bank, send this picture to Sasha and Imani."

The bank pauses. Then there's a *whoosh* and a "Sent" message on the screen.

Feeling lighter, I call Uncle Bryan's landline.

Uncle Griffin answers and says that he isn't home yet. "Guess where he is right now."

"The gym?"

"And I didn't have to say a word. This month's billing statement did it for me."

"Yay for ridiculously expensive gyms. Could you ask him to call me?"

"This an emergency?" Uncle Griffin asks.

"Nope. Just wanna find out if he knows anything more about this store owner who died. And what I should do about some weird texts I got."

"Of course, sweetie," he says. "Your mom told me about all the drama. I'll tell Bryan to call you back after he takes a shower and has a drink."

I drank plenty today, and so I shower. I hum "Jingle Bells" as my electric toothbrush does its thing for two minutes. Then I follow that brushing with robust flossing and Listerine. With a mouth this clean, I will not have an interesting or dangerous night.

I wipe flecks of toothpaste off the mirror, then study my reflection and one of my face's imperfections: the crescent-shaped scar on my left cheek.

I've asked my parents about this scar, but no one remembers its origin story. *Probably a playground accident,* Mom said once. *You had chicken pox,* Dad had recalled, *and you used to scratch at them all the time.* Chicken-pox scars aren't crescent shaped, though.

"Does it matter?" Sasha asked last Christmas. "It's old. It ain't like a man's ever close enough to see it."

That used to be true. But then I met Chris at that barbecue, and after our first kiss on the bluffs above the ocean, his finger had traced that mark. "How'd you get that?" he'd asked.

"Dunno." Light-headed, I had closed my eyes, loving my scar for the first time, and I caught his finger between my teeth. I peeked at him, and said, "Tell me about the scar on my left cheek."

He'd squinted as he thought of a story. "It was the second day of first grade. Eva Washington, the school bully, liked your red plastic Snoopy lunch box, and she told you, 'Gimme that lunch box or I'm gonna beat you up.' Since you had a crush on Snoopy, you told her, 'No, it's mine. Keep your hands off my stuff, you creep.' At recess, you got coffee cake and a carton of chocolate milk. That's when Eva ran over and tried to take the lunch box out of your hands. As she dragged you around the playground, you held on to that lunch-box handle for dear life. You finally let go once a metal jack left on the playground cut your left cheek, scarring it—and your heart—forever. And you've been beautiful ever since. The end."

He kissed my scar, and I told him that I loved his stories. I truly believed that we would be together forever. Yeah.

I wrap my hair in Mom's ancient Hermès scarf, then retreat to my bedroom, grabbing from the coffee table a family photo album I liberated from Mom's living room credenza. The pages are sticky and smell of bubblegum.

There I am, ten years old, wearing a tin grin and a Mickey Mouse hat. Scar on my cheek.

Six years old, in the kitchen with Dad, baking cupcakes, wearing a Minnie Mouse tank top, frosting all over my face. Scar there, too.

Christmas morning 1998, three years old. Mom and me wearing Santa hats, mugging for the camera. Scar? Yes.

Mom, Aunt Angie, and two-year-old me wearing matching Adidas gear, three pairs of big brown eyes, and judgy eyebrows. Triplets, if you ignored the age differences. No scar.

So. Some childhood accident in my second or third year. Maybe a rock hit my face. Or a zipper from a jacket caught my cheek. Since I attended preschool, the scar still could've been the result of a playground mishap.

After ignoring them all day, I read those *Payback* and *Do not fuck with me* texts. I've never received threats like these before, and reading them now . . .

The shakes return and my breathing strains.

I have screenshots of these messages. Dad and Uncle Bryan also have copies. The phone company keeps records. There's no reason to keep this *poison* on my phone, and whoever's sending it doesn't have the right to be nestled between Mom's Love you, Mouse; Dad's Want me to bring you one of these cronuts?; and Imani's Gurl, he's FINE texts.

And so I swipe left and tap "Delete" twice to disappear those texts.

Then I climb into bed and grab my Magic 8 Ball from the night-stand. "Will that asshole leave me alone?" I shake the ball to read my fortune.

Better not tell you now.

"Will I live happily ever after?" Another shake.

It is decidedly so.

Uncle Bryan's picture brightens my phone minutes before midnight, just as I turn over in bed a third time to finally get down to the business of sleep.

"They think it's suspicious," he says.

A chill sweeps over the bed, and I pull my comforter closer to me. "Huh?"

In the kitchen, the refrigerator hums and clanks. Ice cubes fall into the bucket. Rain pelts the windowpanes, and that loosened window screen starts to rattle, and strange shadows twist against my bedroom walls. One shape resembles a shaft of sunlight, but there is no sun. Another shape looks like the main demon from *Fantasia*, with horns and white spaces for mouth and eyes, the "Night on Bald Mountain" demon Chernabog, who looked down on that village with ghosts and fires and . . .

"The old woman's death at the store," Uncle Bryan says. "Don't know more than that right now."

I tear my eyes away from the demon shapes. "So she *didn't* kill herself?"

"I mean . . . *probably*? But we investigate deaths that look a little janky—"

"And this looks hella janky."

"And since there are rumors that someone threatened her a few weeks ago . . . Whatever. A lot of drama over at that crappy little shopping center."

"Yeah. The owner of the diner is filling me in. What did her suicide note say?"

"Which one?"

"There were *two*?"

Uncle Bryan doesn't say another word.

I say, "Hello?"

"You did *not* hear me say that." His voice is hard, cop-serious.

"Okay. What did the one note that I knew existed say?"

"Typical stuff. How she hated losing her memory, the challenge of being a store owner, how it's been stressful . . ."

I tell him about Peter Weller and his plans to tear down the plaza.

"Eh," Uncle Bryan says. "He's a cool cat."

"You know him personally?"

"Played golf with him once. His dad and Pop knew each other back in the day. Weller's not as cool as his old man, but he still gets a bad rap cuz he's a white boy—"

"Taking Black and brown people's land away from them? Yeah, poor guy. So misunderstood. Guess he will find comfort in his millions of dollars."

"Have *you* ever patronized those shops before this week?" Uncle Bryan asks. "Have *you* ever eaten at that diner?"

"No."

"So let him tear down space no one cares about so that we can have more good restaurants and a SoulCycle."

I rub my jaw. It aches from my uncle's jab. "Don't wanna talk twenty-first-century urban colonization at midnight, Uncle Bryan." *Although a SoulCycle spot five minutes away . . .* "The text messages," I say.

"*Unfortunately*, not much I can do about them right now." He explains that the law on the books in California about harassment and text messages specifies that the sender must intend to annoy or harass, that the language must be obscene and graphically violent, and that there must be a credible threat. "And from the way this person wrote it," Uncle Bryan continues, "it seems like *you're* the instigator."

"That's ridiculous," I shout. "I don't even know who this person is."

"And that's the other problem, Mick. Whoever sent this could contend that they thought your number was the right number, but it was actually the wrong number and they had no clue. Ridiculous, but you understand what I'm saying, right?"

"Yeah." I slump in bed, then groan. "So what do I do?"

"If it continues," he says, "keep a record. Save them and send them to me. Other than that, be careful and be aware of your surroundings. Call me. Text me. I don't care if it's fifty times a day. If I'm not around, I'll send a patrol car or I'll send Griff over. I'm here for you. We're *all* here for you. Okay?"

"Okay. Thanks." I trace my cheek. "Random question. Do you know how I got this scar on my cheek?"

For several seconds, he doesn't speak. "Am I supposed to know?"

"Thought it may be part of our family story."

"What did your folks say?"

"Dad said chicken pox. Mom said playground accident."

He chuckles. "No one remembers half of what they think they remember."

"Very profound, Uncle."

"It's late. That's all I got."

Those shadows on the walls twist. My bedroom window rattles from the storm, and that chill slinks around my bed again. Somewhere outside, helicopter blades thwap against the wet sky. My heartbeat speeds up to match its song. Mom says my first big word was "helicopter."

"You okay, kiddo?" he asks.

My eyes burn. "No. Yes. Tired." I pause. "Oh—my friend knew that woman found in the suitcase."

"The one with 'DD' carved in her back?"

I open my mouth, then close it. The article we read didn't mention "DD."

"Yeah," I say. "She and Sasha were booth girls at conventions."

"When was the last time they talked?"

"February." I pause, then ask, "You all figure out what 'DD' means?"

"Nope. And I wouldn't tell you anyway."

I suck my teeth. "And I thought you were the cool brother."

"Give Sasha my condolences." Once again, Uncle Bryan tells me to be careful, to be aware, to make sure someone knows my location at all times.

I'm barely listening and say, "Okay" and "Uh-huh," because . . .

What is "DD"?

Why was there a second note?

What did that note say?

After I end the call with Uncle Bryan, something thuds beneath me in the garage. A single *boomp*, like someone has smacked into our broken elliptical machine.

I sit up from the pillows and watch the walls.

A creak, like a door is opening slowly . . . slowly . . .

A flashlight beam runs across my ceiling.

I gasp and sit up in bed.

Puddles and splashing.

Someone is outside my apartment.

I grab my phone and push the comforter off my legs and slip out of bed. My heart will quit me before I reach the door—but it doesn't quit me. It just bangs crazy hard in my chest. I call Mom as that flashlight beam roves, as I listen to wet leaves and the burp of shoes in mud.

"What's wrong?" The first words out of Mom's mouth.

"Someone's outside my apartment. There's a flashlight."

Mom is whispering to Dad, and I hear her say, "Gun."

"Mom?"

"Call Bryan," she tells me. Not 9-1-1. Not yet.

I call Uncle Bryan. "I know I just talked to you . . ." I tell him what's happening.

Another thud and my floor shakes.

With my back against the hallway wall, I inch closer to the living room. I try to breathe through my hair, my fingers, through any body part that's less noisy than my mouth and nose.

There's another flashlight breaking up the night. The beam is stronger than the one on my bedroom walls.

I skitter over to my kitchen window.

Rain pours from the heavens.

Dad is creeping along the wet yard, flashlight in one hand, gun in the other.

Mom, satin bonnet in place, stands in the doorway holding a knife. She's ready, too.

The trespasser's flashlight beam shines on the glistening crab apple tree.

Dad notices and points the gun in that direction.

That flashlight beam brightens and grows . . .

Bam!

The floor beneath me vibrates.

Dad, soaked now, drops the flashlight and uses both hands to hold the gun.

The trespasser rounds the corner of my apartment.

I gasp, then shout through my closed kitchen window, "Don't shoot!"

Our neighbor Trent has his hands in the air, his eyes squeezed closed.

Dad booms, "What the *fuck*?"

Mom bangs out of the kitchen. "You—why the hell . . . ?"

I rush down the stairs and into the rain. "You fucking scared me," I shout at the man.

Trent's eyes shine with fear. His usually tanned face is wet and pale as the moon. His chestnut hair is plastered to his skull. "Kiki got out again, and we can't find . . ." He bends to rest his hands on his knees.

Dad curses as he covers his eyes with a hand.

The roar of Uncle Bryan's truck growls over the downpour. Mom hurries to greet him in the driveway.

Dad glares at Trent. "I coulda killed you, dude."

Trent is still doubled over.

Something bumps, thuds, and whines in the garage.

"I think I know where Kiki is," I say.

After holstering his own gun, Uncle Bryan walks his still-anxious brother around the yard as Mom lifts the garage door. I make kissy noises into the shadows. Trent stands beside me and says, "Kiki, here, girl."

A tiny bark, and the little cinnamon dog bounds from the garage. Little lost Kiki had been the source of those bangs and thuds in the garage beneath me. She jumps into Trent's arms and licks his face. "We missed you, girl. How did you get out, huh? How did you get out?"

Mom rolls her eyes, then watches Dad and Uncle Bryan talking near the fence.

Trent apologizes to us again, then hurries past the two pissed-off Black men.

I wrap my arms around Mom's neck. "You okay?"

She kisses my forehead. "No. I thought it was . . ." Her pulse still bangs against my wrists.

"You thought it was . . . who?"

She says nothing, then tries to smile at me. "We need a drink."

"Could you make . . . hot buttered rum?"

Mom nods, then takes my hand. Together, we head to the kitchen. She never answered my question.

Who did she think it was?

11.

Even after a mug of hot buttered rum, I can't sleep.

Guess it could've been worse.

It could've been "DD," the predator who killed Allison Cagle in Simi Valley and carved those initials into her back. Though Simi Valley is fifty miles away from my front porch, Allison was just a second-degree connection away from me. *I know a girl who knew a girl . . .*

How did Allison meet "DD"? Why did "DD" choose Allison? Was it because she was blonde? Because she was working late and alone? Had "DD" left YOUR PRETTY notes at her apartment door? Sent her threatening Payback is gonna come text messages?

Don't know.

I *do* know that I cannot say, "Oh, that happened far away. We don't have murderers like that around here." Because the Black Dahlia's mutilated body was found in Leimert Park, just two miles east of my house. And the killer had carved "BD" into her left thigh! The Grim Sleeper—he killed and mutilated the bodies of sex workers around South Los Angeles. He was caught, though, and now sits on death row in San Quentin.

I have to tell Mom and Dad that Sasha knew Allison Cagle.

Breathless, I roll over in bed and grab my laptop from the carpet. I type "DD carved in back" into the search engine. I click on an article, one of few results.

Donnamarie Queneau went missing from New Orleans, Louisiana, on June 3, 1978, and her remains were found in the Rigolets off Lake Pontchartrain. Reports that the initials "DD" were carved into her back remain unconfirmed. Authorities have confirmed that her neck was broken. At the time of her disappearance, Queneau worked as a cocktail server at the music venue Tipitina's in New Orleans.

The second result leads me to an even briefer article on Beverly Prescott from Galveston, Texas. Found January 1, 1979, she was discovered near the Farmers Export grain elevator as investigators combed through debris after an explosion that killed eighteen people. But Prescott's autopsy confirmed that her death happened before December 29, and that the initials "DD" had been carved into her back.

Both of these women were killed more than forty years ago. The "DD" who killed Allison couldn't be the same one from way back then and from way down there in Texas and Louisiana . . . could it?

Artifact 2: Gold-plated circle hair clip. Acquired on December 3, 1979.

Location of Acquisition: Taos, New Mexico, is located in the Sangre de Cristo Mountains, the southernmost subrange of the Rockies. Its Rio Grande Gorge Bridge was recognized in 1966 as the most beautiful long-span steel bridge in the United States.

Last Owner: Darla Schoelerman.

Memory: You spotted a dusty-red Karmann Ghia with its hazard lights blinking parked on the side of Highway 64. A young woman with long black hair wearing a black T-shirt and cutoff jean shorts paced nearby. The stranded driver smiled and waved her arms once she saw that a woman was behind the station wagon's steering wheel. You looked safe.

The stranded driver's smile made you pull in front of the KG. She looked safe, too.

It was a little past four thirty in the afternoon, and the sky wore a magnificent display of blues, oranges, and purples seen only in deserts and canyons. The stranded motorist ran to your station wagon and leaned into the open passenger-side window. She'd run out of gas and hoped you either had a can of it in the wagon or could tow her to a gas station using a bungee cord she kept in the trunk.

"This has happened before," the woman explained, blushing. "The gas gauge is broken."

You said, "I don't have any gas on me, but I can drive you to a station."

"I'm Darla," the motorist said. "Just like the cute girl from *The Little Rascals*."

This Darla was also a rascal. Her smile. The wink. The little shoulder shimmy she made at the end of nearly every sentence.

After attaching several bungee cords from the Karmann Ghia's front bumper to the station wagon's rear one, Darla slid into the passenger seat. Over twenty miles, she shared her story: She was running away from her boyfriend, Rudy. He had hit her and forced her to do all kinds of sick, perverted things. She was now driving to California to be in the movies. "Skin flicks," she said with that rascal smile. "Since I do it anyway, might as well get paid."

She didn't know: the porn industry was a bunch of Rudys, just wearing better clothes.

Darla needed money to complete her trip to California, so she offered you a choice of two items to buy: a jar of her mother's peach preserves or the gold hair clip she wore to complete her half-up, half-down hairstyle.

You selected the clip and watched as Darla's onyx hair fell past her shoulders, freed now from that fancy gold fastener. Later, you tried to use that clip but could never style your hair like Darla's. Some women were just better at things like that.

12.

Did Darla Schoelerman ever reach California?

Did she star in a porno flick?

Did she take a stage name since "Schoelerman" isn't very sexy?

I want to search for movie credits, but my computer is making those woodchuck sounds again. Don't wanna push it any more than necessary.

It is almost ten thirty, and I've worked on one artifact: Darla's gold hair clip.

The memory finally uploads. I let out a whoop.

Thunder booms, and I peek out the window to see a river of rainwater racing through the breezeway down to the parking lot. Since my bladder weighs as much as a piano, now is the time to take a break. I set the gold-plated hair clip back on the table and stretch. My bones creak, and the sugared, buttered grits and crisp bacon that Anna cooked for me roll around in my belly.

Earlier at breakfast, Anna didn't share anything new about Nadia's death. I told her that detectives were putting a little more time into the investigation since Nadia had been threatened. Anna had only grunted and then nodded toward a booth on the other side of the diner. That's where a thick-necked, yellow-haired white man sat with his plate of pancakes and cup of coffee. He looked as comfortable in that booth as a Morehouse man at a Waffle House in Coeur d'Alene, Idaho.

"Who's he?" I whispered.

Anna whispered, "I'm thinking he's one of Weller's spies. Guess he's gonna come after me next."

That was just an hour ago.

Right now, Riley is leaning on a display case of crystal bells and reading a newspaper.

I sidle up to the case. "What are you—"

Riley "eeks" and hops away from the cabinet. "A little warning next time?"

I hold out my hands. "Sorry. Didn't mean to—"

"You *scared* me." Her face flushes, and she's as crimson as her turtleneck.

"I was just going to say that you seem captivated by today's front page."

She rakes her fingers through her hair. "The cops found a dead woman. Some administrative assistant up in Simi Valley. She was stuffed in a suitcase, and someone carved the letters 'DD' into her back. That's just like another girl three months ago."

"Her name's Allison," I say. "My best friend knows her. We found out last night."

I lean forward to scan the article—there's more here than in last night's brief story. *Allison Cagle . . . last seen alive . . . storm . . . text sent to her friend Jessica . . . phone has not been found . . . police are looking for any security camera . . .*

"Your friend?" Riley asks. "What's her name?"

"Sasha."

"Oh—not this Jessica, then?" Her eyes flit back to the picture of Allison Cagle in the article. "She looks like one of those stuck-up pretty girls who's constantly posting on Instagram."

"Eh," I say. "Doesn't mean someone had the right to kill her."

Riley frowns. "Did I say that?"

"No, I'm just . . ." I force a smile even as my cheeks burn.

"Can I help you with something, or did you stop by to annoy me?"

"I need to use the facilities."

"How is that my concern?"

"I haven't used the bathroom here yet," I say. "Where is it?"

"Upstairs." She flicks her hand at me, then goes back to Allison Cagle's murder.

Curiosities hang on both sides of the staircase walls: a frame of pinned silkworms, the mounted head of a taxidermized rabbit, fading regatta pennants, a vintage *Cabaret* Broadway poster signed by Judi Dench and Kevin Colson. If 90 percent of this place is crammed with mummified ravens and apothecary jars, what will Nadia's apartment look like?

My jaw clamps in anticipation of weird smells and strange stains. Cobwebs. Broken picture frames. More dead animals pinned to blue velvet or posed on papier-mâché boulders. I reach the closed door at the top of the landing and tell myself to lay off the liquids. I throw open the door and . . .

Light from a window spills across the blue carpet. A gold couch and armchair sit in front of a floor-console television. A guitar on a stand perches near the radiator. On the coffee table, Baby Ruth candy bars sit beside a vase of pink roses.

Yes. The old woman wearing the BluBlockers brought Nadia flowers back on Wednesday. My skin crawls with that memory and how Nadia's best friend had stared at me.

Over in the space designated for dining, an armoire displays china. The small oak table is set for two with stemware and cutlery as nice as my mother's.

Nothing needs dusting. Everything sparkles. Normal. This apartment is free of the freakiness found in the space below.

My phone vibrates. A text from Mom.

I told her about Sasha knowing Allison Cagle. Mom's eyebrow had lifted, and then . . . nothing. She didn't think there was any connection to my note-leaver, and since she is my canary in the coal mine, I surrendered some anxiety about "DD."

Fence guys just left, she shares now. They'll start tomorrow

Wonderful, I text back.

I peek in the refrigerator: bottles of wine and vanilla Ensure shakes, a loaf of bread, a pack of cheddar cheese, and browning bananas. A shelf is dedicated to tubs of vitamins and supplements: vitamins E and B12, CoQ10, and ginkgo biloba. The freezer is stuffed with packs of salmon and trout.

In another room, the heavy scent of Pine-Sol makes me nauseous. The full-size bed is covered in a vintage blue-and-white quilt. Did Nadia lie here just days ago, gasping for air? A black leather duffel bag sits open at the foot of the bed. I peek inside the bag: a sand-colored scarf and a floral-fabric journal, its flowers fading, pages swollen, and the index card taped to its cover—"Recipes" handwritten in dying ink—yellowing. I imagine someone leaving this collection in a box put aside for the weekend garage sale. The pashmina scarf, though, looks too new to be left in anyone's yard.

There's a piece of paper on top of the bureau.

INCIDENT REPORT

CRIME: Assault

LOCATION OF INCIDENT: 111 Marlton Road

PREMISES TYPE: Parking lot

DATE/TIME RECORDED: 10.30.19, 10:07 p.m.

VICTIM: Denham, Nadia

. . . reporting officer Rivera met with victim. The victim advised that a truck occupied by one male pulled up beside her and pointed what appeared to be a shotgun at her. The victim states the suspect left the car and proceeded to kick and hit her. A passerby saw the assault and intervened. The suspect

fled and the victim waited for officers to arrive. Officers were unable to lo-
cate the suspect vehicle. The victim declined medical attention. This investi-
gation is ongoing.

The last page of the report lists the suspect as a white male possibly driving a Chevy or GMC four-door, white pickup truck.

This may be the reason Anna doesn't fully embrace the suicide theory. Nadia was jumped right outside her shop and the suspect hasn't been caught. Will detectives still investigate the assault now that she has passed?

I stop snooping and hustle to the bathroom to do my business. The blue subway tile is mildewed but otherwise spotless. A curly hair has dried into the bar of soap on the sink. I ignore the soap and run my fingertips beneath the weak flow of cold water.

Behind me, a shadow blots light in the bedroom. I spin around, half expecting Nadia in her blue pinafore to poke her head in and smile her yellow-teeth smile and say, "I could just eat you up, you little busybody."

But there's no one up here. Empty bed, empty couch.

The stairs groan beneath my weight as I descend into the shop.

Riley is no longer stationed at the display case. She stands near the entrance with crossed arms. Towering over her is a Black man in an olive-green Henley shirt, its sleeves pushed past tattooed, muscled forearms. He scratches his jaw and scrutinizes Riley with tired eyes.

"You know I'm being nice, right?" His voice is rich, barrel cured. "Standing here and asking your opinion? All courtesy." His eyes flick back at me.

My heart goes *POW!* Strong chin. High cheekbones. Brown eyes that may be too small on other men, but on *this* man . . .

The moment ends as his gaze stabs Riley's face. "This is bullshit. You're not her blood. You don't get to make decisions."

"You weren't around," Riley spits back. "You flew in *today*. Nadia died on *Thursday*. Decisions had to be—"

"Not. By. *You*." His finger jabs at those words. "Manage the store. That's your job. Step back if shit ain't got nothing to do with *this* shit." He spreads his arms. "You understand me? Do you hear the words coming out of my mouth?" The thick vein in his forehead pushes at his skin.

I want to possess Riley. I want her to yell: "Who the hell are you talking to? You better get some of that bass outta your voice." I will Riley to clap back at this dude.

But she nods. "I didn't mean to overstep, Dex. It's been hard managing the store and watching Nadia forget her life and finding her after she's wandered away, and I've been doing it all by myself. And *then* I find out she's letting some strange woman wander around the store, looking at our things . . ."

"I know," the man says. "Thank you. Maybe there's still time . . ." He glances at his watch, a traditional, expensive-looking timepiece with an otter-brown leather band. "Wow, Riley . . ."

"I didn't know when you were gonna get here," she explains, "and I wanted to do right by Nadia. That's all."

He chuckles without humor. "Can you just say you were wrong? For once?"

His words scratch at me, sympathy pains for Riley.

She swallows but says nothing.

He rolls his eyes. "Fine. I'll go down, and I'll call you when I find out more." The man—Dex—glances back at me again, then stomps out of the shop.

The entrance bell tinkles and the door slams.

Riley flinches, then glares out the window at the retreating visitor. "It's fine," she says to herself. "You'll figure it out. You'll—"

"You okay?" I ask.

She rolls her head between her shoulders, then exhales.

"Unhappy customer?"

"No. That was Dexter, Nadia's son."

"Well now. Nadia liked Black men?"

Riley trudges past me without comment.

"He seemed pissed," I say. "I had to control myself and keep my mouth shut. One more minute, though, I would've had to jump in the ring and start swingin'."

She gives me a sliver of a smile. "You know how some folks lose their minds cuz they think you're wrong, but you're not—they are? So they lose it? That's Dexter now." She heads over to a basket of belts and starts to separate heavy black ones from thin, metallic ones. "He wants to start planning her funeral, but he can't, and like always, he's blaming me for being efficient."

I hold up a chain-link belt that would look great with my high-waisted mom jeans. "What could you have possibly done that got him that heated?"

Riley stops sorting the belts. "None of this concerns you, Memory Bank. Your job is that way. Go . . . *curate*, since Nadia thought you'd be better at it than me."

"Ohmigod, relax," I say, and drop the belt back into the basket.

Poof. Solidarity crushed underfoot.

Where was this bravado three minutes ago?

As I walk back to the office, I wonder about the scene I just witnessed.

Maybe there's still time. That's what Dexter said.

Time for what?

. . . when I find out more.

Artifact 3: Miniature brass kaleidoscope with colored crystal beads and optical mirror on a gold chain. Acquired on June 3, 1990.

Location of Acquisition: Portland, Oregon. Named on a coin toss in 1845 Oregon's largest city is located on the Columbia and Willamette Rivers. Portland is known for its strip clubs—more per capita than any other city in the country—and for its breweries.

Last Owner: Shawn Eckert.

Memory: You'd put off buying a new tire and jack for months. You didn't want to spend the time or money. On a rainy night in June, the front left wheel of the station wagon went flat during a shopping trip across Oregon. You didn't know where you were or if anyone would ever find you stranded on the side of the road.

But a woman driving an electric-blue Chevelle saw the wagon's hazard lights blinking and pulled behind the car. The Good Samaritan in Flannel shouted from the driver's-side window, "What's the problem?"

"A flat," you shouted. "Mind driving to a gas station for a tow truck?"

"I can do better than that." The driver owned a jack and had just purchased a new spare tire that sat in the trunk. She introduced herself as Shawn, and with hands as big as her heart, she helped change out the flat tire for the new one in less than ten minutes.

It wasn't until Shawn said, "Oh, she's awake," that you noticed a little girl in the passenger-side seat.

The child resembled Pippi Longstocking, the heroine of those strange Dutch children's books. The girl had been taking pictures of you and Shawn throughout the tire-changing with a cheap Kodak Star 110

35-millimeter camera. You waved at little American Pippi and offered Shawn the hundred dollars in cash you'd allocated for the shopping trip.

Surprisingly, Shawn took the money. "Gotta replace that tire," she said.

You asked to buy dinner for Shawn and the little girl.

Shawn said, "No, thanks. I'm hurrying down to an art show in Eugene. I stopped cuz I want the universe to smile on me for a change."

With that, the Good Samaritan in Flannel hopped back into the Chevelle, tooted the horn, and roared down Oregon Route 80. During the tire-changing, Shawn's chain holding a mini-kaleidoscope had broken and fallen to the asphalt. You plucked it from the highway and raced (thanks to Shawn's new tire) down the road to find that kind woman, but you never found her.

The kaleidoscope and its unlimited color patterns helped ease your mind as you looked to the light for guidance.

13.

How cool would it be to find American Pippi's pictures of Nadia and Shawn changing a tire? Did those rolls make it to a developer, or are they sitting in Shawn's kitchen drawer stuffed with old keys, dead batteries, and yellowing decks of playing cards?

Last week, I found old rolls of film inside a rarely opened credenza in our garage. What's on those rolls, I have no idea, but now I think I'll have that film developed. If any of the pictures are good, I'll add them to Mom's memory bank.

Near the front of Beautiful Things, three old ladies wearing overcoats of pink, green, and blue browse through a stack of *LOOK* magazines. Using the dying light as a filter and the display case of costume jewelry as a backdrop, I'm taking pictures of a small felt mouse wearing a tin crown. At the register, Riley ends a phone call. Her skin turns so milky, the freckles on the bridge of her nose disappear. "He's gonna be pissed, but he should step up and lead. Shit."

She doesn't say this to me because she doesn't talk to me. The store's quiet exaggerates her cursing, and "shit" clinks off the cabinets and jukeboxes like a grenade pin. She drags her fingers through her hair and chews her bottom lip until it turns bubblegum pink. Her cell phone rings. She forces herself to smile before answering. "Hey."

A man's shouting pulses from the phone. He is *nuclear* pissed.

Riley's knuckles whiten as she grips the phone. Her mouth is a tightrope as the shouting man throws hot coals at her through the earpiece.

I tap "Record" on my phone and pretend to take pictures, shifting the mouse in light that doesn't change.

Finally, Riley says, "Dexter, listen to me—"

More shouting.

Even the old ladies sneak peeks at her. They look over to me with question marks in their eyes. My jaw clenches and I shiver. Her pain is splattering all over us.

Teardrops tumble down Riley's flushed cheeks. Dexter has broken her. As she listens, she dabs her runny nose with her knuckles and fingertips. "Nadia's only mentioned cremation to me," she says pitifully to Dexter. "And so, when they asked—"

Dexter shouts again.

Riley squeezes her eyes shut. "Yes . . . yes . . . okay."

One of the old women tiptoes over to Riley and hands her a pack of tissues.

Riley mouths, "Thank you." She turns away from us to blow her nose. "Okay . . . yes . . . That's fine, Dexter. You should—" She sighs. "He hung up on me."

My own phone is now shaking in my hands.

She wanders over to me and slumps as she stands. "In her note," Riley says, "Nadia said that she wanted to be cremated. And since Dexter is always on the other side of the universe, and because neither Nadia nor I can ever count on him being here, I . . ."

Her facade twitches but refuses to crumple. "It's done, but he's mad because he didn't want that."

A flare cracks in my head. *What?*

"And now he's being a drama queen." She covers her mouth with a hand. "It was the last thing she requested. I made the right decision."

I clear my throat, knowing that I'd slash hers if she'd pulled that with *my* mother. "You still have the note? Maybe show it to him, and that way, he'd see for himself. That way, he sees without question that you honored Nadia's wishes.

Riley mews again and dabs tissue at her eyes.

"You wanted to do right," I whisper, ignoring the niggle of guilt for recording her breakdown. "Dexter's upset. He probably feels a little guilty for not being here."

She nods. "The detectives took the note, so I don't have proof." She blows her nose again. Pushes out a few breaths. Shakes anxiety from her arms, then lacquers on her everyday scowl. "The service is Monday morning, so I'm closing the shop that day. You're free to attend if you want. And . . . umm . . . I'll go tell Anna and what's-her-face at the hair salon."

Riley tromps to the front door, stepping over the corpse that was her pride before Dexter ripped her a new one in front of a room of strangers. *Again.* "Stay around for a minute? Watch the customers?"

"Sure," I say. "Take your time."

"Anna can cook a few things for after . . ."

The doorbell jangles and she's gone.

The old ladies let out a collective breath and scatter about the store. I wilt against the cabinet and tap the red button on my phone to stop recording. This won't go into the Memory Bank's cloud. No, this one I'll keep for . . .

What?

No idea. But I will keep it like bacon grease or a Canadian penny because I may find myself in Canada or have a hankering for a spinach salad.

"You're really into this 'memory' thing, huh?" Anna flips over my hamburger, and the music of sizzling meat joins the smoky goodness of jukebox Gladys Knight singing "Neither One of Us."

"I love history and I love stories, and my job combines it all. My world is one of those lovely charcuterie boards."

Anna squints at me. "A *what* board?" She sets a club sandwich in front of the customer sitting across the counter from me. Helene, the third ex-wife of some long-ago prizefighter, separates the ingredients of the sandwich and eats them like a salad. Her perfume—lilac or freesia—is stronger than the smell of fried food.

I nod toward the old woman with the sandwich and whisper to Anna, "I'd *love* to hear about all the craziness she's seen."

Anna snickers. "Helene is a mess. A different kinda mess than Nadia, who ain't gonna see this thing you're working on so damn hard."

"Well," I say, "there *is* Nadia's son. He can take the box if he'd like."

Anna grins as she drops a slice of American cheese on top of my patty.

I waggle my eyebrows. "What he's like? Is he a mama's boy?"

Anna's brown eyes shine like buttons. She says nothing as she sprinkles seasoned salt onto my fries.

"Come on. What does he do for a living?"

"He travels around the world taking pictures. That's why Nadia didn't see him as much as she wanted. She was so proud of him, though. He got a little frustrated with her sometimes. Wanted her to retire and sell the store, but . . ." She sets the plate of burger and fries before me.

"Is he single?"

She nods and smiles.

"He like Black girls?"

"Dexter is an equal-opportunity ho." She dips her chin. "I thought you had a man."

"I don't know *what* I have." I take a big bite from my burger. Pepper, garlic, and salt dance on my tongue. "You should've heard it. Dexter was totally pissed at Riley. Right before I came over here, me and the customers heard him screaming at her from across the room."

"He's *always* pissed at Riley. If you haven't noticed, she's . . ."

"Bossy? Abrasive? A know-it-all?"

"So you've noticed."

"I'm thinking of finding his number and calling him." I hold up a hand. "About Nadia's memory bank. Maybe he can share some memories of her with me. I'm sure he has stories."

She winks. "He'll be by later. When he's in LA, he always stops in and lets me cook for him. And now that Nadia's gone . . ." She frowns, busies herself with cleaning the cutting board. "What were he and Riley arguing about?"

I squeeze the bottle of ketchup to cover my french fries. "You did *not* hear this from me—but Riley had Nadia cremated without first telling Dexter."

Anna gasps, then touches her heart-spot. "No, she *didn't*. That girl came over here, asking if I can cook for the repast, but she ain't said one word . . . I didn't think . . . Oh my goodness. That wasn't her right. She ain't Nadia's child."

"According to Riley," I continue, "Nadia requested cremation in her note, and the detectives now have the note."

Anna says, "Hmph," then narrows her eyes. "Mr. Kim, the locksmith across the way?"

"I haven't met him yet." His is a cramped shop with flecked, red-painted letters and security bars. In the few days I've been here, I've seen him shuffle to Anna's around two o'clock every day for coffee and a doughnut.

"Mr. Kim didn't like Nadia," Anna says. "Not that he wanted her *dead*, but they weren't each other's cups of tea. Anyway, he told me that those detectives questioned Peter Weller."

Shock makes my spine straighten. "They think that Weller . . . Why?"

"Cuz one of Weller's guys jumped the owner of the club that used to be on the corner."

Link's Lounge, just twenty steps from the diner's front door, is now boarded up.

"They put Link in the hospital," Anna says, "and that's when the lounge closed. He was basically forced to sell. Link still stops by for breakfast sometimes, but he can't eat much since he can't really taste his food. They broke his nose. He ain't been the same since."

Mob shit. Yikes.

"But they . . ." I begin. "*You* found Nadia with a bag over her . . . She left a note."

Anna leans close to me. "Before he went over to yell at Riley this morning, Dexter stopped here. *He* told *me* that the detectives let him see that note. Dexter says that the writing ain't Nadia's."

"*What?*" I gape at Anna.

She lifts my dropped jaw to close my mouth. "Chew your food, baby."

I do as I'm told, then say, "Not her writing? Is he sure?"

She wipes down the vinyl-covered menus in the nearest holder. "He would know his mama's writing, wouldn't he?"

"But she was probably distressed," I offer. "She was about to kill herself. Her hands *had* to be shaking and . . . What if she forgot that she wanted to die? What if her disease screwed everything—her thinking—screwed it all up?"

Anna taps her earring. "You may be right, but Dexter's talking about filing a wrongful-death suit against Weller. He thinks—and he's right—that Weller either forced Nadia to kill herself by harassing her until she broke *or* he had that white man that was eating here this morning kill her and make it look like a suicide."

"All so he could . . . ?"

"Take the store and the land beneath it."

Something craters in my belly. This version of Weller does not track with the version presented by Uncle Bryan, that of a benevolent businessman wishing to build high-priced condos, high-end restaurants, and a SoulCycle.

Anna eyes me. "You don't think so?"

"No idea. It's a lot to believe."

"Anyway, Weller's got to deal with Dexter now." She pours herself a cup of coffee. "Poor Nadia. Ran away from an abusive marriage to become a successful store owner, and now . . . That woman just wanted to sell antiques and take care of her son."

Abusive marriage? No wonder she stopped to help women in distress. She *was* a woman in distress. As I head back to Beautiful Things, I'm determined to see that suicide note. Since I'm now immersed in Nadia's world, reading pages filled with her skinny, slanted writing, I want to compare that script against her farewell to this world. I want a glimpse into the mind of the woman I met two days ago, a woman who seemed enthusiastic about capturing her most precious memories before her mind collapsed.

Back in the office, I shake my head as I stand over the project table filled with her collection. Because it *doesn't* seem right that this same woman wanted to die. Maybe months from now, but over four hours?

Maybe Anna and Dexter are right.

Maybe Nadia Denham *was* murdered.

Maybe Peter Weller, greedy land baron, killed her.

14.

I grab my belongings and turn off the office lights.

Riley sits behind the cash register. Her face is ashen, her lips a twisted line.

"I'm gonna head out now," I tell her, "unless you need me to stay."

She grunts. "No."

"See you tomorrow, then."

She doesn't nod or say goodbye as I leave the shop. She just sits on the stool and stares at her phone.

I'm glad this day is done.

Storm clouds build in the sky. The air is thick and smells of salt from the Pacific Ocean. Since Anna's Place is closed, there's no competition against the aromas of burger grease and cake batter. Over on King Boulevard, a car's stereo booms out a song. I don't know the title or any of the lyrics, but that slow, slinky bass line is Proustian. Oh yeah, Tiger stripped to this beat last weekend. I'd been sipping the nastiest dirty martini. Sasha had stolen my only olive.

The sound of scraping metal pulls me back to the Santa Barbara Plaza. It's the locksmith pulling a security gate across his small storefront.

I say, "Good evening. We haven't met yet. I'm Mickie Lambert."

A tall whip of an old man, he nods, and the fishhooks stuck through his cotton fishing hat tinkle. "I am Jae Kim. Hello." His skin is thin and liver spotted. His calloused hands tug at the shiny padlock until he knows it will hold fast. "Goodbye."

"Wait. Anna told me—"

He waves a hand at me. "I am not involved."

"Right. I—"

"You need keys, you come to me. Gossip? I am not involved." He peers at me through his wire-rimmed glasses, waiting for me to understand.

A smile builds on my lips like pushed-back sand. "Have a lovely evening, Mr. Kim."

He hurries off without another word.

In the parking lot, my car sits alone beneath a sodium light closer to the lot's perimeter. A man stands beneath a bright-white light closer to the stores. I know him—not because I *know* him—but because he's one of the detectives investigating Nadia's death.

With his rich ebony skin and hooded eyes, he resembles an African totem wearing a lead-colored suit and black wing tips. He flashes his badge and kinda smiles at me with teeth as bright as his detective's shield. "Hi there. Detective Keith Winchester."

As I move closer to him, I walk into a stench so full and rich that I gag.

"The RVs," the detective calls out. "Someone's crapper crapped out."

My eyes water. I stop in my step even though it isn't my policy to talk to strange men in strange parking lots. But he is a cop, which means . . . nothing. I love my uncle, but cops can be worse than the monsters who attack young women in parking lots like this. I have protection, the can of Mace in my glove box, but that will do as much for me right now as a flux capacitor.

"And you are . . . ?" he asks.

"Michaela Lambert."

He offers his hand. "Nice meeting you, Miss Lambert."

The detective's hands are supple. He believes in lotion and exfoliation.

"How can you stand this?" My face twists, and I take in air through clenched teeth.

"I'm used to bullshit, Miss Lambert. Folks shovel it in my direction all the time."

"Guess we're all warriors in our own way."

"You knew Nadia?" he asks.

I shake my head. "Just met her on Thursday. I'm doing—*was* doing, *still* doing—a project for her."

"Uh-huh." He pulls a little notepad from his jacket pocket. "What kind of project?"

I give him the elevator speech that Chris drills into every employee. *What is the Memory Bank? Why is a memory bank so special? How can a memory bank change your life and honor the lives of those you've lost?*

Detective Winchester simply writes in his pad. "Did Nadia seem distressed or . . . *uneven* during your time together?"

I think back to Thursday morning. The old woman's eyes had sparkled as she talked about the travel journal, about the Japanese map, about the collector's edition of *Anna Karenina*. She was chatty and lively as we toured the shop, and she cracked jokes as we stood in the basement with its white powder and yellowing plastic.

"She was chipper," I tell the detective. "Sad that she was losing her memory but excited that I'd be working with her to preserve some special experiences."

Interest sparks in his eyes. "*Special experiences* . . . got it. Back on Thursday, what time did you arrive to the store?"

"Around eleven that morning."

"And you left . . . ?"

"That first time, I left a little before noon. She told me to come back at five that evening. She'd planned to close the shop and help me get started." I tell him about going home for an hour or so, then seeing a movie at the theater across the street and shopping in the mall. "After shopping, I walked to my car—"

"When?"

"After four o'clock. I came out of the mall and saw all the emergency vehicles here."

"Do you have a movie ticket stub or receipt from shopping?"

I blink at him, and my heart beats one strong *boom*, and then it dies. "Am I a suspect?"

"Movie ticket stub or receipt."

My face numbs as I thrust my hand into my bag. "Umm . . . I . . ." My fingers slip around my wallet, a hairbrush, my digital recorder, a tampon . . . "They're in here somewhere . . ."

He watches my hand move around in my bag. "If you can't find it now, find it tonight and send me a picture." He points his pen across the street. "You said that theater, correct?"

"Yes." My hand continues to scour the depths of my bag. That stub has to be here. "Am I . . . ? Did I . . . ? But didn't she . . . suicide?"

"It appears that way," he says.

"Even though she pushed the button on her medic-alert bracelet?"

"Who told you that she pushed the button on her medic-alert bracelet?"

I freeze. "I . . . can't remember. I barely know anyone's names here."

"I smell bullshit." Detective Winchester's eyes peck at my face, my shoulders, my hand still lost in my bag. "Ms. Denham is dead. Why are you still here?"

"She paid for the bank, and it isn't cheap. I'm told that her family still wants it." I try to swallow, but a ball of fear lodges in my throat. My voice is quivering. I'm terrified, and yet I haven't done anything wrong.

"Her family," he says. "Meaning . . ."

"Her son. I think his name is Dexter." A lie—I *know* his name is Dexter.

"And what do you know about Dexter?"

"Not much. Anna, the woman who owns the diner? She told me that he's a photographer. Riley says that he's not around much. He was here today, though. Right now, it seems that he's angry at Riley for something, I guess. Other than that . . ."

"If I were to go into the store," the detective says, "and find out that some things are missing, I wouldn't find those missing things in your car, would I?"

I shake my head so fast that its motion tilts the earth's axis by an inch. "Why would I . . . ? And really, there's nothing valuable in there. At least, not valuable enough to *kill* someone for."

He eyes me. "The land on which it sits is worth millions, though. A *lot* of people would kill to have it."

"I wouldn't—I'm not into commercial property."

He lifts an eyebrow. "Maybe not property, but I bet you're into money. And someone interested in this land could've paid you to do a job."

"A *job*? You mean a *hit*? You think I'm a—" My laugh sounds like the clang of pots in a church sanctuary, as jarring to me as it is to the cop. "Just so you know, my uncle is Bryan Lambert. He runs the Missing Persons Unit over at Pacific Station. And my grandfather—Bryan's and my father's father—was a sergeant at Southwest."

"My bad." He grins, but malice rests in his eyes. "I didn't know that people with law-enforcement families couldn't break the law."

My skin hurts. His words swarm like horseflies. "That's . . . that's not what I mean."

"I know your uncle. I still need you to find that movie stub, though."

"Okay."

"And if you notice anything strange—"

"Have you actually *seen* the inside of Beautiful Things?"

He holds out a business card. "Strangers, any interesting conversations, I'd like to know."

My hands shake as I take that card.

"Anything else?"

I blurt, "Nadia was jumped back in October."

He gazes at me, waits for more.

"No one was arrested, I believe."

"Anything *else*?"

"There was someone here earlier. A white guy—he's not a normal fixture around here," I say. Then I describe the man who ate breakfast at Anna's Place, the one she thought to be Weller's spy.

Detective Winchester flips back a page in his steno pad. "According to my notes, you've been working here all of . . . three days, since Thursday. Correct?"

"Correct."

"So how do *you* know he's not a normal fixture?"

My tongue feels fat and stupid in my mouth, but my mind has finally shaken off its fear. "Then why did you ask me to tell you to report anything or anyone strange if three days is not enough time for me to make that determination?"

He grins, and this time, the lights in his eyes dance. "Good night, Miss Lambert. Give Lieutenant Lambert my regards. Oh, may I have your number in case I have any other questions?" He chuckles. "*In case.* No, I have *lots* of questions."

My voice quavers as I recite my cell-phone number.

"I'll be in touch."

I offer him a "good night" and shuffle to my car, the stink of human waste blossoming with each step.

"You parked far," he shouts at my back.

"I'm a crappy driver," I shout over my shoulder. "This way, no one gets hurt."

A minute later, I'm behind the steering wheel of my car. But the weight of . . . *him* still cramps me in my own space. Wrung out, that's how I feel right now.

Detective Winchester hasn't moved from his spot beneath the light. He isn't watching me. He's watching the store. Watching the store as though some secret is buried somewhere between the busted jukebox and the cracked-cover journals of mezzo-sopranos.

As I turn left onto King Boulevard, my phone buzzes with a text— Detective Winchester.

What if I were to tell you . . .

Tell me what?
I watch ellipses bubble . . .

. . . that someone says . . .

Says what?
Ohmigod. I'm shaking so much that I pull into a 7-Eleven parking lot . . .

. . . they saw the man you described leave the store right before Nadia's body was discovered?

15.

Detective Winchester doesn't suspect me of killing Nadia.

Thank you, God!

Because I am *many* things.

Smart.

Curious.

Scattered at times, even.

But I am a dolphin—dolphins don't *kill*.

The man in the diner, though . . .

Was I *that* close to a possible murderer? What if he returns?

Who saw him that night?

I tap the detective's phone number as the world brightens around me.

His line rings . . . rings . . .

"You can't text me shit like that and not answer!" I shout into the void.

Finally, the line quits ringing and his voice mail message plays. His calm, recorded voice tells me to leave a message.

At the beep, word vomit pours from my mouth: *who said that, danger, am I in danger, description, police artist, surveillance, protection, please call me.*

Does Anna know? What do I do *now*?

Drizzle covers my windshield. It's the kind of rain that I hate, the not-enough kind of rain that makes the roads slippery, the slip-and-slide kind of rain that abetted my father's car slamming into the ass of that trash truck. And now, my stomach clenches. I'm already panicking, and I tell myself to loosen my grip around the steering wheel.

I can't, though.

Car headlights creep behind me as I leave the 7-Eleven parking lot. Because of Winchester's text and my frantic voice mail, I've been distracted, and now, I can't see the driver of this car. Whoever it is drives so close to me that the reflection in the rearview mirror is a glare of light. Whoever it is must see my hands, white-knuckled and squeezing the steering wheel.

I veer left and turn onto Coliseum Road.

The car behind me also turns left onto Coliseum Road.

Together, we head into the grove of densely packed apartment buildings.

At the light, King Boulevard again, I turn into the grocery store parking lot.

The car behind me also turns into the grocery store parking lot and leaves the lot just as I have to drive north on La Brea Avenue.

I'm being followed.

I snake from the right lane to the left. At the last minute, I gun the engine and race through the yellow signal at La Brea and Jefferson. The Benz's ass fishtails, but the tires snatch back their grip to keep me from hydroplaning.

The car behind me lurches through the intersection and runs the red light.

Who is this?

There are three shields in the car's front grille.

What car has three shields?

A Buick.

I am soaked in my own sweat—didn't know that I could sweat so much. My body can't stop twitching and jerking—didn't know that I could be as scared as I am right now. My eyes sting with gathering tears, too many tears for my eyes to hold. But they must hold those tears because I cannot be blinded, not right now.

I thrust my hand toward the center console. My phone. Where is my . . . ?

A car horn blows.

The sound forces air from my lungs.

Did I cut someone off?

Did I—

The world around me wobbles, and my cheek stings from the heat of a single teardrop.

The rear of a metro bus is coming fast at me and I stomp the brake pedal. My tires squeal to a stop. An inch. That's how much space there is between me and the bus. My car's cabin glows red with the bus's brake lights.

Breathing hard, mind spinning, I glance in my rearview mirror and those headlights . . .

The glare has dimmed, and the lights aren't so bright in my mirror.

I swipe at that fallen tear on my cheek, then bat my hand around the car to find my phone in the passenger seat.

In front of me, the bus moves forward, and so do I. At the next red light, other cars pull behind me, and now I can't see those headlights at all. I count the seconds between the back-and-forth flicks of the windshield wipers.

I make three turns and find myself back on Obama Boulevard. Disoriented. That's how I feel right now. In the Upside-Down. I am soaked in sweat, and my body won't stop twitching. My eyes won't stop darting from my car's rearview and side mirrors to the road ahead.

Time isn't slowing my racing pulse, and my vision is screwed. I can no longer distinguish the front grilles of cars. A silver pony? Buick. A cosmos of stars? Buick. Because the only thing that I know about this madman is the make of his car. Hell, I don't even know if a man was sitting behind that Buick's steering wheel.

I need to get home. Get home before he finds me again, rams my car from behind, and captures me for . . . *What?*

Did the Grim Sleeper ever have a good reason? The BTK Killer? The monster roaming the city right now and carving "DD" into women's backs—what reason could he give for that?

Christmas lights around the eaves of my family home welcome me and promise safety in our small herd. Even with those sycamores now trembling from the wind and somber wet sky, no monsters can touch me. Not anymore. Still, I throw nervous glances behind me as I climb out of my car. I crouch near the hood and peek past the front house to the street. With a prayer of thanks on my lips, I wait to hear the crunch of tires against asphalt or the strained whine of an old American car climbing the hill.

No headlights. Just rain and Debussy.

I shiver from the chill of cold slipping past the fibers of my sweaty clothes.

Except for my panting and the boom of my heartbeat . . . silence.

Has this happened before—someone following me—but tonight's the first time I noticed? Noticed because I tore my eyes from the phone and from the stereo to actually pay attention to the world around me?

What scary shit have I missed simply because of Snap, Twitter, and 'Gram? Is this how "DD" grabbed Allison? Why was I chased? Who's watching me? Is it the note and text sender? *Why me?* Any reason I come up with makes no sense. I have nothing, I know nothing, I'm just a digital archaeologist, a high-end scrapbooker, a gussied-up geek, goddamn it.

I push out breaths to calm my nerves. As I wait for Buick headlights to slink past my house, the cold pulls me back from the brink of full panic. My heart, though, beats louder than Mom's piano playing.

Am I imagining all this? Is it possible that no one driving a Buick is coming for me?

I talk myself off the ledge as I head upstairs.

No return call or text message from Detective Winchester.

By the time I dump the contents of my satchel onto the living room couch, I have almost convinced myself that yes, I *did* imagine that Buick following me, I *am* overreacting.

Anna Karenina has tumbled out along with the flotsam and jetsam in my bag. The bookmark sits in the chapter where Anna feels guilty for thinking less of her husband.

I'm a wicked woman, a lost woman . . .

No, I am an *innocent* woman.

Here's my proof!

The movie stub from the two o'clock showing is smeared with lip gloss and is somehow now peppermint scented. The store receipt—four fifteen p.m., paid with a debit card ending in -3910—shows my purchase of a sweater and leggings. Security cameras from both businesses will show me entering and exiting.

I take pictures of both alibi documents and slip them into my wallet. Then I release a long, shaky breath from my lungs. Something—my sanity, my . . . optimism, *something*—has frayed inside me and is now torn at the corner and wants to entirely rip in half.

No. I will *not* lose control. I will *not* rip. I will *act.*

I text Uncle Bryan. Could you send a patrol car to check the area?

He immediately responds. Did something happen?

Maybe? I'm paying more attention and a car seems suspect. Not sure if it was following me.

What kind of car?

A Buick. Older. Black or purple. Blue? Couldn't see.

One more deep breath and my shoulders sag.

My mind turns back to Detective Winchester's suspicions.

It's a privilege to walk the earth without watchful eyes scratching at one's skin. As a Black woman, I will never know life without that type of disregard or caution. I am automatically a thief and a whore, and I cannot prove that I'm neither to those who would automatically think the worst of me. Neither ticket stubs nor store receipts matter to some. But no matter how much I'm worn down, I refuse to break, not for phantoms driving Buicks, not for strangers sending texts and leaving notes.

Detective Winchester, he knows the deal. He's just paid and trained to be skeptical, to ask questions. To formally cock an eyebrow on behalf of truth and justice. He's doing his job, nothing personal.

Uncle Bryan has always told me that he could spot a liar the moment they walked into a room. Shifty eyes. Fingers raking through hair. Suspects scanning your face to see if you believe them. Their words, "I didn't do it," never matching their hands. And if *he* thinks Weller is a good guy, then maybe Nadia *did* die by her own hand.

But Winchester, he's just as trained as my uncle, and he thinks Nadia's death is suspicious. If Nadia didn't do it, who does he *really* think murdered . . . ?

What do you know about Dexter? That's what Detective Winchester asked me.

Does he think Dexter did it?

I don't know much, if anything, about Nadia's son. But this could change because I now type "Dexter Denham" into a search engine on my phone.

My eye catches my kitchen counter. The quart of vanilla latte sits there. I forgot to put it back into the fridge this morning. Damn it. Moving too fast again.

Before I do anything else, I upload all my recordings to the Memory Bank's cloud. Riley's argument with Dexter has nothing to do with Nadia's bank . . . unless it does.

I boot up my laptop.

Photographer Dexter Denham | Buy Photos | AP Images

Born in Hartford, Connecticut . . . Studied photographic illustration at Santa Monica Community College and California State University Los Angeles . . . compelling images of off the beaten path . . . major assignments include Hurricane Maria, the Rio de Janeiro Olympics, and the 2016 presidential campaign . . .

Not the bio of a man who just committed matricide.

Other hyperlinks take me to more photographs taken by Dexter Denham.

Spokeo has found twelve records. Of those listed possibilities, three could be Nadia's son. Was it the guy living in Granada Hills? Pittsburgh, Pennsylvania? Los Angeles? In the Related To section, though, Nadia isn't listed in any of these records. So maybe not?

I scroll to the bottom of the screen.

Statistics for all 35 Dexter Denham results . . .

The results are 100 percent Caucasian. Spokeo is no good. Maybe—

Something skitters above me. The wood creaks . . . Sounds heavier than a mouse, heavier than a raccoon. Scratching . . .

I stand still, breathing but barely, praying that those sounds and the creature making those sounds go away. All of me aches from sudden clenching over the last hour and—

Now, my apartment is too quiet. Hollow even though I am sitting *right here*. Not that my fear—*am I fearful?*—is unjustified. Once I left my front door cracked and a gust of wind blew it open enough for a cat to skulk in, only I didn't know that until eleven at night, when a thud and bang from my kitchen yanked me from sleep.

But this scratching and skittering doesn't sound like a cat. I grab the remote control to turn on the television. The next episode of *The Bachelor* is ready to watch. A banner from the *Los Angeles Times* brightens my phone. "Video taken from a security camera on Cochran shows last time Simi Valley victim Allison Cagle was . . ."

Was what?

That curiosity gene wants to thumbprint into the story, but I won't, especially after tonight's adventure. And I already know the ending: Allison Cagle is dead. I also know the moral: a girl child ain't safe in the world of men. I understand my mother's fears—bad things happen to *someone's* daughter every day. She teaches public school in South Los Angeles, and so girls in her classes die, are beaten, get pregnant, or disappear altogether, and that's why she's playing piano *right now*. Don't have to "do" anything for bad things to happen. You can stand in the rain after a long day and someone decides to follow you out of a parking lot.

In the bedroom, the window screen rattles. Frustrated, I growl and say, "I'll tighten the damned thing myself." As I pull open the window, chilled air rushes past and the rattling intensifies. The screw that belongs in the bottom left corner of the screen is missing. Also? I can't make any repairs from the inside—I'd need the ladder, a screwdriver, and another screw. And all this would require me to futz around in the cold darkness.

Yeah, I'm not doing that tonight.

Right now, I want to take a shower, change into sweats, drink wine, and start to read a novel that I've read before. *The Stand* or *The Mist*, far-fetched, trapped-inside apocalyptic tales.

Tomorrow, tomorrow, I'll handle it all tomorrow.

Saturday, November 23
Chili's
Torrance, California
8:08 p.m.

"At least it isn't raining."

"At least." Chloe places the customer's glass of Dr Pepper on the table.

No, it isn't raining, but she's drowning in disappointment and her lungs feel tight. Feels like she's drowning beneath the reds, blues, and golds of the restaurant's lights. She tries to look out the windows, but glimpses of the mall's parking lot, of freedom, have been blocked by the wide bodies of men with sticky hands, dirty mouths, nasty burps, piggy eyes . . .

PARADISE IS NOT A PLACE—IT'S A STATE OF MIND. Yesterday's tear-off calendar for the twenty-second.

She fights the desire to weep and slides a lock of curly blonde hair behind her ear.

A NEGATIVE MIND WILL NEVER GIVE YOU A POSITIVE LIFE. That is today's calendar.

A good tipper. That cheers her up, and this customer in the Army Ranger hat and thick black glasses always tips well. The soldier's been here three times since Friday and sat in Chloe's area each trip. Same Ranger hat tonight. Same glasses, too. New shirt, though, plain black.

A Chicky Chicky Bleu sandwich the first two visits, and this evening . . .

"Steak fajitas," the customer orders.

"Good choice," Chloe says. "Sorry that we're out of ribs."

The last slabs had been ordered by the locals now crowding the bar. They're hooting and hollering because the Rams just scored against Baltimore. Not even touching the ribs.

The customer's eyes flash behind the thick lenses. "Don't you ever get a night off?"

Chloe chuckles. "I'm off tomorrow. What about you? I've never seen you in here until this week, and now I see you all the time. You don't have someone cooking dinner for you?"

The customer blushes. "My mother's dying, and I flew in from North Carolina. I'm stationed at Fort Bragg. Since it's just me and her, my sergeant lets me leave."

Chloe leans on the booth. "I'm so sorry to hear that."

The customer holds out a hand. "I'm Dale. Thanks for making sure I don't starve."

Dale's thin hands have a few calluses, just like Chloe's. Zach's hands feel like sandpaper. Both his good touches and angry ones scuff her skin. Lately, his touches have all been angry, and so she doesn't mind working so many shifts. Any excuse not to be at home.

"You okay?"

Chloe's spine stiffens. She's spacing out again thinking about Zach.

Dale stares at her, eyes soft with concern.

Chloe flinches. Something inside her stings. "I'm sorry," she says. "Just thinking about something. Someone."

"Whoever it is must upset you. Your face . . ."

Chloe taps the pad against her thigh and tries to smile. "Sorry about that. Let me go put in your fajitas." TRYING TIMES ARE NOT THE TIME TO STOP TRYING. That calendar page is taped to her locker in the breakroom.

Dale motions to the other side of the table. "Sit, if it'll make you feel better. And honestly? I'd rather you cry now than cry into my fajitas. They're salty enough as is."

Chloe howls. Honey gold, that's the color of her inner joy right now. Tonight, she'll note that in her journal. Maybe do a new vision board with only honey gold–colored things.

Dale holds up the soda glass as a toast. "Storms don't last forever. Remember that."

"Ohmigod," Chloe says, eyes bugged. "I have a key chain that says that, about storms."

Two tables over, a thick-necked man wearing a Rams jersey waves his menu.

Chloe yells to the Rams fan, "I'll be over in a minute, sir."

"I'm getting you in trouble," Dale says.

Chloe wags the order pad at her customer. "You *are*. He's not gonna tip me."

"He looks like a tight-ass. He wasn't gonna tip you anyway. Men like him suck."

"Sounds like you have a story to tell," Chloe says.

"You'd never believe my story," Dale says. "Key words would include 'bong,' 'bloody footprints in the snow,' and . . . 'restraining order.' Not against *me* but against my jerk of an ex."

Chloe gapes, touches her heart. "Ohmigod, now I *have* to know. After my shift?"

Dale gives Chloe a thumbs-up as she rushes over to Table 4.

YOU ARE RESPONSIBLE FOR YOUR OWN HAPPINESS. That is now on her phone's lock screen.

At Table 4, the man's face is red as the sauce covering Chili's famous baby back ribs. He growls, "It's about time."

"Sorry for the wait, sir. We're a little busy. Monday Night Football." Chloe pushes a smile to her face. At least some of that tightness in her chest has fizzled.

Yes. Men like this guy *do* suck. Also, men like Zach suck, too, and later, she will tell Dale about the time Zach pretended to push her off a cliff while hiking up a trail in Griffith Park. *It's a joke,* he'd said. *You're too sensitive,* he'd said. *Why would I kill you in front of all these people?* And then he laughed and told her that she didn't have a sense of humor.

Chloe's pulse races just remembering that day high above Los Angeles.

Maybe Dale could introduce her to some guys. Maybe Chloe could start over again, here or in North Carolina.

Every new day is a chance to change your life.

She cannot see. Too dim. But she sees the shadow of a large bird perched above. Her head hurts. Sharp and dull together. Like that time Zach elbowed her in the nose.

Where is she?

Crying. Someone is crying.

"Hello?" Her throat hurts, raw from screaming.

The crying stops.

Somehow, she knows that is worse.

A bright light blinds her, and she tries to turn her head, but she can't move. On the floor—wood, dirt, she can't tell. In that light, she glimpses scratched walls, walls stained brown.

Footsteps . . . until a figure in shadow stands over her.

Chloe looks into the shadow. Can't see eyes, can't see lips or hair, but she knows. "Please let me go," she whispers. "I won't tell anybody. I don't even know where I am."

"I have to," Dale whispers. "I said that I would."

Before Chloe speaks again, she hears a rustle, and now, there's something over her head. A bag. The world fuzzes through the plastic. And now, something squeezes her throat and she can't breathe. Hands? A rope?

Please let me go. Please let me go. She can't speak but she can think it and maybe Dale will hear her thoughts and maybe Dale will stop. *Please let me go. Please let me go.*

Maybe Dale will . . .

16.

On this Sunday morning, the kitchen is so quiet that I hear raindrops patter against the windows. Mom blinks at me from the breakfast nook. Her coffee cup wobbles in her hand. "Why?" she asks now.

"Because it matches." I'm wearing a long gray wool skirt. I twirl for her, and the skirt goes, *Whee!* "So. Let's go. I gotta get to work."

She sets down her mug, then pulls herself out of the nook as though I've asked her to burn down the house instead of to borrow her fluffy white sweater. "So you're confiding in Bryan now?"

I trail her up the staircase. "Huh? Oh. The Buick. I didn't want to worry you."

"And cop cars slipping up and down our street late at night doesn't worry me?" She slips the key from her sweatpants pocket into her bedroom's doorknob. The door opens and cool perfumed air washes over us.

Mom stays in the doorway while I plod to her closet. "It's his job. It may be nothing."

She doesn't speak, but her twisted lips tell me that she's displeased.

"Like you tell me everything all the time," I say.

"Not the point."

I throw up my hands. "Sorry. Won't happen again. Where's Dad?"

"Running over at the park."

"He has to fix that screen today. I almost did it myself, but rumor has it that I'm no good on ladders." I turn to the closet. Black sweater, blue sweater . . . white sweater. "There you are, my precious." I tug the cardigan from its hanger and turn around to face my mother.

Her arms are crossed, her chin tucked to her chest.

"So speaking of telling each other everything . . ." My pulse races because I now have the nerve to ask. "Why do you still lock the door?"

"Habit." She says this without looking at me, and that single word teeters on the air.

I shake my head. "Nuh-uh." I pull off my T-shirt and toss it at her. I slip the sweater over my head and plop onto their bed. "I need a better response than that."

She sucks her teeth. "Thought you needed to go to work."

I lay back on the pillows and place my hands behind my head. "I'll get there. Answer the question, please. I am twenty-four years old and you still lock that door. Why?"

"We have a gun in here," she says. "You *know* that."

"I do know; that's why I call bullshit. Try again."

"You tell me, Michaela, since you know so damn much." No twinkle in her eyes. No sparkle in her words. Her anger is real.

"Whoa." Surprised, I sit up and hold out my hands. "Why so hostile?"

She leans back against the doorframe. The shadow passes, but her mouth remains tight.

"And since you're already mad and since I'm already asking questions . . ." I scoot off the bed and join her in the doorway. "This." I point to the scar on my cheek. "How did I get it?"

Mom's nostrils flare again, but tears swell in her eyes.

I startle and reach out to grab her hand. "Mom, it's okay. You don't have to—I'm sorry." I lift her chin. "I don't mean to . . . I'm just . . ."

A teardrop tumbles down her cheeks, and she flicks it away. She shakes her head, pushes out little breath after little breath. "I just feel like . . . like . . . I'm losing control and I just . . ."

Her sadness rips at my heart, and shame bubbles in my chest like hot grease. I want to take back my questions. Too late.

"We had a lot of people over when you were little," she says, dabbing now at her eyes. "A lot was going on that night, and . . . there was a glass coffee table with sharp edges and your little face . . ." She holds back a sob, but her face twists in the effort.

"I cut my face on a glass table?" I ask.

She nods. "Blood everywhere. You needed six stitches." Something between a chortle and a sob breaks from her chest. "I've never stopped feeling awful about that." With her finger, she traces the scar on my face.

I pull her into a hug, and she shivers beneath my hands. "It's okay, Mom."

She and Dad were young. They'd never own a glass table ever again. That's probably the moment both became safety nuts. Child-protector covers still cover our range top knobs. No matchbooks sit out in the open. Our smoke detectors and carbon monoxide monitors receive fresh batteries every eight months. My parents swung from one extreme to the next.

"Why didn't you tell me before?" I ask.

"You got eleventy-thousand scars on your knees and elbows. I remember how you got some, but not all. Just because I haven't told you the origin story of every blemish on your body doesn't mean there's a secret."

Mom makes another strange sound in her throat, then squeezes me tight. "Mouse, I need a vacation." She kisses the top of my head over and over again.

I take her hand and walk with her down the hallway. My head hurts from our sudden argument, but my heartbeat slows because we're fine now. Nothing between us is broken. "Christmas. I'll be done with this memory bank. Dad can set up people to do year-end tax stuff, and school will be out on winter break. And the back fence—that'll be done, too."

Bleary eyed, she says, "Yeah," and tries to smile. That smile is disfigured and damp, but it bubbles there, waiting to be revived by midnight buffets, limbo contests, and a luxurious stateroom with a balcony.

Yes, we're fine now. And soon, we'll be even better.

17.

Early-morning sunshine fills Beautiful Things. Riley stands with a small group of women dressed in draping, velvet frocks. She bugs her eyes at me as her Renaissance faire customers cluck over the buckets of amulets, brooches, and dragon eggs.

I mouth, "Good luck," as I weave past the tables filled with Victorian toothpaste pots and deer's-foot bottle openers.

The office is freezing. "What to work on today?" I ask the room. Before I start, I pick up the music box and turn its thin silver crank. The space, with its peeling paint, solitary window, and wood-beamed high ceiling, fills with the tinny rendition of "You Are My Sunshine."

Up in the store, the bell over the door tinkles.

Yes! Another customer! The store is hoppin' today!

Nadia's dream to share beautiful things with other people must be fulfilled. There's some theater geek out there who'd worship that signed *Cabaret* poster. There's an Elvis fan who needs that slotted spoon with the King's face on the handle. Maybe the Memory Bank *could* somehow partner with Beautiful Things—there are too many untold stories here.

I unpack my work tools, taking a moment to make sure that I'd uploaded all my recordings to the Memory Bank cloud.

Someone knocks on the door.

I slip the digital recorder into my skirt's pocket and shout, "Yeah?"

The door opens, and Riley stands there with Detective Winchester behind her. "Sorry for the interruption."

"Hello, Miss Lambert," the detective says.

I force my lips into a smile. "Hi. Again."

"Again?" Riley says.

"I talked with Miss Lambert last night." The detective's eyes dart around the office and land back on Riley. He smiles at her and says, "Thank you."

She returns the smile. "No problem."

He stares at her.

Her face reddens. "Oh. I should go. Let me know if you need anything." She backs out of the office and closes the door.

Detective Winchester waits until we can hear Riley's footsteps tapping away from the office and back toward the showroom.

I grab the ticket stub and store receipt from my wallet and thrust both at him. "You wanted these. I texted them to you last night."

He takes my alibi documents without comment and slips them into his coat pocket.

"You never called back," I say. "Who says they saw the guy? Should I be worried? Too late—I *am* worried. See, I think someone is following—"

He holds up a hand. "It was a simple question, Miss Lambert. Sorry for scaring you. We're looking in all directions." Then he wanders over to the map filled with colored pushpins.

"That's it?" I blink at him. "What if I see him again? I think he's following me."

He says, "What if you see *who* again?" Then he studies that map for a while. He turns to face the project table and waves a hand at the collection. "So those things are . . . ?"

I clear my throat. "The items that Nadia wanted to include in her memory bank. And I'm talking about the guy—last night when I left here, I noticed that a car, a Buick . . . It followed me west on King, then north on La Brea."

He peers at the miniature kaleidoscope. Reads the page beneath it. Detective Winchester has no interest in last night's car chase. But he's very interested in this collection.

I drop a hand into my pocket and press the button to activate my recorder. "I'm concerned about my safety, Detective Winchester. Shouldn't you be just as concerned?"

"Did you call 9-1-1?"

"Not while racing through the streets of LA. I called my uncle once I got home."

"And I assume he sent patrol cars over?"

"Yes."

"Sounds like you handled it like a pro, then." He points at a slip of notepaper. "This is Ms. Denham's handwriting?"

"Yes, sir."

"All of these notes, they're in your care now, correct?"

"Correct, sir. I'm working from—"

"Mind if I take one for comparison?" he asks. "Otherwise, I'd need to obtain a warrant, and that's time consuming and really not necessary since I'm just using it to compare and you just told me that she, for sure, wrote these herself. So may I?"

"Umm . . . can I give you notes that I no longer need? I don't want to stall my progress."

"Of course. Don't want to be a burden."

I pass over the notes to the music box and select the notes linked to the gold-plated hair clip. To keep the ink from smudging, I ease the pages into a white catalog envelope before handing it to the detective. "As you'll see from my ticket stub and store receipt, I wasn't in the plaza on Thursday around the time Nadia died."

"Who's to say that you watched the entire movie?" he asks.

I pause, then say, "Excuse me?"

"I left *The Big Lebowski* twenty minutes in. Never saw the rest of the movie. But I had a ticket stub . . ."

My cheeks tingle. "Are you *still* saying that I—"

"I'm not saying anything. I'm simply poking holes in the hull of your very certain ship." He holds up the envelope. "Would you mind not mentioning to anyone that I have this?"

I nod. "Something wrong?"

He about-faces and heads to the door. "The service for Miss Denham is tomorrow."

"Yes," I say. "I was planning to attend."

"That part of the Memory Bank package?"

"No, it's free. Comes with being a human."

He chuckles. His face isn't so hard now.

"There was one last person who came here back on Wednesday night," I add.

"Really?"

"I think it was Nadia's best friend."

Detective Winchester tilts his head. "Around what time?"

"Five o'clock. I saw her in the parking lot. She was carrying groceries and a bouquet of pink roses. The roses are still in a vase upstairs in Nadia's apartment. I didn't know she was the best friend until Anna at the diner mentioned that the best friend always stopped by with food and flowers."

Detective Winchester pulls his little memo pad from his pocket. "A vase?"

I nod.

"Upstairs?"

I nod again.

As he writes, he asks, "This best friend, you know her name?"

"Anna said she thinks her name is Esther."

Is my recorder getting all this?

I cross my arms and step closer to him. "You think she may have done something? To Nadia, I mean?"

It takes forever for Detective Winchester to look at me. "Is there reason for me to think that she has?"

I blink at him. "Frenemies?"

"You meet Ms. Denham's son yet?" he asks.

"Dexter?" My cheeks burn just saying his name. "No, not formally."

The cop's eyes flicker. "Can you show me where you were standing when you spotted Esther the best friend?"

A minute later, we've left the office. Filled with light too intense for my eyes, the store feels unfamiliar. Blinking, I toddle past the butterfly and beetle collections and drift from the Tiffany lamps to the postcard rack. As my eyes adjust, I alter my course to the entrance.

Riley watches us as she leads an old woman around the display case of crystal bells.

Detective Winchester follows me to my car. We don't talk as we walk. A low fog hangs over the lot. The RVs are mirages except for the orange racing stripes of one mini-Winnebago.

I stand at my driver's-side door. "I saw her from here."

The cop slowly turns 360 degrees. "Could you describe her?"

"Old white lady, maybe late seventies? Red hair. She wore one of those snappy blue fedoras with the bird feather in the brim. A blue trench coat and . . . She drove a . . . I'd call it a Brady Bunch station wagon. Big. Long. Wood paneling on the sides?"

"Got it." He clicks his teeth as he stares at the plaza's landscape, a white sea bobbing with crappy campers, weeds pushing past broken concrete and a random collection of cars.

I stand there, also looking at the plaza. "There are no security cameras here," I offer.

"You'd be surprised with what I can see, Miss Lambert." He chuckles and shakes his head. "You have a good afternoon." He stalks back toward Beautiful Things without saying another word.

What does he see that I can't?

Esther. Is it possible that *she* killed Nadia?

If she did, will she still show up for Nadia's memorial service tomorrow?

Artifact 4: Felt gray mouse wearing a gold foil crown. Acquired on April 3, 1978.

Artifact 5: Vinyl Bohemian-laced checkbook cover. Acquired on April 3, 1978.

Location of Acquisition: Syracuse, New York. The fifth most populous city in New York, Syracuse gets more than 120 inches of snow each year. Syracuse is home to the Erie Canal and the longest-running state fair in the United States.

Last Owners: Christina Spiro (item 4) and Renee Spiro (item 5).

Memory: Renee was a single mother, and Chrissy was her sweet brown-haired three-year-old. Even in April, the nights are cold as sin in Syracuse, sometimes getting down to thirty-two degrees. You lived in a one-bedroom unit in an ugly brick-and-shingle apartment on the second floor. Renee and Chrissy lived in a single.

Neighbors for all of three days, Renee knocked on your door with Chrissy on her hip. Both looked too thin, and Chrissy shivered so hard, you thought the girl suffered from a disease. "My radiator's been broken for a week," Renee said. "That stupid-ass landlord promised to fix it, but he hasn't. My comforters from Florida aren't thick enough for this cold. And Chrissy, she's potty training, so I can't put a lot of layers on her without having pee everywhere. And my ex, he took my little radiator and . . ." As she ended her litany, tears stood bright in her eyes. "Guess I'm asking if you got any blankets or a space heater you can lend me?"

You had a space heater, and it was turned up to the maximum. Because Charlie, that stupid-ass landlord, had promised to also fix your broken radiator but hadn't.

Chrissy started to cry. "Mommy, I don't wanna go home. It's too cold."

You couldn't let a mother and her child suffer while you, a single, healthy person with a heater and three electric blankets, sat in an easy chair and watched *Barney Miller*. Like any decent person, you offered Renee and Chrissy one of the electric blankets and the space heater. You rolled the heater up to the tiny studio apartment, a place so cold that white clouds puffed from your mouth to surround your head.

Through tears of joy, Renee said, "I don't have any money to give you."

Little Chrissy ran over to her toy chest and plucked out a mouse made of gray felt. The sweet brown-haired girl ran back and placed the toy in your hand.

You pointed to an empty checkbook cover on the wobbly kitchen table. "How about that? Mine went missing in the move."

Renee laughed. "Sure. I ain't got no use for it. My ex cleaned out my checking account, too. Hope you know just how grateful I am—whatever you need, just ask."

18.

After I watch Detective Winchester drive out of the parking lot, I pull my recorder from my skirt pocket and listen to our conversation. Is he planning to compare that notepaper against the two suicide notes? Does he think Nadia wrote only one of those letters?

My eyes adjust to the silvery fog, and now I see all the gritty RVs along with their bags of trash, dilapidated bikes, and shopping carts. I hear voices but see no bodies. It's like listening to sea lions at the pier even though they're miles away, sunbathing on big rocks.

I tromp back to the store. Feels like forever ago when I left Beautiful Things with Detective Winchester.

Riley waits for me at the entrance. She's blinking like a hair is trapped in her eye. "What did he want?"

My lips burn. Winchester doesn't want me blabbing about our discussions around the notes and Nadia's handwriting. "He asked to see where I was parked on the day Nadia passed. He also wanted my alibi for that day."

Her shoulders drop. "Ah. Oh."

"And he asked if I was attending the memorial tomorrow."

Riley has lost interest. She wanders back into Beautiful Things.

I follow her into the store with its musty air and cramped spaces. I shuffle to the office, idling in the doorway because it's ten degrees colder here than it is in the showroom. Crunching from my computer cuts through the layers of quiet.

Oh, to be relaxing at the Sagebrush Inn right now with a lover, a plate of chilaquiles, and a fiery Bloody Mary.

I work in between my computer stalling and Sasha's frantic texting.

Did Uncle B catch the guy in the Buick??

U should buy one of those cute lady Glocks!!

It may rain on Thursday OMG!!!

I think I gained a pound!

The zipper on my dress is already suspect!!!

The bell above the store's entrance rings. I don't peek out to see that customer on the hunt for ceramic chickens. My stomach growls, but with my computer cooperating, I don't want to leave it. I push through my hunger to photograph the checkbook cover and upload those pictures into the CMS. Tension bundles around my shoulders and lower back.

The hourglass icon on my computer screen turns and turns and turns . . . then crunches.

"That's it. I'm done." I close the screen, pack up my stuff, and turn off the lights.

Riley sits on the stool at the cash register and stares out at the dimming plaza. She isn't crying. She isn't smiling. She's just . . . *sitting there*. Her skin is so pale that her veins, blue and wild, push against her face like a vampire's.

"See you tomorrow?" I ask. "Inglewood Park Cemetery, right?"

Expressionless, she blinks at me. "Yeah."

Outside, the fog has faded, and the twilight sky pulses with flocks of crows. Sad, I turn to look back at the store and gasp.

The white guy with the spiky yellow hair, the one who was eating breakfast at Anna's, stands beside the store with a lit cigarette between his lips. He eyes me through the smoke, then shifts to his other foot.

Startled, I jump and spin away from him and hurry to the parking lot.

Detective Winchester or one of his team, they *must* be watching this man. But if he killed Nadia, would he be standing around the store like this?

Residents of the RVs watch me approach my car. A dude with waist-long dreadlocks grills meat on a little hibachi and pays me no attention. An older Black woman smoking a cigarillo from her beach chair calls out, "Have a blessed night."

"You too," I say before climbing into my car.

How many people live in these campers? What disasters—random or self-inflicted—shoved these folks into a parking lot?

That man is still loitering near the store.

And he sees me watching him, too. He grins and leans back against the building.

My gaze skitters around the parking lot. I don't see a Buick.

I find the number for Anna's Place, and I call to let her know that the strange white guy is hanging around again. "Maybe you and Riley should walk to the parking lot together." After she agrees, I swipe to the screen to make an emergency call if needed. My thumb is ready.

The stranger tosses the cigarette to the ground, killing it with a twist of his shoe.

Anna leaves the diner with her purse and a large Styrofoam cup. She pokes her head into Beautiful Things, then stares at the man while she waits at the door.

The stranger shoves his hands into his pockets and strolls north, passing her as he moves toward the now-shuttered Link's Lounge.

Lights in Beautiful Things shut off, and Riley pops out to grab the sandwich board from the sidewalk. She sets the sign inside the store then locks the doors. With the crazy jumble of buildings behind them, Riley and Anna walk to the parking lot. Anna climbs into her Honda, and Riley climbs into her Prius.

I release a long breath. I'm free to go.

And now, I need coffee so sweet that it makes my teeth hurt.

At the coffee shop on Crenshaw Boulevard, hip-hop music blasts from the shop's speakers. Old men at the back tables nurse tall drips and ogle pretty girls ordering upside-down caramel macchiatos. I can't hear myself think over the music and the hiss of the steaming machines, but I can smell roasted beans, warming croissants, and the body odor of the shaggy Black man standing in line behind me.

He shuffled in moments after I did, and like Uncle Bryan has always instructed, I looked the man in his eyes like I would a sweet-smelling human being. Since Los Angeles has a homeless problem, I look plenty of men like this guy in their eyes.

"What do you tell 'em when you just want coffee?" he now asks, scratchy-voiced.

Who is he talking to?

I glance over my shoulder. He's looking at me.

I offer him a conservative smile. "Say that you'd like a drip and then the size you want."

"A drip. Cool, cool." He pauses, then asks, "That's what you get?"

"No," I say, head half-turned. "I order this drink with espresso, milk, and caramel."

"You look like somebody I used to know."

Eyes on the menu board, I say, "I hear that a lot." Like the actress on the DC fixer show. Like homegirl from that reality show. Like the pastor's daughter over at that megachurch.

"You don't recognize me?"

"No." My voice sounds flat, but my insides are flickering. My eyes hop from the exit by the napkin counter to the defensive-back type seated at a table with his laptop and iced tea.

"You ain't even look at me full in the face." He sounds playful, but there's an edge of resentment in his tone.

Shit. Here we go.

I'm doing my best, Uncle Bryan.

I hold my breath as I turn to look at him. His eyes are a vivid green-blue and bright against his scarred toffee skin. There are two blue teardrops beneath his left eye. He wears ancient Adidas with shoelaces blacker than coal. His khakis will never be khaki colored again. He looks to be around my parents' age. Old—like, fifty. Handsome, maybe, once upon a time.

Looking him in the face, I say, "You don't look familiar."

The barista beckons me and asks, "What can I get started for you today?"

Dry-mouthed, I order, pay, decline the receipt, then head over to the waiting area and closer to that exit. As is the custom of women everywhere, I find my earbuds in my purse and slip them into my ears. I bring up Lauryn Hill as anxiety snaps at me like hungry koi.

Teardrop Tats claims his drip at the register but then shuffles in my direction.

Dread weighs down my heart and pinches my lungs. *I just want my hot beverage, dude.*

A woman wearing cheap yoga pants and a hot-pink thong joins the line. Conversation at the AARP tables stops, but Teardrop Tats doesn't tear his eyes from me, the woman who looks like somebody he used to know.

I pull up Twitter on my phone—the president did *what?*—and I pray. *Please don't throw your coffee on me, please don't throw your . . .*

"This woman I used to know," Teardrop Tats says with some urgency.

Can't he see the buds in my ears? Can't he see the phone in my hand? Can't he see hard disinterest on my face? And now I'm angry, just as I would be at any man who's ignored my body language. Fury burns my heart, and I want to scream because why can't I just . . . *stand* here and be left alone?

"I used to be in love with her," Teardrop Tats says, with that hot drip in his cup close to sloshing over the rim. "I used to be in love with this woman and she hurt me."

"Vanessa!" the barista shouts.

Vanessa is my coffee name, especially because I look like somebody too many men used to know. I say, "Excuse me," to the man I *certainly* don't know and claim my drink.

Teardrop Tats watches me place a cardboard sleeve around my cup, then says, "That woman I used to love, the one you look like? She's dead now." His coffee sloshes past the rim of the cup and splashes onto the tile floor.

I hop back. Heart pounding, I say, "Sorry to hear that," and march to the exit. "Hope you have a good night."

Behind me, the man shouts, "I killed that bitch!"

I shudder. The coffee shop shudders, too, and for a brief moment, silence hangs over coffee shop. The old guys stand from their table, and one man says, "That fool need his ass beat." The defensive-back type leaves his table and iced tea to step in front of Teardrop Tats. He turns to me with an assuring smile, and says, "Head out, shorty. You good."

I whisper, "Thank you," and push open the door.

Teardrop Tats tries to push past the big guy to grab my coat, but one meaty arm from Defensive Back stops him.

Frigid air stings my cheeks as I rush through the parking lot. My eardrums throb. Did his shouts burst them? What if he'd thrown that coffee in my face?

Like Lot's wife, I dare to look back over my shoulder.

Unlike Lot's wife, I do not turn into salt.

156

Defensive Back has Teardrop Tats cornered as customers flutter around the store. Guilt for escaping niggles at me as I safely reach my car. Though I'm relieved that Teardrops Tats hasn't followed me, my throat is dry. My hands won't stop shaking, and I can barely grip tightly enough to pull the car door handle. Once I do, I fling myself into the driver's seat, almost forgetting that I'm holding a cup of hot coffee. After three attempts, I set the cup into its holder, lock my doors, and squeeze my eyes shut.

Please God. Protect any other woman he meets tonight.

SIGNS POINT TO YES

19.

Even though Mom gets the week of Thanksgiving off, she's sitting at the breakfast nook at nine forty-five Monday morning already dressed—a fresh ponytail, leggings, my Adidas sweatshirt—and reading the newspaper. Her perfume fills the kitchen. She lifts her head as I bang into the kitchen and gives me the up-and-down. "Where *you* going?"

I'm sporting her black pin-striped pantsuit with the flared leg. The steel-colored blouse beneath the jacket is also hers, but the Tahitian pearls belong to me.

I grab a mug from the cupboard, then help myself to the still-hot pot of coffee. "I'm headed to the memorial service for the shop owner. Then I think we go back to the diner for lunch. Your sweater is hanging up in my closet, stain-free. I'll take it to the dry cleaner's tomorrow. And where *you* going looking like Beyoncé?"

"Out," she says. "A few errands. The fencing guys are pulling down the old wood behind the apartment today."

"When will they be done?"

"By Wednesday, I hope."

I shake my head. "You mean tomorrow. We're driving down to Temecula on Wednesday, remember?"

She rubs the bridge of her nose.

"Or they can wait until we get back from—"

"No," she says. "They're doing it now. I want it done, and I don't want to think about it any longer than I have to."

There's a heaviness in the kitchen. Even though it's sunny, there's no gleam of sunshine on the stainless-steel refrigerator, range, and faucet. On the other side of the nook, a half-eaten slice of boysenberry-jam toast sits on a paper towel beside an entire veggie meat patty—Dad didn't finish eating breakfast.

Wary, I dump cream and sugar into my cup.

Mom sips her coffee and stares at the newspaper.

In the quiet, I can hear her heart beating. I can hear her lungs straining as she holds her breath. "You okay?" I ask.

Eyes still on the paper, she says, "Umhmm."

"You and Dad fight? He didn't eat . . ." I point to the breakfast patty and toast.

The space between Mom's eyebrows crinkles. "So what are your plans for the day?"

I blink at her because I just *told* her my plans for the day. "The memorial service and then lunch. You?"

"Mall—I need a dress for Sasha's wedding and . . . Where's the service?"

"Inglewood."

Her face tightens. "Ah."

"Want me to place any flowers?"

She thinks about my offer, shakes her head, then goes back to the newspaper. Without looking up, she asks, "So you and Chris?"

"Are not together."

"Friday night, then?"

"He's hot combined with top-shelf alcohol mixed with the fear of being alone."

She takes a sip of coffee. "I've told you about alcohol-fueled booty calls."

I take a sip of coffee. "Yes, I remember that morning. You bought me my first Bloody Mary and then guided me over to the craps table at the Bellagio. I wore your black halter jumpsuit and Tory Burch wedges."

She looks up and smiles, and that smile is true. "Seriously, though. Chris—"

"I know." I finish Dad's patty in three bites. "You should get a massage or something. Enjoy your downtime."

Her phone vibrates from the table. The sound makes her sigh.

"Work even though it's break?" I ask.

She nods, giving me a tired smile. "Barney's is going out of business. Maybe I'll see what I can get for two hundred dollars."

"A belt?"

"One shoe." Mom's phone vibrates again, and her eyes slide down my face to the table.

"You're depressing me." I gulp more coffee, then bend to kiss the top of her head. "See you later. Love you."

"Love you, too, Mouse." She clasps my wrist. "Be careful, Mickie, and watch yourself. Something's in the water."

My throat tightens and keeps me from telling her about the man in the coffee shop and the one at the plaza right now. I don't want to add more stress to the burden that already has her moaning and jumping and, now, thinking about her loved ones buried in the cemetery I'll visit today.

Mom's phone vibrates again. She catches the startled gasp from fully escaping her lungs.

I grab her phone and waggle it. "Ignore this today. It's freaking you out."

She takes her phone. Her thumb accidentally unlocks the screen, and the notification banner is replaced by a blue screen with white letters: $V \ldots I \ldots N \ldots E$.

"What's VINE?" I ask.

Mom gazes at me, then looks at her phone. "It's just a notification system."

"For?"

She swallows, bites her upper lip. "Crime."

"You're still worried about those notes someone slipped under my door? Or are you actually really freaking out that Sasha knew Allison Cagle?"

"I'm . . ." She sits back in the booth.

"Are you thinking how it's always someone else, right? But what if 'someone else' is us this time?"

Mom cocks her head. "*This* time? When Angie died, we *were* 'someone else,' and I'm not interested in living through that again."

I take her hand and kiss it. "You're right. I'm sorry. You, Dad, Uncle Bryan . . . You guys won't let anything happen to me. And there are lots of Good Samaritans in this city. One helped me out last night when a homeless guy was trying to keep me from getting my coffee in peace.

"But I'm gonna start arming my alarm at night and whenever I leave, and I'll be okay. That's what I'm saying." I rub her shoulder—the muscle there is harder than our granite countertops. Mom's eyebrows sit high. She's trying not to cry. "Has anyone else on that VINE app reported strangers stalking the neighborhood?"

She shakes her head, whispers, "No."

"Take it off your phone. You're already high-strung. If you were a macaw, your beautiful feathers would be all over the breakfast nook. And nothing's sadder than a bald bird."

She laughs.

I hug her tight. "You be careful, too, today. Don't talk to weirdos. Don't get in cars with murderers. Share your destination anytime you take an Uber, and keep a dime in your shoe."

"Calls cost a quarter now." She decides to smile. It's a poor replica of the one that exploded across her face just moments ago.

I wag my finger at her. "No true-crime shows today, either—you don't need to know about *all* the evil. You're gonna wear down the piano keys."

Her gaze wanders to the window. That space between her eyebrows crinkles again, as though she's spotted something strange and inexplicable in the backyard.

Like she's seen a ghost.

Twenty minutes later, I'm surrounded by ghosts.

My maternal grandparents, Rosalind and August Craig, are buried here at Inglewood Park Cemetery. Their side-by-side plots sit across the street from the Forum. Grandpa loved the Lakers of the eighties and wanted to be close to them during his eternal slumber. Aunt Angela, who died years before them, is buried in a midtier crypt closer to the front of the park. She was killed in a drive-by shooting in front of her apartment. She'd been only twenty-two years old. Mom keeps a few of Angie's things in her bedroom closet: my aunt's favorite Starter jerseys, some swap-meet bamboo earrings, an "Angie" nameplate, her diaries . . .

People look at my mother—hell, *I* look at my mother—and assume she's lived a quiet life. Piano recitals, music comp classes, Chopin. Coretta Craig Lambert, though, understands the pain of losing her best friend in a burst of violence. She knows the agony of never seeing someone she loves ever again. Her entire immediate family, eternally slumbering.

Guess that's why Mom always sinks into silence anytime we drive past this place. She thinks of Grandpa's heart attack, Nana's ovarian cancer, and Angie's murder. I don't know if Mom comes here to visit Aunt Angie or her parents. I don't bring it up. Neither does she.

Even still, Dad taught me how to drive at Inglewood Park Cemetery. The winding roads; the large, unobstructed parking lot; and the constant reminder of the results of speeding and texting while driving made for a perfect practice spot.

This morning, six cars are parked in the lot closest to the Chapel of Palms, the location of Nadia Denham's eleven o'clock service. It's windy, and the palm trees that line the cemetery's perimeter sway and swish. There's no fog this morning, and the sky flecks silver with airplanes.

My cheeks tingle as I hurry to the chapel's glass doors. As soon as I cross the threshold, warm air greets me, as do the crypts of a hundred people. Colored light from the chapel's stained-glass window shines on the single column of pews. "The Old Rugged Cross" drifts like smoke from hidden speakers.

I head to the wood stand that holds a guest book and sign my name, adding "from the Memory Bank" after "Lambert."

The chapel smells of jasmine and roses, stemming from the fresh bouquets at the front and from the blooms sitting in the holders bolted to each granite cremation niche. A blown-up picture of Nadia—gold-rim glasses, imperfect row of bottom teeth, stark white hair—sits on a tripod. A platinum-and-brass urn rests on a round table at the front of the chapel, surrounded by an arrangement of sweet-scented roses, tulips, and hydrangea.

Riley sits in the second-row pew. She wears jeans and an orange Patagonia nylon jacket.

Compared to her, I'm the Duchess of Sussex on her third job interview.

Head down, Dexter Denham stands to the left of the stained-glass window. He wears a blue dress shirt, a gray sports coat, and black Air Jordans.

Riley motions for me to sit next to her.

I give her a "one moment" finger and approach Nadia's son.

He's inches taller than me. He's taller than Chris. His cologne smells like grapefruit.

I offer him my hand. "We haven't officially met yet, but I'm—"

"The woman from the Memory Bank." His large hand is soft and warm. "Dexter Denham. Thanks for coming."

"Michaela Lambert. I'm so sorry about your mother. I only met her once, but she was very kind to me. Very excited about us working together. I was thrilled to see all her . . . stuff."

Stuff? Ohmigod.

"I'm glad you're still working on it," he says. "Especially now that her memories are all that I have. If you need any help with anything, let me know."

I smile a little too brightly. "I may take you up on that."

"Please do." There's a sparkle in his eyes the size of a mustard seed.

Back in the pew, Riley glares at me. "You look very formal. It's just a memorial service."

I slide beside her. "Just how I was brought up. Always look your best when you go to jury duty and funerals."

She crosses her arms. "I don't know why you came—you didn't even *know* Nadia."

I hear . . . resentment. And I hear . . . jealousy. It sounds like gurgles of volcanic mud.

A few more people straggle in from the cold. Detective Winchester of the inscrutable face stands near the guest book. He catches my eye and nods at me. He continues scanning the chapel. Jae Kim, the lock-smith, hasn't arrived yet, but Anna comes to sit next to me. The woman who owns the hair salon—Anna's told me that her name is Pepper—comes to sit next to Anna. Her platinum-gray wig matches Nadia's urn. Anna's also told me that Pepper inherited the hair salon from her mother (and Anna's best friend), Big Pep(per).

As we wait for the service to begin, I search for VINE: *Victim Information & Notification Everyday.* If Mom is using this notification system, who's the victim? And who's the offender?

A minister wearing a white robe enters from a door beneath the stained-glass window. After he and Dexter shake hands, Dexter settles in the front pew, a reach away from Nadia's urn. An older Black woman sits in a chair placed before an electric synthesizer. Peter Weller, hair purposely and perfectly mussed, sneaks in as the musician sings and plays "Amazing Grace."

Anna and Pepper notice and start whispering to each other.

Once she finishes the hymn, the woman steps over to the podium. She picks up greeting cards that have been placed there and reads aloud.

Gone but not forgotten . . .

Wishing you peace and comfort . . .

Our memories build special bridges . . .

Dexter's eyes are closed and his chin quivers. A nerve pops in his temple. He must have all his father's genes—he does not have Nadia's thin lips; nor does he have her bulbous nose. Those high cheekbones, those may be a gift from Nadia, but since I met her only once . . .

The minister approaches the podium and offers a few words of clichéd comfort. *No more pain . . . lived life to the fullest . . . chose her own path . . . inspiration to everyone here.*

He didn't know Nadia.

The minister stands in the corner as Dexter takes his place at the podium. Before speaking, he shoves both hands into his pants pockets, then lifts his face to the ceiling. After taking deep gulps of air, he squares his shoulders and faces us. "I tried to write a few remarks about my mother, but . . ." He covers his mouth with a hand, and his eyebrows crumple. He finally pushes out words: *no one in the world like her . . . fascinated by things some would call junk . . .*

Riley mews like a hurt kitten. She dabs her wet eyes with tissue and nods at the end of Dexter's sentences.

Nadia's urn is placed into its niche. Some of us leave the chapel for fresh air.

Anna's mascara is gummy from crying. So is Pepper's. After we all hug, she says, "You see the detective is here?"

I nod.

"If he's gonna arrest anybody," Pepper says, "he needs to arrest Peter Weller. My client's best friend's sister is a dispatcher, and that's what *she* heard they're gonna do."

"Well," Anna says, "my daughter's ex-boyfriend's father also works at Winchester's station, and *he* heard that the man who jumped Nadia in October came back and finished the job."

My stomach growls. "Should we get moving? What did you make for lunch?"

Anna shakes her head. "Dexter told me that he didn't want a repast, so . . ."

"We're going to the Olive Garden," Pepper says. "You wanna come?"

I tell them that I'll meet them there, then head to the parking lot.

"Hey, Memory Bank!" a man shouts.

I look over my shoulder. I'm the only person here associated with my ex's company.

Riley and the minister are still standing at the chapel door. She may be hearing the minister talk, but her attention is focused on Dexter Denham.

That's because Dexter Denham is jogging toward me.

"Sorry for calling you that," he says now, "and this is going to sound absolutely awful, but I can't remember your name. My apologies."

"Michaela—Mickie." I blush. "You have a lot going on, and . . . I actually *do* have a few questions. There are a couple of items your mother left on the project table back at the store that didn't include background information."

"Yeah? Like?"

"There's an earring and a fountain pen. I have no clue what to write."

Detective Winchester strolls out of the chapel. As he slips on his sunglasses, his head swivels in Riley's direction. He stares at her, and she watches me.

Dexter sees my eyes shift and glances back over his shoulder. "Got crowded out here."

I say, "Yeah," and then: "I thought your mom . . . I thought . . ."

"Why is Detective Winchester here if she did it herself?"

"Yeah."

"Long story." He pauses, then says, "I can tell you over dinner. And maybe I can give you more information about the earring and the pen. That is, if you'd like . . . I mean . . . I don't know if I'm stepping on someone's toes or . . ."

"No toes. And if I said yes, would *I* be stepping on toes?"

Dexter shakes his head. "Nope. How about Alta Adams?"

Upscale soul food.

"Perfect," I say. "Six o'clock?"

A no-pressure time.

"Sounds good."

"Cool."

He smiles, and his lips do this . . . *thing* . . .

Beneath me, the earth rolls.

He says, "See you then."

I say, "Yep." I'm light-headed, as though I'm standing atop Pikes Peak.

Where did I park my car?

As I amble through the parking lot, I spot Peter Weller.

He doesn't see me, and he holds his phone to his ear as he tromps to a red Lamborghini SUV parked one row over from my car. He slips out of his suit jacket, and sweat stains discolor the underarms of his violet dress shirt. ". . . most pitiful funeral I've ever attended. Raggedy, just like that shop . . . Well, she's gone now . . . The others . . ."

The Lambo's lights blink and the doors unlock. Weller tosses his jacket into the passenger seat. "Who? Dex? Ha. Lemme tell you why he—" He climbs into the driver's seat and slams the door behind him.

Nadia Denham kept Peter Weller from his goal, and now she's dead.

Is *that* why Detective Winchester came today?

The cop stands at his Crown Victoria. Only his head moves as he watches Peter Weller's SUV race out of the parking lot.

"I don't know your face." A man's garbled voice comes from the dusty black Cadillac parked behind me. The man himself is brown skinned with permed hair and a lower jaw that doesn't align with his upper jaw. He's leaning against his open driver's-side door.

I say, "Excuse me?"

"I *said*, I don't know you."

"And *I* don't know *you*."

"My friends call me Link."

I nod. "Link's Lounge. Right by Anna's." And now his crooked jaw makes sense—he was jumped and forced to sell. "Did you hear Peter Weller just before he got in his car?"

He grins at me. "Uh-huh."

"I hear that he may be arrested."

Link flicks his many-ringed hand. "Nah. Men like that don't go to jail."

"Then who are they gonna arrest?"

His eyes scan the parking lot. His head stops, and his gaze stays fixed. "But you ain't heard it from me."

I turn my head in the direction of his gaze.

He's looking at Dexter Denham.

20.

Only one of the fencing panels behind my apartment has been disassembled, and now there's a gap—anyone from the park can just . . . *walk the fuck into our backyard.*

"It's raining," Jerry the Fence Guy explained. "And since we need to use jackhammers to break up the concrete blocks that anchor the old posts, *blahblahblah.*"

Dad and Uncle Bryan are nailing thick sheets of plywood across that empty space as I pull out of the driveway.

Once I reach Alta Adams, I stop thinking about stalled home improvement projects. Instead, I commit to enjoying the restaurant's soft golden lights. Lights that make every person here look like an extra in a big-budget, Black Hollywood rom-com. With that light, conversations look more intense: "Baby, I love you," or "That stock that I bought a long time ago . . . ," or "I'm leaving you," or "Yeah, I'm not feeling it anymore." Morris Chestnut could play the guy reaching across the table to taste Gabrielle Union's shrimp and grits.

On my second date with Christopher, I brought him here. I wore Mom's strapless black tank dress that night. We sat at a window table and ordered the plantain chips and the chicken. As we snuggled, I explained to him—a Brentwood boy—what okra was, and then we canoodled. I had never canoodled with anyone during dinner. I had dreamed of canoodling and snuggling, and finally, there I was! Doing both!

Tonight, I'm wearing that strapless black tank dress again—I want to get lucky . . . *I think*.

Because I don't know . . .

Dexter is hot, but is he smart?

Dexter is hot, but is he kind?

I will canoodle with a dumb man, but I won't snuggle with an asshole.

What about a murderer—is that a canoodle or a snuggle?

I don't believe Link. I don't even *know* Link. Not that I know Dexter Denham. Still . . . just how Anna talks about Dexter . . . He couldn't have killed his mother.

My mouth goes dry as I think about this while sitting in the restaurant's small lobby. And I worry about this because it is now ten minutes past our agreed meeting time.

A black Jeep pulls in front of the valet stand. Dexter climbs out from behind the steering wheel and tugs on a black jacket.

He's here! And he's driving!

I take deep breaths to calm the nervous energy snaking from my toes to my belly up to my temples.

Dexter finds me sitting in the lobby. His smile is tinged with remorse. "Sorry," he says. "Some of Mom's favorite customers kept dropping by the store."

I touch his elbow. "It's no problem. If you need to reschedule—"

"Nope. I'm good."

We walk to the reception station. The hostess seats Dexter and me at the window table where I snuggled with Christopher back in May. Beyond the plate glass, Pico Boulevard flickers, and it feels like we're sitting in a café on the seventh arrondissement and the Seine is right there, and Notre Dame Cathedral is over there.

The server welcomes us. Fortunately, she's not the one who flirts with every male diner who sits at her table. Sasha and I hate that Janelle Monaé wannabe. No, this server reminds Sasha and me of Rihanna, her lip gloss shining in the light like diamonds.

I order a cocktail that boasts star anise, whatever the hell *that* is.

Dexter orders a cocktail that celebrates fresh Fresno chile.

"Have you eaten here before?" he asks.

I nod and sip ice water.

"First time for me," he said. "What's good?"

I tell him, and the server returns with our drinks. We order plantain chips to share. I order the fish. He orders the hanger steak.

And now he's staring at me.

I flush and say, "What?"

"I'm guessing you were here with a guy, and I'm guessing that you and whoever he was didn't work out."

"Nope. Came here with a Memory Bank client. She lived in this area before it became 'Historic West Adams.'"

"Ah." He lifts his glass. "Here's to Nadia Denham, who is now in heaven's garage, looking for Captain Kangaroo electric blankets."

"Cheers," I say.

He keeps his gaze on me as he sips.

My hands are so sweaty that I fear dropping my fancy cocktail all over Mom's dress. Nervous, I clear my throat, and say, "I'm sorry about your mother. What a shock."

"She'd been depressed," Dexter offers, "which would've been unusual a long time ago. But when she started forgetting . . . And then, when she was diagnosed . . . Alzheimer's—that disease is just *cruel*." With his finger, he catches a bead of condensation running down his cocktail glass. "She kept asking me about the right to die."

"Like the law in Oregon? The Death with Dignity Act?"

Dexter had done research. There was a similar law in California, the End of Life Option Act. If Nadia had sought out physician-assisted suicide, her life insurance policies would have still paid out. Nadia wanted to take care of her son.

"And you would've been . . . okay with that?" I ask.

"Physician-assisted suicide?" He nods. "If that's what she wanted, yes."

I slump in my seat. "I don't think I could."

He smirks. "Well, let's hope that your mother is never diagnosed with a devastating disease and that you won't have to see her suffer and slowly die." He sits back in the chair as Rihanna places the basket of plantain chips between us.

I pluck a chip and Dexter plucks a chip. "I'm sorry for saying that," I whisper. "I don't wanna ever experience that."

He brushes off my apology. "So what kooky thing did you say my mother left behind in the office without explanation?"

"This." I unlock my phone and find a picture of the fountain pen and emerald earring. "Not so kooky."

He says, "True. Not so kooky. I have no idea why she chose those things. But then, I don't know what you're supposed to be doing."

I tell him how the Memory Bank works.

He says, "Got it. That reminds me . . . Have you seen a ruby necklace around the store? My mother wore it all the time and I can't find it."

I remember that red-stoned teardrop, so bright and sassy against Nadia's horrible blue pinafore. "I haven't," I say, "but I'll keep an eye out for it."

"Funny," he says. "It's the most basic and traditional thing she owns, and I can't find it."

"Was she as eccentric as the store?"

"Yep. In elementary school, though, I thought my friends' parents were unconventional because they cursed a lot and smoked joints in front of us."

"But?"

He rubs his jaw. "My mom was actually the weird one. And she never chaperoned field trips or allowed me to have friends over. She never came to school programs, either. I never knew what it was to share your mother with other kids. To be *embarrassed* like my friends were embarrassed by their parents trying to sound and act cool."

Frowning, I say, "So she didn't get to see you free the slaves for Black History Month or lip-synch Michael Jackson for the middle school talent show?"

He shakes his head. "Anna always came, though. She drove me most times."

"Graduation?"

"Never marched."

I gape at him. "So you were *that* kid. Ohmigod, I can't imagine missing out on walking across a stage wearing a cap and gown, hearing my family scream my name like crazy, loud Black people." I cover my eyes and giggle. "Graduations were actually the only times my family acted like crazy, loud Black people."

Our meals come.

Dexter clutches his knife and fork like clubs. Nadia never taught him the correct way to hold cutlery. He also salts his food before he tastes it. I cock an eyebrow at that because Mom would cock an eyebrow, too. She's told me the story about Henry Ford inviting job candidates to dinner and watching them eat. He never hired the man who salted his food before tasting it.

On the other hand, Ford, an anti-Semite, counted Hitler as a fan.

I ask Dexter about his career as a photojournalist.

Camera in my hand longer than I've been able to walk.

Almost got my ass kicked at that rally where he pointed at us in the reporters' pen . . .

Funeral in Gaza City . . .

March For Our Lives . . .

Impressed, I say, "So you've done absolutely *nothing* in your life."

He laughs. "I'm rarely home. Guess I got that from my mother. Whenever and wherever I travel, though, I find a flea market and I search for some curio that Mom would love, and I ship it . . ." His eyes glaze. For a moment, there's nothing or no one around him. He's alone. "One of our few traditions." He focuses. "I miss her."

Dessert comes, and we move our spoons through the bowl of warm bread pudding.

"Your father?" I ask.

"Never knew him," Dexter says. "It's just been Mom and me— that's not so different than a lot of people, right?" He chuckles. "What about you?"

"My parents have been married for twenty-five years."

Now it's time for him to gape at me. "What does *that* feel like?"

"To have two parents in one house?" I sip my cocktail. "Normal? Balanced? I don't know any other way."

"Siblings?"

"Nope."

"All to yourself, then, huh?"

I cock my head. "*You're* an only child."

"Kinda. Riley. One day, I woke up and there she was, sleeping in the twin bed across from mine."

Dexter tells me that Nadia basically saved Riley's life. She'd spotted this tiny, frazzled seven-year-old girl sleeping in a bus terminal by herself and brought her home. Riley's mother had been murdered right in front of her—a home invasion. Something happened with Child Protective Services . . . he didn't know the details. Ultimately, though, no one else wanted Riley, so Nadia adopted her.

"Just one more of Nadia's beautiful things," I say. "Weird that no family stepped forward, but lovely that Nadia did."

"So now I'm being told that this strange girl was gonna be my sister. Riley looked nothing like me, and my mom looked nothing like me . . ." He squints at the near-empty dessert plate. "Riley fit better with Mom than I did. That was fucked up, to be an outsider with outsiders."

"Did the cops find out who killed Riley's mom?" I ask.

"The cops didn't give a fuck about a dead, drug-addicted . . . Sorry for cursing. So forgive Riley if she's acting . . . *off*. It's because she *is* off. Like I said, Nadia Denham was not the most traditional mother."

I asked him if Nadia also skipped Riley's special programs and graduations. According to him, Riley didn't even have to attend school. Nadia was scared that the people who killed Riley's mother would also come for the surviving girl.

I cock my head and narrow my eyes. "Huh. That's . . . a choice to make."

Dexter chuckles. "Yeah. But whatever, right? I have a sister, and despite our differences, despite our mother's crazy decisions, I love her."

"You ever think about finding your father?" I ask.

"Sometimes. I never wanted to betray my mother or have her think that she wasn't enough. But in some ways, with me being a Black man . . . she *wasn't* enough." He sighs. "Now that she's gone, I think about it a lot. But then, I'm like, he doesn't deserve to know me now. Since he didn't do the hard work, he shouldn't get the prize. Anyway, I have enough to worry about right now with the store."

I lean forward. "Detective Winchester's been hanging around. Peter Weller's people, too. This white guy with short blond hair? I've seen him twice now, at Anna's for breakfast and last night, just hanging out by the store. I told Anna he was there, and she and Riley walked to their cars together."

Dexter grunts and spoons the last morsels of bread pudding.

I tell him that I saw Weller at his SUV after the memorial service. "He was talking smack. He mentioned you, but I didn't hear the rest. But he said something about 'the others,' now that Nadia's gone."

Dexter sucks his teeth. "Peter Weller can kiss my Black ass."

"Winchester seems to think—"

"And I agree," he blurts.

"That someone . . . ?"

"Killed my mother? Definitely."

I'm knocked back in my chair. "Her MedicAlert bracelet . . ."

Dexter tells me that Nadia pressed that button. It was the only way she could let him know, let the *world* know, that she didn't wanna end like that. That she wanted to live.

I blink at him with feverish eyes, unable to speak.

"I kept telling Mom to buy a security system," he says. "But she hated the thought—"

The server drops off the check.

I reach into my purse, but Dexter holds out his hand and says, "No."

Mom would like that. His generosity makes up for the cutlery club-hold.

I exhale. "Shit, Dexter. Who do you think would do something like that to her?"

He slips his silver credit card into the folio. "I'd rather not say, but Winchester's on it. They're looking for fingerprints on that bag that was over her . . . you know. And the letter they found—"

"Yeah, he asked me for a sample of your mom's handwriting."

Oops.

Dexter frowns. "Why did he ask *you* for her writing?"

Crap.

I swallow, but my foot is the size of a mammoth. Voice tight, I explain: "The notes for her mementos? She wrote them, so those notes are, *technically*, the last samples of her writing."

Sorry, Detective Winchester.

Dexter works his jaw back and forth—he's pissed—then says, "Well, those notes won't match that letter."

Which letter? But this time, I keep my mouth shut. Instead, I ask, "Did you ever go with her on trips to collect?"

He nods, and his smile is as bright as fire. "When I was little and could afford to miss school. I'd wander around someone's junky front yard or around a stadium parking lot. Mom always gave me twenty bucks to buy whatever I wanted during those trips. I remember falling asleep in Nebraska in the back seat of the station wagon and waking up in Colorado . . ."

As he remembers, he scratches his cheek with a thumb. "I bought my first camera at an estate sale in New Orleans—a Nikon with a sticky shutter. And I started collecting tossed-out photos. I'd buy my own albums and place the most interesting shots in them, and I'd write these totally made-up captions and that would be my thing. Mom, she'd sit and listen to my stories, and she'd ask questions about the people in the pictures."

Nadia had never rushed him or got bored. She'd been genuinely curious. Sometimes, she'd brought Dexter pictures and told her own stories. Her tales, of course, were better than a young boy's. "They were so detailed and scary sometimes," he recalled. "'Never blink while telling a tale. People will always believe you if you don't blink.' She'd always say that."

"And now, look at you," I say. "A professional photojournalist."

"All because I'd been around a woman who taught me to look for interesting stuff and to think of the story behind it. But then, I stopped going on those trips. She didn't want me to miss school or basketball games. She'd take Riley, but I had to stay home, which, you know, made me a little jealous."

He lived with Anna sometimes, and other times, he'd live alone, with Nadia leaving all these rules. He had more freedom staying with Anna than staying by himself in the store.

Dexter asks about my life, and I tell him that it's average and uneventful. My mom teaches music, and my dad is an accountant. My extended family are cops and doctors. Everyone attended my plays, my games, my graduations. My parents completed their mandatory volunteer hours at my school. Dad took me to father-daughter dances once a year in high school. Black Excellence. No drama, not really.

"No drama can be a good thing," Dexter says. "Parents work hard so that their kids never have to experience too much drama."

"I guess." I want to say, *My aunt Angie was killed in a drive-by*, but that would seem a little . . . *greedy*.

"Wanna go to a movie later this week?" he asks.

"Yes," I say, even though I will be in Temecula later this week.

I'll figure it out. I always do.

It's drizzling as we wait for the valet to bring our cars around. There's no traffic on Pico Boulevard now. The air smells of damp earth and simmering garlic, and the light rain melts across my face. I usually hate this kind of rain. Not tonight.

Dexter kisses my hand and looks deep into my eyes. "Meeting you was unexpected. A real-life Denise Huxtable."

"So if I'm Denise, then you're . . . ?"

He blushes. "I'm still trying to figure that out, but he has a camera with him at all times."

The valet parks my car at the curb.

"That you?" Dexter asks.

"A hand-me-down from my mother."

"I know a little something about that hand-me-down life."

I hug him. "Thank you for dinner. I had a great time. And I'd love to see those photo albums of other people's lives. It's basically what I do for a living."

"We'll come up with a time to hang out. Oh yeah, I'm stopping in the store tomorrow. Gotta check on Riley." He pauses a beat, then adds: "You know she hates you, right?"

I nod. "But I don't know why."

"Probably because Mom wanted you to handle those beautiful things instead of her."

I flick my hand at that. "I'm getting paid, and I was far from being Nadia's daughter."

Dexter grins. "I'm glad Mom got to meet someone else who could appreciate her stories."

I squint at him. "What are you gonna do about the store?"

"Annoy the hell out of Weller, who *did* threaten my mother. She told me about it."

I gasp. "Poor Nadia."

"I was in Caracas, so I could only call him and talk to him about it. Maybe I should've gotten in his face. Anyway, thanks for giving me the heads-up. I'll prepare for battle."

"May the odds be ever in your favor."

He kisses my cheek, and his breath warms my face. He gives me butterflies. My fingers drift from his cheek to the chain that peeks from beneath his sweater. He's sexy. Creative. Loves adventure. A few of my favorite things. It's only seven forty-five, but I decide then.

Tonight, I will dream of Dexter Denham.

21.

Giddy with lust and star anise, I navigate La Brea Avenue with one hand on the wheel and the other clutching my phone. The sky is swirly with rainwater, and lights from cars and fast-food restaurants spill like ribbons across the street. No one is following me. No one is sending me nasty messages.

At every red signal, I text with Sasha.

OMG he's 🔥🔥🔥

R U driving to his place or is he coming to yours???!!

I'M NOT SLEEPING WITH HIM!
It was our first date geez

U slept with Chris on your first date

Shut up Sasha

Christmas lights twinkle bright around my parents' home. A new lake glistens in between the house and garage. My mother's reflection shines in my rearview mirror. She's looking out at me from her bedroom window. By the time I climb out of the car, her shadow has slipped across the ceiling.

If—no, *when*—I become a mother, will I hover and clasp my hands like Mom? Will I curse the lurking shadows that follow my girl around the city?

Upstairs, I glance out my bedroom window, janky plywood now where there used to be fencing. Back in the living room, I glance out *that* window and see nothing except for Christmas lights. I feel Mom's eyes even when she's not looking at me. Her gaze is a weighted blanket. If I were stressed or anxious, that would be a good thing. But right now, I'm not stressed or anxious, and so it's a bother, but it's a single–fruit fly bother instead of a hornet's nest worth.

The steady hum of falling rain is better than the silence or the scratching of rats. After tonight's adventure, the ordinariness of my life—boxes in the corner, TV remote control on the couch cushion, charging cables tangled on the coffee table—seems more . . . enigmatic. There's more to me than my S'well water bottle and the nail clippers beside it.

Huh. My parents—they were more than that before they had me, before they became "You're Mickie's mom," and "You're Mickie's dad." Coretta "Cori" Craig, a.k.a. C.C., had boyfriends and, as I've seen in her library, read Black erotica books. Funny, sarcastic, and able to sing a pitch-perfect middle C.

If Alzheimer's took all that away from Mom, and then away from me . . .

Would I be okay with watching her diminish, or would I think like Dexter and Nadia? Ending life with dignity?

Thinking about Nadia's end and the two suicide notes . . .

"Crap." I hurry over to my purse and find my recorder. My interaction with Detective Winchester—I forgot to upload that very important conversation into the cloud. As I wait for the recorder's purge, I wash my face, brush my teeth, and change into another pair of boxer shorts and Dad's ancient Body Glove T-shirt. I Febreze Mom's dress, and then I text Dexter.

Home safe

Thanks again for dinner

If u need to talk I'm here

I swan-dive into bed and pull my comforter around me. I'm not tired—blame the star anise and the electricity of a new romance.

My phone chimes. Dexter!

Thanks Mickie

Have a good night

My sultry smile denatures into a tangle of skin and muscle. My heart dips. I hoped for something more, like . . . *I wanna make you take some PTO* or *I'm not sleepy. R U?*

I'm cold now. The walls of my bedroom are no longer painted urban mist but colored stupid gray.

I'd forgotten the man said goodbye to his mother today.

Who can properly sext during a time of grief?

Acid sizzles up my throat and blisters the middle of my chest.

Heartburn.

I paw through my nightstand, searching for antacids but finding a book of matches, a deck of UNO cards, and condoms. *Tums!* I grab the roll and pop three.

My phone chimes again, and I hope that it's Dexter with a more creative text message. At this point, I'll take *Sweet dreams* or *Dream of me* or . . .

This text did not come from Dexter.

There's no name. Just a number with a 402 area code.

I don't know anyone in a 402 area code.

And where the hell *is* 402?

I thought I'd blocked this number back on Friday night, but Christopher had interrupted with booty-call plans.

I read this newest text and—

IGNORE ME AND I WILL ANNIHILATE YOU!!

22.

Last night, I searched that 402 number.

No name, but I learned that 402 was the area code for Omaha, Nebraska.

I don't *know* anyone from Nebraska—I've never even visited the state.

Ignore you?

Who are *you?*

The Buick. Is this the person who chased me through the streets back on Saturday night?

Is this the note-leaver?

Near tears, I tapped "Block This Caller" and swiped "Do Not Disturb" before turning off the lights. Then I sent a screenshot to Uncle Bryan.

What the fuck, he texted. I'll see what I can do. Get the geeks on it.

Minutes after receiving that "annihilate" text message, I showed it to Mom and Dad, and they demanded that I sleep up front with them.

I retreated to my childhood bedroom again, where I slept like crap. Woke up every twenty minutes. Rolled over so much that the corners of my flat sheet unsnapped. Kept hearing creaks and leaks as shadows crept along the walls and ceiling. I swung between volleys of panic and exhaustion. *Is that him? Which him? How did he get my number? It's nothing. Just sleep. What's that sound?*

Somehow, I fell asleep. My eyes popped open hours later. It was nine o'clock.

Late.

No more weird text messages, but no resolution from Uncle Bryan on the origins of the threats, either. *Get on it, geeks!*

And now I'm achy and my eyes scratch. My feet hurt, and the thought of wearing clothes makes me recoil. Mom's car is gone. There's no hot coffee in the pot. Damn it all to hell—there are no breakfast patties in the freezer, and the bread smells too sweet. And the fence won't be finished today, either, because the type of rain that I hate drifts from flat clouds. The sky is wet enough to halt home-construction projects, but the roads aren't wet enough for oil to wash off the asphalt.

At the intersection of La Brea Avenue and Obama Boulevard, a truck has smashed into a motorcycle. Minutes tick by on my car's dashboard. In the Notes app, I tap out a list of things I'll need to do before my drive down to Temecula: hair appointment, laundry, pack, Target run . . .

My heart should feel lighter today. I should be wearing Dexter all over me like pollen. I should be blushing as I remember our evening together. But none of that is happening because . . . so many things.

Sasha texts.

Maybe u should get a new number??

Leaving in 3 hours!

Pray for perfection!

Buy that lady Glock!!

See u in Temecula!!

I don't wanna rain on her parade, but it will rain on her parade.

Thursday's Thanksgiving forecast: another winter storm.

My typical eight-minute drive lasts forty minutes. I reach Beautiful Things fifteen minutes before eleven.

The store bustles with customers. An older couple points at flasks in a display case. She's wearing a rose-printed rain bonnet and a bright-pink raincoat, and he's sporting a black fedora and patent-leather shoes. A young mother in a wrinkled trench coat holds her son's hand as they browse through the selection of board games. A hipster girl in a fuzzy purple sweater and denim shorts swipes at the carousel of vintage sunglasses.

Riley is polishing an Elvis Presley tea service complete with a pot, four cups, and matching saucers. Her skin shines as though she's using a steel-wool pad on her face instead of Noxzema. Her sky-blue turtleneck matches the chamois in her hand, which moves like a quick bird against the white porcelain teapot.

Yesterday, I spotted the crate holding that set. The label is written in Nadia's neat handwriting: LOVE ME TENDER. NEVER BEEN USED— 6/100—STRAIGHT FROM GRACELAND. I wanted to snicker and ask, "Who the hell collects Elvis tea sets?" but my grandmother owned cups and saucers shaped like peacocks.

"Didn't think you were coming in," Riley says now.

"There was a car accident."

She notices my jeans and bright-white Adidas. "Casual Friday on a Tuesday?"

The jeans are snug and butter-soft, and the sneakers inject much-needed spring into my step. "Not feeling high fashion today."

She grunts, and says, "You have mail. Someone left an envelope for you. I put it on Nadia's desk." She waits a beat. "Dinner not go well last night?"

I tilt my head—how does Riley know about my date with Dexter? Did he tell her after I'd left the cemetery? And anyway, her question slips into my nostrils like the stink of sour milk. "Dinner went *great* last night," I say. "We had a lovely time."

"Who paid?" she asks, mean-girl grin on her lips, virtual shiv in her hand.

Fire flares in my belly. "Why is that your business?"

She dismisses my question with a quick wave of her hand. "Since you're the type who expects a man to pay, and since Dexter has mega money problems, I figured—"

"Oh, so you know me now," I say, cranky and brittle because . . . *so many things*. "What if I said that you're the type who stands on the porch to watch other women live their lives and then has tons of snarky things to say? How would that make you feel?"

She blinks at me and smiles. "You'd be correct."

"Whatever. Dexter is a great dinner companion *and* a supreme kisser."

Pop, pop, stab.

Riley's glee shatters like cheap glass.

Because I'm also *that* type of woman.

I hurry to the office to claim that envelope. Did Dexter write me a love letter? Did I miss his morning visit?

The office is cold, dreary. I turn on every light. I keep on my puffy nylon jacket because I now work in the California Arctic. I spot the envelope on the desk. Just as Riley said, my name is typewritten across its face.

The envelope isn't sealed. I quickly pull out a slip of folded paper.

The answers you need start here: 1831 W. Washington Blvd., No. 372017. The note was signed by Jae Kim. The locksmith? Why would he leave me this?

And: The *answers*?

I don't know the *questions*.

I stare at the note, hoping that my fixed gaze jars a memory. Staring doesn't work. Fine—I'll go over and ask him, and then maybe I'll take a field trip after working on a few items.

Riley stands in the doorway with her arms crossed. "Apologies for being a hag," she mumbles, head down. "I shouldn't have said that about Dexter. You're right—it's none of my business, and if you're cool with him, then

I'm cool, too. Wow, it's cold in here." The redhead slinks into the office. She opens the closet door and rolls out a space heater. "This should help."

My body starts its melt in advance. "Thanks, Riley. And I'm sorry for snapping at you. I'm having a hard time sleeping lately."

"Me too." She plugs in the heater and flicks the "On" switch. "It's difficult being here. Without Nadia, I mean. Even when she was traveling, the store never felt *empty*, you know? It was a living thing, and now that she's gone . . . I don't know."

"Dexter plans to keep it open."

She rolls her eyes. "Sure, he'll make Peter Weller beg for it, and he'll drive up the price, and *then* he'll sell. He needs as much money as he can get."

Riley wants me to ask about Dexter's financial woes, but I ignore the bait. Instead, I plop into the chair over at the project table. The items I'm done with sit in the corner of the table, only five. I need to step this up.

Riley comes to stand over me. "You must think this store is strange."

I pick up a key fob shaped like a hedgehog. "I don't judge. Well, I *do*, but not this."

She flicks her hand. "That's a political answer. It's okay—Nadia and I both talked about the weirdness of curios. Who collects porcelain bells shaped like Betty Boop's head? Am I right?"

I tug an elastic band from my wrist and use it to pull my hair into a ponytail. "People like their stuff—I mean, storage units are a boom business. I read that the industry makes about thirty-eight billion dollars a year."

Riley picks up the kaleidoscope. She's a wisp of a woman, and her cheekbones jut against her face. She looks too thin, probably because she's stressed from managing the store alone.

I watch her, then say, "You all cater to people who'd rather sell their stuff than store it."

"That's a good way to see it. Guess I was always scared that Nadia . . ." She smiles as she looks through the kaleidoscope.

"Scared that Nadia *what*?"

She sets the artifact on the table. "I was scared that Nadia would die in this store. Not because of a robbery or some external force but because a big pile of *Encyclopedia Britannica*s had fallen on top of her. If you haven't noticed, there's a lot of junk here."

Yes, there are towers of record albums and stacks of handbags, but those records aren't old, flattened Chevys and rusty Packards. Those handbags aren't sharp-edged and swimming in tetanus. Upstairs, Nadia's apartment shines and smells of Pine-Sol. There's no danger here. Riley's distress seems displaced.

"I've wanted to quit so many times," she says. "Really, out of all the retail stores in LA, there are better places than *here*. But I didn't want to leave Nadia alone in this place."

She puffs out her cheeks like a balloon, then pushes out the air. Her shoulders sag. "Dexter hates the store, so he would've never worked here. He says Nadia and I had a codependent relationship. For once, I think he's right. I stayed to keep Nadia happy—she'd done so much for me—and the one time I finally go on a collecting trip . . .

"Guess I'm mad at Dexter. Nadia and I may have had an unhealthy relationship, but he's partly to blame for that. He never helps, always complaining. Swoops in and makes everyone feel bad for *him*. But he gets to travel and meet new people, and I'm . . . here."

She picks up the kaleidoscope and runs her finger along the barrel. "Girls are getting killed, and here I am, miserable, not growing because Nadia never thought I could handle being away from her. All because I promised her that I'd never leave her and I didn't because I would've felt guilty after she saved me, y'know?

"But she's dead, and I'm still scared of what she'd think if I broke my promise. She loved this stupid store and she fought to keep it open and I'm complaining. Why am I complaining?"

Sad for her, I chew my lip, then say, "Maybe you can convince the original store owner to come back."

Riley's eyebrows knit together. "You mean Sarah Park?"

"Maybe she's tired of South Korea. Maybe she'd be interested in getting back in the curios game. Oh—better suggestion: maybe you should open an online store. Like your own eBay business. That way you can leave sometimes and do what you've always wanted to do."

"First of all," Riley says, dropping the kaleidoscope back onto the table, "Sarah Park will never come back here. Second, the online store is a good idea, but Dexter . . . He'd think it's stupid and expensive, and he doesn't want me wasting time or money."

I suck my teeth and shake my head. "I can talk to him if you'd like, and he'd be wrong. Online stores don't have to be too costly. It's not like you don't have anything to sell. That tea set you were polishing—how much will someone pay for that?"

"About three hundred dollars."

"See? And you charge the buyer for shipping and handling. More people will see this stuff on the internet than the four people who walk through that door every day."

Riley's eyes shine with hope, and she covers her flushed cheeks with her hands. "Would you? Talk to him for me, I mean?"

"Sure."

She smiles, squeezes her cheeks, then takes in a deep breath. After exhaling, she lets her shoulders drop. "I should let you get back to work. Lucky me, I have another tea service to polish. This one is Dolly Parton. If you need anything, just holler. And if there are start-up costs for an online store, let me know. Since I haven't gone anywhere or done anything except work, I've saved up a lot of money over the years."

I give her a thumbs-up.

She offers another thankful smile, then pads out of the office.

I text my web-designer friend Kendrick.

How much would you charge to set up an e-commerce site for a small business?

During our senior year in college, Kendrick and Sasha dated. Because he'd been my friend since middle school, I got to keep him.

Estimate I'll do for free, Kendrick responds.

Basic site averages about 12k yearly.

Friend discount 10k.

eBay is cheaper a basic store costs about 20$ a month

Twenty dollars a month sounds better than several grand a year.

I'll tell Riley later. As for Dexter bashing the idea . . . I hate that men bully women to keep them from innovating and thinking big. He gets to wander and "do art," but Riley's dream of being an e-commerce curios queen is stupid?

Ugh. If that's true, then strike one against Dexter Denham.

He needs as much money as he can get.

Last night, I didn't pick up on any financial problems he might have.

Blood pushes at my face because that's not an accurate observation. He *did* mention Nadia's life insurance policies and her scheme—is "scheme" a fair word?—to die lawfully, so that Dexter could receive that payout.

Does Riley know about that? Will he give her any money he receives? Did Nadia leave her adopted daughter *anything*?

Huh.

I pluck the hedgehog key chain from the project table. Riley is abrasive, a little cold, and arrogant, but she's just trying to be great. And I fear that she's being shafted in the process.

Should I say anything? Is any of this my business?

Why is Dexter trying to stop her?

He needs as much money as he can get.

Artifact 6: Teakwood hedgehog key chain engraved "DESTINY." Acquired April 3, 1993.

Location of Acquisition: Fresno, California, sits in the center of the San Joaquin Valley in the middle of the state. Fresno started the raisin industry in the US—the grapes withered because of hot weather. Nearly 100 percent of all raisins in the states come from Fresno County.

Last Owner: Bonnie Hargreaves.

Memory: You were hooked on that day's episode of *Guiding Light.* The storms had finally stopped, and the other residents in the trailer park had come out to sweep away the mud. You needed to do the same, but the soap opera was so good.

Someone knocked on the door. At first, you didn't answer because, earlier, neighbors had demanded that you help with the cleanup. The person knocked again, politely—nothing like the hard, coarse knuckles of the drifters living in the neighboring trailers.

A young lady, eighteen or nineteen, with a button nose and hair the color of summer wheat, stood at your door. "Hi. My name is Bonnie, and me and my company, California Publications Circulation, are selling magazine subscriptions." Her eyes were fresh-air blue.

You thought it unwise that Bonnie was traveling alone through mobile-home country.

"Oh, I'm not alone," Bonnie said. "My friends are also working. They're at the next mobile-home court and the next one after that."

As you listened to the young woman's sales pitch, Bonnie finally noticed that the coffee table was filled with magazines. "Although *technically*," the young woman said, studying the subscription label of *TV Guide*, "Lucia Montez subscribes to these magazines."

"We're roommates," you explained, "which means I don't need two copies of anything."

Bonnie dug into her backpack for a different catalog, taking out all her belongings to find the second in the bottom of her bag.

You signed up for *Amazing Stories* and *Science Digest*.

The young woman was so excited—her first sale! Preparing to leave, she shoved her belongings back into her bag.

Later, you found a hedgehog key chain. It had missed Bonnie's bag and landed in the trailer's shag carpet. You kept it, expecting the girl to return since keys were on the ring.

Bonnie returned, and she sat with you to watch a few minutes of *The Simpsons*.

DESTINY.

You never received any issues of *Amazing Stories* or *Science Digest*.

23.

My hand hurts.

This computer sucks.

The rain has stopped.

Can we talk?

A text from Christopher.

I hold my breath, not sure that I want to talk to him—which means that I don't.

Can't. Working

Later then?

I don't respond. Later, then. If at all.

Time for a new adventure.

I grab my keys, my bag, and the envelope that Mr. Kim left for me.

The answers you need start here: 1831 W. Washington Blvd., No. 372017

Up in the store, Riley is selling an old Black couple a Last Supper wall clock. Outside, there's no sun, only layers of clouds and flocks of seagulls and crows. The air smells like rainwater and hamburgers. Anna's diner is filled with the lunch crowd. My stomach growls as I stroll over to the locksmith's shop. I knock anyway, then peer through the dingy windows.

Empty. No answer. Maybe he's on a house call.

I hurry to my car. Before I leave the parking lot, I text Chris.

Going out on a field trip for client

1831 W. Washington Blvd. No. 372017 fyi

Will let u know when I'm back at the store

I'll call you later

I throw my eyes around the parking lot. No Buick, no Teardrop Tats, no shadows. Relief.

Cars, trucks, and buses crowd the streets. A day without a million vehicles on La Cienega Boulevard in LA is the day the Big One shakes California into the Pacific Ocean or a pandemic sweeps across the globe and forces Angelenos to shelter at home. I'll shapeshift into an old white lady before *that* happens.

I know these passing neighborhoods. Mom's favorite Korean barbecue place is right there and will be a wonderfully savory stop on her memory bank ROAD TRIP! My play-uncle, Kip, got shot by his wife in that grocery store parking lot over there. My elementary school took field trips to the public library right over there. After story hour, the librarians handed out sugar cookies and warm Hawaiian Punch in small wax cups.

1831 W. Washington Boulevard.

I slowly drive past the destination, then look again at the address on my telephone to compare it against my real-time place on the block.

Across the street is 1828—a sign and banner shop. A mechanic at 1830 and a storefront church at 1832.

I drift back to 1831.

This is it. This is my destination.

Angelus Rosedale Cemetery.

The answers you need start here.

Located across the street from the all-boys Loyola High School, Rosedale is one of the oldest, creepiest cemeteries in Los Angeles, with large tombstones shaped like pyramids and giant Celtic crosses. Famous people are buried beneath those stones—"Hurricane Hank" Armstrong, Hattie McDaniel, Rasputin's daughter Maria, and Anna May Wong, just to name a few. Old Los Angeles is also buried here. Southern California streets, high schools, and cities have been named after the Slausons, Burbanks, and Fremonts now interred at Rosedale.

"Looks like a memorial identification number." That's what the old man in the cemetery office tells me about the numerical sequence in my note. "Lemme get you the . . ." He taps into his computer, then scribbles on a memo pad. "Here you go. It's located in the more recent burial sites. I suggest you drive over there." He rips off the sheet from the pad and hands it to me: SECTION KK, LOT 395.

Only a few groundskeepers wander the cemetery. Their backhoes whine and their rakes scratch against the wet brown grass. Some of the tallest palm trees in the city surround the cemetery's perimeter, their swishing fronds creating white noise. Moss, grit, and rust cover the older memorials. No one tends those obelisks and pyramids.

I've now visited two graveyards in just over twenty-four hours.

In this newer section, the grass is greener. The air smells less of mildew and decay. Pinwheels jammed into the grass around some plots spin and click in the wind. The modern, flat markers are cared for, although they are less dramatic than the giant angels and crosses found in the older sections.

I locate Section KK, Lot 395.

In God's Care
Joaquín Reyes
August 6, 1951–July 22, 1980

The name doesn't mean any more to me now standing here than it did when I first heard it spoken by the old man in the office ten minutes ago. I snap a few pictures of the black granite marker and then take in the park around me. Those swaying palms. This sea of gravestones, mausoleums, statues, and benches. Those heavy clouds building over the city. Cigarette smoke heavy enough to make me think someone is standing nearby.

But I'm the only living person here.

Am I the only living person here?

Also, why am I standing over Joaquín Reyes's grave?

I find the number to Mr. Kim's shop and call.

No answer.

Raindrops fleck my phone's screen. The palm fronds are louder now. Gusts of wind are pushing in the next storm from the Gulf of Alaska. That cigarette smoke smells stronger. The burning tobacco tweaks my sinuses.

A man stands in another section. He's wearing a blue hoodie, and his hands are hidden in his pockets, so he's not the smoker. He wears sunglasses, and I feel him looking at me.

That makes me twist inside.

The air feels thick and heavy. Something is happening here that I don't understand. My gut tells me to move, and so I do. My footsteps slap at wet grass and then wet pavement as I tromp back to my car. Every two yards, I throw a cautious look behind me.

Though the man in the blue hoodie doesn't move, his shadow still chases me.

Back in the car, a cyclone is banging inside my head. Why am I breathing so hard? Why is my heart banging like this? Why am I freaking out?

With shaky hands, I try calling Mr. Kim again. Still no answer. This time I leave a voice mail. "Hi, this is Mickie Lambert. You left me the note about Joaquín Reyes, but I'm not sure why." I recite my number and ask him to call me.

Cold sweat makes my shirt stick to my back. My pulse pounds in the quiet.

A knock.

I bark and jump in my seat.

The man in the blue hoodie is standing at my car window.

This close, I still cannot see much of his face. The world is fuzzy.

He knocks again.

I shout, "Yes?" behind my closed window. Stuck between the steering wheel and center console, I'm curled away from him as much as I can be.

He holds up a piece of paper. "You dropped this."

It's the note Mr. Kim left me. When had I dropped . . . ?

The man in the blue hoodie slips the note beneath my windshield blade.

I stare at the sheet of paper. Like me, it wants to move, but it, too, is trapped.

I turn my head to thank the man in the blue hoodie.

He's gone.

He isn't walking to his car. He isn't standing by the graves. He isn't lurking at my door anymore and staring at me through his sunglasses.

No—the man in the blue hoodie is *gone* gone.

Like he was never here.

24.

"Who's that?"

I gape at Riley and point to the front door. "He owns the locksmith shop right there."

Behind me, the world has disappeared in a silvered rain. Around me, Beautiful Things glows with warm light burnished by the copper, brass, and glass antiques.

"What about him?" Riley looks up from the coin collection on the counter and to the paper fluttering in my hand.

"He's the one who left me the note. Have you seen him?"

She cocks her head.

"Is he out on a job? I've been trying to reach him."

"Am I a psychic? A secretary?" She narrows her eyes. "I'm guessing here—and it's only a guess—that I . . . don't care."

I clutch the edge of the counter. It's keeping me from being swept away in a river of crazy. "The letter mentions this guy—not *exactly*, not *directly* . . . Does the name Joaquín . . . ?"

She's smirking at me.

I release the counter and square my shoulders. "You know what? Never mind."

At each red light between the cemetery and the store, I searched the internet, and the World Wide Web didn't have a direct answer for my

Joaquín Reyes question. He was a doctor, an actor, a meme, a general manager, a basketball player, and a cyclist.

Riley stares at me. "You look totally *chaotic* right now."

Bugged eyes. Clenched fists. Hair trapped in a damp and messy ponytail. My lips are a twisted line across my face.

Riley, on the other hand, is the picture of calm sitting there with her coins, sleek edges, and dry turtleneck. She notices my sneakers and grimaces. "You take a walk in a park?"

"A graveyard," I say, my heart close to popping.

Riley flinches. Emotions aren't her jam. "Why?"

Tears build in my eyes, and I don't care if she's uncomfortable seeing them. "It feels like I'm constantly being watched, being followed, and there's a mouse in my roof, and there's some nutjob in Nebraska who keeps texting me bullshit, and I . . . I . . ."

Riley pats the counter. "Let me show you something." She holds up a heavy-looking silver coin. "This is an 1893 Queen Isabella commemorative quarter. And this one—" She picks up a smaller bronze coin. "This one is . . . some other nineteenth-century coin. Ha." She waves her hand at the collection. "About 140 coins here."

"How much are they worth?" I clamp my tongue between my teeth to keep from crying.

"About five thousand dollars."

"You're telling me this because . . . ?"

"These coins aren't impressive or important enough for Nadia to include in her memory bank. What something is *worth* isn't always tied to money."

Her distraction is working, and my skin doesn't hurt as much, and the glass crunching through my veins has softened. I direct my eyes to the mounted bull horns hanging above butterflies in glass domes.

As I focus on controlling my breathing, Riley returns to her coins. Whistles as she works.

"So . . . I noticed something about Nadia's memorial service yesterday."

"What?" Riley slips the Queen Isabella coin into a two-by-two clear pocket.

"There was someone missing. Someone who didn't come."

"You knew Nadia for all of one hour and now you think you knew all of her friends?"

"Her best friend, she didn't come. At least, I didn't see her."

Riley sits motionless, then says, "How do you know Nadia had a best friend?"

"Anna told me. Her name's Esther, right? I saw her—I'm assuming it was Esther—bringing Nadia roses back on Wednesday night."

Riley blinks at me.

"The roses in the vase upstairs."

She blinks again.

"What's wrong?" I say.

She tells me that the roses aren't upstairs anymore. Detective Winchester stopped by while I was out and took the vase. "He didn't tell me why he wanted them."

"Cuz Nadia's BFF brought them, and she may have been the last person who saw her alive. You know who I'm talking about, right? She's old, white, wears a fedora—"

"Yeah, yeah."

"Does she know that Nadia . . . ?"

"I haven't told her yet."

"You sure you know who I'm talking about? Her name's Esther—"

She closes the coin binder. Strands of hair lift from her head. "I know."

"Why haven't you told her?"

"She's in the hospital," she says. "Heart attack. She was admitted on the morning that Nadia . . . She had one back in April, too. She's old, you know? I didn't want to . . . kill her."

I blink at her. "Really?"

"Really. Old people get sick a lot. I know that's hard to believe," Riley snarks.

"Did you talk to Esther after she was admitted, or did someone tell you that she'd—"

"Someone told me." She nibbles the cuticle around her thumb. "Does Winchester believe that she . . . *hurt* Nadia?"

"Don't know," I say. "I think he's curious since the old lady saw her last."

Riley reopens the coin binder. "How would you know that, though? That she saw Nadia last? You weren't here the entire night. You weren't here the afternoon it happened. Someone, *anyone*, could've walked inside this store after Esther left. Hell, Peter Weller could've dropped by. And old-lady murderers? Really, Michaela? You believe that, but you find it hard to believe the old lady had a heart attack? I could easily believe that *you* were the last person to see Nadia alive."

I pick up a dime stamped "1969." "I know. You're right. A lot of time had passed. I didn't think before I spoke—I let my nerves get to me. But . . . Detective Winchester should probably talk to Esther anyway. Which hospital is she in?"

The edges of Riley's face turn cherry-blossom pink. "No idea."

"Who told you she was in the hospital, then?"

"Whoever it was that answered her phone."

"Do you know that person's—"

"I'm a psychic and you're LAPD. Funny, cuz I thought you worked for this strange scrapbooking company as a digital archaeologist."

"I didn't mean to—"

"I don't know, all right? Nadia rarely talked about Esther. I found her phone number upstairs somewhere. I called, someone answered, and they told me that she'd had a heart attack. I didn't want to upset her since she was already in the hospital, so I didn't mention Nadia dying. The end. Back off me, okay?"

My cheeks burn as though she's slapped me. I take a step back from the counter.

Her eyes flare with anger. "You act like I know everything about Nadia, but I don't."

Neither of us speaks for several seconds.

My fingers curl inside the sleeves of my jacket. "May I ask a *work-related* question?"

Riley massages the back of her neck. "What? Of course. I'm sorry."

"The fountain pen and the earring: Did you include those with Nadia's other items?"

Riley waggles her head. "I don't understand . . ."

I tell her that neither item has Nadia's write-up—they're on the table without any context. She said, as I was starting the project, that she wanted to include more things.

Riley's mouth opens and closes. "Maybe Nadia put them there first, but she ran out of time. Maybe she didn't have the chance to write something before she . . . You know."

I will myself to go cold, to not take any of this personally; Dexter warned me last night that Riley was a little . . . *off.*

"I don't feel like telling Esther what happened and breaking her poor heart," she says. "I'm no good at things that require . . ."

Emotion?

"Patience," she says, smoothing her hair with a flushed hand.

"Let's do this . . ." I rub the bridge of my nose. "You find Esther's phone number, and I tell her the bad news. But I'll couch it with good news, that I'm capturing special memories of Nadia's, and then I'll ask her for a few thoughts, and I'll offer to curate a Nadia-related thing of hers for the bank. How does that sound?"

"Deal," she says.

"But it'll have to wait a few days. I'm out for the rest of the week. My friend's getting married in Temecula and I'm in the wedding."

Riley lifts an eyebrow. "She's getting married on Thanksgiving weekend?"

"She's getting married on Thanksgiving *Day*."

Brighter now, Riley says, "Call her whenever, then. She loved Nadia like a sister. I agree with you. She should know."

We stare at each other.

"Esther's number?" I say.

"Oh. Yeah." She springs from the stool and hurries to the cubbies in the back of the shop. As she rummages through her purse, she says, "This may take a moment."

"It should still be in your phone's call history."

"I called her from the store's landline." She keeps digging through her bag. "I wrote it on a slip of paper, then dropped it in here . . ."

"What's her last name?" I ask, making a new contact record in my phone.

"Umm . . . Little, I think."

I send Christopher a quick text—Back safe—as the bell over the entrance tinkles. An old white woman with cotton-candy hair shouts, "Riley. Sweetie." Glorious in a sequined deck-of-cards duster, she shuffles over to peer at me through her oversize black glasses. "You're not Riley. Did that old Singer sewing machine come back from repair?"

I offer an apologetic smile. "Sorry, I don't work here. Love your coat."

"Thank you, dearest. Where's—"

"I'm back here, Mrs. Fleckenstein." Riley has now emptied her bag onto the counter.

The old lady turns and leaves, and I'm left bobbing in a spicy wake of Shalimar.

Riley waves a sticky note. "Found it."

"Riley, sweetie," Mrs. Fleckenstein shouts, "did the—"

Riley says, "One moment," to her customer, and to me, she says, "Ready?" She calls out Esther Little's number as I tap it into my phone. Then she turns to Mrs. Fleckenstein to discuss the sewing machine.

As I head toward the office, Riley says, "Hey, Michaela. If I were you? I'd take a break. This project isn't worth the stress you're feeling."

I inhale and then loudly exhale. "I'll be fine. Thanks."

She clucks her tongue. "Whatever. Just don't bring your crazy stalker to my store."

I roll my eyes. "In other words, ask him to murder me somewhere else?"

She winks, then turns back to Mrs. Fleckenstein without another word.

Artifact 7: Handmade Mexican art earrings. Acquired on March 3, 1993.

Location of Acquisition: Fresno, California, sits in the center of the San Joaquin Valley in the middle of the state. "Ash tree" in Spanish, Fresno is the closest major city to Yosemite National Park.

Last Owner: Lucia Montez.

Memory: You did odd jobs and repair around the trailer park—there were always things to fix at a trailer park! Your roommate, Lucia, came from a family working in one of the many strawberry, almond, and garlic farms scattered around the San Joaquin Valley. The young woman hated that backbreaking labor and had found work as a babysitter around Fresno. She slept on the pull-out couch in the trailer's tiny living room.

You were happy to share the trailer. Lucia paid in produce if she didn't have money. You also began to learn Spanish since she didn't speak much English. To help in her studies, Lucia subscribed to every American magazine she could afford, and those publications were stacked all around the trailer.

One evening, you spotted earrings on the kitchen sink. *How perfect, how beautiful,* you thought. You didn't tell Lucia this. The language barrier forced you to keep many of your thoughts to yourself.

Lucia was set to soon embark on the next leg of her journey with her family—leaf-lettuce harvest. To celebrate her departure, you grilled a special very-American dinner: steaks, baked potatoes, and ears of corn.

Lucia's emotions were everywhere that night. Fear, panic, relief, sorrow. Somehow she found enough calm in her last moments at the trailer park to offer you the earrings as a gift.

"Because you love them," Lucia said in her halting English.

You gladly accepted.

After Lucia left, for you, Fresno was never the same.

25.

As I sit beneath the hair dryer, I text Christopher.

What did you want to talk about?

He doesn't respond. As I wait, I tap "LUCIA MO—" into the search engine on the Charley Project. I hold my breath as the results fill my phone's small screen. Lucille Montell. Lucy Morris. Lucia Monroe. Nadia's old trailer roommate is not among the cold cases.

I click on Lucia Monroe's link—foul play suspected, never heard from again.

Lucille Montell—drugs and alcohol may have been a factor in her disappearance.

Lucy Morris—few details are available in her case.

I am going to believe that Lucia Montez harvested all that leaf lettuce with her family, and now, almost thirty years later, has retired and is surrounded by grandbabies, love, and light.

By the time I drive up my street, the city has been blessed with skinny cirrus clouds. With that break in rain, my neighbors flock to the streets: jogging, dog-walking, baby-stroller-pushing. The bright-red and yellow windbreakers they've typically worn just three times a year now look war-tired and dull from the constant rain. We smile and wave at each other, thrilled to be outside and beneath the puce-colored sky.

I haven't figured out why Mr. Kim left that note or why he directed me to the grave of Joaquín Reyes. And the Buick—haven't identified the driver. And the sender of those Nebraska-numbered text messages—haven't identified the sender. Oh, and those notes slipped under my door—no idea.

I quickly glance out my bedroom window.

No progress on our fence. It will have to wait until we return from Temecula.

I must pack regular casino clothes and fancy casino clothes for Sasha's wedding. And just in case Christopher shows up in Temecula, I toss lingerie, gifts from him, into my suitcase. Then I pull my brides-maid dress from the closet and lay it across the bed.

It's gold.

"In honor of the Thanksgiving holiday," Sasha claimed.

It's V-necked.

"Cuz your neck is short," she told me. "I know you're always trying to lengthen it."

It's chiffon, with an asymmetrical hem.

Sasha offered no explanations for that.

I change into a sweatshirt, boxers, and thick socks, then head to the front house.

Tonight, Mom has taken her AP music class to UCLA's big-band concert. Dad has provided dinner for himself and me—Fatburgers, fries, and vanilla shakes. He wears his favorite black Nike shorts and matching T-shirt. His skin is still damp from a shower, and he smells like cocoa butter.

Together, we travel to the den. The couch is covered in Dad-tritus: thousands of electronic devices, left-behind socks, notepads, and maga-zines. After he pushes some of his junk to the floor, he plops into the plump pillows with his Fat Meal and aims a remote to turn on the Xbox One and the large-screen television.

"Minecraft?" I ask, grabbing the game controllers from the charger.

"Sure."

Before playing, we uphold tradition by dipping our first french fry into our shakes.

"Mom pack for you yet?" I ask.

"She's still doing laundry." Chili from his burger tumbles down his T-shirt, and he scoops it up with a french fry.

If his employees could see him now.

"Your anniversary's coming up," I say. "You guys doing better?"

He wrenches his eyes away from his avatar now tunneling through the earth. "She's mad at me for something?"

"She's been acting strange lately. She bit my head off when I—"

"Asked about the scar on your face? Yeah, she told me."

"And this morning, you didn't finish your breakfast."

"Oh. Yeah. That wasn't a fight." His cell phone rings from between the couch cushions.

"What was it, then? Why is she freaking out?"

He pauses, then says, "Work. The stress of living. The fence. Those notes someone left you. That Buick. Polar bears. It's all good. No worries." He digs into the cushions, finds the phone, and answers.

A man shouts from the speaker.

Dad's face tightens, and his sentences are restrained fragments. "What about . . . backup . . . accounting cycle . . . This isn't Quicken, dude . . ." He rubs his eyes, curses again. "I'll be there . . . I'm coming now." Jaw twitching and forehead vein thumping, he ends the call and shoves three fries into his mouth.

"That sounded a bit troubling," I say.

He stands and stretches, and his growing belly pokes from beneath his T-shirt. "The server freaked out and data files are missing. And the end of the year is . . . when? Five weeks from now?"

"They try turning it off and turning it back on again?"

"Ha. I'll be back. Remember to lock up." He drops his burger and fries back into the bag and grabs his shake from the floor. "You doing okay?" he asks.

"People are weird."

He frowns. "What does that mean? Did something happen?"

"Not really."

He's staring at me.

"Okay, don't freak out. People *are* weird. Just an observation. Like, 'women be shopping' and 'white people walk like this.'"

He's still staring at me. "You're not gonna tell me about that last text message?"

"Ah. Oh. Uncle Bryan is looking into it cuz that's what he does for a living."

"And my job as your father—"

"Is to save the numbers!" I nudge him with my foot. "Go! Hurry! Save the numbers!"

He kisses my forehead. "Let me know next time?"

"Yep."

"You'll be okay by yourself?"

"Uh-huh."

"Bryan may stop by on his way home," he says. "I'm turning on the alarm."

"Tell him to let me know if he does," I say. "He could get a face full of Mace if he surprises me."

"Ha." One last kiss on my forehead and Dad rushes out of the den.

I shout, "Good luck, Number Man."

"Lock up," he shouts as he leaves out the front door.

The security system drones, "Arming. Stay," and then it beeps three times.

I finish my Fatburger and complete the Minecraft house I've been building. I feed my virtual pet pig, Smokey, a carrot and log off. In the kitchen, I pour bourbon into the rest of my vanilla shake, then call my father. "Let me know if you need my help with anything. I can sit with you like I used to a long time ago."

I'd bring my books or his ancient iPad. I'd bring a hundred Barbies and a bag of popcorn popped by Mom and sprinkled with sugar just for this occasion. I'd sprawl on Dad's office floor, happy to have him to myself even if he was busy doing grown-up math stuff.

He smiles through the phone, also remembering our Back-Then. "Thank you, Mouse. This may take a while. At least there's not a lot of traffic. Leave lights on for Mom."

I flick on the porch light, and then I turn on two lamps in the living room.

The heater whooshes. Warm air swirls from the vents and washes over me. The bourbon warms my belly and the bottoms of my feet.

I'm alone.

I climb the stairs.

The thermostat clicks off.

The house drops into silence. No—not complete silence. I hear . . . the gurgles from boiling water in the watercooler . . . the hum of the fridge and the ice maker . . . I hear the slight rattle of a . . . don't know what that is.

I tiptoe down the hall and stop at my parents' open bedroom door. Steeling myself, I peek in as though Mom's robot guard is patrolling her space.

In the glow of lamplight, shadows play against the light-gray walls, the white ceiling, and the Ed Ruscha print won at a high school silent auction. The bed is made. A tissue box and the Vegas flashlight I gave him sits on Dad's nightstand. Mom's water bottle sits on her bedside table alongside a novel and the television remote controls.

No mess. No robots.

A car engine roars as it races up the hill.

I turn my head toward the sound in the streets and wait . . . wait . . .

Out the window, my apartment shines against the foggy parkland behind our house.

Holding my breath and expecting resistance, I tug the knob on Mom's nightstand.

The drawer slides open.

I gasp so suddenly that I get a stomach stitch. This drawer has *never* opened for me.

The smell of gun oil billows from the now-open space. The silver, matte Smith & Wesson .357 revolver sits on top of its case.

But the gun doesn't hold my attention.

The picture sitting beneath it does.

A teenage girl I've never met poses in one of those rattan Huey Newton / Black Panthers chairs. She wears a Los Angeles Dodgers Starter jersey and jean shorts, and her long brown legs end in white high-top Nikes. Purple, feathered hair. Gold bamboo earrings. Fuchsia lipstick.

Aunt Angie.

Pretty. Flyyyyyyy.

Looks just like my mother.

I pull the picture from beneath the gun. My love for a woman I've never met fills me, and I kiss the photograph. With my phone, I snap a picture of the photo for Mom's memory . . .

This box in the drawer isn't a gun case.

This box is large, almost too big to fit in this drawer. Light-colored wood with coffeewood trim. There's a keyhole in its center.

I touch the top of the box. My sweaty fingers leave prints on the wood's glazed finish, then evaporate. I try to open the box, but it's locked.

The key isn't in the drawer. It wouldn't make sense to keep the key too near.

I search my parents' bureau. Underwear, socks, T-shirts, gloves, and scarves . . . I run my hand beneath the mattress and the box spring—Mom's hunting knife and . . . nothing else. I head to Mom's vanity and search the cubbies and containers. Foundations, powders, earrings, and . . .

A key!

It's small enough to be the key I'm looking for.

I rush back to the box and stick the key into the lock.

Shit.

This isn't the key I need.

Tuesday, November 26
Baldwin Vista
Los Angeles
7:48 p.m.

Christmas bulbs brighten those places that lights in the kitchen or living room can't reach. The wind makes the branches of the big trees creak. The next storm will hit the city on Thursday. The porch light snaps on.

Michaela is a shadow behind the curtains as she flits from one room to the next. Lamplight glows as her shadow moves. Light on the second story glows as her shadow . . .

Where did she go? Why is she alone tonight? Why has the little elephant separated from the herd? Is tonight the night to take her?

Tingling scalp . . . Sizzling blood . . . Tonight certainly *feels* like the night.

Nylon rope. Duct tape. Chloroform. Knife. All in a knapsack, and the basement is ready.

A crash. Wind has toppled something heavy and metallic down the block.

Breathe.

Relax.

It's just the wind.

Where's Michaela? What's she doing? Working? Watching TV? Making memories?

What's the plan?

Hop out of the car. Run over to the house. Ring the doorbell and just . . . tell it all. About the female in Simi Valley. About the female in Torrance. About the others.

A dog barks. A cat screeches. Even the city's quiet places pulse with sound.

Headlights brighten the narrow street. Seconds later, a light-colored truck swings into the driveway and parks beside the Benz.

No!

A middle-aged Black man climbs out of the Ram and strides to the porch. He's as big as an oak tree.

The night's chill vibe splinters.

Who is he? A lover? Is he—

The front door opens.

Michaela smiles up at him.

He waggles her head, musses her hair.

Not a lover.

Muffled voices—what are they saying?

Don't look over here. Don't look over here . . .

A thousand heartbeats pass, and the man is still standing on the porch. He looks comfortable. He's not leaving anytime soon.

Tonight is not the night. But the time will come for Michaela, and she will then record it all *properly*. Beautifully.

And then?

26.

Sasha and Tyler are now Mr. and Mrs. Westmore and are vacationing in Fiji.

Back on Wednesday afternoon in Temecula, Christopher and I met at the furthermost table in the brightly lit Lobby Bar. Beer for him. Bloody Mary for me. I wore brick-colored lip gloss that smelled like chocolate. He wore the beginnings of a beard but had left those stupid fake glasses in his costume trunk.

"You look great," he told me.

"You look great, too," I told him.

We looked incredibly great together in that incredibly bright bar.

"So what's going on?" He leaned forward, focused on me.

"I was chased through the streets of LA."

"*What?* Michaela."

"It's weird." I shook my head. "But I don't wanna talk about that right now. You have some words to say."

Christopher gave me a small smile, and I loved how he looked at me. As though I were the only person in the room, as though I were the only person who mattered. He took my hand and told me that I couldn't leave the firm. That he was close to figuring things out. That he'd never had a problem avoiding relationships so that he could focus on his business until I came into his life. All he'd wanted to do was spend his days and nights with me. That's when his cell phone rang from the table. I recognized the number—the Memory Bank—and I watched his temples pound as he tried to decide whether to answer.

He answered the phone.

I gulped my cocktail.

He ended the call. After a quick kiss and hug, an apology, and a nuzzle, he hurried to his room, grabbed his unpacked bag, and beat it to his car to head back up the 15 North. He sent apologetic text messages every few miles.

I am so sorry

You know I'm always on call

This couldn't wait

They needed me back

You need to tell me about being chased! Later tonight OK?

Imani found me sitting in the bar, numb but not numb enough to keep from crying, drunk but not drunk enough to black out and forget. I'd been kinda reading a news alert on my phone—"Torrance Woman Found Dead"—but the words kept losing their shape. I'd retained enough to understand that there were worse things than getting white-girl-wasted in an Indian casino.

And now, days later, Anna sucks her teeth as she refills my coffee mug and listens to my tale of woe. Lunch rush over, the diner is cool and quiet. Her last two customers linger outside the entrance, smoking cigarettes and telling tall tales. Their drifting smoke and heavy cologne remind me of Sundays after church at my grandparents' house.

"Your daddy's right," Anna says. "You're *not* a priority to him."

"Chris needs to belong to everyone. *Everyone* is important to him, which means *no one* is important to him. We used to have these deep conversations and he'd tell me about his fears and secrets, and I thought he'd saved that special space just for me."

"But?"

"My best friend Imani knew about the time his dad left him alone in the car to pick up a prostitute."

"So your girl knew what you thought he only told you."

"Yeah. I want to feel special . . ." I shake my head. "Maybe . . ." I rest my chin in my hand.

"Maybe *what*?" Anna asks.

I bite my lip before a grin breaks like warm molasses across my mouth. "Maybe Dexter is up to the challenge. We're having dinner again tonight."

Anna whoops. "And is that why you had me baking this cake? What time is dinner?"

"Seven."

She eyes my wide-legged trousers and turtleneck. "That gives you enough time to change into something more . . . *less*."

"My classic Katharine Hepburn look isn't sexy? A glimpse of my ankle won't get him hot and bothered?"

"All that wool will get him hot and itchy." Anna eases the lemon cake I ordered into a pink pastry box. "Wear something that's more than your butt cheeks hanging out and less than *Little House on the Prairie*."

"That was a TV show, right?"

Anna rolls her eyes.

I sit up on the stool. "There's something I've been wanting to ask you. Do you know the name Joaquín Reyes?"

"Joaquín . . . Reyes . . ." She squints as the memory flutters in and out, then snaps her fingers. "Oh yeah . . . I remember him. He used to work at Beautiful Things way, way back in the day. Back when Sarah

Park was the owner. Nice Latino gentleman. A little older. Always did a good job of fixing things. One day, he just stopped coming in, and then a few months later, his daughter stops by out of the blue asking for his last paycheck cuz he'd died."

"Ah. Riley didn't recognize the name."

"That's because Riley wasn't born yet. She doesn't know everything, don't matter if she thinks she does." Anna brings the cake over to the counter. "Well?"

Glazed. Bundt. Goodness. Thin slices of candied lemon twist and swirl around the cake. The fragrance makes me swing my feet beneath the counter.

Anna closes the box. "Why are you asking about Joaquín?"

"Mr. Kim, who *still* hasn't called me back and isn't at the shop. He left me a note last week that directed me to Joaquín's grave at Rosedale Cemetery."

"That's strange." Anna sits the cake box before me. "Enjoy."

"If I had a to-go cup of coffee, I'd sit in my car and eat this entire thing."

"But then you wouldn't get to share your cake with Dexter tonight."

My face warms. I plan to share my cake with Dexter, just not the one in this pink box.

Heh.

Anna waves at Kangol Man now shuffling to the parking lot with a new cigarette hanging from his lips. "How's it going over at the store?" she asks me.

"Making progress."

"You're gonna keep stopping by after you're done, right?"

"Of course. If you start making mimosas and Bloody Marys, I'll bring my friends here for brunch." I point to her. "Ooh, that's a change that you can make. We *love* brunch. Get a liquor license. Put some dog bowls out there. I'll bring you my *New Yorker*s and *Vanity Fair*s, et voilà. Anna's Place, now a brunch destination!"

She taps her fingers against the counter. "That's a good idea."

"My friend Sasha, the one who just got married? She's in special events. She could help you promote things here. Readings, listening parties, guest chefs, all kinds of obnoxious, buzzy stuff. I'll talk to her if you'd like."

"You wouldn't mind?"

Phone in hand and texting already, I say, "Nope, not a biggie." A whoosh and the message—CALL ME WHEN U GET BACK. EVENT IDEA! SMOOCHES MARRIED LADY—is sent to a cell tower somewhere in Fiji. "Speaking of Sasha . . . you hear about the girl who was killed in Simi Valley last week?"

"Young white girl?"

"Uh-huh. My friend Sasha knew her. Between you and me . . ." I lean over the counter and whisper, "It could be a serial killer."

Anna's eyebrows lift. "I thought it was a boyfriend."

I shake my head. "There were letters carved into her back. Two *D*s."

Anna takes a breath. "Reminds me of the serial killer back in the day."

"The Dashing Devil?"

She gapes at me. "They never caught that fool. He's back?"

"Dunno."

Anna sucks in a breath and flicks her hand at her face. "Back when I was living in Louisiana, I remember being terrified whenever there was a story in the paper about some woman being found with 'DD' carved in her back. Fished out a girl from one of the levees, I think. But they were all white, so my daddy told me to stop worrying so much." She shudders. "Can't be the same man. He gotta be almost a hundred years old now."

"Maybe he hired an intern." I cross my eyes.

Anna laughs as she pours coffee into a to-go cup. "Joaquín the handyman. The Dashing Devil. You bringing back *all* the memories.

I like you being here. Riley doesn't come over at all anymore. And I watched over her, too, just like I did Dexter. You'd think she'd treat me a little better, but . . ." She clucks her tongue. "I got a daughter. Don't need Riley."

"And you have me. I'm like the cool niece." I grin the widest grin.

"What thing of Nadia's are you working on now?"

"Artifact eight—the deed to Beautiful Things."

It's a weird item to include, but I'm guessing Nadia was proud of the deed. Nothing interesting, though. The shop was originally purchased by Abram Horowitz. He owed the developer $2,000 or something. And then Sarah Park bought it from Horowitz, real estate jargon, *blahblahblah*. This is no hedgehog key chain, but it's Nadia's box.

I dump cream and sugar into my coffee. "Any memories from those days with Sarah?"

Anna hands me a lid for my cup. "She was happy. Quiet. Her English was so-so. Every morning, she'd buy her breakfast here—coffee, four slices of bacon, and an apple with a wedge of cheddar cheese. She said it would help her become more American."

After work, Anna would help her and Mr. Kim learn English. They'd sit right where I now sit, and they'd watch *$10,000 Pyramid* or *Wheel of Fortune* on a little television Anna used to keep on the counter. That's how Sarah and Mr. Kim learned basic words and phrases.

"On those nights," Anna recalls, "Mr. Kim's wife would bring us Korean food for dinner. Ooh, I love me some bulgogi and samgyetang!" She taps her belly as she remembers.

The door to the diner opens.

Anna's eyebrows lift.

Riley stands there, Q-tip skinny, hard lipped, peering into the darker space, one minute from demanding that we turn our music down or she'll call the police.

"I was telling Mickie that you don't come over here anymore." Anna gives me a look.

I give her a look back, then pat the stool beside me.

"Nadia didn't want food smells in the shop." Riley sits. "May I have a slice of cherry pie and coffee, please?" She turns to me. "Are you done for the day?"

"Nope. Just picking up a cake for dinner before Anna skedaddles."

"Miss Mickie here has a date tonight." Anna sets an empty mug at Riley's hands.

"Very cool," Riley says, plucking a packet of Splenda from the holder. "If you don't wanna drive all the way home, you can change upstairs. Nadia has a full bathroom. Good lighting to do your makeup and hair."

"You wouldn't mind?" I ask. "Not that I live far away."

Anna sets a plate filled with pie next to Riley's mug. "You're in Baldwin Vista, right?"

"Where's that?" Riley asks.

"The hilly part off La Brea," Anna says, "right in front of the park."

Riley fluffs out a napkin across her lap. "Michaela's gonna help me figure out a plan to open an online store."

"You call my friend?" I ask.

She grins. "Yep. I just need to figure out a few things first."

To Anna, I say, "What were we . . . ?"

Anna leans back on the counter. "So I was real tight with Sarah and Jae—that's Mr. Kim's first name. But then . . . Sarah was here one day, and all of a sudden? *Poof.* Gone. Never saw her or heard from her again."

"Yeah," I say, "Nadia told me that Sarah's mom back in South Korea was really sick. The note for the deed says that Sarah decided to stay and that she sold the store to Nadia for some ridiculously low price."

"Is that what *you* heard?" Anna asks Riley. "That she sold the store to Nadia for a song?"

Riley cuts her pie with a precision that rivals the Blue Angels'. "I wouldn't say a *song*."

"Sarah sold for ten thousand dollars," I say.

Anna sucks her teeth. "Like I said: a song and not even a good one. Anyway, I don't know what to believe. I *still* don't believe Nadia committed suicide."

"*What?*" Riley barks. "You *saw* her, Anna. You saw the bag on her . . . You *saw* it."

"I did, but . . ." Anna shakes her head.

"You're being ridiculous," Riley proclaims.

My eyes bug out and my hand covers my mouth. *No, she did not.*

"You think you know it all," Anna says, voice tight, wanting to chew her up but not chewing her up because she doesn't want sinewy Riley-meat stuck in her molars. "You ain't got one clue about *nothing*, especially when it came to Nadia."

Riley flinches.

"Ooh!" I say, smiling mostly to ease the tension. "Nadia had secrets?" My heart pounds in fear of Riley's edges being snatched by Auntie Anna.

"There are *always* secrets," the older woman says now. "I adored Nadia, but she was shady, especially in the beginning. She conned Sarah out of that store."

"You think?" I ask.

Anna swerves her neck. "Ten thousand dollars for a thriving business?"

"It was the *seventies*," Riley says with a flick of her ponytail. "Sarah was desperate."

"And if Nadia *did* swindle her," I add, "she made up for it by facing down Peter Weller, who still has that man following us."

"Following us?" Riley snorts. "Nuh-uh."

I snort. "Uh-huh."

Riley gapes at Anna.

Anna nods.

"But that only proves my point," Riley says. "A woman who owns a business in this city has to be tough. That makes Nadia a hero in my book."

Anna glares at the redhead. "Child, I own a business in LA, too. I've been robbed, threatened—all of it. I'm not talking about *that*. I'm talking about . . ." She sets both elbows on the counter and leans toward us. "I got this letter back when Sarah left for Korea. Her brother sent it. The family was looking for her because they wanted to tell her that her father had a heart attack. The brother had called the store, but Sarah never called him back. By then, though, Sarah was gone, and I figured that his letter came but Sarah was already in South Korea. Remember, this was before cell phones and answering machines existed."

The back of my neck tingles. "Do you still have that letter from her brother?"

Anna slips the bill for the cake on top of the box. "It's at home in a file somewhere."

I reach into my pocket for money to pay for the cake.

"I don't understand," Riley says, face grim. "What's the point of this conversation? To tarnish Nadia's reputation? To . . . *blame* her for doing what men have done since the beginning of time?" She sounds shrill.

Anna accepts my twenty-dollar bill with a wink. She eyes Riley, and says, "Girl, ain't nobody tarnishing nothing about no Nadia."

"So what's the point?" Riley asks again.

Anna puts a hand on her hip. "You weren't even *in* this conversation until you brought your narrow ass through my door. You ain't gotta know the point."

I lightly tap Riley's wrist. "I was just asking Anna about the store back then. I'm working on the deed for Nadia's memory bank, and I just wanted more context."

Riley rolls her eyes. "That's all you had to say, Anna."

Anna scowls at Riley, then smiles and waves at Pepper. The stylist is out in the breezeway, beneath perfect sunlight, snapping pictures of her client's new lavender weave.

I tap the cake box and ease off the stool and head toward the door. "Work calls. Thanks for baking this, Anna."

"You have fun tonight," Anna calls after me. "I wanna hear all about it in the morning."

And I want to hear more about Sarah Park and Joaquín Reyes.

I know where *he* is right now.

Where's *she*?

Artifact 8: Deed to Beautiful Things: A Curiosities Shoppe. Acquired on May 10, 1980.

Location of Acquisition: Los Angeles, California. The Santa Barbara Plaza, also known as Marlton Square, played a vital role in the Black community. Thriving in the 1940s and 1950s, businesses in this twenty-two-acre shopping center met the needs of thousands of consumers across South Los Angeles. From the Broadway and May Company department stores to Woolworth's and J.J. Newberry's, the plaza has transformed from a vibrant shopping hub to a now nearly abandoned plot of land.

Last Owner: Sarah Park.

Memory: You'd recently relocated to Los Angeles and answered a want ad Sarah Park placed in the classifieds. Hired on the spot, you worked full-time, from acquiring collectibles and fixing broken things around the shop to handling business dealings and advertising materials.

Early one morning, Sarah received a call from her family in Seoul, South Korea. Her mother had been diagnosed with stage 2 liver cancer, and Sarah needed to immediately return home. A dutiful daughter who always sent the bulk of her earnings back to her family, Sarah closed the store and left for South Korea. She didn't expect to be away for long, but soon, days turned into weeks.

Sarah called two months after she'd left to attend to her mother. "Do you want to buy Beautiful Things?" she asked. "You are the only one I trust to run the store like I did."

You were honored. The store was a special place. There was a problem, though.

"I don't have much money," you told Sarah.

She agreed to sell the store for $10,000 paid over ten years. "And if you find my favorite ruby pendant, please send it to me immediately."

You *did* find that pendant but never got an address from Sarah Park. So you kept those payments in an account, the least you could do to hold up your end of the bargain. Unfortunately, you never heard from your business partner again.

Forty years later, Beautiful Things: A Curiosities Shoppe has more than seven thousand items and loyal customers. For you, this store deed is the second most beautiful thing you've ever acquired.

27.

Dexter lives on the sixteenth floor in a high-rise apartment on Grand Avenue. I had a tough time deciding on an outfit. The pleather jeans and slinky sweater that I'd bought from my favorite boutique weren't comfortable. So I returned home and grabbed a slinky, innocent-looking summer dress . . . even though the thermostat hovered at fifty degrees.

As soon as Dexter ushers me in, I spot the silver curves of Walt Disney Concert Hall over there, and the deep-space-blue Chavez Ravine, home of Dodger Stadium, over there. A series of black-and-white photographs—a river snaking through a canyon, children running through sprinklers—lines the taupe walls.

Though difficult to do with the pink cake box in my hands, Dexter and I hug.

Beneath the black Henley, his body is a range of lean muscle.

"You smell incredible," he whispers.

"Lemons?"

He comes in for a kiss. "Umhmm."

"It's my cake." Hoping he'd pick up the double entendre I dropped, I close my eyes as his lips touch mine.

He tastes of bourbon and oranges, like an old-fashioned. Because delicious cocktails always make me goose pimple, my skin does that now as his lips travel along my neck.

Dexter doesn't pick up that play on words; nor does he want to wait until after dinner for dessert. And now, he closes his eyes as he devours . . .

Anna's cake.

Not mine.

I eat a slice—the dessert is sweet, tangy. My lips are covered with lemony glazed sugar, but Dexter doesn't notice that I'm now a sweet treat. "She baked it this afternoon," I tell him.

"Anna's lemon cake will always be my favorite dessert," he says, finishing his second slice. "So how was your friend's wedding?"

"Rainy but perfect. She was a beautiful bride, and I looked like an Amazon tree frog in my shiny gold dress."

"I wanna see."

I show him pictures on my phone and make a face. "Ribbit."

"You look amazing, Mickie." He taps a perfectly lit selfie of me posing near the wedding cake. "Send me this one so when I'm in Yemen next month, I'll be able to pull up this picture of you in tree-frog gold."

I giggle. "No man has *ever* said those words to me."

He kisses me again, and my heart flutters in my chest.

After all I've experienced in the last several days, being caressed and complimented is the breather I freakin' deserve. I will soak up every bit of this night—the hard times *will* come again, but I will be able to draw from the glory of this evening to pull me through.

"Something to drink?" he asks. "I can make anything you want."

"Surprise me."

He ambles over to the open kitchen. "How's Mom's memory bank going? You ever get more info on that pen and earring?"

"Not yet. But I'm halfway through the rest of the collection."

"Word?" He places a sugar cube in a short glass and grabs bitters from the cabinet.

An old-fashioned!

"You have to show me the photo albums you mentioned last week," I say. "We were talking about other people's pictures, remember?"

Over at the floor-to-ceiling windows, I gaze out at nighttime in Los Angeles, and the city, as always, leaves me breathless. The lights, the towering buildings, that sky, the sea of cars, the march of airplanes coming and going . . . Other cities have these things, but none of them have these highways, this smog, and a theme song written by Randy "I Love LA" Newman.

"I'm learning a lot about your mom," I tell Dexter now.

"Like?"

"Like how she was incredibly generous. The little vignettes that I'm writing? They're stories about how she shared anything she had. Electric blankets, space heaters, gas money. And that ruby pendant you can't find? Did you know that it used to belong to Sarah Park, the store's original owner? Sarah forgot it when she returned to South Korea. Anyway, once Esther gets out of the hospital, I'm hoping she can tell me about the other side of Nadia, the silly-girlfriend side."

Dexter joins me at the window with two glasses filled with golden booze finished with a twist of orange peel. "What silly-girlfriend side?"

"You know: Did she and Nadia go bet on the horses in Del Mar? Did they stuff dollar bills into strippers' thongs? Talk about boys late at night on the phone? Silly-girlfriend stuff."

"Ah." He holds up his glass. "To making new memories."

We click. We drink.

Icy bourbon glides down my throat and splashes into my belly. *Kapow!* I shiver as liquid sunshine spreads throughout my arms. This is a delicious, perfect cocktail.

"So . . . Esther?" he says.

"Yeah—the night before your mother passed, I saw Esther leave the store and come back with groceries and flowers." I sip my drink, then add, "I told all of this to Detective Winchester. He didn't mention anything to you? Cuz he took the vase of roses last Tuesday."

Dexter shakes his head, lifts the glass to his lips.

"Riley told me that Esther's in the hospital. Heart attack. That's why she didn't attend the funeral. She doesn't know anything about Nadia dying. Riley gave me her phone number."

"*Esther's* phone number."

I nod and sip more bourbon-backed joy.

Dexter drains his cocktail, then says, "Let's call her."

"*Now?*"

"It's been a week today since the funeral. She should know that her best friend died."

I pluck my phone from my purse and find the number Riley shouted at me from across the store as she helped cotton-candy-haired Mrs. Fleckenstein with her Singer.

Dexter dials, then puts on the phone's speaker.

The line rings . . . rings . . . clicks.

"Hello?" A woman.

"Hi," Dexter says. "May I speak with Esther—" To me, he whispers, "Last name?"

"Little."

"May I speak with Esther Little, please?"

The woman says, "I think you have the wrong number."

Dexter apologizes and ends the call. "Let's try again." He dials, slower now.

The same woman answers. "Me again."

He hangs up and blinks at me.

I shrug. "It was chaos in the shop that day. Riley was helping Mrs. Fleckenstein while she was trying to talk to me. We probably messed up."

"Probably." He takes my hand, and together, we plop onto the couch. He stares at the melting cube of ice in his glass, then says, "I don't know Esther. I had no idea my mother had a best friend. And now you're telling me that she was there the night before . . ."

My face burns. "I'm sorry. I thought you knew."

His hand scrubs his jaw. "Riley is always so quick to tell me about my business, but she didn't tell me *this*?"

"Maybe it was a new friendship," I suggest. "Maybe Esther was a customer at first, but then she and Nadia bonded over Graceland toilet brushes or something. Maybe your mother forgot to mention her—she *did* have a memory disorder." I squeeze his knee. "Isn't it a comfort, though? Knowing that she had someone else who loved her?"

His jaw clenches, and the nerves in his neck twitch. "I should've been there for her."

"I'm sure she was proud of you, that you're now the explorer that she was."

He peers at me, and a slow grin breaks past his sorrow. "What was that?"

Stomach noise has interrupted the moment.

I giggle. "Is that your belly growling or is it mine?"

Ha. I already know: it's mine.

He turns on the stereo and selects the soundtrack for tonight—Maxwell, good choice—then escorts me to the dining room table near the windows. He's cooked spaghetti, and unless it's fresh pasta and a twenty-four-hour bolognese sauce, spaghetti is pretty much spaghetti. He's selected a good Chianti. Mom has bottles of Cantalici in her collection. As we eat, we talk about politics, the Lakers, the worst traffic accidents we've ever seen, and the rib eyes at Mastro's.

As we clear the dishes to eat the rest of Anna's cake, Dexter and I bump into each other. Just like that, my mouth is on his, his body presses against mine, my hand drops to the fly of his jeans—he's ready.

I lift his shirt over his head.

A half-heart-shaped locket hangs from a silver chain around his neck. I run my fingers over his bare chest and the copper scar that crisscrosses his right shoulder blade. He kisses my neck. Somehow, my dress unbuttons and falls to the ground.

Newton was right. Every mass *does* attract every other mass in the universe, and the gravitational force between two bodies *is* proportional to the product of their masses and inversely proportional to the square of the distance between them. Physics be real.

Outside, beyond those windows, only God—oh, and the residents in the apartments across the way—can see Dexter and me.

Whoever's watching?

Hope you like my cake.

Dexter's smashing it.

As we lie naked on the couch, we talk about politics again and the worst Christmas gift we've ever received. Then he pulls out an album of found photographs from the coffee table.

Four men posed before an old Cadillac convertible and a Black boy crying on Santa's lap . . . A little girl eating a melting ice-cream cone and an accidental double exposure of a flapper wearing opera gloves . . . A couple—he looks at the camera; she tucks her face in his shoulder—dressed to the nines in a crowded dance hall. Just two shots on each page.

"So that they can breathe," he explains. "So that I can appreciate the juxtaposition. Have enough space to create my own story of Black lives."

"I was thinking about getting some old rolls of film developed," I say.

"There's something special about holding an actual photograph. Sorry, but it's better than your fancy holograms."

My eyebrow cocks. "Um, excuse me? You haven't *seen* my fancy holograms."

He pauses. "True. I'll reserve judgment until then."

"You ever think of looking for any of these people?"

He shakes his head and takes the album from my hands. "They'd mess up the story."

Sounds familiar.

He pulls me onto his lap.

His cell phone rings from the coffee table.

"You want that?" I ask as he plants kisses on my shoulder.

"Mmm . . . Maybe. I'm expecting an important call."

His hands are full of me, and so I reach back. I glimpse VINCE RADER on the screen before handing him the phone.

His eyebrows crumple, and he says, "Gotta take this. Sorry."

I bristle. This is the second time in less than a week that a creative, hot man has chosen to take a business call over sharing a quiet, *creative* moment with me.

Into the phone, Dexter says, "Hey." He listens, then squeezes and kisses my hand. "Hold on, hold . . ." To me, he says, "I need to—"

I tug his ear. "Yep."

Dexter strides to the bedroom and closes the door behind him.

"Strike two, Dexter Denham." First strike: criticizing Riley's dream. And now this. I pop up from the couch. With quivering legs, I snatch my bra and panties over by the kitchen counter. While I'm up, I pour myself another glass of wine and peek at the stack of opened mail on the counter: electric bill from Department of Water and Power, notice of health insurance privacy policies, legal papers . . . United States Bankruptcy Court, Southern District of California . . .

Oh. Boy.

Back on the couch, I grab my phone to text Riley.

Was she right about Dexter's money problems? I don't ask her that, but I do ask about that number for Esther. As I await her response, I tap into Google and search "VINCE RADER," the man luxuriating in my dinner date's attention right now.

The search engine finds more than fifty thousand results in 0.51 seconds.

Rader Consulting, Los Angeles Private Investigator.

Where am I?

My mind wobbles in and out of shadow, then throws up its hands. *No clue, girl. Good luck.*

The digital clock on the dresser—*whose dresser?*—glows with red numbers.

5:48 a.m.

It is colder here, wherever I am.

Hot pink, atomic green, and golden lights dance across the ceilings. *Vegas?*

No. Those are lights from digital billboards.

A man's arm drapes across my breasts.

Christopher?

No, this man's skin is the color of bourbon.

Dexter.

His bed.

His apartment.

His body.

Oh yeah.

My brain locks, and the rest of me relaxes.

Something has pulled me from sleep.

But it wasn't Dexter. He's knocked out. His half-heart locket hangs from the chain and nestles in the scoop of my neck.

Who's wearing the second half?

Is it an ex-girlfriend he met in Kuala Lumpur, who keeps it in a mementos box? Or maybe there's a daughter he left behind in Reykjavík and she has it.

I shift in bed so that my head rests on his forearm. Those lights from the billboards play against our skin. This shoulder scar.

How did he get it?

Is it as mysterious to him as my cheek scar was to me?

The nightstand vibrates. My cell phone.

Probably Mom just noticing that I didn't come home last night and . . .

Not Mom.

I SEE U WHORE

I KNOW WHERE U LIVE

◆ ◆ ◆

"Could be a wrong number." Dexter pulls his shirt over his head, then sits beside me on the bed. "You tell them that?"

"Of course I did." My skin burns and I can't catch my breath. I pull the comforter around me because now I am *cold* and breathless. Even with that brilliant blue sky and those puffy white clouds beyond his windows. Even with these flannel sheets bunched around me. Even with this hot guy curled at my hip. I am cold.

Dexter takes my hands in his and squeezes. "You're freaking out over a phantom, over a person who isn't brave enough to say this shit to your face."

"I don't want them to say this shit to my face."

He asks me a question.

I shake my head, even though I'm no longer hearing him, no longer hearing anything except this weird humming in my ears and my heavy breathing and my pounding heart. His mouth is moving and I'm nodding, but I don't know what he is saying because . . .

This is not the Nebraska number. This one starts with 310—an LA number.

"Block it."

I blink—I heard that. "Huh?"

"Block the number." He takes the phone from the nightstand, finds the number, and taps "Block This Caller." He hands me the phone, and his lips twist into a wry smile. "Done."

"But they say they know where I live. It doesn't matter if it's blocked or not when whoever it is can roll up on me and . . ." I close my eyes and take deep breaths. *You have resources. You are part of the LAPD family.* I push out a breath, calmer now. Another slow breath in, another slow breath out. "I'll tell my dad."

Dexter lifts an eyebrow. "I thought your dad was an accountant."

"He's an accountant with a gun and a brother who's a cop."

Dexter sits up. "Oh. I didn't know that."

"Half of my family is LAPD, and my uncle is already looking into the Nebraska number. But now there's *this* one."

He stares at me, then catches himself staring. "You gonna be okay?"

"Eventually."

He brushes my hair away from my face. "This wasn't the morning I had planned for us. Can we get a do-over?"

I say, "Yeah," and he pulls me onto his lap.

Even with my eyes closed, I can still see that text message glowing from my phone.

So many keys.

In this line of work, doors always need to be opened.

Stealing keys is easy. Every day, people leave them with valets, with mechanics, with the parking attendants . . . Sometimes, folks just leave their keys sitting around.

This new key is the same color as the heavy clouds over Los Angeles. And the air smells metallic, just like this new key.

What weird alchemy is this?

The elderly locksmith took forever. He wanted to chat and catch up. He was being nosy. Again.

The old man will have to die.

At almost eight in the morning, the mother and father have both left the house, and the new key successfully slips into the apartment's lock. The door swings open, sending out a cold breeze infused with jasmine and oranges, toast . . .

A *beep-beep* and "Front. Door."

Shit.

An alarm . . .

The security panel above the light switch is green.

Disarmed.

Good to know.

"Hello? Anyone here?"

The only sound is the refrigerator humming.

She must still be asleep.

A flight of carpeted stairs leads up to the living space.

Two steps groan.

Also good to know.

In the living room, a blue suede couch. A folded quilt sits on the ottoman. There's a sixty-inch television. On the coffee table: magazines, an iPad, and a novel with a faded red cover. The kitchen has white appliances. Boxes pile near windows that look out to the park.

Those boxes . . . Is she coming or going?

In the refrigerator, there's a small carton of milk, a bottle of white wine, bagels, cheeses, and . . . *that*. A liter of vanilla latte with a top that screws off easily. The mouth of the jug is big enough to drop as many Rohypnol tablets as needed. Michaela will drink it without even realizing . . .

Outside, a door slams.

A quick peek out the kitchen window: Michaela is standing beside her car in the driveway. She's talking on the phone.

What the fuck?

She didn't arm the system? She didn't come home to sleep? Where has she been?

Do it now.

Take her now.

The rope, the knife . . . all the tools are in the backpack.

Michaela, talking to someone who makes her smile, wanders closer to the door. She tosses her head back and cackles. She holds a grocery bag.

Fear and surprise would make any person's legs weak. Fear and surprise would send the bravest soul rushing down the hallway to hide in a closet. And that happens now. Waiting, the knife comes out, and breathing becomes harder. Like breathing is a new thing. Like *killing* is a new thing.

The front door creaks and the security system's sensor chimes.

"Ohmigod, Imani, you're *so* ridiculous." Michaela is still talking on the phone. "No lie—I *did* wanna run a credit check on his fine ass." Her voice is like heavy silk, even when saying stupid things like—

"Of *course* I brought condoms. You think I'd leave it to a man?" She chuckles, and those two steps groan beneath her weight. "No, they weren't expired. They're the ones we got from the Hustler Store last . . ."

Anxiety overtakes the sizzling thrill of the hunt.

"I just walked in," Michaela says. "Yeah, I bought bacon, so I'm still stopping by before heading over to—"

Silence.

What is she doing?

Just standing there or . . . ?

The vanilla latte—the container is sitting on the counter, and the refrigerator door . . .

Is open.

Those two steps groan again.

Michaela says, "Lemme call you back."

She sees!

She's probably dialing 9-1-1 right now.

There's only one exit now.

Outside the window, there's a short ledge and a giant tree with branches that reach so close . . . Fortunately, the back fence is down . . .

Just open the window.

Just kick out the screen. It looks loose enough.

And then what?

A siren cries in the distance.

There are only two choices:

Jump.

Stay and be caught.

Make a choice.

The siren sounds closer now.

Jump!

The hang time lasts for only a second, and it's followed by a crack against the face, a crack of a branch, and then, down, down, down, ending with a crack in the ankle. There's a kaleidoscope of hurt, but that must be ignored for now. Now it's time to scramble past that open fence and into the bramble of the park's sage and chaparral.

Focus. Focus.

Success. For now.

In addition to the knife, rope, and packets of Rohypnol, the knapsack also holds a white short-sleeved dress shirt and a black necktie. *I'm just a Mormon on a mission and I'm lost. What's in my knapsack? Just a few copies of the Book of Mormon, pamphlets, and a small painting of the first vision.*

The park is a soggy valley. No hikers. No joggers. No dogs off leashes. The dull roar of traffic grows during the agonizing trek east. The adrenaline is wearing off, and painful twinges shoot up, down, and zigzag. By the time Obama Boulevard looms ahead, the ankle pain hasn't eased. A visit to urgent care was not in the plan.

But the plan keeps changing.

To the hospital and then . . .

Try, try again.

BETTER NOT TELL YOU NOW

28.

After leaving Dexter's apartment, I head home.

"You didn't leave your wallet and debit card laying around this time?" Imani asks.

"Ohmigod," I say to her, "now you're being petty. One guy steals my ATM card—"

"—because you got distracted by his pretty eyes."

I close the door to my apartment behind me and climb the stairs. Two steps creak beneath me. Dad thinks we'll need to tent the apartment for termites.

I swipe away unread WhatsApp messages from Christopher, then check out Sasha's Instagram honeymoon pictures. "Yeah, I bought bacon, so I'm still stopping by before heading over to—" I reach the top landing and freeze. "Lemme call you back."

The refrigerator door is open.

I don't remember leaving the refrigerator door open.

I don't remember leaving the jug of vanilla latte on the kitchen counter.

I creep into my kitchen. No, I don't remember leaving that door open or . . .

Was my front door unlocked?

Did I disarm the security system? Did I even turn it on before leaving last night?

I can't hear myself think over the racket of fire truck sirens coming up the hill.

So this jug of vanilla latte . . .

I run a shaky finger against the jug's plastic.

It's still cold.

Would it be this cold if it had been sitting on the counter since . . . *when*? Last night?

I force myself to stick the jug back into the refrigerator, and with deliberate intent, I close the fridge door.

No.

No one's come into my apartment. Because my television is right there, and my iPad is still on the couch. Both are easy, pawnable things. I hear myself pant as I creep down the hallway to my bedroom. My hand-me-down designer handbags and shoes—they're still in my closet. The TV on my wall—it's still hanging there. Those are also easy, pawnable things.

Nothing's been stolen.

I say this—*nothing's been stolen, nothing's been stolen*—like it's my only line in a school Christmas play.

No one's come in. Not the note writer. Not Kiki, the neighbor's dog. Life is just moving too fast; that's what's happening.

I change into leggings and a sweater and . . .

Quiet. No *knick-knick-knicking* at my bedroom window . . . Sunlight shines unfiltered from outside and streams across the bed's comforter.

Did Dad finally fix the loose window screen frame?

I shuffle past the bed to inspect his handiwork and pull open the window.

The silver screen isn't here.

Did Dad just take it off completely? Was the steel frame too bent to repair?

Before closing the window, I peek at the yard below.

There it is. The white screen frame looks bright against the dark, wet ground.

The wind must have whipped it off.

Makes sense even as dread makes my stomach cramp.

How long has the frame been down there?

I try to think as I shut my window. Not sure, since I cared about that creepy knicking only at nighttime. Any other time, I didn't pay attention. I text my father that the screen is now lost in the bushes. Fortunately, the apartment is on the second story, so I don't have to worry about someone climbing in that window. Still . . .

He texts immediately. **Sorry. Too much going on. I'll get to it today!**

He's right. There is too much going on. He'll fix the screen, and I'll do better, too. I'll pay attention to what's in front of me, charge myself twenty dollars anytime I fail to arm that security system, and I'll starve my distractions and feed my focus like that fortune cookie told me to last week.

That jug of vanilla latte, though. Still cold. Like someone just plucked it from the fridge.

Giant yellow beasts have sprung like after-rain mushrooms in the parking lot of the Santa Barbara Plaza. The RVs have limped to the western perimeters of the lot, and their occupants huddle together, hands on hips and arms crossed in confusion and anger. One of the men resembles the homeless guy I met in the coffee shop, but I'm too far away to know for sure. The presence of the bulldozers tells me that Peter Weller is serious about his takeover.

"He wants that land," Dexter tells me over the phone. "He owns the parcels where you see the heavy machinery."

"Should you hire a lawyer? I mean, you haven't sold. Anna hasn't sold, either." Maybe this is the reason Dexter's hired a private investigator, to gather dirt on Peter Weller. A mistress. A love child. A dead mistress. A dead love child.

"He's trying to pressure us," Dexter says.

I turn off the Benz's ignition. "And do you feel pressured?"

He laughs. "I feel . . . *splendid*. See, there's this girl I know. We spent the night together."

"And she rocked your world?"

"Burned it to the ground."

One of the hard hat–wearing bulldozer operators is staring at me. His red-faced buddy points toward the shops. Dexter is saying something, but I'm not listening. I want to tell him about the refrigerator door and the jug of vanilla latte, but there's nothing to tell . . . except only maybe there *is*; maybe someone is stalking me, but I have no idea who that would be.

After Dexter and I say our goodbyes, I rush through the parking lot, passing Beautiful Things. Anna will talk me through this. She'll either tell me that the open-fridge-door episode is serious enough to tell my parents about or she'll shake her head and comment on how tender I am, how quickly I jump at shadows because my folks have been overprotective. *You doing too much, Mickie. Your phone is always in your face. You don't look up. Kids these days.* And then she'll put a bowl of grits in my hands and say, *Eat your food, child.*

The windows in the diner are lightless, the door locked. No one answers when I knock.

Riley, alone in the store, sits at the back counter. She's wearing work gloves grimy from sorting through a tub of toy cars. With her sleeves rolled to her elbows, she runs a cotton swab along the bottom of a lime-green car. "I saw you walking to the diner."

"Yeah," I say, "but Anna's not there yet."

She says, "That's weird."

"It's been weird all morning."

"You okay?" she asks.

"I think someone was in my apartment."

Riley gasps. "While you were sleeping?"

"No. I wasn't there."

"Then what makes you think someone was there?"

I shake my head, and my throat closes, and now my warm face tingles. "A feeling . . . Just . . . I'm losing my mind." My eyebrows crumple.

Riley says, "We all go a little mad sometimes."

I say, "Yeah," but I'm not going mad because I'm premenstrual or because someone's gaslighting me. *Something* is happening. But I can't collapse into Riley's arms, because she'd say, "Ew," tighten into a ball, and kick me in the corner next to the owl-shaped cookie jars.

"You look like you had a better night than me," I say now. "A meeting or a lunch date?"

She gapes at me. "Huh?"

I point. Foundation now hides her freckles. "Cuz you're wearing makeup."

Riley blushes, and says, "Oh. Yeah."

"Looks good, girlfriend."

"Maybe we can do an e-store test run with this." Her blush deepens, and uncomfortable, she holds up the green car. "This is a rare 1973 Matchbox Rod Roller. Part of a three-model set, according to the daughter of the man who collected these things."

"How much is it worth?"

"Nothing. The other two aren't in the box."

"So maybe not start with worthless items. Find something . . . *one of a kind*. Something a person would kill to have. I know there has to be something like that in this store."

She sets the car on the other side of the tub. "How was your dinner date with D. D.?"

"Who is D. D.?"

"Dexter Denham—Anna told me that you two had a date."

I twirl a lock of hair around my finger. "Magical. Wonderful. Almost perfect." Talking about Dexter loosens the knot in my stomach.

"*Almost* perfect?"

I give a coy smile. "He can always do better. What did *you* do last night?"

She motions toward the toy cars. "You're looking at it."

"C'mon. Pretty thing like you, no special someone in your life?"

"I'm in the early stages of something new right now."

"And?"

She blows into a car. "Rather not discuss it, don't wanna jinx it. I'll tell you when I'm ready." She blushes as she smiles at me.

The office is how I left it, with six artifacts that need cataloging on the project table. No—three don't have notes, and that doesn't include the hair-clip notes Detective Winchester took. The three without notes are the pen, the earring, and . . .

Huh.

D. D. That's what Riley just called Dexter.

Because those are *his initials, duh.*

Still . . .

Up in the store, the doorbell tinkles and I hear the murmurs of a visitor.

I sit there for a moment more—*D. D.*—then tell myself to stop being silly. I hesitate before moving on and clicking into the content-management system to create a new record for a pipe that came from a woman in Sky Valley, California.

"Where the heck is Sky Valley?" I roll over in the chair and peer at the map above Nadia's desk. A blue pushpin sticks in Sky Valley, which sits next to Joshua Tree National Park in the Mojave Desert. A stone's throw from Coachella Valley.

"Hey, Mickie?" Riley stands in the doorway.

I twist around in the chair. "Glad you're here—I have a question. Did you put—"

"When was the last time you talked to Anna?" Riley asks.

"Not since yesterday. Why?" I roll back to the table and point to a key chain that's been there only since. . . I don't know when.

Riley's eyes glaze as she stares past me. "The diner still isn't open. Mr. Kim just stopped by and asked if . . . Well . . . Anna's not at the diner. She's not answering her phone. No one knows where she is."

29.

Without the aromas of frying bacon and percolating coffee, without the familiar melodies of "Chain Gang" and "My Guy" drifting from Anna's jukebox, the Santa Barbara Plaza is a living exhibit of neglect. Like a sick, ragged woman wearing months-old makeup, this parcel of land needs the energy that only comfort food and a strong cup of coffee can provide.

But Anna isn't here.

Those bulldozers—Peter Weller's steel beasts—*are* here.

Anna's Place is closed, and a small group of us, including Kangol Man, Cigarillo Guy, and Third Ex-Wife of That Old Boxer What's-His-Name, circle the breezeway like zombies.

Pepper waggles her platinum head. "I'll call again. Maybe she's sick." She dials, then puts the phone on speaker.

The line rings . . . rings . . . clicks. Anna's recorded voice tells us to leave a message.

Pepper says, "Hey, Auntie. It's me, again. Where you at? Call me cuz we all worried about you. You ain't never missed a day. Folks hungry over here. Okay. Love you."

A sick silence settles over the breezeway.

"She probably had to make a stop," Pepper says with forced cheer. "She told me before she left last night that she had to buy stuff to make chili."

"Oh yeah," the boxer's ex-wife says, "she *did* say that."

I can't tell whether Helene is bullshitting or drunk. Maybe she's both.

"You'll let us know when she calls back?" I ask Pepper.

The stylist nods. "Yeah. I ain't stressed."

But I see worry in her eyes. And I see fear, too. Both shine like the sun.

Riley hobbles behind me as we return to Beautiful Things. The Matchbox cars now sit on the back counter, and Riley's laptop screen saver swirls with multicolored butterflies. She settles on the stool and says, "I hope she's okay."

My heart feels raspy in my chest. "I hope we're just being extra sensitive."

"I can't help but think the worst."

"Peter Weller?" I ask.

"Yeah."

What would Weller do to claim this land? Would he follow shopkeepers around the city? Intimidate them until they finally surrendered? And if they didn't surrender, would he go nuclear and have them murdered?

Nadia—she resisted and now she's dead.

Link, the owner of the lounge, who also resisted, has a metal plate in his head after supposedly being jumped by Weller's men.

Anna's resisting, and now she's . . .

Alive. She's at the grocery store, bickering with the butcher about his fatty ground beef and scrawny sirloin.

I plop into the chair. My soul moans, exhausted already at eleven in the morning. After taking several cleansing breaths, I type "PETER WELLER" into a search engine.

He has his own Wikipedia page. American businessman . . . philanthropist . . . CEO and founder of the Weller Group, an American real-estate company . . . former real-estate attorney in his father's firm . . . Board of Trustees at

Stanford University ... 55 years old ... spouse is Vivienne, a former model ... children are Peter and Lily ... wanted to bypass environmental laws to build a mall ... wanted to cement over the wetlands to build condos ...

Just as I thought: rich asshole. Why would Uncle Bryan defend Peter Weller the other night? Because what Weller's doing right now, tearing down the plaza and forcing people out? A classic David-versus-Goliath story. In today's world, Goliaths like Peter Weller are winning, and the Davids like Nadia and Anna are dying.

"Stop," I say. "Anna is okay."

That feels like a lie.

Dexter should know.

Know *what*, though? Dexter's been through enough with his mother's death. We're not even certain that Anna is hurt.

Instead of texting Dexter, I search for Esther Little's phone number.

There are about 128 million hits on the name on Google and in our People Finder. None of the results have phone numbers close to the one Riley gave me.

There's an Esther Little in Maine.

Esther Little in Beverly Hills is forty-four years old.

Esther Little who lived a few miles from Beautiful Things died in 1982.

There's one more Esther Little, and she lives in Leisure World, a retirement village down in Orange County.

"Hello?" Her voice is as brittle as ancient clay.

"Hi, Ms. Little," I say. "I'm calling about Nadia Denham."

"I'm not done with *what?*" she says, sounding whittled down, moments away from breaking free of her mortal chains to be with the Lord.

Slower and louder, I say, "I'm calling about Nadia Denham."

"What's that?"

"Do you know—"

"Hello?" A younger man has taken the phone.

I introduce myself and tell him that Nadia has passed and that—

"My mother doesn't know Nadia Denham. Mom doesn't know *me* anymore, and I haven't let her out of my sight for two years now."

"So she doesn't drive—"

The man laughs before I can finish the sentence.

Which means *this* Esther Little isn't the redhead I saw in the parking lot two weeks ago.

"Sorry to bother you and your mom, sir," I say before hanging up. I sink in the chair and rub my temples.

This day . . .

"No word yet on Anna?" Riley hovers in the office doorway.

I shake my head. "I'm sure Pepper will hear from her by the end of the day." As she turns to head back to the front of the store, I blurt, "I just got off the phone with Esther Little."

She scratches her cheek. "She's out of the hospital?"

"Yep. Just a little scare. She's gonna stop by today."

"Ah." A flush creeps up her neck. She's wearing God's red turtleneck.

"She wants to include something in the memory bank."

She says, "Mm."

Neither of us speaks, and several seconds pass before she says, "I wasn't being all the way truthful about Esther."

"Yeah, I know that now. Care to explain what's going on?"

She hides her face in her hands. When she looks up at me, her cheeks are wet, and her tear-filled eyes are starting to swell. "Since Nadia died, I just feel . . . *lost*. I don't know how to . . . *be* anymore. My mind gets all tangled, and I find myself . . . I don't know."

She swipes at her cheeks. "I'm here crying in front of a stranger. And no one's around to take some of this . . . *pressure* off my shoulders and—"

I pull her into a hug.

She goes rigid at first, but then her body relaxes.

I pat her back, then reach into my bag for a pack of tissues.

Riley whispers apologies as she blows her nose and dries her face. "I'm sorry," she says. "I don't know *where* Esther is or even if that's her last name. Maybe it's Lyden or Linton . . . I wanna have all the answers so that Dexter doesn't decide to fire me and sell this place."

I understand that. I'm sorry she's in this position. Once Riley shuffles out of the office, I consider Nadia's memories at my hands, things that she valued, things she hoped Dexter would also see as valuable. But there's a possibility that he, too, sees that music box as junk.

Whatever my mother has in her treasure box is valuable to her. Yet here I am, trying to break into it. If I ever find the key, I may find a felt mouse or a gold hair clip or a music box, and I'll wonder, *What's the big deal?*

My cell phone rings. I don't recognize the number, but this could be Anna.

A man introduces himself.

I hear him, but say, *"Who?"*

"Peter Weller." He sounds like the ocean and Mount Everest. He sounds like a blue whale and Son Doong Cave. He sounds like he owns this phone, like he owns *me*. Doesn't matter how Peter Weller got my number. He owns that, too, because he is Goliath.

"How may I help you, Mr. Weller?"

"I was just curious. Who you were, why you were in that shop. So I asked around and I found out. Very interesting, what you do."

"I think so, too, yes." My hands shake. I grip the phone tighter.

"Two things," he says. "Number one: I'm interested in learning more about this memory-bank device. I may reach out to Mr. Fenton about investment opportunities. Maybe we can make it a more *communal* activity, an attraction at one of my commercial properties."

Awful idea. "Great idea," I say.

"Second: You ever go to Vista?"

"The restaurant?"

"Yes."

Smoky cocktails. Grilled lobster. Fresh . . . everything. "I have. It's one of my favorite places."

"Mine too."

Please don't ask me out, please don't ask me out . . .

"The executive chef is a good friend of mine, and he wants to open Vista II right here in the city." Weller is probably pacing right now in his big corner office, his Testoni-clad feet lost in carpet made with the wool of baby vicuña.

"Another Vista would be awesome," I say now. "Malibu can be hard to reach."

"Exactly! I want to build Vista II for him, and I know the perfect location."

He doesn't say it, but his intention hangs there. Santa Barbara Plaza.

Airy! Hanging plants! Beachy-cool! I already picture Sasha, Imani, and me drinking crisp morning cocktails and sharing plates of everything. But I can also picture a transformed Anna's Place. Renamed A.P. Sleek. Modestly lush. White tiles. Colored walls that pop . . .

Peter Weller hears me thinking. "Consider the visibility. Think about the increased value of the homes in the area. Folks are always saying that the Crenshaw District is a food desert. I'll change that with Vista II. Salads galore. Best mixologists in the city. Possibilities are endless."

"But?" I force myself to stand.

"You know the 'but.'"

"Why are you calling *me*?"

He clicks his tongue. "In the short time you've been there, you've become an influencer. Convince Anna to take the deal. Because guess what? Dexter Denham will, and she'll be left out in the cold. No diner, no money, no future."

I glance out the window. The yellow-haired man is leaning against Mr. Kim's key shop.

My stomach drops as acid burns up my throat. "So convince Anna or . . . ?"

"Or nothing. Me getting my way is just a matter of time, Miss Lambert."

261

Artifact 9: Handblown, pearlescent pink pocket pipe. Acquired on October 3, 1980.

Location of Acquisition: Located 1,060 feet above sea level, Sky Valley, California, sits outside Joshua Tree National Park. While there's not much to say about this small town, much can be said about the park next door. Named after the twisted trees that populate more than twelve hundred square miles, the park boasts rocks that are 1.7 billion years old. With 191 miles of hiking trails, the park is popular for its rock climbing and dark-sky stargazing.

Last Owner: Brenda "BB" Barton.

Memory: Some folks just pass through Death Valley. Others pitch tents or park RVs. BB was an "other." She was a life-loving, loud-laughing barrel of a woman who threw the wildest parties out there in the desert.

You had been traveling from Phoenix, caught the flu, and came close to passing out behind the wheel of the station wagon. You spotted a small settlement off Highway 10. RVs and shotgun houses that shouldn't have been standing welcomed you. Wind chimes and the aromas of sage and marijuana eased your mind.

BB, wearing cutoff denim shorts and a white Carter-Mondale '76 T-shirt, tromped barefoot over to the station wagon. "You sick, babe?" Her voice was as coarse as the desert.

"I just need to rest." And then you passed out.

Over the next six days, BB nourished you back to health with soup, rice, and eggs. And from your place on the fever-drenched couch, you watched her steal antiques from the back of the station wagon as well as money out of your wallet.

On day seven, BB almost died after overdosing on heroin. You found the woman on the kitchen floor of that filthy RV, bent burned spoon in hand. You saved her life.

Though BB never returned the stolen antiques or the $1,000 she'd swiped, she begged you to take her favorite pocket pipe. She swore that she'd never smoke again.

You helped BB keep that promise.

30.

Maybe writing corporate communications wasn't so horrible after all.

After Peter Weller's phone call, I sit and stare at the project table.

What the hell am I supposed to do now?

My mind scrolls through its library of movie scenes that may help navigate this moment, but I keep replaying Ripley wearing a suit of pneumatic armor, battling the Mother Alien. I'm Ripley, which is awesome, but I can't shoot a grappling hook through Peter Weller's head.

Right?

I find myself closing my eyes and tilting my head. The bell over the front door rings. A police helicopter thunders above the store. A siren cries from the firehouse a few blocks away. None of that first-responder power is for Anna, though. We don't know if she's actually missing. What we do know is this: No Sam Cooke. No raucous laughter. No clink of knives, glasses, or ketchup bottles.

It is almost four o'clock, and my shoulders and stomach burn from holding my breath all this time, from waiting to hear *anything* about my friend. Raindrops fleck the concrete sidewalks of the breezeway, and cold seeps into the office.

Pepper is looking for the phone number belonging to Anna's daughter.

I haven't heard from Dexter since this morning. After our night together, I expected a call, a text, flowers, some acknowledgment of *something*.

His mom is dead dude

Imani is right.

He's an emotional wreck

OK I get it

But I'm worried about many things, like . . . the old text messages from the Nebraska number. The new text message from the Los Angeles number. The notes slipped beneath my apartment door. That jug of vanilla latte. And . . .

DD.

Dashing Devil.

Dexter Denham.

Also, my throat is raspy, and I'm crampy, and my hair feels like straw, and I'm working on the narrative for this Zippo lighter, but I can't focus. I wrote a decent first draft, so I tried moving on to the next item. But I can't find those items. According to the notes Nadia prepared, I'm supposed to be cataloging a pair of crocheted baby shoes and a matching hat. She acquired the set, originally owned by Sharleen Bosler, in Palm Springs in February 1985.

But there are no hats or shoes on the project table. I thought that I'd counted . . .

"Hey, Riley?" I shout.

"One minute," she shouts back.

I search beneath the project table—nothing but boxes of bracelets, mugs, pot holders, a View-Master, Bing Crosby cassette tapes, and an embroidery loop filled with commemorative Olympic pins. I'm pushing down panic. I can't find this set, and I don't want to be blamed for losing it. Maybe Detective Winchester took the items like he took the vase of roses.

"What's up?" Riley's skin shines—she looks better than she did this morning. She's smiling at me as she leans against the door. Smiling. *At me.*

"Have you seen a baby hat and shoes?" I read Nadia's note. "They're not here."

Riley tugs at her ear. "Maybe Nadia forgot to put them out."

"Winchester hasn't been by recently, helping himself to Nadia's things?"

"Nope."

"Could you help me look?"

"Later. A guy is out here—he's buying that coin collection." She gives me a thumbs-up.

"Would you mind if I—"

She's gone before I complete my request.

"Okay. Well . . ." Hands on my hips, I survey the office. "Where would Nadia keep a bunch of baby clothes?"

Near the box of wooden ducks? Inside the box of battered Barbies?

My stomach growls. I'm back to bad habits again. I haven't eaten and want a burger from Anna's.

I reread the sheet of notepaper.

Sharleen . . . grocery store . . . abuse . . . aspiring entrepreneur . . . good at crochet . . . Nadia wanted to support her . . .

This story snags my heart—maybe because I'm cold, tired, and hungry, or maybe because Sharleen had only these things left and she gave them away.

How could Nadia stand to meet so many dejected women?

Did she ever meet a woman who was doing "just great" in her life?

I need to find those baby shoes and that hat. I dig through the box of children's books and find an illustrated edition of *Charlotte's Web*. I paw through a crate of ceramic spoon holders and find one shaped like a bat from Carlsbad Caverns. I search the nook beneath Nadia's desk.

A box.

I peek inside.

The baby shoes and hat! Pink flowers, slightly yellowed, hand crocheted. Sharleen's—

Something else in the box glints and catches my eye.

I push aside cassette tapes, ashtrays, candleholders . . . I pull the handle of a knife with a black blade as long as my forearm. Hard, brown stuff is stuck to the blade.

Is this . . .

Blood?

31.

Maybe it's an old hunting knife and this blood belonged to an eight-point buck. Maybe this "blood" is actually corn syrup mixed with red food coloring, and the knife was a prop in a high school play. Yeah.

The brick in my belly means that I disagree. But why would I assume the worst? Especially since 99 percent of the junk around me came from flea markets and backyards? Nadia plucked boxes, crates, and bags without a discriminating eye. Out by one of the six jukeboxes, there are . . . *fucking* . . . red cardinal toilet tattoos and a set of clothes for concrete geese next to a stuffed life-size beaver.

The cry of seagulls circling above the parking lot interrupts my thoughts. In the store, the customer's laugh jangles the quiet like spoons crashing against a hardwood floor. My phone vibrates from my pocket: a text message from Christopher.

Just got off the phone with a potential investor!

Peter freaking Weller!!

Christopher's excitement pulses over the radio waves.

He says he's talked to you!

Said you're my best ambassador

I told him U were special

His words squeeze me. Pressure, so much pressure. My hands shake as I type.

I am special

Why would Nadia have this knife?
Why *wouldn't* Nadia have this knife?
I mean, c'mon—my mother stashes a hunting knife beneath her mattress.

Can u imagine if Weller invests??

I will give you the world.

And this knife, it doesn't matter anyway. This box came from Connecticut. It says so in thick black marker. Oh! Crushed rats—that's where that blood could have come from, if it is, indeed, real blood. I've seen that before with another client's box of stuff.
The cry of seagulls fades behind the growl of heavy machinery. A truck beeps . . . beeps . . . as it backs up. Peter Weller is a cruel man.
My stomach rumbles.

U there?

Where did u go??

And I remember again: We can't find Anna. And Esther, Nadia's best friend—she still doesn't know that Nadia is dead. I don't know what to do about that. Or if I even *need* to do anything about it. Esther Little-Linton-Lyden is not my responsibility. I've been here only a few weeks, and I don't know *any* of these people.

My numb legs sting, and so I complete six deep knee bends and walk over to the door. I take a few seconds to listen to Riley talking about the coin collection to some guy with a skunk-colored mullet. Then I close the door and return to the box with the knife.

I'm working hard for us.

Oh, Christopher. Who is this "us" you speak of? You and me "us" or all of us at the Memory Bank "us"?

And who owned this knife before Nadia found it?

A hunter or . . . It was Halloween, and he was Jason Voorhees from *Friday the 13th*.

No, I don't know this world; nor do I know these people and what is normal and what is just effing strange. I'm gonna find out, though. Starting with the ringleader.

Who was *Nadia Denham?*

The search engine results tell me what I already know: proprietor of Beautiful Things: A Curiosities Shoppe. She was awarded a business commendation from the Chamber of Commerce in 1996 and received recognition from a women's council in 2007. Her only listed address matches the store's address. No listings of a birthplace, credit history, bankruptcies, or that marriage she left behind. No driver's license, no phone number. No criminal record. Nothing.

But then, my grandmother used to fix me hot chocolate with whipped cream and sprinkles, and she made my buttered toast beneath the broiler, and she loved me, and she was very real, but at almost eighty years old, she isn't googleable.

Aunt Angela—she died a violent death and wore designer athletic gear and shared a bedroom with my mother. She was *very* real, and as

I type her name into this search engine, none of the results match the woman now buried in Inglewood Cemetery. She, too, isn't googleable.

Why should I expect Nadia to be?

Michaela I love you

I stare at this last text message. My breathing—I've stopped breathing. Christopher has said these words to me before, and yet . . . I drop the phone back on the table, then peck at the laptop's keyboard to type a name.

The stuffed owl on the bookshelf is watching me. The harlequin puppet hanging from its strings from the doorknob—he's watching me, too, as I type this name. I'm nervous beneath the stares of dead and inanimate things.

There are countless results for Sarah Park.

I add "Beautiful Things" beside her name.

Last known address: 111 Marlton Road.

I blink, then say, "Huh." Because 111 Marlton Road is . . . *here.*

Shouldn't her last address be listed somewhere in Seoul?

There's a second hyperlink. I know this website. The Charley Project listed Katrinka McLaren as missing, but then her remains had been discovered somewhere in a national forest in New Mexico.

Like Katrinka, Sarah Park has her own page.

The words there chill my heart.

Missing since 1980.

32.

Sarah Park is missing.

A Sarah Park is missing.

I've never seen a picture of Beautiful Things former owner Sarah Park, so I don't know if this woman in the picture, squinting into the sun, is her. Well . . . no, it's not. *This* Sarah Park was last seen in Reno, Nevada, driving a gray Datsun. And *this* Sarah Park grew up in Garden Grove, California, not Seoul, South Korea.

"Different Sarah Park." The tightness in my chest loosens, and I exhale the longest breath I've ever released.

For a brief moment, I wonder: Was Nadia like the white-woman equivalent of Harriet Tubman? Instead of helping slaves escape, had Nadia tried to help women in danger escape? Did some of these desperate women find hard-fought freedom, while some—like the unlucky slaves— were caught and killed? If so, that would make a helluva memory-bank narrative. I'd just need to somehow find the survivors . . .

What if . . . ?

What if Nadia interfered with the Dashing Devil's attempts to murder one of the women she eventually saved, and he vowed revenge? What if he played the long game and waited until Nadia was old and suffering from a memory disorder? What if *he* killed Nadia? He's in the Southland right now and left his mark on Allison Cagle.

The knife is back in its box. The crocheted baby clothes have taken their rightful place on the project table. I straighten the notebook pages, lingering on those items that still need stories. *Storms don't last forever!*

I consider that map filled with pushpins on the edges of the country. Those pins never punch through the heartland. Why? There must be plenty of crappy flea markets in Kansas. I don't know firsthand since I've never visited Kansas, but if crappy flea markets exist in Tinseltown . . .

Done for the day, I gather my things and leave the office. The store is empty, but something is creaking. I stand still and listen to Beautiful Things make noise. I think about following that creaking sound to its source, but then I see Riley standing in the breezeway with Pepper. Both look distressed.

Anna!

I rush out of the store and ask, "What's wrong? You find Anna?"

"Still no word," Riley says.

"You talk to her daughter yet?"

Pepper shakes her head. "No one's answering."

"Maybe we should drive to her house," I suggest. "Doesn't she live over in Inglewood?"

Backing away, Pepper says, "Yeah, but I gotta rinse out color from my client's hair."

Over in the parking lot, the bulldozers sleep like watchdogs. There's a chill in the air, but the cold hasn't stopped the RV community from grilling, from riding their bikes in small circles, from smoking cigarettes and passing joints.

Is the blond man, Weller's spy, watching us at this very moment?

Riley paces and gnaws her thumbnail. "I don't know *what* to think."

I tap her shoulder. "Think positive thoughts."

"Somebody needs to call Dexter. Anna's like a mom to him. And he knows where she lives." Riley stops her pacing and stands before me.

"Didn't you used to stay with her, too?"

"She's moved since then. Anyway, you should call him."

"What? Why?"

"Aren't you two a thing?"

So loud in my head now. Like millions of birds are chirping and thousands of cats are screeching . . . I rub my face and sag even though I'm standing. My throat hurts worse than ever, and my cramps have amped from a three to a six.

I pull my phone from my pocket, and text: You around?

No ellipses on Dexter's side of the conversation.

I do the old-fashioned thing and tap the telephone icon next to his name.

Still no answer.

"Well?" Riley asks.

"Nothing." As we showered this morning, Dexter told me that he had afternoon meetings at CNN and Condé Nast. My head falls back, and as I watch wild parrots circle above the parking lot, I debate whether to tell Riley about my call from Peter Weller.

But she's made the decision for me. She's shuffled inside the store without a goodbye.

The drive home should take only eight minutes, but the lights on La Brea Avenue are on the fritz, and cars are everywhere and going nowhere fast. This type of traffic leaves plenty of time for thinking. About Anna— where is she? About Dexter—where is he? About Peter Weller—why are rich men such assholes? About that bloody knife and Sarah Park.

Aren't you two a thing?

For a moment, I'm irritated by the old woman's gossiping. But then I say, "No. No bad Anna thoughts." I just want my friend safe behind the counter slinging burgers and fries.

Our house sits somber among the sycamores. No Christmas lights razzmatazz along the eaves. More fence slats have been assembled. The video feed shows no one strange lurking around our property. No one is home. Perfect time for snooping. I want to find that key to Mom's treasure box.

No little key in the kitchen's bunch-of-crap drawer. No key in the hallway closet.

I close my eyes and picture Mom, key in hand, wandering the house in search of a perfect place, a meaningful—

My eyes open, and I dart to the living room and to her at-home away place: the piano. I lift the bench and push aside sheet music and compilations and . . .

"Yes!" A thin silver key nests in the seat's crushed green velvet. I jam up the stairs and hurry down the hallway to my parents' room. The door is unlocked. The bed is made. Dad's red Sixers jersey is draped on the bed's footboard. I sit on Mom's side of the bed and pull the nightstand drawer.

The box is still here. The gun is gone. The picture of Aunt Angie is still here.

If she'd lived, would she have taken me to Claire's to get my ears pierced instead of Mom? Would she have driven me to soccer practices on Thursdays and given me bawdy advice about boys? Would she have thrown raucous block parties and danced the Wobble in the middle of the street with a red cup filled with Courvoisier and soda?

I'd like to think so.

The bastard who stole her life—hope he's six feet under right now, rotting in a potter's grave beside other demonic men. *This is my prayer, amen.* I push out a breath and return my gaze to the box on my lap.

This better be worth it. I better find something more than a Zippo lighter or a mini kaleidoscope. With a shaky hand, I stick the key into the lock and turn.

Click.

I feel like I've just defused a bomb. Giddy relief floods through my arms and hands.

I lift the lid. The box smells of pine needles, peppermint, and a woman's perfume.

Outside, tires crunch on asphalt.

I freeze.

The car keeps driving up the hill.

I gotta hurry.

The box is crammed with papers.

Mom and Dad's marriage certificate—wed on December 1, 1994. While in Temecula for Sasha's wedding, my parents took a luxury winery tour to celebrate their twenty-fifth anniversary. I snap a picture of this certificate—it will go great in Mom's memory bank. Since it's a public document, I can always claim that I ordered a copy from the Hall of Records.

You shouldn't be doing this.

There's another manila envelope in the box, and this one is overstuffed.

I ease out the thick sheath of papers and find my birth certificate. Born April 25, 1995—Mom had been pregnant with me when she and Dad married. That's never bothered me. But this certificate . . . This certificate looks different from the one I've used for my passport, for school forms, for work. This paper is thin and slick like old fax paper. I scrutinize the print, not because the ink is fading but because I don't understand what I'm . . .

I throw my eyes to look at something else—my apartment, also lost in the canopy of trees. No sinister figures crowd at the one slat of bright-white fencing that remains.

My vision resets and I turn back to the certificate . . .

There it is. In black-and-white print.

FINAL DECREE OF ADOPTION . . . On the 21st day of December 1998 . . . The petitioners Coretta Craig Lambert and Orson Lambert are husband and wife, and are qualified to adopt the child in interest . . . name to appear on the child's birth certificate as MICHAELA ELYSE LAMBERT . . . It is hereby ordered, adjudged, and decreed as follows . . . So ordered . . .

Mom and Dad . . . aren't . . . ?

The shakes come first, and then tears sting . . . My breath . . . I can't breathe . . . I can't . . . breathe . . . Feels like I'm sliding . . . sliding face-first . . . sliding fast . . .

The room fades all around me, and I close my eyes and try to think of calming things like swaying palm trees and waves and rolling soft water and cashmere blankets and slowly . . . slowly . . . My lungs . . . I can breathe . . . I'm breathing after the sucker punch to my stomach. I smell my own sweat, and now I taste blood. I've bitten my tongue.

Satisfied?

Mom and Dad . . . They aren't . . . ? Then who?

It's too warm in here. It's too bleak outside. This smell . . . mint and ink and . . .

Slower now, I shuffle through the papers to read that slick-paper birth certificate again.

NAME OF FATHER: Michael Anthony.

Who's Michael?

NAME OF MOTHER . . .

Angela Craig.

REPLY HAZY,
TRY AGAIN

33.

Colors around me have washed out. The gray walls, the red Sixers jersey, the manila envelope . . . All of it blends, becomes . . . oatmeal. The truth about my origin has made me color-blind. And paralyzed. I can't move. Can't feel my face. I . . . want to cry but can't. Want to yell—at something . . . My heart isn't working. Eyes not seeing. Lungs . . . what lungs? I'm . . .

Shattered.

I peek at those words . . .

Final decree . . . adopt . . . so ordered . . .

Trembling. Finally. The air inside me burns and I cough it up and it comes out as a sob and another sob and now I'm weeping freely and I ball up on the bed and I cry and think of nothing and everything and Christmases and sweet sixteen and New Mexico and first-day-ofs and soccer and Fatburgers and Minecraft and all my life not being my life. The lies, the secrets, how could they, why would they, how is this possible, it isn't possible, but it is possible because the State of California wouldn't *lie*.

My weeping stops.

The house finds silence again.

I rest on that bed, those official documents now damp and crumpled beneath me. Wobbly, I sit up and wipe snot with my shirt. I had no idea. None. Why would I believe that I'm not . . . ? That Angela Craig—Mom's *sister*? That *she's* my biological mother? That means that Mom *wasn't* pregnant when she and Dad married, that I was three years old once the state approved my adoption.

Michaela Elyse *Anthony*?

Who is Michael Anthony? Where is my biological father? Why isn't he here with me? Why didn't he keep me and raise me? Why hasn't he reached out to—

Wait. Does he know about me? That I exist? That Aunt Angie, Angie . . . my mother . . . was pregnant? Or was I a secret? *Another* secret, because secrets tend to be a thing for this family. And that makes me throw my head back, and I scream, and I kick the nightstand.

New anger swirls through my veins. I'm twenty-four years old. When were they going to tell me that I was adopted? What else have they lied to me about? Now it makes sense why this box was locked, why their bedroom door was almost always locked, why—

My phone chimes from somewhere beneath the papers and the comforter.

Dexter. What's up?

I use my phone to take pictures of the slick-paper birth certificate and the adoption decree. I have no clue what to do beyond confronting Mom and Dad, Cori and Sonny, Mom and Dad, I don't know. My hands still shake as I shove everything back into the manila envelope, as I shove the manila envelope back into that box. No felt mouse. No music box. Just a whole new identity and entirely new parents.

Satisfied?

My bones feel broken as I try to lift that box from its place on the mattress, so I leave it there on the pillows. Mom will notice it first and she will know. Weak kneed, I stumble to their bathroom. I wash my face; pop three ibuprofen for my headache, cramps, and sore throat; and then trudge down the hallway, down the stairs, and back out to my car.

At least there's no more rain, just flat, heavy, lavender-black clouds and streetlights to show me the way. At least there's gas in my car, although the needle has dropped precariously close to *E*. It's the grace of God that protects other cars from mine. My guardian angel guides me through the streets of Los Angeles and to Dinah's somewhere on Sepulveda Boulevard.

Dexter waits for me in the diner's lobby, and his smile slips like rainwater off his face. He pulls me into his arms, and whispers, "You okay?"

I was okay but now I'm not okay and I can only shake my head.

The hostess senses that we need the farthest booth possible and leads us past the families and their tables filled with sandwiches and waffles. I sit facing the rock wall so that I have some privacy. Dexter sits across from me. He takes my hands and kisses them. "Tell me."

"I'm . . . adopted." It's the first time I've said these words, and they sting my lips and I clutch my heart because it hurts, and tears stream in familiar paths down my cheeks. My face will soon be the Grand Canyon.

The waitress, a solid-looking woman with a mass of black, curly hair, sets glasses of water and a stack of napkins on the table. "Let me know when you're ready."

I inhale until my lungs can't handle any more air. Thick tongued, I tell Dexter everything. He catches my last teardrop with his knuckle. I take a napkin from the pile and dry my face. "What should I do?"

He slumps in the booth. "No idea."

"Should I find him? My biological father? Should I ask him why he left me? Why he never reached out to me?"

He opens his mouth to speak, then closes it. His head falls back, and he stares at the diner's craggy ceiling.

I blow my nose, then grab another napkin. "You're older, wiser. I'm . . . lost, so . . . lost."

He sits up, then gives me a lazy grin. "I'm five years older than you *and* I'm a man, which means I have the wisdom of a six-year-old." He grabs his water glass and gulps until it's empty. "Maybe he didn't have the tools to raise you alone. Maybe he wanted you to have the best shot at life, some stability, y'know? And maybe he *did* reach out—you just didn't know he was your father."

I nod, but then I shake my head. "I don't know what to do."

"Forgive your parents," Dexter advises. "Whatever the reason they kept this from you, forgive them. Angela died, and they took you in and made you theirs. You were and *are* loved. Many kids get dumped into the system and don't make it out. You, though. You're a princess. You're your mama's best friend and you're a daddy's girl and you ain't gotta ask him for nothin' cuz he got you. I'm not mad at that—that's, like, *goals*, you know what I'm saying? That's Black love.

"I've only known you for, what, two weeks, but you . . . *They* made you one of the most interesting women I've ever met. And you love them, right?"

"Yes. I love them. They rescued me. They chose me." They hadn't even been married for a year before they became my parents. But my love for them is pushed aside by my dragon-anger. It swirls near my heart, bright and dazzling.

We order: a pastrami Reuben for him, pancakes for me. I tear at napkins and watch as the flakes pile around my wrists. My thoughts have calmed, but they're still there, like electric-blue dragonflies buzzing around my head.

Dexter tugs at my pinkie finger. "Is this why you texted me?"

"No. Just . . . Anna—no one's heard from her. The diner was closed today."

"That's strange."

"I wanted to get her address from you and drive by, but then my own life kinda . . ."

He texts me the address. "I'll stop by. You have more important things to do tonight."

I say, "Yeah," barely tasting the heavily syruped wedge of pancakes in my mouth, barely swallowing the mush in my mouth because my throat is tight. "Did Nadia keep any secrets?"

"Hell yes. Take a wild guess."

"Your father?"

"Yep."

"Did she even tell you who he was? Why she left?"

"Nope. She'd get angry anytime I brought him up, so I stopped bringing him up." He pauses, then says, "Your biological father, do you really want to find him?"

"I wanna say no because what if he's a monster and couldn't give a damn about me and resents me because I somehow messed up his plans?

"I wanna say yes because that's me, naturally curious, and I'd wanna at least know who he is. My father—Orson Lambert—he's my dad. He's . . ." I try to smile because I can't talk, because if I talk, I'll start crying.

Dexter reaches out to squeeze my hand. Together, we sink into silence and focus on eating.

Once the buzzy threat of weeping bumbles away again, I ask, "You hear from Detective Winchester lately?"

Dexter nods. "They're still investigating whether it was suicide or not." His face clouds, and he tosses the french fry he was eating back into the pile. "I'll never forgive Riley for having *my* mother cremated. She's un-freaking-believable. Winchester and the coroner would've seen the truth by now if she hadn't . . ." He hunches over his plate, picks at the meat.

"She sees things different," I say. "She thinks that she—"

"Was closer to Mom than I was? That Mom depended on her more than me?"

I nod.

He bats his hand. "She ain't blood, so her opinion—" His eyes widen, and he reaches for my hand. "My situation with Riley is totally different from yours. Sorry."

I nod but I cannot smile, not yet.

He shrugs. "Closure. That's what she's keeping me from having." But something clouds his eyes and that word.

I want to say, "Is that all?" because "closure" doesn't seem to be all that he wants to have. "It's only been two weeks," I say instead. "I'm sure the cremation complicated things, but with Nadia's death being suspicious, they probably kept what they needed to analyze before releasing her to the mortuary."

Around us, people laugh, talk with full mouths. Children hop on the red Naugahyde with crayons in their hands and mouths. On the monitor above the counter, numbers for Keno and the lottery blink from screen to screen.

I say, "Did Winchester talk to Esther yet?"

Gloom spreads across Dexter's face as he nibbles pastrami.

Anxiety beetles across my scalp. "I can probably work with a police sketch artist—"

"You remind me of a puppy." He says this amused and irritated.

Popped on my nose with a newspaper, I sit back. "I just wanna help."

"He will come to you if he wants your help." He tries to smile to soften his rebuke.

I try to smile, always a good sport, but his disapproval is sticky like the syrup on my fingers.

He looks at his phone. "I need to head out. Go check on Anna, and then I have another appointment with Condé Nast."

"This late?" I tap my phone. It's almost seven thirty. Mom and Dad have called and texted me over a million times.

"Would *you* say no to Condé Nast?"

I wouldn't say no. I don't say no when he pays our bill. I won't say no if he invites me back to his apartment, and I hold my breath as we leave the diner hand in hand.

Outside, the cold air feels like sweet water. A bank of clouds has drifted apart so that I can glimpse a clear black sky. A moment of grace.

"Feeling better?" Dexter asks.

I nod.

"Those threatening text messages stop?"

"Yes."

He hugs me tight. I can feel his heartbeat against my cheek. He's alive. So am I. There are worse things. I kiss him long and hard, as though I'll never see him again.

Back in the sudden quiet of my car, I check the messages on my phone.

Mouse call me

Mick Honey call us

Dexter's Jeep rolls out of the parking lot. Instead of turning right, in the direction of Inglewood, where Anna lives, the Jeep turns left.

Isn't he going to Anna's?

But then, he didn't seem too alarmed after I told him that we hadn't heard from her.

Why not?

I speed out of the parking lot and turn left as the light turns yellow to red.

The Jeep is a light ahead of me—enough space to follow Dexter without his knowing.

We drive west on Jefferson Boulevard, getting closer and closer to the wetlands. But then he makes a right turn onto Lincoln. My phone glows with MOM CALLING and DAD CALLING and text messages between those calls.

We drive through the fog, through Marina del Rey, too close to the beach, too far from Anna's house. He finally pulls into a strip mall. I park at the curb beneath a fat magnolia tree. My pulse bangs against my skin. Why are we here?

Dexter doesn't enter the doughnut shop. He doesn't stop in for a mani-pedi. There's nothing he wants in the Indian restaurant. It's the State Farm insurance agency he seeks. A white man wearing a red polo shirt and dad jeans is happy to see him, and they shake hands.

Life insurance.

Closure.

And Nadia's death investigation is stalling the issuance of a death certificate.

He can't receive the benefits from her policies without a death certificate.

And that death certificate has to say that her manner of death was . . .

Homicide.

34.

Maybe Dexter called Anna and she answered and told him not to come over. Maybe Anna asked to meet him somewhere in Marina del Rey. Maybe he's a liar.

But why would he lie about something as silly as checking in on a friend?

I watch Dexter from my spot at the curb. Maybe this is a quick stop and he'll soon be on his way to Inglewood. But the man in the red polo shirt and dad jeans brings Dexter a cup of coffee, and Dexter sits back in the chair and sips his hot beverage like he has no place else to go.

Life insurance—that's what he cares about right now. Not being honest with me.

And who am I?

I'm just a girl who didn't know she wasn't a Lambert by birth. I'm just a girl who barged in on her aunt's marriage, making that aunt a mother when she'd barely become a wife. I don't know anything, and my heart hurts almost as much as my head.

I do know that I don't want to go home. Not yet. I'm not ready to have that conversation with Mom and Dad. Because they *are* my mom and dad, through state decree. Through love and depleted checking accounts, through splinters, splints, and fever-flu nights. No, I don't want to cry any more tonight. I don't want to feel the sting of truth any more tonight. But my body aches, and I want a shower and my bed.

So I creep onto the 405 freeway instead of taking the surface streets. That means the glare of red brake lights as far as my eye can see. That means surrendering all brainpower to avoid fender benders and side-swipes. That means I will never reach my destination.

The text messages from my parents have stopped filling my phone screen. I don't listen to music—any meaningful lyrics will disintegrate what's left of me. After merging onto the 10 East, after forty minutes of complete silence and squeezing the steering wheel, I exit at La Cienega Boulevard.

It is ten minutes after ten o'clock.

The house sparkles with Christmas lights. They turned them on before reaching the bedroom and seeing that box . . . I pull in front of the garage and see the lights burning in my apartment kitchen. My pulse kicks. Did I leave on that light? Does it matter?

My gaze drifts up to my parents' bedroom window. What are they doing? Do I care?

No.

Inside my apartment, I stand at the bottom of the staircase with my eyes on strange shadows twisting across my ceiling. My head buzzes and my bladder cramps. I arm the security system and listen to "Alarming. Alarm. Stay," until the final *beeps* and *boops*. The need to pee forces me up those steps, and I flip on every other light switch to chase away the gloom. I leave my phone on the coffee table and head to the bathroom and turn the shower handle. As steam fills the room, I peel off my clothes. I reek of diner smells, sadness, and musty underarms.

Christmas is just weeks away. Am I still part of a family that listens to soulful Christmas songs as we decorate our tree, special ornaments first? Has anything *really* changed?

Near tears, I whisper, "Memory Bank: tell me about Christmas," even though the device can't hear me, even though I can't see the pictures I uploaded months ago. But in my mind's eye, there are scrolling pictures of Mom, Dad, and me wearing Santa hats as we opened gifts. Pictures of ten-year-old Mickie sprinkling brown sugar over the yams and Dad slicing apples for his once-a-year apple pie. There are holograms of tiny presents wrapped in big boxes, and stockings heavy with summer sausage for Dad, new earbuds for Mom, gift cards for—

What was that?

I remain still beneath that cascade of hot water.

A moan or a cry or . . .

I twist off the shower handles.

The drip of water . . . The shower drain gurgling . . . There it is! A whine or a . . .

I hop out of the shower. Still wet, I pull on my clothes. With no weapon close, I ease off the toilet tank cover for protection. Then I tiptoe out of the bathroom and—

Thump!

Something up in the living room.

Every hair on my body stands straight, and I grip the heavy tank cover tighter.

The alarm didn't go off. No one could've come in . . . unless they were already here . . .

That whine, it's deep now.

Lights still burn bright throughout my apartment.

Good. Okay.

Closer . . . closer . . .

The living room looks empty . . . That sound again . . .

I drop to my knees.

My phone. It's fallen off the coffee table onto the carpet, and now it's vibrating. Mom and Dad have been sending frantic texts, and Dexter just called.

The phone. I'm freaking out and it's just my phone. I push my hair back and hide my face in my knees. I am a wreck. I hold my breath as

I swipe past the frantic text messages sent by Mom and Dad to read the others.

Please call when you have a chance—Detective Winchester.

Thinking about you—Christopher.

Thinking about U—Dexter.

After replacing the toilet tank, I pour red wine into my biggest glass and find an unopened bag of Ruffles in the cupboard.

Let the healing begin.

My apartment feels different now. Those unpacked boxes filled with my love life—that life was led by a woman who didn't have daddy issues, and while her daddy may be an accountant, her biological father is named . . .

Michael. I'm named after a mystery.

Standing at the kitchen sink, I eat a quarter of the bag of chips and drink all the wine in the glass. The buzz in my head dims as wine warms my belly. I'm filled now with liquid courage. That's why I grab my laptop from my bag, dive onto my couch, and type "ANGELA CRAIG" into Google's search engine.

No relevant results for a dead woman with that name.

MICHAELA ANTHONY.

None of these white women are me.

MICHAEL ANTHONY.

There are over a billion results on that name. I click on a few and surrender my quest. I'm sure Angie didn't date the bassist from . . . Chickenfoot and the Circle.

I click over to LexisNexis and search for the hub that stores legal cases. Somehow, I land at "Easy Search," and there's a box. *Look up US Cases. Citation number.* I don't have that information. *Or by parties.* I know only my family's name, but I don't think it would be Craig versus . . .

"Versus who?" I ask aloud because I don't know who shot her. Still, I try and aim my cursor at the box.

Nothing happens . . . More attempted clicks . . . Still nothing . . . Seconds pass and a black box pops onto my screen: "Page Unresponsive." A few more attempts, an equal number of "Page Unresponsive" black boxes. Easy Search ain't so easy, and it sucks.

I find nothing about my aunt in the Gale Biography and Genealogy Master Index. Nothing in the *Los Angeles* or *New York Times*. Smithsonian Library sure as hell has nothing on Angela Craig. To all my best depositories of information, she's just another anonymous and dead Black woman.

Fuck all of 'em.

Outside, car brakes squeak. Tree leaves rustle. Something scratches. Something creaks.

Though I feel wrung out, the wine leaves me free of anxiety. "Now's the time to come kidnap me," I announce to the room. Then I finish my second glass of wine in two gulps. I say, "Rrrruffles have rrridges," and jam four chips into my mouth to keep from crying.

Since Detective Winchester is the only man who hasn't lied to me, I call him.

He answers on the first ring. "Miss Lambert, what a pleasant surprise."

"Why? You called me."

"Of course I did. I'm hoping that you could help."

"Only if you help me. Nothing to do with what you're working on."

He doesn't speak.

I say, "Hello? This thing on?"

"You've been drinking."

"Not enough."

"So how can I help, Miss Lambert?"

I tell him I discovered that I was adopted, that my biological mother was dead, that I had no clue who my birth father was. "There are no records or articles on the internet. So maybe you can find something the police may have, and maybe you can share it with *me*."

"Huh."

"You don't sound surprised."

"Hard to surprise me in this line of work," he says. "Can't your uncle help?"

"Nah. Nope. Nuh-uh. I gotta theory."

"Okay."

"What if he's hunting me?"

"What if *who* is hunting you?"

"The man who killed my mother? Omigod. What if he's the Dashing Devil?"

The detective sighs, then says, "So what can you tell me about the store and its owners?"

"So . . . you don't think so?" I crunch a few more potato chips and think about that. And as I think, my eyes fill with tears. Because I don't know anything *at all* anymore.

Heavyhearted, I tell him that Dexter talked to a private investigator last night, that I saw bankruptcy papers in his apartment, that he and Nadia talked about life insurance, that he wants the medical examiner to find that Nadia was murdered because he needs the death certificate to collect on her policies.

The cop chuckles. "With a girlfriend like you—"

"I'm not his girlfriend, and will you find all the stuff for me? About my bio parents?" My voice is flat—the wine has kicked in 100 percent, and now I wanna sleep. "No one cares—no one wrote an article about her. Not one blip, not a mention, and that's fucked up cuz she existed, y'know?" And then I drunk-cry into the phone. After a few moments, I collect myself and dry my face with my shirt. I offer strangled apologies between nose-blowing and hiccups.

"I'll see what I can do," Detective Winchester says. "You okay?"

I shake my head, but he can't see that. Because what is okay?

"One last thing: a handwriting expert compared the note pages against the suicide note, and the writing matches. That's why I called you. I'll bring that note back sometime this week."

"Anna's missing," I blurt.

"Who?"

"The diner—Anna."

"How long has she been missing?"

I think and blink and think and blink some more. "Today."

"Less than twenty-four hours?"

I say, "Uhh . . ."

"Anything else, Miss Lambert? You should probably get some rest."

"I wanna see the note."

"Can't do that."

"I wanna see the note, pretty please?"

"Ask Dexter. He has a copy."

Detective Winchester has no answers for me.

What if it's the Dashing Devil in the Buick? What if he's come to finish the job? He's sent me text messages as warnings and slipped notes beneath my door, and now . . .

And now I'm coming undone . . . right?

Just like Nadia. Thinking about her, I wanna cry again, and I don't know why. It's not like I *knew* Nadia. *How* she died shouldn't matter to me. She ended her life because of the prospect of losing her mind. But not on that afternoon she called me as I sat in the movie theater. She wanted to keep adding to her memory bank.

That's why I'm crying.

Because Nadia's death matters. My aunt, my *mother*, her death matters.

And I don't think I'll ever be able to move forward until I fully understand both of their lives—and their endings.

Outside, car brakes squeal again, and an engine rattles and whines . . . It's still rattling, still whining . . . Silence. By now, that car's tires are either supposed to crunch up the hill or crunch going down. That crappy engine is supposed to huff up the hill or groan going down. I know the noises of my neighbors' cars. The growl of Brent's classic Mustang. The nervous whinny of Samara's old Lexus . . . This car's sound and now its silence . . .

Do Mom and Dad hear it?

My insides twist as I slip to my kitchen window. Without light, I can't see much. With my parents' house blocking my view of the street, I can't see anything at all.

I grab a knife from the block, then tromp down the stairs. I disarm the system, throw open the door, and ignore the chill of December. On rubbery legs, I creep through the driveway, ignoring the soberer voice yelling for me to take my drunk ass home.

Breathing deeply, I peek from behind Dad's Audi to see the rest of Mantova Drive.

I know that silver Corolla.

I know that brown Subaru.

I know . . .

Shit.

That car—I know that car, and it's not supposed to be here.

The park provided a perfect escape, and now, with the back fence gone? A front seat to the show. A bit windy and cold now as those clouds overhead march across the sky. But the perfect murkiness of this free space and the absurd brightness of the apartment across the way . . . Suffering through a few minutes of shivers is worth it. Because from here, it's easy to see:

Michaela's been drinking. Michaela *is* drinking. Michaela is *drunk*. She sways on her feet, traipsing around the living room while talking on the phone. She keeps pushing her messy, long hair off her face and pulling it away from her neck. She's probably forgotten to check the lock on the front door . . .

Goose pimples watching this.

There's something delicious about a sad and lonely drunk.

The sharp tang of trees, shrubs, and bushes makes the nose itch, and the urge to sneeze intensifies. Cigarette smoke rides along the breeze. Is someone nearby? Do homeless people sleep in this park?

Michaela peeks out the kitchen window.

Does she sense a stranger? Does she smell a wolf?

It's bedtime, but she hasn't brushed her teeth. She hasn't pinned up her hair. She hasn't washed her face. Zits, tangles, and plaque—is this how she looks when no one's around? Before the makeup, the designer shoes, and the hair?

Fuck this princess and her sadness. She has everything anyone would ever want in life. Life doesn't always work out. And? So?

This could end now.

But the parents . . . They're probably standing in their bedroom window, looking at her stumble around—

What was that?

Something moved in the darkness.

Or did it?

That . . . What was that?

Nothing's here except skunks, raccoon, possums, other night creatures.

Michaela's father shuffles out the kitchen door from the main house wearing sweatpants and a basketball jersey. He glances up at his daughter's apartment, then shakes his head. He carries a flashlight and shines it around the yard.

No. Not a good time. Eyes everywhere.

The father stomps down the driveway. Shines the light up that way, then down that way.

What is he looking for?

He turns right and disappears.

Shit.

Should've taken her before. Should've taken that chance. Could've worked. Could've come up with a good explanation. A surprise, a check-in, a delivery . . . Dry mouth just thinking of all the excuses that could've been made.

But what if no one had believed those excuses? May not have walked away with just a sprained ankle. May not have walked away at all. Dead just like that.

The father walks in the opposite direction, passing the driveway.

The shop. That's a good place.

One fewer pair of eyes there now.

Hide Michaela in the shop, bury her beneath all that clutter.

Not like it's never been done before.

Artifact 10: Silver case Zippo lighter. Vintage 1950s. Acquired on December 3, 1970.

Location of Acquisition: Burlington, Vermont. Nestled forty-five miles from the Canadian-US border, Burlington is the first city in the nation to source 100 percent of its residential energy from renewable sources. In 1978, Ben Cohen and Jerry Greenfield opened an ice cream shop here in a renovated gas station—this was the birth of Ben & Jerry's ice cream.

Last Owner: Steffanie "Steffie" Minsky.

Memory: Working on the janitorial staff at the University of Vermont, you met Steffie at a bus stop. It was the dead of winter, and the girl wore slinky pants and a rainbow ski jacket. You noticed the lighter because it kept busy lighting all those cigarettes Steffie chain-smoked.

"Where'd you find that beauty?" you asked the girl.

Steffie shrugged. She didn't care, she didn't know, or she didn't want to say.

You soon learned that Steffie had been living in the broken-down VW Beetle across the street from your apartment. You had suspicions that Steffie was a "working girl," and every month, she came across all types of men, including those who'd own such a rare item. You took the young woman blankets, pots of soup, loaves of bread. Right before a particularly bad storm, you invited her to share space in front of the radiator in your apartment.

Steffie always thought you had been judging her in those early days, but eventually she relaxed and enjoyed your time together. "I feel so safe around you," she would often say.

That's because you weren't trying to "date" her or steal from her. Steffie had already faced the trauma of assault and abandonment—her father had kicked her out of the house six months before. Then she'd dropped out of high school.

"I'm okay in the Bug," she said. "It ain't much smaller than my room at home."

But winters in Vermont are cruel, and you hated the thought of this poor girl living in a car. You invited the seventeen-year-old to stay, at least until spring.

Steffie, grateful, had nothing to offer as rent except for the lighter.

You never found out how a girl like her came to possess a classy Zippo lighter. In 2018, you had the Zippo appraised. It's worth $6,000.

35.

For the first time in weeks, early-morning sun shines into my bedroom. Dad has also fixed the window screen frame.

None of this improves my mood. The sunlight highlights my swollen eyes, my cracked lips, and my hair. Oh *crap*, my hair. Can't see my throat, but it must be ragged and red as fresh roadkill.

Like Nadia back on the day she straggled into Sky Valley, I must look like a fresh version of hell. I think about BB, the original owner of that pink pocket pipe. Is she still alive? If so, has she kept her promise of staying clean? I considered searching for "Brenda Barton," but the thought of even *one* news story popping up on an off-the-grid, hard-living heroin addict—while there's nothing on Angela's murder—would send me spiraling into another bottle of wine.

By now, the world has started its Wednesday, and my stomach growls. I wear my own clothes today. This black turtleneck has hung, unworn, in my closet since junior year at USC. It's tight around my breasts and made of scratchy dog fur. And I wear slacks that pinch my bloated middle. If I'm near an open flame today, these poly-blend suckers are gonna melt. Not wearing Mom's clothes, I'm naked, open to attack, vulnerable to the cold and rain. Her closet is filled with protective armor, but my anger still moves through me like sludge, and part of me wants to mope at home.

"No," I say. "I won't let them win."

But who is "them"? Don't know, but *they*—my parents—have left a note out on my kitchen table.

We're ready to explain everything. We love you more than you know.

No one was sitting in the old Buick by the time Dad checked it out. After I explained to him that *this* was the car that had followed me the other night, he took a picture of the license plate and sent it to Uncle Bryan. I thanked him, then returned to my apartment.

Now I fold my parents' note in half, then scratch my dry scalp. Flakes drift onto the front of my turtleneck. For food, I decide to pick something up at Anna's—

Oh. Yeah.

I buy a bacon-cheese-egg biscuit meal from McDonald's and continue my drive east. Text messages from my parents fill my phone screen. So do news alerts—the president did this, the Lakers did that. A Torrance woman named Chloe was found dead with the letters *DD* carved into her back. COULD THIS BE THE SAME DASHING DEVIL WHO STALKED WOMEN IN THE '70S AND '80S? the *Los Angeles Times* asks.

Crap. Torrance is closer to me than Simi Valley.

"He's circling," I tell Imani over the phone as I drive.

"You're trippin'." She slaps a wet blush brush against her palm. "You're Black."

"And? So?"

"The victims are white, blonde, and blue eyed—he obviously has a type." Softer, she says, "Sorry about all of that adoption stuff. I would've never thought Sonny wasn't your biological dad. You two are so freaking alike."

I say, "Yeah."

"Wanna grab drinks later? We can even watch *Mamma Mia* if you want."

A smile trembles on my lips. "You'd do that?"

"That's how fucked up all of this is."

We laugh, and I tell her that I love her and send her back to cleaning makeup brushes.

The hash brown patty is salty and delicious, so hot that it burns my tongue.

I *am* alive.

Bulldozers rumble at the western edges of the Santa Barbara Plaza, and a jackhammer pounds into old asphalt. Men wearing orange shirts and hard hats toss chunks of broken-up concrete into larger piles. Anna's Place is still quiet. No customers hang around like alley cats, waiting to be fed.

Riley stands at the register with a ledger and a calculator. Her laptop sits on the stool beside her. She, too, wears a turtleneck, but hers is soft rose and free of dandruff. She looks over at me and freezes. Her gaze drops to my hands. "Whoa. *And* McDonald's? You okay? You and Dexter break up?"

I blink at her.

"I don't want to pry, but I need to warn you about my brother. He uses girls like you."

"Girls like me?"

"The rich kind."

"I'm not rich."

Riley blinks. "Guess we all have our definition of 'rich.' Whatever. Just be prepared."

"For?"

"Being asked for a loan. No, an *investment* opportunity. An art gallery, most likely. There's a girlfriend who lives somewhere in Europe who bankrolled a gallery for him last year."

My scalp blazes with heat and makes my dandruff as crispy as my hash brown patty. I clear my throat to say, "I'm not sad about Dexter." Although Dexter *did* call me a daddy's girl last night, and he got testy with me for wanting to help Detective Winchester, too. And oh, yeah, he *did* lie to me about going to see Anna, driving to a State Farm agency instead.

"Sit." Riley moves the laptop from the stool to the counter.

If she's being this nice to me, I must look like death on a graham cracker. "I really don't feel like talking . . ."

"Then don't. Like Anna would say, 'Eat your food, child.'"

I plop onto the stool and pull out my biscuit. I offer Riley some and she declines. I bite into the sandwich—more salt, more butter, and now cheese. My soul rejoices.

"Guess you found the baby clothes that you were looking for," Riley says.

"Yeah, I'll get to them today."

"Looks like you're close to being done, at least with this part."

I grunt and pull off a piece of bacon glued to the wax paper by bright-orange cheese.

Riley turns back to the ledger. It's a beastly thing, thick, swollen pages between green leather. "You find anything interesting when you were looking?"

"I'm only looking at items Nadia left out."

Her eyebrows knit together. "Oh." She noticed that I rummaged through boxes. Did she notice that I found the knife?

"I did look through boxes but only to search for the booties and hat." A flush creeps across my face. It's shame, even though I'm allowed to look for work product around the store.

"A few weeks before you came, I found this broken watch in one of the boxes in the office," Riley says. "I gave it to Nadia—it was a nice watch—and she sold it to a watchmaker for ten dollars. He came back to tell us that it was a rare Rolex, the ones that had been given to the

Italian Navy during World War II. He got close to a hundred grand for it. *A hundred grand!* And Nadia sold it for ten dollars. The old Nadia would've never . . ."

She shakes her head. "*That's* why I'm asking. If you find anything worth anything, let me know. We can put it in a safe place."

"The shop isn't safe?"

Riley frowns. "The construction guys out there, I don't trust those bastards at all. And we've been broken into before." She opens a photo album on her laptop. "Look at this."

"This" is a silver necklace that looks like it's made of flattened spoons.

"That's . . . something," I say.

"This necklace was designed by a famous sculptor, something Calder. As ugly as it is, it's worth three hundred thousand dollars. We have this piece and a matching bracelet."

And now those pieces belong to Dexter Denham.

"I'm thinking they can go into our future online store," Riley says.

"You may get more through Sotheby's or Christie's."

"You think? I'd have to get permission from you-know-who."

You-know-who will agree since he has money problems.

And may have thought of killing his mother, but she took herself out before he could.

Ohmigod.

Why did I just think that?

My underarms go clammy. More shame.

"I told my neighbor about your memory banks," Riley says now. "She's turning eighty. She has boxes of junk everywhere. A painting that looks important. She has an old Holly Hobbie Oven and Ansel Adams negatives . . . How much for a bank like Nadia's?"

"Five thousand."

She makes faces as she thinks about the cost. "And you'd come to her? Like I said, she's old and can't move around much."

306

"Of course. I go where the client is. That's why I'm sitting next to you right now."

She smiles. "Ha. That's right. Awesome. Can I request you, specifically?"

"You can."

"Maybe you should come and, like, do a consult first. Look at a few things and tell us if there's a story there. You know, before I spend all that money."

"Sure. Just tell me when."

"How about . . . sometime this weekend? Like Saturday morning?"

"Sure," I say again. What happened to my plan of Nadia's being the last memory bank I worked on for Christopher's company? What happened to striking out on my own?

"Thanks, Michaela." Riley's eyes soften. "You're actually pretty cool."

I smile, not sure what to say.

That's when the bell over the front door tinkles.

"Y'all will never guess what happened to me."

My eyes bug out.

Riley gasps.

Together, we shout, "Anna!"

36.

"We've been worried about you!" I hop off the stool, chest sunbursting with relief, and rush over to Anna. Tears fill my eyes, and as I hug her, they plop onto her sweater.

"Not too tight, not too tight." The old woman laughs and eases out of my grasp.

No autumn-colored knitwear for Anna today. No chunky pieces of jewelry or oversize sunglasses. She looks pared down in comfy sweats and old-lady nurse shoes. She looks her age, with jowls, swollen hands, and tired eyes. She looks . . . *alive*, and that is the most beautiful thing.

Riley, behind me, gives Anna a quick hug. "Where have you been?"

Anna's eyebrows crumple. "Pepper didn't tell you?"

"Pepper doesn't know anything," Riley says. "She's just as worried as we were."

Anna rolls her eyes. "My daughter left a message on Big Pep's phone."

There's a butterfly bandage along Anna's hairline and a shaved section in her scalp, hair replaced by purple-black skin and stitches. The white of her right eye is red, and there's a gash across her bottom lip. "You get in a car accident?" I ask.

She catches her breath as I take the bags from her hands. "Child, somebody jumped me."

Riley and I shout, *"What?"*

She nods. "Back on Monday night. Knocked me out cold. I woke up in the emergency room. My head was killing me and I kept throwing up."

"Concussion," I say.

"Uh-huh. So they kept me overnight and let me go last night. And I'm here cuz I already lost one day. Mickie, baby, you look worse than me."

"That's what I was thinking," Riley says.

"Whatever," I say. "*Who* jumped you? Was it the guy who came to the diner?"

Anna grimaces as she flicks her hand across my shoulders to sweep off dandruff flakes. "The police came to see me in the hospital. You know, to take a report. All I know is this: I was pulling into my carport on Monday night. I got out my car, this hand came over my mouth, and . . . Mickie, you sound sick. You catch a cold?"

"Probably," I say. "Was he tall, short? Did he wear cologne? Did his breath smell?"

"He was definitely taller than me," Anna says, nodding, eyes shining. "And he may have been left-handed, but . . . I must've said the Lord's Prayer six times in a minute while we tussled." She flaps at her face and pushes air through her pursed lips. "Ooh. Makes me want to take up smoking again."

"Did he say anything?" Riley asks.

Anna slowly shakes her head. In the last few minutes, she's looking stronger. More erect. Like she gave as much as she got and now she's remembering that.

"He take anything?" I ask.

"Nuh-uh, and that's the strange part." Anna glances back at the entrance. "Now that I think about it, now that I see those machines out there, it could've been him. I know you don't think so, Riley, but Weller's trying to scare me. He killed Nadia, and now he's warning—Mickie, what's wrong?"

My cheeks tingle as I tell them about Peter Weller's phone call. "I wish I'd recorded it," I say, "but he caught me off guard."

"Why didn't you say something?" Riley shouts, red-faced.

"I was going to," I shout back, "but then Anna went missing and . . ." My stomach growls, knowing that Anna is back.

The old woman grins and asks, "Want me to make you some grits and bacon?"

A feeble smile finds my lips. I nod, then grab her bags from my ankles. "And for real: you should've stayed home and rested for a few days."

Anna sucks her teeth. "And let that man win? He already gave me PTSD. He ain't gettin' to do nothing else. We gotta turn my diner into a—" She lifts her chin. "A *brunch destination*."

I nod. "We do!"

She puts a hand on her hip. "You know the saying 'Never let another woman live in your house'? Well, this here plaza is *my* house, and Peter Weller is a simple *bitch*."

Riley and I laugh. Anna tries to laugh, but it comes out strangled. We're all on the edge of panic.

"Nah," Anna says, "he ain't take nothing from me, but I sure as hell took something from him. I found it this morning in my carport." She plucks a plastic baggie from her purse and holds it up for Riley and me to see. "I'm taking it to the police later."

It's a gold chain with a half-heart pendant.

Just like the one Dexter wears.

Artifact 11: Crocheted baby shoes and hat with pink flowers. Acquired in February 1985.

Location of Acquisition: Palm Springs, California. Located in the Sonoran Desert and only a two-hour drive from Los Angeles, Palm Springs boasts the world's largest rotating tramcars from the desert floor and up one of the steepest mountain ascents in the world. Palm Springs claims to have more swimming pools per capita than anywhere else in the country.

Last Owner: Sharleen Bosler.

Memory: It was grocery-shopping day. A sudden winter rainstorm blanketed the desert, and as you waited in line for the butcher, you spotted a man and a woman arguing in the frozen foods section. Angry words made a few shoppers stop in their steps. You ignored the shouting. The desert had its rich, and the desert had its trash, and that's what this couple was. His Confederate flag belt buckle. Her Iron Eagle leg tattoo. The bad teeth, the crinkly hair, the cursing. These two were not the Bob Hope and Dinah Shore of the desert.

As you ordered a pound of ground round, Sir Trash shoved Lady Trash into the freezer of frozen pizzas. He left her there on the linoleum floor. You took the package of ground beef and pushed your cart over to the weeping woman. "Are you okay?"

"I think he sprained my . . ." The dirty blonde blanched as she tried to move her shoulder.

You helped her stand. "What's your name, dearest?"

"Sharleen," the woman said.

"Who was the man you were with?" You offered Sharleen a handkerchief.

"My husband, Mac. We're driving in from Tucson, and we been arguing all the way here and now he's gone. I ain't got no money. He took the car and . . ." She sobbed into her hands.

You patted the injured shoulder of the crying woman. "It'll all work out."

"No, it won't," Sharleen cried. "All's I got are . . ." She pointed to her satchel and pulled out a set of crocheted baby clothes. "I'm making outfits for my little girl, Treasure, but I'll give you these and everything else I'm making if you drive me to a bus station in the next town or . . ."

You didn't like Sharleen *at all*. Sharleen was a con, and Mac hadn't injured her shoulder. This was all a setup. You'd seen the couple around town before and heard that they'd been robbing, beating, and sometimes raping citizens of the desert. You also knew that Mac was Sharleen's partner in crime—he'd be waiting for Sharleen to bring you. Still, you played along for a bit as you drove Sharleen to a better place. A place where Mac would never find the white-trash Bonnie to his redneck Clyde. And after you'd left Sharleen at that better place, you took the crocheted baby shoes and matching hat from her satchel as payment.

37.

Is Dexter's chain gold, or is it silver? Is the heart pendant flat like this one or rounded? I can't remember, and it's hard to focus on anything else. Because why would Dexter *mug* his second mother? But then, why did he lie to me about checking on her?

I rub my face and take several deep breaths.

Focus. Breathe. Focus.

I reread the narrative about Sharleen Bosler.

You drove Sharleen to a better place . . . took the crocheted baby shoes and matching hat from her satchel as payment.

Something dense and gooey swells and pulses around me. It's not the weather. Pure sunlight arcs through the office window, and almost an entire day has passed without clouds in the sky. No, that dense, gooey thing is . . . this memory. There's something *nasty* about it. Yes, Sharleen was a con and Nadia was her mark, but . . .

Outside the store, Kangol Man hobbles up the breezeway to Anna's Place. Sam Cooke sings "A Change Is Gonna Come." Once she opened the diner, Anna's alley cats—myself included—returned. Soon, every stool had a butt and every break in silence was filled a second later with jukebox music and laughter.

With a belly filled with the most food I've eaten since Sasha's wedding, I now boot up my laptop. As I wait for its screen to flicker on,

I wander the office holding Sharleen Bosler's page. I pace in a slat of sunshine and stop to study the map above Nadia's desk. There's a green pushpin in Palm Springs. I've visited Palm Springs countless times. The shopping outlet, the Indian casinos, that tram . . . with girlfriends, with parents, with Christopher.

Where did Nadia drop Sharleen? What "better place"? Salton Sea? Coachella Valley? In 1985, there weren't many better places way the hell out there.

How did this story end?

"Knock knock. Special delivery." Riley stands at the door holding a vase of white roses.

Delight skitters up to my heart like a golden retriever. This day is improving. "For me?"

"Yep." She plants the vase on Nadia's desk. "There's a card."

The roses absorb sunlight, and now they glow, their sweet aroma surpassing my diner smell. Another small blessing. I pull the small white card from the envelope.

I should've sent this sooner, but time stands still whenever I think of you. DD

"So?" Riley says. "Are they from your ex?" She plucks the card from my fingers and reads . . . and pales. She hands back the card. "Ah."

My lungs pinch, not because Riley knows about Dexter and me for sure now, but because . . . *ugh*. Less than twenty-four hours ago, I sold Dexter out to Detective Winchester. And less than an hour ago, I thought he had maybe, perhaps, possibly assaulted Anna, who snatched his chain during their tussle. And also, he'd possibly stalked me in an old Buick.

I exhale, releasing a breath I didn't realize I've been holding.

What do I do now?

Riley taps a rosebud. "We talked earlier, but . . . can I say something else? As a friend?"

Friend? Since when?

"Please, please, please," she says, clasping her hands before her mouth. "Be very careful. Stay away from him."

"Because . . . ?"

"He's not who you think he is."

Don't say it. Don't say it.

Riley pokes her tongue at her cheek as she thinks. "Okay, so here's the thing. In her last days, Nadia didn't trust Dex. She loved him; of course she did. But . . . Dexter rarely came around the store. He was always traveling, always working. Or so he said. Like *months* would go by and we wouldn't see him. Wouldn't hear from him. We'd get post-cards, sometimes.

"But then, when Nadia got diagnosed with Alzheimer's . . . That's when he started coming around again. And he'd ask her weird questions about the store, about money. Once, I saw him talking to Peter Weller. What the hell, right?"

"But *I've* talked to Peter Weller—"

She shakes her head. "Not the same thing. I know. I'm talking about weird things that, separately, don't sound weird, that actually make *me* sound paranoid, but I'm not paranoid."

Riley looks me in the eyes and tries to smile. "I don't know what you have that he wants, but it's something, Michaela. Something more than money. Something more than sex. Just . . . keep one foot in this world, okay? That way, I can pull you out. Like the mom did to Carol Anne in *Poltergeist.* Ha."

My heart is beating three times faster. She's making him sound lethal. But then, I'd just thought about him as dangerous, too. For now, though, I muster enough calm to ask, "Why didn't you tell me this earlier?"

"Because I was hoping it would just come to a natural end. But now, he's sending you roses, so *obviously* . . ."

"You've lied to me, too, you know."

"I have not."

"Nadia's best friend, Esther? You told me that—"

"That's different." She's pink-faced again.

I tuck the card in my pants pocket, then move back to the crocheted baby hat and shoes at the project table. "I appreciate the warning and your honesty. I really do. Some things are starting to make more sense to me. Thank you." Now all that sunlight hurts my eyes, and the office is too hot, and my dandruff-flaked turtleneck feels as heavy as bear fur.

Riley nods at the roses. "They're really beautiful." She slips out of the room.

My laptop is taking forever to load. The CMS will soon take my computer to a better place, and Sharleen Bosler will disappear along with it.

A better place. *A place where Mac would never find . . .*

I grab my phone and tap "SHARLEEN BOSLER" into the search field. The Charley Project is, again, the first search result. She looks just as I imagined. Scuzzy blonde hair, blemished skin, mean eyes. A walking, sentient yeast infection.

> Sharleen Bosler disappeared from Twentynine Palms in February 1985. Her remains were found in Idyllwild, California, in 1986 but weren't identified until 2004. No suspects have been identified, and officials can't determine if her death was foul play or natural due to exposure in the desert.

My stomach drops.

Nadia said that she took Sharleen to a better place, a place Mac would never find her. Did Nadia—pissed that she was being taken advantage of—drive Sharleen way out into the desert and abandon her on the side of the road? Knowing Nadia's kind spirit, I wonder: Did she calm down and drive back to pick up Sharleen, but the woman wasn't there?

I reread those final sentences from Nadia's note. There's nothing to suggest that she abandoned Sharleen.

There's a second link to another search result in the *Desert Sun*. According to the reporter, the case was still pending in 2004. Forensic pathologists had determined that Sharleen had been stabbed several times before dying on that mountainside in Idyllwild. The blade was estimated to be about thirteen inches, but they don't know for sure since no weapon was ever found. Her brother and partner in crime, Ernest Macklemore—known as Mac—was also killed in 1985. No suspects have been identified.

A thirteen-inch knife. In a box nearby, there's a long black blade encrusted with . . .

Had Nadia . . . ? Could Nadia . . . ?

DD. Dexter signed the card as . . .

That news story about the dead waitress who had the letters *DD* carved into her . . .

Where was Dexter last night, after he left the insurance agency?

. . .

No.

My phone buzzes in my hand.

I "eep" and fumble the device, and it drops to the worn carpet. My stomach cartwheels as a text message brightens my screen.

I'm here.

38.

Weller's guys are no longer beasts lurking at the edges, eyeing us warily from the shadows, revving their bulldozers and glowing like killer bacteria in fluorescent orange shirts. No, they've come closer. From my booth at the diner, I see them standing at the curbs near the shops, pointing at things while holding blueprints. One shakes a can of orange spray paint, but he never marks the pavement.

I don't notice Uncle Bryan walk past. I don't see the plate of towering french fries sitting between the young couple at the counter. I don't hear Donna Summer singing "Last Dance" on the jukebox. I haven't taken a single bite from the pastrami sandwich on my plate. No, I'm watching the predators at the curb. The sunshine gives them power.

"And good afternoon to you, too." Uncle Bryan has slid into my booth. He's wearing a tie and a sports coat. The waves in his hair look like how my stomach feels. His eyebrows lift as he takes in my scraggy appearance. He clears his throat and loosens the tie. "I was happy that your text referred to me as 'uncle.'"

"Black family means that I'd still call you 'uncle.'" My words have not warmed with the weather. And my eyebrow is cocked so high, my butt hovers an inch off the banquette.

"Mickie—"

I hold up my hand as Anna sets a cup of coffee and a slice of sweet potato pie on his place mat. Uncle Bryan thanks her, and she lingers, expecting introductions. I say, "Anna, this is my uncle Bryan. Uncle Bryan, this is Anna. She's the owner." The two engage in small talk and niceties. Once she's had her fill, Anna flits back to the grill.

Uncle Bryan tries again. "Mickie—"

"I'm not ready to talk about my family situation yet."

Silence settles between us. He clears his throat, then offers: "They're pouring concrete for the fence out back—"

"I asked you here because I need something, and seeing that you've lied to me my entire life, you can't say no for a very long time."

He says nothing as he sweetens his coffee with two packets of sugar.

"A lot, *too much*, is going on right now, and none of it is good." I grip my glass of Diet Coke tight.

He moves his fork through the pie custard. "Okay. Tell me."

"I found something strange at the store."

He nods back at Beautiful Things. "That store over there? No way."

I ignore the sarcasm and reach into my satchel for the plastic bag. "Can you test . . . ?" I place the bag in the space between us.

A new song from the jukebox plays, and now Diana Ross purrs about no mountain being high enough. The young couple at the counter feeds each other french fries. The Boxer's Third Ex-Wife stumbles to her booth by the restroom and shouts, "Diana Ross is a *back-stabbin' ho!*"

Uncle Bryan, chewing slowly, leans forward and stares at the knife in the bag. He sits back, still chewing, still staring at the artifact.

"I think there's blood on this," I whisper.

"And this knife belongs to . . . ?"

"A dead woman. Nadia Denham."

"The store owner?"

I nod.

He steeples his hands before his face. "You suspect it's blood because . . . ?"

I tell him about Sharleen Bosler, Ernest Macklemore, and the baby clothes. I tell him about the con they ran. How Nadia knew she was being conned and drove Sharleen to a "better place." That Sharleen went missing and was found and had been stabbed with a thirteen-inch knife. How her brother was killed the same year that she disappeared.

Uncle Bryan stares at the knife.

Nervous, I wriggle in my seat and twist my fingers around each other. "I'm not saying Nadia *killed* her . . ."

"What *are* you saying?" His eyes—eyes that I thought looked like mine—bore into me.

I swallow my words because I don't know which ones to use. I lift my ponytail off my neck and exhale. "People lie, for good and bad. I need to know the story about this knife. The *true* story, not the one I've been paid to write. And even though you haven't been truthful with me, you can help me learn the truth about something meaningful to someone else."

"Mickie . . ."

"Will you help me with this or not?" My icy tone surprises me. I grip my glass even tighter to keep from swiping the plate, napkin holder, salt and pepper shakers—all of it—to the floor.

Uncle Bryan takes possession of the bag.

I ask, "How long will it take?"

"If this were an active homicide case, a week. Seeing that it's a possible cold case—"

"That could be solved with this evidence."

"Which may not even *be* evidence."

"But it is," I say with a nod.

"And you know this because . . . ?"

Something flickers in my chest. *Where is Sarah Park?*

"How long?" I ask.

He rubs the bridge of his nose. "I'll see what I can do."

"Thank you."

"May I ask a question? I know you said that you aren't ready to talk about it yet, but . . ."

My tears blur the man seated across from me. My head hurts as though someone has clocked me in the face.

"How did you find out?" he asks.

"I wanted—" My voice cracks as a hot teardrop tumbles down my face. "I wanted to give Mom something special for her birthday and I went looking and . . ." I'm vibrating, and I switch from gripping my soda glass to gripping the edge of the table. "And I found all the papers."

"Have you talked to them at all?"

I swipe at my cheeks, then slide out of the booth. "Let me know what you find."

"Your pastrami."

I shake my head and leave him there. I can't handle any more than this. My origin story is as chaotic as Nadia's shop. Not beautiful at all.

39.

I've said it before—in help desk tickets, in bed with Christopher, to myself at my desk—and I'll say it again to this empty office: the Memory Bank's content-management system is a buggy piece of trash. And now its Linux-DOS-UNIX-defective *x*'s and *o*'s are killing my computer. I need to complete my time card to be paid, but the laptop's screen is now a glaring blue. The damn thing won't even shut off as I hold down the power button.

This day sucks. This office with its single window, flaking paint, and boxes of other people's crap, it sucks, too.

How the hell did I get here?

The perfume from Dexter's roses could soothe me. His note of sweet words could soothe me, too. But I don't want to be soothed. I wanna throw this computer across the room. I wanna tear down that map with all those pins and burn it and everything else down. I wanna crash my car into other cars, into plate glass, into toxic lies.

But I don't. I can't.

I am stuck. In all things.

I look out the window. Honestly? This plaza is an eyesore. No single architectural theme carries from Nadia's store to Anna's diner to Mr. Kim's key shop. This place needs a singular vision to restore it. Unfortunately, Weller has the money to not only restore it but transform it into a place with synthesized moxie and Botoxed good looks. No warmth. No charm. But then again . . . Vista makes a fantastic grilled lobster.

Weller's men have left the curbs to return to their bulldozers in the parking lot, and—

"Dexter?" I gasp. Not just because I see my lover outside the store, but because he's laughing with Weller's construction crew. Why is he laughing? I stare at him, at them, at the group, all smiles, all hands clapping backs, hands giving pounds . . .

Up in the shop, the bell over the front door rings. It's not Dexter visiting, because I'm staring at him in the parking lot. I fumble in my pocket for my phone to text him.

Thank you for the roses!

If you're around stop by

He's still standing with them, but he looks at his phone, then slips it back into his pocket. He climbs into his Jeep and races out of the parking lot.

He didn't come to see *me*. He came to talk to *them*, to Weller's . . .

Riley warned me. Two times today, if I'm counting.

My heart is pulverized, and I wanna cry. Every day has ended in lies and betrayal.

My laptop is still whirring, but it's also crunching. Woodchuck sounds should never come from healthy electronics.

In the shop, Riley is talking to a man with Elvis sideburns. They hang out in front of the cabinet of Elvis memorabilia. This guy has visited before and has left with the Elvis ceramic spoon holder and the Elvis toilet seat cover. Riley's MacBook sits on the rear counter and glows a healthy white. Would she let me borrow it to complete my time card?

I wander over to the counter as Riley tells the man about her last collection trip to a flea market just a stone's throw from Graceland.

The MacBook's tabbed up to a website: Websleuths.com . . . The Dashing Devil, USA.

Riley's fascinated, too. Is it because she thinks Dexter . . . ?

"You need something?" Riley calls over to me.

"Could I use your laptop for a quick minute? Mine just died and I need to—"

She shakes her head. "I'm downloading a program, so maybe later?"

I return to the office.

My computer is still dead.

I text Christopher. That bug in the CMS just killed my computer!!

I send him a picture of the blue screen. I can't do my timecard!!

As I await his response, I search "WEBSLEUTHS DASHING DEVIL" with my phone.

An internet community focused on crime and crime victims. Visitors in the forum talk crime and unsolved cases. One discussion thread: unidentified possible Dashing Devil victims. Another: DD Timeline— No Discussion—Scroll Down for Updates.

> Fresno Police Investigating Possible Link in Disappearances

> Donnamarie Queneau went missing from New Orleans, Louisiana, on June 3, 1978, and her remains were found in the Rigolets off Lake Pontchartrain . . .

> Person of interest Norma Diefenbacher Questioned in the "Dashing Devil" Murders . . .

My phone vibrates.

So sorry Mick

Stop by tonight

I'll have another computer. Gilbert will save your data.

Okay thanks Chris

I miss you babe

Umm . . .

Hello?

The voice in my head is screaming, "No, girl, no!"
My body coos, "Hit that again for old time's sake."
My heart flutters like a butterfly.

I'll stop by tonight

Kill the butterflies.

Christopher met my parents once, at our annual Labor Day barbecue. Yet I've never met his parents, who live high in the hills of Brentwood. Not a drive-by visit, not a texted picture. They don't know me from Whoopi Goldberg. "Why is that?" Imani asked.

Even as I pull on my coat and close the dead laptop, I'm not sure where I'm headed. Even as I say good night to Riley, still talking to the Elvis fan, and the night air chills my face, I'm not sure where I'm headed.

Home to my family in Baldwin Vista?

Miracle Mile to Christopher?

To the beach, where I can just sit and stare at waves crashing against the shore?

Imani is in Miami, and Sasha is still in Fiji, so I can't go see them.

Out in the parking lot, near the RVs, a man stands with his back to me. He's unkempt—uncombed hair, stained pants, run-over shoes.

I slow in my step and hope that he ambles into one of the trailers. I hope he doesn't turn around. I hope he doesn't see me.

I've so had enough.

My Mace is in the glove compartment along with my Taser.

The man shuffles toward the mini-Winnie but stops before opening the door.

I become as still as possible and will myself to fade into the night.

The man twists his head to look behind him, but he stops. Instead, he opens the mini-Winnie's door and lumbers inside. *Crack!* The sound of the closing metal screen door echoes across the plaza like the blast from a gun.

If I hadn't seen it, I would've thought he'd shot me.

40.

The sycamore trees that surround our house sway as the wind pushes in an oncoming storm now gathering off the coast. A few branches have cracked and crashed to the lawn, and the torn wood is bright and fleshy. Every bulb in my parents' house burns golden-bright. The reds, yellows, and blues of the Christmas lights reflect on the silver truck parked at our curb.

Uncle Bryan, sitting behind the steering wheel of that Ram pickup, ends his phone call as I pull into the driveway. He climbs out of the truck.

"I know it's too soon to ask, but are the results back?" My voice is clipped, business-only for the man who's been a second father to me.

"I loved her." His voice quavers.

Annoyed, I scowl at him. "You loved *who*?"

"Angela Craig." He swipes at his eyes. "Not like . . . *that*. But . . . Angie and I met the same night that Cori and Sonny met. At a fraternity house party up at the Kappa house on Crenshaw." He bops his head as though he can still hear Heavy D and the Boyz, as though that thump of bass still hits his chest and the leather Africa medallion hanging from his neck.

"Angie wasn't supposed to be at that party," Uncle Bryan continues. "She was seventeen—a year younger than me and four years younger than Cori, who figured it would be good for her little sister to be around positive, college-aged Black men."

I picture Angie and Mom wearing those LA Dodgers Starter jerseys, spotless high-top Air Jordans, silver hoops in their ears, Fly-Girl flyy.

"That girl could rap, and she could dance. The wop, the Cabbage Patch, Running Man . . . As for yours truly, I could only do a sorry-ass two-step. Anything more than that, and I'd just . . . freeze." He shakes his head, embarrassed. "So I watched Angie do all these routines, and I couldn't take my eyes off of her. She was so . . . *free*. So joyful and irreverent . . ."

Mom has found us, and she stands in the living room window, hands pressed before her face. Dad, pacing behind her, refuses to look out to the street.

Uncle Bryan gazes at the house. "I finally got up the nerve to ask Angie out."

"Did she say yes?" I ask.

"She said, 'Bryan, I can't figure out if you're cheesy or lame.'"

I snort. "Sounds like a no."

"I was too *boring*, she said. I couldn't dance, didn't smoke, didn't drink. I was a cop's kid, right? Hell, preachers' kids are rowdier than a cop's. But I wasn't cheesy or lame because I was a cop's kid. I was lame because I was trying to force myself to be someone I wasn't."

I drop my head, understanding.

"Angie and I hung out a *lot*," he says. "People assumed we were a couple, which I didn't mind." He swallows. "She was the first person I told."

"Really?"

He chuckles. "Her first reaction was disbelief. 'You don't *look* gay.' That's what she said. Remember, this was, like 1990. I drove my souped-up Charger and played football . . ."

"Did she ever say anything to anyone?" I ask.

He shakes his head. "She was scared something would happen to me. I graduated from high school and went to Cal State LA. When I enrolled in the police academy, she hooked up with some dude she met at the skating rink. He was way older than her, and he banged—Hoover Crips. He had a record as long as you are tall. Nothing but trouble." He rubs his jaw. "Man, Cori and Dr. and Mrs. Craig absolutely hated that bastard."

"Was he my . . . ?"

"Biological father?" Uncle Bryan nods, but his attention shifts over to the walkway.

Dad is gliding toward us. "Can we talk about this inside? Your mother—"

"Has lied to me every day of my life," I snap.

"And has loved you like she carried you herself for nine months," Dad snaps back.

"This is a private conversation." I move away from him.

Michael Anthony—does he resemble my father Orson in any way? Does he have light-brown eyes, a narrow nose, and long fingers? Does he dunk his fries into his milkshake? Does he have a kind smile? He can be a Crip and still have a kind smile.

To Uncle Bryan, I ask, "So then what happened?"

"Angie and Mike started hanging out on the DL."

"Cuz your grandparents forbade Angie from seeing him," Dad adds.

"And then *you* happened," Uncle Bryan continues. "And we knew then that she would be tied to Michael Anthony forever."

"So what did you do?" I ask.

He shoves his hands into his pockets. "I finished college and police academy. Watched Angie drift between Cori and Sonny's apartment and Mike's duplex. He started hitting her. And she caught him a few times shaking you because you wouldn't stop crying."

"What?" I know I just shouted that single word, but I can no longer hear my voice.

"Angie begged Mike's mother to intervene," Uncle Bryan says. "To talk some sense into him. But What's-Her-Face . . ."

"Rita," Dad says. "She was a sanctimonious drunk and she saw the Craigs and she saw you, Mickie, as a ticket out and . . ."

How did *she* look? Did she wear big church hats? Did she scowl or smile? Was her bosom hard and her big purse devoid of candies with noisy wrappers? I close my eyes and hold up my hand. "Rita. My grandmother . . . She didn't love me?"

Dad gives a single headshake.

Uncle Bryan continues. "Angie, who was just, what, twenty years old? She freaks out and starts calling me. She'd stay with me sometimes while Cori and Sonny kept you. And it was like that for a few months. Mike was in and out of jail. Pop had cops looking for *any* reason to arrest him. Littering, loitering, driving over the speed limit. You had a room at Cori and Sonny's that you shared with Angie, when she wasn't staying with me."

"Staying with you. As in . . . *dating*?" I ask.

"No, but Michael Anthony didn't know that. He thought we were together and . . ." His voice catches, and he covers his mouth with a shaky hand.

"You and Angie spent the night at our apartment," Dad says to me now. "Mike was out of jail again, and he was pissed that Angie had broken up with him. You weren't even two years old yet. He came to our apartment and demanded that Angie leave with him. Angie told him no, and he grabbed you from her arms and threw you across the room. You crashed into the corner of our glass coffee table."

Dad's finger traces the mark on my cheek. "Your scar there . . ."

"Mom said it was a glass table," I whisper, "but she . . . she said it was her fault."

"You're screaming," Dad continues, "and I'm holding Cori back because all she wants to do is claw Mike's eyes out. Angie rushes over to you, and that's when Mike pulls out a gun. And he threatens to kill you, but Angie and Mike's sister . . ."

"Cookie," Uncle Bryan says. "I can't remember her real name."

"Angie and Cookie calm him down," Dad says, "and Angie promises to go with him if he puts down the gun. So he shoves it into his back pocket, and she assures Cori that everything's gonna be okay."

"And then," Uncle Bryan says, "Angie hugs you tight and uses the scarf she wore around her hair to stop the bleeding on your cheek. She kissed you and told you to stop crying and that she'd see you in the morning."

"As soon as Angie, Cookie, and Michael Anthony left the apartment," Dad says, "I called 9-1-1. By the time they reached the end of the walkway, Michael pulled out a gun and shot Angie in the head. She was dead before she hit the ground."

It's cold out here, and I can't feel my face. It's quiet, and I can hear only my thundering pulse. The world around me is slick. Drizzle falls from the sky like silver tinsel.

"We got Mike before he reached Crenshaw," Uncle Bryan says. "His trial was quick—he pleaded and got a lighter sentence. Twenty years. He was sent to Pelican Bay up near Oregon."

"Twenty years?" I screech. "That's all? It's *been* twenty—" I gape at Dad. "Is he out?"

Dad nods. "We received the alert about three weeks ago, right before Thanksgiving."

"Do you think he's still . . ." I gulp. "Is he still violent?"

Uncle Bryan runs his hand over his mouth. "A buddy that works at Pelican told me that Mike hadn't gotten in trouble in over ten years. No fights, no shots. Not a model prisoner but not a dangerous one."

VINE. Victim Information and Notification Everyday. Mom has that alert on her phone. On the morning of Nadia's memorial service, I'd noticed the blue screen . . .

Panicked, I ask, "Do you know where he is?"

"He's here in LA."

My eyes bug out. "And?"

"Sometimes we have a location," Uncle Bryan says. "Sometimes we don't."

The latte left on the kitchen counter . . . My open refrigerator door . . . Could that have been . . . ? Light-headed, I say, "Ohmigod," then sink to sit on the curb. "Has he been here? Does he know where we live?"

"We . . ." Uncle Bryan looks at Dad, then drops his gaze to the asphalt. "We don't know what he knows. He hasn't shown up on your security system's video feed, but we've received reports of him being spotted in a few places, and . . ."

"That Buick that parked near the house," Dad says. "Bryan ran the plates, and . . ."

"It's his?" I whisper.

Dad nods. "And that handwriting on the notes you found—"

YOUR PRETTY and YOU LOOK LIKE HER.

"He left them?" I can barely hear myself speak.

"We're not one hundred percent sure," Uncle Bryan says, "but I'd say yeah."

Stunned, I can only shake my head. "The text messages?"

Uncle Bryan rubs his neck. "Not sure. The phones are burners bought at Walmart."

"We've been overprotective sometimes," Dad says, sitting beside me. "It wasn't because we didn't trust you. It was because we didn't trust *him* or his family. We tried to give you as normal a life as possible. But we've also done a few things you have no idea about."

"Like a bodyguard," Uncle Bryan says.

"What?" I shout. "When?"

"Elementary school through high school," Daddy says. "Tracy Pickman."

"My *babysitter?*"

"Who knew how to make a great cup of cocoa," Uncle Bryan says, "but also had a black belt in karate and was a deputy in the US Marshals Service before she retired."

Behind us, the front door creaks as it opens.

It's Mom. Her eyes are red and swollen from crying. Her jeans hang off her hips, and her T-shirt is wrinkled and stained. She's come undone. And now she trudges off the porch and onto the walkway. "Mickie," she says, her voice as creaky as our door. "Mouse . . ."

I hop up from the curb and back away from her.

Mom hurries toward me, her eyes and her love as wild as stallions. "Please don't go. Please don't leave me."

But I've escaped to my car. I'm leaving her even though I love her. And I race down the hill, rushing to Christopher even though I don't love him.

41.

The soft rain that I hate is back, and the flat slabs of clouds responsible for this horrific weather press down on the city. My hands hurt from their death grip around the steering wheel. My head hurts as it imagines Angie's last moments alive as she walks down that pathway, right before her lifeblood spills onto the pavement.

I have a whole other family in this city. They are the opposites of the Craigs and the Lamberts. I also have a murderer's blood in my DNA. He gave me this scar. He killed my birth mother and wanted to kill me, too, and he's now out of supermax prison, and he's slipping notes beneath my door and stalking me around LA. The text messages—he *must've* sent those.

He is not the Dashing Devil. He is Michael Anthony, my biological father.

Texts from Mom blow up my phone.

Please come back

We didn't want to lie to you

We just wanted to protect you

You are my daughter

You are MINE

Christopher is shocked to see me even though he told me earlier to come for a new computer. That was then, and this is now, and now his eyes widen seeing me at his front door.

I say, "Chris," and a sob rattles from my aching chest. As I weep, he pulls me into his condo and kisses the top of my head.

There are thousands of people crammed inside the living room. I can't see their faces because I am ugly-crying after holding on to these tears during a seven-mile drive on rain-soaked streets. I kept it together, and now I am all misery and naked hurt. I smell . . . prosciutto and . . . I smell pizza . . . and beer and . . . I want Christopher to send these people away.

His voice rumbles against my cheek as he tells the group, "I'll be right back." He whispers to me, "It's okay, it's okay," as he guides me down the hallway to the bedroom. He settles me on the couch, then grabs the tissue box from the nightstand. He kneels before me, dabs my tear-soaked face, and brushes my hair from my eyes.

The room hasn't changed. The Ed Ruscha print I selected because it reminded me of home still hangs above the headboard. The walls are still painted bright blue. Our picture on the dresser, taken at Alcatraz—that's gone. And since Temecula, Christopher has shaved the beard. His skin is flushed from drinking. His lips are dry from not hydrating. And those lips are now moving, but I can't hear him over my crying.

"Breathe, breathe." That's what he's saying to me.

I finally manage to push away hysterics long enough to pluck a tissue from the box.

"What happened?" he asks. "What's wrong?"

"I—I interrupted-rupted you," I hiccup. "I'm so-so-sorry."

He flicks his hand. "They can wait a few minutes."

A few minutes. What I have to tell him, what I've just learned about my family, about my parents, about *me* . . . All that will take more than a few minutes. I want him to send those people away. "Do they have-have-have to stay?" I ask.

He offers a sad smile and apologetic eyes. "It's pretty important. They flew in this morning from—" Something must be happening to my face, because he flushes and says, "But I'm not rushing you. Talk to me, Mick. Take as long as you need."

Out in the living room, someone is laughing. A woman's donkey bray. Out in the living room, someone is shaking a cocktail, martinis, or old-fashioneds. Out there in the living room, laissez les bon temps rouler.

I gaze at Christopher, at his perfect hair and soft blue eyes. He's wearing the white Aran sweater I bought him for his birthday. Its cable stitch depicts fishermen's ropes, symbolizing a bountiful day at sea.

He sneaks a peek at his Apple Watch.

His impatience smacks me hard, and I want to vomit.

Mom and Dad are right: I *am* the fucking flower. Time should stand still for me.

"What's going on?" he asks.

I push him away and stand. "Never mind."

"Mickie, come on. You can't be mad at me." He folds his arms. "It's not like we're even together like that."

"But I'm a *human*, Christopher. If you can't show me basic courtesy without an expiration date, then . . ."

"Here we go." He lets his head fall back.

"*You've* been texting *me*, Christopher," I shout. "Every single message, you tell me how you love me, how you miss me, how you miss us."

"Calm. Down."

"You came to my best friend's wedding." I jab his chest with my finger. "You were in my bed two weeks ago. *You* calm the fuck down."

He drops his head. "Mickie, I . . . It's complicated."

I hold up both hands and toss my crumpled, snotty tissue in his face. "You know what? Fuck you. I don't love you."

He pales, and says, "You're upset about something, and I don't know what it is, but you're upset and you're saying things that you don't mean." His eyes become as shiny as the sea.

"No? I don't?" My brain scrambles to make sense of what's happening. My legs are forced to do the most pressing thing—get me out of there. I throw open the bedroom door, and it bangs against the wall. I charge down the hallway to the front door.

A woman shouts, "Hey, Mickie. Everything—"

Christopher follows me to the elevator and rides down with me. He follows me to my car and doesn't speak as I slam into the driver's seat. He doesn't wave as I squeal onto Wilshire Boulevard. He doesn't do anything he *should* do because he doesn't love me, either.

42.

My drive through the stormy streets takes less time. My hands are tight around the steering wheel again, but my driving is more certain in heavy rain. I keep my eyes fixed on the reflective strips on the road ahead of me, peeking at my phone only during stops at red lights.

Christopher keeps texting me.

Please come back

I don't know what you want from me

You know how I feel about you

He calls.

I answer. "What?"

He says, "Mick—"

I press "End" and toss my phone on the passenger seat. His words, his voice—all of it makes me sick. They stink up my car, and I roll down all four windows for fresh, wet air.

I turn right onto my street. The black sky is lit up around my family home. After the long drive in the rain, it is now my harbor. Before climbing out of the car, I read one last text message from Christopher.

Let me know if you can finish the memory bank

No, he doesn't love me.

True love is waiting in my apartment.

Mom has changed the sheets on my bed, and she's opened a bottle of our favorite red wine and popped popcorn. I can see butter glistening on kernels from where I stand.

I shower, scrubbing hard even though all of me, inside and out, feels brittle. Mom has brought me one of her fluffiest towels and creamiest lavender lotions. Clean and scented, I trudge back to the living room.

Mom, sitting on my couch, waits for me. "Wanna talk?"

I'm wearing her Prince sweatshirt and ancient Lululemon leggings. She's wearing my Dwight Schrute *Office* hoodie and track pants, both of which I thought I'd left at that condo on Miracle Mile.

I grab one of the wineglasses, then sit beside her. "No, I don't." I take a sip, and the wine warms my throat. "Not right now." I grab the remote control from the coffee table.

She watches as I scroll through Hulu's menu to find *The Golden Girls*. She plucks the second wineglass from the table and takes a long gulp.

There's a small cocoa-colored birthmark on the white of her right middle finger. I have the same mole on the same finger. Together, we eat popcorn and watch Dorothy, Rose, and Blanche compete against each other in a dance marathon.

I lay my head on her shoulder.

She strokes my hair.

Her love is like a cashmere blanket. Her love is like this wine. Her love is like the sun.

She is my mother.

"There's this guy," I say, now that the wine has untangled my nerves.

She says, "Umhmm."

"His name is Dexter, and this memory bank I'm working on? It was for his mother."

"The store owner who died?"

"Yeah. I really like him . . ."

"But?"

"But I'm not sure if he's . . . good. I'm not sure if he's . . . safe."

"Not sure he's safe because he's dangerous? Not sure he's safe because someone wants to harm him or because he wants to harm you?"

I look up at her. "I don't know. My judgment . . . It's broken right now. I see murderers and dead people everywhere."

She's the one who taught me that saying "my bad" and "I'm sorry" defuses a sticky situation, that *Living Single* came before *Friends*, that cheap shoes will give you bunions, and that wine spritzers are the devil's folly.

And now she says, "You've known him for, what, three weeks? Which means that you *don't* know him or what he considers normal. He grew up around other people's things, had a mother who traveled the country digging through boxes in strangers' front yards. And *you*?"

She pokes my nose and forehead with her finger. "You've been kept in a safe environment for twenty-two years, and you've never lived more than ten miles away. Your upbringing has also been weird. Which means that anything unlike that can seem dangerous."

"So what do I do?"

"Pay attention. If you see something off, take it at face value and don't try to explain it away. You have a gut—I know you do cuz I helped build it. You were right about that Buick, so your gut still works. You knew something had been bothering me, that I wasn't being open and truthful with you. So, again, your gut works. Listen to it. If it's saying, 'Dude is shady'? Then dude is shady."

We polish off the bottle of wine and the bowl of popcorn.

"Michael Anthony," I say. "Should I be scared?"

"You should *always* be cautious. We got you that Taser—carry it. If you want a gun, Dad and Uncle Bryan can help you get a concealed carry license. We took out a restraining order against him, but a maniac that gives zero fucks about the law ain't gonna heed no restraining order. And you can always stay with Dad and me in the front for a while. It's up to you."

She holds the bottle up to the light. Still empty. "As for Christopher. He may be fine as hell, but he was a shitty boyfriend. I never liked his ass."

I cackle. "You're extreme."

"Did he ever write you a bad poem?"

I make a face. "No."

"Did he ever mess up his hair or his shoes to get something you dropped in the trash or in a fountain?"

I shake my head.

"He ever bring you a cool towel while you're sick and on the toilet?"

"Oh no, never. But then I wouldn't *want* him to see me—"

"Being human?" She smirks. "Be wary of a man who you don't want bringing you a cool towel when you're about to pass out from explosive diarrhea."

Her observations peck at me, and I understand her point. "Yeah."

She kisses my forehead and stands.

I take her hand, and the electricity from her touch settles me. "Can you sleep back here with me?"

She smiles, musses my already-mussed hair. "Of course. I'll go get my supplies."

The house gun, the hunting knife she keeps beneath the mattress, and her charger.

Because she—*my mother*—will face down the devil to protect me.

And tonight, I need that kind of comfort.

OUTLOOK
NOT SO GOOD

43.

It is Sunday and the sun shines high and bright, and after three days of ignoring most of the world, I almost feel normal again. The frizzy quivering is gone. The achy uncertainty is also gone. All I needed was sleep, home-cooked meals, clean hair, and time—with my parents, with my television, with myself. I didn't see Christopher when he stopped by on Thursday with a new computer. Nor have I opened the envelope he left for me with Mom.

"He begged me to beg you," she told me afterward.

"And you said?" I asked.

"That I wouldn't because he treated you like a secondhand, refurbished iPod." She cocked her head. "I started to say 'purse,' but he wouldn't have understood. Anyway, he denied that, of course, and so I asked him how many times my daughter had shown up at his parents' house, because I've lost count how many times he's come here."

"None," I said. "I've never met them."

"He didn't answer the question," Mom said. "He didn't have to."

"And then?"

"He apologized and professed his love for you again."

Mom and I both howled, rolled our eyes, and then crunched into our tacos.

This morning I opened Christopher's letter and immediately saw the words "love" and "forgive." Without reading it in its entirety, I held that letter over the lit front burner of my stove. Nothing he says to me—except *you're fired*—matters to me now.

This weekend, my parents also showed me the stay-away order forbidding Michael Anthony to come within three hundred feet of them or me. No contact—no calling, texting, emailing, or stalking. Violating these orders would be a felony.

Am I still scared that Michael Anthony may pop up at any second, a Negro Rumpelstiltskin aiming to finish the job of killing me? Yes, I am. But now I am armed—with weapons, with Mom and Dad, with the whole armor of God.

The sound of rain tapping the leaves and pitter-pattering on my roof was hypnotic during my time away, and the downpour drowned out the beeps and rumbles from my cell phone. And that's why I kept my phone turned off . . .

Until now.

Text messages fill my screen.

Sasha: I's married now and back in LA

Imani: Flew back from Miami and boy are my arms tired

Christopher: Hey

Now I am ready to meet the world again. Dressed in Mom's buttery-soft jeans and fuzzy pink sweater, I leave my apartment, ready to work, ready to apologize to Riley for not showing up at her neighbor's house on Saturday morning for that memory-bank consult. Ready to boot up a new laptop with an improved CMS.

Out in the back, the fencing company eases one post into a cup now cemented in the trench. Jerry tosses me a wave, and shouts, "We're getting there!"

I give him a thumbs-up. Not his fault that LA is being deluged with strange wet stuff from the sky.

The main house is quiet. I don't smell veggie breakfast patties, coffee, or laundry detergent. My parents don't sleep in, and I figure that they went for a walk in the park behind the house. But I'm not alone. Uncle Bryan walks up the driveway. He carries a box that contains manila envelopes and a big blue binder. He hasn't slept—bloodshot, baggy eyes, and stubble on his cheeks and chin.

I try to hug him. "Thank you for *everything*. I mean it."

He shifts the box and uses one arm to hug me. "No one wanted *any* of this to happen."

I give a one-shouldered shrug. "I lucked out. I know that. Some kids get dumped into foster care, but I lived with wonderful people who gave me a wonderful life, who do absolutely everything they can for me. And I also have an uncle who's been my personal bodyguard since Eva Sutter pushed me off those monkey bars back in second grade. So . . . thank you."

He hands me the box. "Winchester and I went through the academy together. After graduation, he went to Southwest Division, and I went to Pacific. He told me that you wanted to read case files."

I run my hand over the envelopes. The heat of my past warms my fingers. "I was looking and couldn't find anything. It's like she was never here."

"And I have something else." He shows me a sheet of paper filled with bars and graphs.

"How the Egyptians built the pyramids?"

"Close. DNA test results. The blood on the dagger comes from two different people."

My eyebrows lift. "Does either set belong to Nadia?"

"We don't know much of anything yet. They're still analyzing. Winchester knows, and he's interested. That's why these tests happened so quickly."

"If the DNA isn't Nadia's," I say, "then that means it can't be Dexter's, either. Right? Because he and his mother share mitochondrial DNA."

"And you know about mitochondrial DNA because . . . ?"

"Mom and I watch a lot of *Forensic Files*. New season starts in February."

"You should probably back off of this, whatever this is."

"'Whatever this is' comes with the job. I'm not Scooby-Dooby-Dooing. I was hired to tell a story, one gigabyte at a time."

That's a lie, though. Nadia didn't select the knife to feature in her memory bank. But I'd needed to find those damned crocheted baby shoes and hat. The rest is history.

I carry the box filled with my violent history back to my apartment, and I set it on my sunlit coffee table. Anxious, I close my eyes and tuck my hands beneath my damp armpits. Why am I now reluctant? The answers are right here, waiting for me in reports, summaries, and pictures. But I can't move. I don't want to know. Not right now.

As I drive to the Santa Barbara Plaza, I wonder about those DNA results because it's easier to think about someone else's life than my own. What if the blood on that knife isn't Nadia's? What if that isn't her DNA? Then whose is it? And are they still alive?

Dexter is pacing in front of Anna's Place. We haven't seen each other since the night I found out that I was adopted. That was the night I also followed him to the insurance agency in Marina del Rey. Here we are, four days later, standing six feet apart, not moving to hug or kiss each other. Is he wearing his locket and chain? Does he have fresh scratches from Anna's fingernails? We're both uneasy, the space between us no longer intoxicating. It's toxic.

I turn on the digital recorder hidden in my coat pocket.

He says, "Hey, stranger," like a dental hygienist who hasn't seen me in a year.

Like a patient who doesn't care about tartar buildup, I say, "How's it been?"

"A lot's going on, and I need to talk to you about it." He opens the door to the diner.

My stomach growls, and even the food that I'd never eat—like Kangol Man's sunny-side-up eggs or Third Ex-Wife's mound of cottage cheese—looks delicious. Anna's Place sparkles today. The grill, the counter, the jukebox . . . The syrup in the pourers looks like liquid gold.

Dexter and I settle in a booth far from the regulars. Anna doesn't speak as she sets cups of coffee down on the table. Her stitches are losing their bruise-purple swelling, and the whites of her eyes are white again. She says, "For you, Mickie. I baked these earlier." She leaves behind a small plate of corn muffins, then stalks back behind the counter to tend to her bacon and eggs.

"She's mad at me," Dexter says.

Because she, too, thinks you jumped her? I don't say that. No, I say instead: "Because she saw you talking and laughing with Weller's guys, too? Oh yeah. I saw you doing that last week. Not a good look, especially when people are feeling threatened." I dump sugar and cream into my coffee, then stir.

He sucks his teeth. "It's not what everybody thinks—"

"It's none of my business," I say, then sip from my mug. I don't see his chain. Where is it? Anna's little baggie—that's where it is.

He settles his chin in his hand. "I don't even know where to begin."

"Did you really have meetings with CNN? Let's start there."

He glares at me. "You calling me a liar?"

"I'm asking a—"

My phone buzzes from the table.

Christopher is texting.

Did you read my letter??

Please call me

Your mother wouldn't tell me what's happened

You can't come here all broken up and leave without telling me shit!!

Michaela!

MICKIE

"Do you need to take that?" Dexter snarks.

I turn the phone face-down and sit back in the booth.

"Yes, I had a meeting with CNN *and* Condé Nast. The hell kinda question is that?" He blows out air, then leans forward with his arms on the table. "Last time we saw each other, you were a wreck. You'd just—"

"Learned my family's big secret, yes."

"But something stuck with me. You'd said that you'd always felt like you *belonged*. You looked like your mom. You acted like your dad. There were no real clues that you weren't biologically their child."

"And now that I've moved past being angry, I still feel that way," I say.

His eyes darken, and he slouches in the booth.

"What's wrong?"

Before he can answer, the yellow-haired white man who has been lurking around the plaza knocks on the window beside our booth.

I gasp and say, "That's him."

Dexter holds up a single finger and says to the man through the glass, "One minute."

The man nods at Dexter and winks at me.

My face twitches. That frizzy quivering raises it head, ready to pace near my pancreas again. "So you *are* working with Weller."

"What?"

"We think he's the one who jumped Anna."

"No, c'mon. Let me explain." Dexter reaches for me, his hands hard and freezing cold. "Remember when you asked if I wanted to find my father? I told you no. That wasn't true. Unlike you, I've never really felt *settled* as a kid. Yes, there was the obvious race thing—my mother was white, which meant my father was Black. But there were times Nadia would say things . . ." He stares into his cup of coffee.

My nerves stretch like tightropes. I'm scared of what he's about to tell me.

"I'd wanted to do a DNA test, but something more than, 'You are three percent Native American.' So I hired Vince Rader's firm to find out. And about a month ago, I stole Mom's toothbrush, and while she was sleeping, I ran a cotton swab to catch spit dripping from her mouth."

"I get that. I don't get why that man out there is following me."

"He works for Vince Rader, the investigator I hired."

"And why is he following me?"

"Because I thought that maybe you had something to do with my mother's death. Or that *you* were working for Weller."

"What?" The accusations push me against the booth, and shock explodes like tiny bombs around my head and heart.

"I thought the idea of a digital scrapbook with holograms and projections was preposterous," Dexter says, "and that a girl like you wouldn't be doing a thing like that."

"A girl like . . . And now you think . . . ?"

He doesn't blink as he says, "Part of me *still* doesn't believe it."

Neither of us speaks for a very long time. Diners come and go as we sit. Anna moves from the tables to the counter, pot of coffee in her hand. She doesn't stop to top us off.

"I'm a digital archaeologist with the Memory Bank," I finally say. "Believe it or not." Then, I pluck a corn muffin from the plate and slather butter on it. "Good to know that you still don't believe me. It's mutual, you know. Part of me thinks you're a liar and that you're trying to get over on me. Are you? Now's the time to live your truth."

His nostrils flare, and that vein in his forehead stands out against his skin. "Who I am or what I'm doing is none of your business. You can tell Detective Winchester I said that. Just like you told him about my bankruptcy, my mother's insurance policies, and everything else."

His words are fiery coals thrown in my face. "He asked me," I say, "and I told him. I don't lie to the cops for any-old-body."

"Oh, so I'm any-old-body now?"

I cock my head. "I don't lie to cops."

"How noble." An amused sneer twists across Dexter's lips. He stands but bends over so that we are face-to-face. "It was hot while it lasted, Miss Lambert. But we're done."

His gold chain and locket swing like a hypnotist's watch from around his neck.

Artifact 12: Gold-plated heart locket on a gold chain. Acquired on December 3, 1992.

Location of Acquisition: Hartford, Connecticut. At almost four hundred years old, Hartford is one of the nation's oldest cities. In addition to having a strong literary pedigree—Mark Twain and Harriet Beecher Stowe both wrote classics here—Hartford is also home to the Colt revolver, invented by Hartford resident Samuel Colt. With a violent past, the north end of Hartford was the location where 160 people died at a matinee performance of the Ringling Brothers circus.

Last Owner: Patricia Kirby.

Memory: Patricia was just twenty years old when you met. Already an old soul, Patricia was a single mother from the conservative Hartford suburb of Middletown. Disowned by her family for her pregnancy and deserted by the child's father, Patricia proudly loved her baby.

She told you that she'd graduated from high school and couldn't find a decent-paying job outside of waitressing. The little money she earned went to the feeding and care of her infant, Joshua. This meant that her apartment in the three-story brick building on Albany Avenue was located in one of the worst parts of the city.

You were brought up to fend for yourself, and that meant knowing how to use a hammer and wrench. You lived next door to Patricia and baby Joshua and would always hear the infant crying through the unit's thin walls. You visited the little family a few times, carrying up mail or bringing over pans of leftover lasagna or pots of chicken soup.

Grateful for your kindness, Patricia would always say, "You don't have to do this."

You'd say, "I just wanna keep you and Josh healthy. It's gonna be a long winter."

Over the next few weeks, you made small repairs in Patricia's unit, from the leaking shower pan to replacing insulation around the windows. You even watched over Joshua a few times when Patricia needed to work a night shift.

"Sometimes," Patricia said once, "I think Josh likes you more than he likes me."

One evening you went over to the apartment to fix the leak in the young mother's kitchen sink. You knocked but no one answered. The door was unlocked. You stepped in. The single closet was clear. Joshua's things were also gone. The only item left was this locket on the kitchen counter.

You later learned that Patricia had moved out of town to live with her high school friend Norma.

44.

I remain in the booth and watch as Dexter marches to the parking lot. He throws a wave at the construction crew and then disappears around the corner. Over at the counter, Anna smiles at her customers, but her eyes are as flat as a doll's. The cops haven't found her mugger yet. She doesn't sway as Sam Cooke sings about the boardwalk; nor does she laugh at Kangol Man's bawdy joke about the zombie hooker. Being mugged has changed her, and I hope that the Anna who fired Dr Pepper at me weeks ago is simply vacationing for the moment. This version is too quiet.

Back at the store, Riley sits at the register and sorts through tarnished hatpins and pince-nez spectacles.

I say, "Good morning."

She says, "Hey," but doesn't look up from her job.

"Sorry for not being around," I say. "Family stuff. I had a semi-nervous breakdown back on Wednesday night." I try to chuckle, but it comes out strangled. I clear my throat to add, "I should've let you know. My bad."

"No problemo." She blinks up at me. "You look better."

"I feel better. Let's reschedule the appointment with your neighbor. Again, apologies."

She shrugs. "Whatever."

I settle myself back in Nadia's office. At least nothing has changed here. I pull out my recorder and listen to the taped conversation with Dexter. The earlier part of our chat is soft, filled with murmurs, but as we move closer to the finale, our voice levels increase, and we sound more like angry neighbors than onetime lovers. I hear in my tone the moment when the light I felt for him dies. And now that I've moved past being angry . . . It sounds like a twig snapping beneath my boot.

Nights ago, Mom told me to listen to my gut, and my gut tells me to stay away from Dexter Denham. We won't need to interact until I complete Nadia's memory bank. Even then, Christopher could handle those final transactions, like handing over the device and walking him through the commands.

The store is too quiet right now. There are the usual sounds—the doorbell tinkling, Riley dry-coughing, the stool scraping against the floor. But . . .

This new laptop works. I'm making good progress on uploading pictures of the locket. My eyes crunch and burn from dust and exhaustion. There's only one text—Sasha inviting Imani and me over for drinks and to open wedding gifts.

I'm so far from that life of china sets and thank-you notes. Thought I'd be the next bride, meeting Christopher at the end of a long aisle somewhere in Descanso Gardens. We'd take field trips each month. We'd lounge in bed, fingers entwined, telling each other stories. But we ended. And just days ago, I thought that maybe there'd be something with . . .

Did I betray Dexter?

Should he be mad at me?

Should I be pissed at Detective Winchester?

Or am I wrong about everything?

Am I the asshole?

The office door bangs open. Riley stands there, her face contorted and lips curled in anger. She charges into the office and snarls, "Get out."

I hop out of the chair because she is stomping toward me. "What's—"

"You need to leave." Her hands are now fists, and spit gathers at the corners of her mouth. "How *dare* you."

Cold sweat breaks over me. Is she about to hit . . . ?

"Riley, what are you talking about?"

She's so angry she's turned purple. "Dexter told me *everything*. About you looking into Nadia's past. About you telling Detective Winchester—"

I hold out my hands as I back away from her. "I haven't done anything."

"Nadia was a good person!" she screams. "And how dare you insinuate that she—"

"I didn't mean—"

"She was good to me. She was good to Dexter, and you talk to the police—"

"Calm down." Dull buzzing fills my ears.

"Poking and snooping around the shop? That knife could've been anybody's—"

"You *knew* I was looking for the baby shoes and hat. I told you. And that Elvis guy—no, the coin collector—was here and you didn't have time to help me look."

"Get your shit and *leave*," she says.

"Nadia hired me—"

"She's dead, and now Dexter's firing you. He doesn't wanna see you in here ever again."

"Let me call Dexter—"

"Get out *now*," Riley growls.

My face burns, and my stomach fills with large black flies. I'm scared and embarrassed even though only Riley is here in the office. I blink—can't see—and I blindly grab at things that should belong to me. Maybe my bag? Perhaps this jacket?

Riley closes in, ready to frog-march me out of Beautiful Things.

I'm quicker, and I rush out of the office, passing the King's collections, the jukeboxes and stuffed ravens, passing the table of old journals and buckets of tangled belts, and jamming out the front door with the bell jangling violently above me and out into fresh, cool air that smells of bacon and cigarette smoke.

Riley turns the lock on the door and flips the **OPEN** sign to **CLOSED**. From his key shop window, Mr. Kim watches me but doesn't leave his store.

I stand alone in the breezeway, trying to understand . . . The men standing near the construction equipment watch as I stumble toward my car. Over at the RVs, no one cares. A patrol car is parked near the mini-Winnie, and a uniformed cop is questioning the man with dreadlocks. Another patrol unit inches into the parking lot to join the call.

Back in my car, I close my eyes and try to catch my breath. My mouth tastes like blood—I bit my lip and my tongue. In my haste to leave the store, I grabbed my new laptop computer, but I forgot the power cord. And I grabbed my bag, but this piece of cloth is not my jacket. It's the little blanket I brought in last week because it was so cold.

That last scene with Riley. I can't understand . . . I don't understand . . .

My hands tremble as I text Dexter.

Riley just kicked me out!

Are you firing me??

The heat of the closed car swells around me, and my blood pressure ticks higher . . . higher . . . as I sit there, waiting . . . waiting . . .

Ellipses appear in the text screen—Dexter is responding.

More ellipses . . . more ellipses and then . . .

. . .

Nothing.

45.

It's a misunderstanding. They're overreacting. This will all work itself out. As I pace from one side of my living room to the other, I keep telling myself this. And I want to explain to Dexter, and I try to call him, but he won't answer.

Prickly from all my wandering and worrying, I open the windows. The breeze carries the voices of people walking the trails in the park. Someone is having a party in the picnic area, because I hear faint Stevie Wonder singing his version of the birthday song. Everyone is out, but I'm here alone. I can call people, but I don't wanna feel their noise against my skin.

I should be working.

Noon approaches, and the sun's light fills the room and falls on the box that Uncle Bryan gave me just hours ago. I wanted to know everything, and now that I *can*, I don't *want* to. I want to go back in time. But I can't even do that.

It's too early for wine, but it is Sunday, which means that I can enjoy a Bloody Mary or a mimosa. Mom isn't here, though, to make a Bloody Mary or a mimosa. I have no champagne, but I have Bailey's and whiskey, so Irish coffee along with *The Bachelor*.

Because this is all a misunderstanding—they're overreacting, and it will work itself out.

As I drink my spiked coffee, I mourn for the naive Mickie, the Mickie before she took the red pill, the Mickie before she peeked behind the wizard's curtain. Throughout her quiet life, she believed that true love was just a day away, and that her job was a meaningful and creative vessel to bring people joy. She'd pursue a steady life like her parents'.

I now know blood, violence, and murder are my very beginnings. My life has bounced between good men and evil men, knights and hoods. I now know that I've been protected by a determined queen who hasn't had a decent night's sleep since Michael Anthony met her sister . . .

. . .

I hear myself cry out. My eyes pop open—I'm looking at . . . I'd been dreaming of . . .

My phone is ringing. That's what awakened . . .

Aunt Angie. I was dreaming of her. She was covered in cobwebs while she, Imani, and I roamed the aisles of Sephora. We carried goblets in our hands.

My phone is still ringing, and I grab it from the coffee table. My belly alley-oops and my head spins.

"Hey." It's Uncle Bryan. "You sound . . ."

"I been sleeping, I been drinking." Drunk but not in love.

My apartment has slipped into complete darkness. The fencing guys are gone—I no longer hear their murmurs, the thump of their sledgehammers, or the whir of their drills. In the quiet, my secret tenant has returned and now scratches at the walls. For a minute, I'm dizzy and can't remember . . . Pain pops in my mouth. Oh. Yeah. Kicked out of Beautiful Things. Bit my tongue and lip as Riley chased me out of the store.

I roll onto my side and turn on the lamp beside the couch.

There's power, not a blackout.

Uncle Bryan is talking, but I'm not listening.

No house or Christmas lights shine at my parents' house. No familiar background noises—no pots banging in the kitchen, no dramatic video game music from the den, no piano.

Where *are* they?

I look at my phone's screen even as my uncle jabbers on about . . . who knows. Messages: Imani, Sasha, Christopher, Dexter . . . Mom and Dad. They've called and texted—

"Are you listening to me?" Uncle Bryan snaps.

Progress on the fence: All panels except for two now stand. Only a horde of zombies instead of a swarm can invade our property.

"No, I'm not listening," I admit as I run my tender tongue over my teeth. "You talk to my parents today?"

"Yeah," he says, "they're trying to strengthen the order against Michael Anthony. They've been in rooms with lawyers all day—"

"Why aren't you there?" I pop down the stairs to make sure the front door is locked.

"I was, but I wanted to call you about the knife."

The security system glows red—I'd armed it as 'Stay'—but the front door isn't locked. The knob wobbles freely in my hand.

My ears burn as I wonder, *What if . . . ?* My breathing catches as I think about going to my parents' house and turning on the lights, but then I think about every scary movie I've ever seen. I'm not that brave or that stupid.

"Hey, Uncle Bryan," I say now. "The lights are off in the front, and the house is still open back here since dude hasn't finished putting up the fence. I'm not ashamed to say that I'm freaked out right now and don't wanna go up there and turn them on."

He will send a patrol car over—Candace and Demetrius. I've met them before at Christmas parties. They'll watch as I make the house bright again, and they will check out the areas around the fence. "Sonny didn't think they'd be away all day," my uncle says. "Anyway, I need to get back to them, so grab a pen."

I grab a pen, but I also grab my Taser from the bedroom. I glance out the window, and in the dusky parkland, I see the ghost glows of cell phones, and I hear the whispers of people talking. No faces, no bodies, just phone light and fog. And flying things swooping in that fog, and those swooping things are too quick to be birds.

"Those DNA hits on the blood from the knife. One name came up in CODIS. Winchester thought that maybe you've seen this . . ." He spells the name.

I stare at what I've written. "Norma Diefenbacher."

"She's in the system for a bunch of petty crimes—burglary, passing bad checks, a couple of DUIs. The DUI was in New Orleans, and that's the one that landed her and her DNA in the database. Have you seen that name in the shop?"

"No, but right now, I'm a little fuzzy-headed. What about the second DNA profile?"

"Nothing yet. Can you look around the shop? Maybe—"

"No, I can't. I've been kicked out." Those words are burs that tear my throat.

"What happened?"

I tell him about Dexter's and Riley's anger at me for snooping around, for talking to Winchester about the knife and about Dexter's financial problems. I rub my face, tired from just *thinking* about Beautiful Things. "I wasn't being nosy, but I'm not supposed to really dig into people's lives, and I did, and now here I am." My shoulders droop. "It's just that . . . writing good stuff requires context, and so I searched on Nadia and found . . . nothing. Not really."

"And finding nothing is strange to you?"

"Nothing is very strange to me. Are Candy and Dee on their way?"

"Should be there in a minute. I love you, kiddo."

"I love you, too, Uncle Bryan. And the security . . . Is that for me?"

He pauses, then says, "It's for you and for your parents." He pauses again, then adds, "Norma Diefenbacher, just in case Dexter forgives you."

Only one other house nearby has lit windows. Did I miss the memo? Has the entire block—except these shadows in the park—been raptured? I back away from the window and return to the coffee table. *Norma Diefenbacher.* Yes, I've seen that name, and now that mystery drifts like a single length of spiderweb . . . *Where . . . ?*

I close my eyes and . . .

Person of Interest Norma Diefenbacher Questioned in the "Dashing Devil" Murders. . .

"Websleuths," I say now, leaving a message on Uncle Bryan's voice mail. "In a forum thread. Call me." My heart races. Why is Norma Diefenbacher's blood on a knife inside a box at Beautiful Things?

Because Norma Diefenbacher, questioned so long ago, could be related to the Dashing Devil. And Norma—

Ohmigod.

Artifact 12, the heart locket.

Patricia Kirby, who left Hartford to live with her high school friend Norma.

As I wait for Uncle Bryan to return my call, I set my hand on the box of case files he gave me. The newest document—back in September—sits on top. It's a transcript from a probation hearing for Michael Anthony.

> *. . . and I went temporarily insane . . . crime of passion . . . What were you doing with your life at the time of the crime? . . . Got my AA . . . disciplinary records show creating a disturbance and continued affiliation with the Crips . . . will participate in anti-aggression/anti-violence counseling . . . I'm sorry all that happened.*

There is a recent picture of my biological father. Fair skin, sandy-brown hair . . .

Those eyes.

Green-blue eyes. Weird eyes for a Black man.

I know those eyes. I've *seen* those eyes . . .

The coffee shop—he stood behind me in line. *What do you tell 'em when you just want coffee?*

That's what he asked me.

I killed that bitch!

That's what he shouted.

He wasn't being delusional. He was being honest. He *did* kill my mother.

He killed Angie Craig, and he knows who I am.

46.

I don't see myself in this man. Not in his eyes, not in the curl of his lips, not in his violent anger. And because I don't see myself in him, nothing rang from inside me during our coffee-shop encounter. Because I am not this man's daughter. Maybe biologically. I am not in ways that matter most.

Does that make him angry?

Who does he hate more? Mom because she resembles Angie and because she's always fought against him? Or Dad because he's the man who raised me, the man I've called "Daddy" all my life? Or does he hate me the most because I'm a reminder of everything that's gone wrong in his?

No matter—he's back. And he's scarring me again.

Hard to believe that Michael Anthony stood less than a foot away from me. He could've followed me out of the coffee shop, and he could've . . .

Don't wanna think about that.

He could be out there right now, watching me from behind the wheel of that Buick. He could be at my door, listening to my panting and heavy thinking, delighting in my fear. I don't wanna think about this because the more I think about the monster, the more I must acknowledge the mess around me. Feels like iron weights pressing down on my shoulders, and it's hard to move, even harder to breathe. What I'd give for one clean, easy breath.

Where are the cops?

I need the lights on in my parents' house.

I need to eat and drink something other than Nutter Butters and Irish coffee. There are only lattes, wilting salad mix, and dying strawberries in my refrigerator. My parents have sandwich meats and tangerines, leftovers in plastic containers, and two types of mustard. There's bread, cheese and wine, salty snacks, and sweet treats. Wasabi-flavored *and* honey-roasted almonds. I need all this but with lights burning bright around me.

I turn off the television. I need to hear. I creep toward the staircase and look down to see that the chain isn't on, but the lock above the doorknob is vertical. *Locked.* But that chain . . .

I place my foot on the first step and then the next . . . the next . . . down, down . . . This step creaks . . . This step creaks, too . . . It's colder the closer I get to the door. I hold my breath as my fingers clunk around the chain, as I try again and again to slip that bolt into its slot, as cold air slips from beneath the door and licks my ankles.

The chain is on.

Shaking, I jam up the stairs. I've never been so scared.

As I pace the living room, I gnaw the cuticle around my thumb. Fear comes like pirouettes, dizzying, spinning fast. Something lurks out there—a monster shaped like a man. I want to peek out the windows and yell, "Go away; please leave me alone," but I don't speak monster. And door chains never keep monsters out.

The sycamores that have forever protected our home . . . I don't trust these trees anymore. Their branches are too strong, too sturdy. The monster could be perched on a bough now.

Fighting hysterics, I keep moving . . . keep moving . . . I hear the low voices of people talking. But my television is off.

Am I imagining voices? Are there men in the part of the park closest to our property? Neighbors? Someone is out there. They've shambled through those spaces no longer guarded by a fence, and they prowl in search of . . . in search of . . .

I wanna look out my living room window. I wanna look out my kitchen window.

Yes, I hear talking.

Effing fence guys. Freaking rain.

My phone vibrates in my hand, and I yelp, caught off guard.

Outside, the night turns bright white.

I gasp again and fumble with the device. My phone keeps ringing. I don't stoop to pick it up from the floor but choose to simply watch it ring—UNKNOWN CALLER. I wait . . . and I wait . . . until it stops ringing.

"Michaela," a woman shouts outside my window. "It's Officer Swanson. We're here."

I peek past my curtains and out into the lit-up night to see Officer Swanson. She's Black and lanky with sunken eyes. Her partner is also Black, also lanky, also sunken eyed. Like an old married couple, they're starting to resemble each other.

Relieved, I pop down the same stairs that just terrified me to meet the cops at the garage. Cool air smacks my face and snaps my spine. I need that hardness.

Minutes later, Christmas lights blink from the eaves of the front house, and the electrical grid wobbles because I've flipped every switch available. In the light, nothing looks out of the ordinary—no toppled-over pictures or vases of dried flowers. Those shadows against the walls have always been here. That hum, it's just the refrigerator.

My phone vibrates from my pocket.

Meet me tomorrow night at the store

A text from Dexter!

We need to talk

I type OK even though none of this is okay, even though I'm not sure that I want to hear from him. My gut tells me . . . nothing right now. No—it tells me to let someone know that I'm going to meet him. *Because you are gonna go.* My gut knows me.

While the cops check our property and the beginnings of the park space at our backyard, I make two roast beef sandwiches with two types of mustard. I will also take the bag of potato chips, the package of cookies, and two cans of Diet Coke back to my apartment because I am a raccoon ready to fill herself with trash.

Officer Swanson tells me that they'll hang out in the front for a while, and they watch as I carry my food back up to my apartment.

Mom texts. **On our way home**

I text back. **You didn't leave the lights on and I worried! When is Jerry finishing??!!** I want to tell her that Michael Anthony found me days ago at the coffee shop—a shiver runs up my spine as I remember that encounter.

No, I won't put all this into a text message. I will tell her in person.

I shove chips into my mouth and wince. The cuts on my tongue and lip sting from the salt. I close my eyes and wait until the pain ends. Because eventually the pain *will* end. I grab my dying laptop from the coffee table. The power cord sits in an outlet at Beautiful Things.

With my belly full, my fear feels silly now. Iron from the roast beef fortifies my blood, and I can think straight.

Norma Diefenbacher: Who is she?

The first search engine result is a hyperlink to the website Riley visited. According to Websleuths, Norma Diefenbacher was born August 12, 1940. A domestic worker and handywoman, she often took jobs in economically depressed neighborhoods. Even though she worked as a cleaning woman, she took pride in her attire—wearing slim-fit pants and turtlenecks one day and paisley swirls and hippie dresses the next. She was thought to have killed at least ten women across the continental United States. After she was linked to the death of a young mother and child in Syracuse, New York, in 1978, witnesses mentioned how dashing she looked in her cranberry-colored fedora. Thereafter, police called her "the Dashing Devil."

DD.

The Dashing Devil is a woman?

There are two mug shots. The black-and-white photo shows a woman with piercing light-colored eyes and thick, wavy hair sprayed in place. The color picture shows a middle-aged redhead with those same sharp eyes but saggy jowls and shaggy hair. There's a picture of a tattoo on her hand: a heart with a pair of dice and the words "Good Luck."

A *woman* is crossing the country to kill other *women*?

Yes, female serial killers exist. Aileen Wuornos, Belle Gunness, and . . . A quick search on the internet gives me Juana Barraza, Jane Toppan, and Nannie Doss. From rat poison to arsenic, starvation to suffocation. Killing husbands, patients, children, old people.

The patrol car's light brightens my windows again. Did Officer Swanson and Officer Hayes see something out there or . . . ?

My hands hover above the keyboard as that light tracks across the curtains.

Is Michael Anthony here?

Has he found me?

The light comes back the other way now. It holds right where my door would be, and then it bobs . . . bobs . . . in that space.

I wait for something to happen—a gunshot, a man screaming, a wiggle of my doorknob.

The light blinks off.

Tires crunch against the pavement. The engine growls. These sounds grow faint . . . faint . . . until there's silence.

Nothing happens.

No one is coming for me.

I exhale and click another link.

Norma Diefenbacher—she's also wanted in the murder of . . .

The young woman in the picture has blonde hair and blue eyes. She's nineteen-year-old Bonnie Hargreaves. Last seen alive in April 1993 at the Thunderbird Mobile Homes in Fresno, California, while selling magazine subscriptions door-to-door.

Bonnie . . . the original owner of artifact number six—the teakwood hedgehog key chain. *DESTINY.*

That tattoo . . . *Good Luck.*

I've seen a tattoo like that before. I remember like it was yesterday, even though it was almost a month ago, when I first met Nadia Denham.

Wait . . .

The death of a young mother and child in Syracuse?

Did that child ever own a felt mouse that wore a gold tin crown?

47.

Renee Spiro and Christina Spiro found after snowmelt in a steel barrel on May 7, 1978.

Steffanie Minsky discovered in a burned-out VW Bug on December 12, 1970.

Katrinka McLaren's skeletal remains unearthed in Carson National Forest.

The Charley Project hosts pages for each of these women.

Checkbook cover and felt mouse. Zippo lighter. Gold-plated hair clip.

Sharleen Bosler is dead. So is Katrinka McLaren. They each encountered kind Nadia. And Bonnie Hargreaves—she encountered Norma Diefenbacher, too.

Something . . . no, lots of things are clicking inside me.

It's a golden Monday morning, but I can't think about anything else except these women. The fence guys are finishing out back, and Mom has fried bacon and brewed coffee, and I smell it all, and yet . . . these women. No zits on my face, Mom's black jeans fit, and yet . . . these women.

On the paper for the gold locket, Nadia noted that Patricia Kirby had left that apartment to live with her friend Norma. Patricia and her son, Joshua, have been missing since 1993. What if Patricia Kirby changed her name to Nadia Denham and then changed Josh's name to . . . *Dexter*?

Ohmigod. No. Just no . . . maybe?

And Sarah Park, where is she?

I pace the living room, trying to think of ways to confirm that Sarah Park is well in South Korea, that she's still on this globe upright and alive.

Park is the third most common name in South Korea—that's millions of people. But only one Sarah Park owned a curiosities shop in South Los Angeles. According to Anna, Sarah's brother called, but he hadn't spoken much English. And I don't speak a lick of Korean that isn't a delicious menu item. Who knows Korean? Who has also spoken to Sarah's brother? Who won't think any of this is completely bonkers?

Mr. Kim gapes at me as I stand before him. Completely bonkers. But as I explain the reasons I've come, his face relaxes. "Yes, good. I'll do whatever you need," he says, stepping back to let me enter. The shop smells of cigarettes and shaved metal. So does Mr. Kim.

I toss a look behind me. Beautiful Things is open. Riley energetically leads an old woman to the table of journals. I duck some to keep her from spotting me—stupid thing to do since there's no place to hide. Stupid thing to do since she doesn't own this plaza.

A Korean-language soap opera plays on an iPad on Mr. Kim's desk. Keys hang from mounts on the walls—skeleton, flat steel, antiques. Towers of doorknobs, padlocks, and deadbolts are stacked in cubbies, and a safe as tall as me and four times heavier hunkers near the entrance.

South Korea is seventeen hours ahead of California, so it's a little after nine in the morning there. "It's fine, it's fine," Mr. Kim says, flicking his hand. He offers me the guest chair as he settles behind his desk.

I dial the number and press "Record" on my digital recorder.

After that weird transcontinental ringing, the phone clicks and a man says, "Anyou?"

Mr. Kim offers a greeting, then picks up the script I've prepared for him.

Is Sarah there? If yes: *May I speak with her?* If no: *Will she be home soon?* I've listed close to fifty questions, but the conversation between the two men is quick. Less than two minutes pass, and Mr. Kim pales as he hands me the phone.

With the digital recorder still rolling, I ask, "So what did he say?"

Mr. Kim's hands are shaking. "Jun, her brother, says Sarah isn't there. He says he talked to her last when she went to a convention in Reno almost forty years ago."

"Reno?" The Sarah Park on the Charley Project was last seen in Reno. "Did she grow up in Garden Grove?" I ask, sounding thin.

Mr. Kim says, "Buam-dong. In Seoul."

Okay, so not Sarah Park of Beautiful Things. Coincidence?

I stare at the timer on my recorder. There's more to this. A man's hands don't shake just because someone isn't at a place to answer a phone call. "Is she still alive?"

"She never returned to South Korea. She didn't know their father was sick because Jun never spoke to her to tell her."

I shake my head. "Nadia said that she went over because of the mother—"

"Sarah's mother died giving birth to Jun."

A shadow obscures the window next to Mr. Kim's desk.

I startle and duck.

A man's face is pressed against the dirty glass. Muffled, he shouts, "You open?"

I exhale and unclench my hands from the arms of the chair.

Mr. Kim shouts, "Thirty minutes," to his customer.

Sunlight returns as the man shuffles toward Anna's Place.

I sit back up in the chair. "Sorry. It's been crazy."

"Yes, crazy." Mr. Kim touches his heart. "This is not okay. I called about Sarah a long time ago, but the police never believed me. *Never.*"

"Do you remember anyone at the store named Norma?"

Mr. Kim nods. "I didn't like her. She came here after Joaquín disappeared. And I . . ." His Adam's apple bobs. "I left you the note so that you could find Joaquín."

My mouth pops open, then closes. "I tried calling you that day and came over a few times. Why did you want me to find him? Why have you avoided talking to me about any of this?"

"Because you are a little . . . What's the word?"

"Inquisitive?"

"In Korean, we say 'koga keun.'"

"Is that 'curious'?"

"Nosy."

"Ah." My face burns and I'm at a loss for words.

"Joaquín, I know Norma killed him. She told me that Sarah hired her—"

"But—"

"Sarah *did* hire, but . . . I call the police on that woman."

"Why?"

"A feeling, that is all. But that is everything. Feeling, sometimes, is all we have."

Mr. Kim and I peer across the breezeway at Beautiful Things. Mrs. Fleckenstein swans into the shop wearing a gold-sequined duster. She carries a small white dog in her arms.

"Norma Diefenbacher disappeared," Mr. Kim whispers. "She disappeared, and Nadia came. I talked to Sarah, and she told me that Norma had scared her. Nadia acted nice with Sarah, but she wasn't nice to me. Sarah knew that and wanted Nadia gone. But she didn't know how to make Nadia leave."

A teardrop slides down the old man's face. "I called the police again, but they told me to stay out of people's business. They told me that they would contact immigration if I kept calling." He swipes the tear, then exhales. "So I gave up and I stayed away. But I know in my heart . . . I know Nadia killed Sarah."

48.

I don't want to believe this.

"You did not know Nadia," Mr. Kim says to me. "And you did not know Sarah. You know nothing."

"You're right," I admit. "And I wish . . ." Where to even start with my wishing? "I'm so sorry. I hate myself right now for pulling you into this adventure."

The old man swipes his sweaty upper lip. "I've been on this adventure long before you arrived, Miss Lambert." As soon as he walks me to the shop's front door, he lights a cigarette. The muscles in his face relax as nicotine swirls through his veins.

I thank him and say, "I'm gonna figure it out, okay? I think we're close to . . . it, and Detective Winchester, I'm telling him everything and he's smart. So . . ." My throat feels raw.

So . . . what? Stay safe? From whom?

Not Nadia anymore because she's dead.

Norma Diefenbacher a.k.a. the Dashing Devil—she's haunting Southern California right now. She's hunting Southern California right now. She is successful because the bodies of two dead women bear her signature.

I enter Beautiful Things. I want my left-behind jacket and the power cord to my laptop computer. The stool at the register is empty.

On the counter, there's a half-full water bottle, an open bag of potato chips, and the swollen ledger.

Did Mrs. Fleckenstein and her little dog already leave? Where's Riley?

My phone vibrates in my hand.

Texts from Detective Winchester.

Got your earlier message about Bonnie

Thanks also

Good news on that DNA

Two cold cases tied to Norma D.

You helped in that

Grateful

My brain scrambles for an appropriate response. There's so much to say, so much to ask, like: Who are those two related cold case victims? But my words don't work, and I can only tap:

I'm at the store now

I stick my phone in one jacket pocket, and in the other, I press "Record" on my digital recorder. I shout, "Hello?" as I wander back to the office. "Riley?"

No answer.

Back at the project table, the last artifact I worked on—the heart locket from Patricia Kirby—sits alongside its note. I'm so close to finishing, so close to understanding. But no closer to determining the origins of that fountain pen or that earring or the *Storms don't last forever* key chain. My eyes scan each note, and something clicks that I didn't notice before.

The music box was acquired on September 3.

The hair clip was acquired on December 3.

The kaleidoscope . . . June 3.

The felt mouse and checkbook . . . April 3.

Why the third of the month?

Was that a day that Nadia, who suffered from a memory disorder, just decided to use? Or was that a day in the month that *an event* occurred?

I pull my power cord from the wall outlet and pluck my jacket from the back of the chair, and that's when I remember: Nadia said something to me during our short visit together. *Sarah's spirit surrounds this place. In some ways, she never left. In every way, she's still here.*

Those words cannot be taken literally. Those words were simply a metaphor, new-age hokum. But what if Norma Diefenbacher and younger, trailer-park-drifter Nadia *did* steal the store from Sarah like Mr. Kim alleges? What if Norma killed Sarah and . . . Where would she leave Sarah?

No better place to hide a body than a shop crammed with boxes filled with old things.

A month ago, Nadia walked me around the shop, proud to show off her vast collection. From the butterfly cases and jukeboxes on the first floor to the boxed-up treasures in the basement. White powder was scattered on the floor near the corner.

"Rat poison," Nadia said.

There'd also been a steamer trunk covered in yellowing plastic.

And now, I stand over that trunk. The old fitness bike still sits to the right, and an old cabinet filled with yellowed apothecary bottles still sits to the left. I poke the trunk's plastic, old and stained brown, with my foot. No pellets of rat poop in the white powder. No gnawed corners or holes. No stink of urine. There's another smell, though, and I don't know that smell. The faint breeze that rustles the hair on my neck carries that smell.

"Why are you here?"

Startled, I try to spin around, but I lose my balance first and fall back over the plastic-covered steamer trunk. My hands knock over something hard. My fingers scramble over something soft.

Riley stands at the bottom of the staircase. Her face is hidden in shadow. "Are you stupid? I told you—"

"Dexter," I say, struggling to sit up but failing. The white powder slips against my palms and makes it impossible to find stability. "He asked . . . that I . . ."

"Did I leave the door unlocked?" With hard, flat eyes, she inches closer to me.

"I do it all the time." I try to smile as I hold out my hand. "A little help?"

She lifts her sneaker and pushes me back against the plastic with a kick. Her skin is pale and ghostly. Scratches are healing on her cheek. When did she get those?

My heart bangs in my chest but does nothing to push away her foot. "What are you . . . ? Let me up."

"Why are you down here?" Riley presses her foot against my chest. She wants to break me in half.

I try to wiggle away, try to kick her off, but I'm breathing that white powder—*not arsenic, it's lime*—and I'm slipping into the crevice between the bike and the steamer trunk.

"I told Nadia this was a bad idea," Riley says. "I knew that you'd try to mess up everything she's built. I told her that I'd work on her scrapbook, that I knew her more than a stranger. But that disease ruined her mind, destroyed her judgment."

Electricity razzes through my body. I can't think. I can only sweat, swat, and scream. And who is that woman screaming? She doesn't sound like me. But she is me.

Riley is standing nearly on top of my chest. Her face is twisted, and glee dances in her black shark eyes. She hasn't raised her voice. She isn't panting. All the noise comes from me and the old plastic crackling beneath my body.

The powder starts its slow sizzle against my sweaty palms. "I don't . . . I'm not trying . . ." I sputter like I'm drowning, but no water is filling my lungs. "I was just looking . . . looking . . ."

She reaches into her back pocket and brings forth a bungee cord and a plastic bag. She slips the cord over my left wrist, which is now wedged alongside me in the crevice. "I think I'll keep you down here with the other one."

The *other* one?

She stretches the cord across my torso to lasso my right hand.

I try to kick but I'm stuck, and I can't breathe, and any minute now, my heart is gonna . . .

"What the *hell*?"

IT IS
DECIDEDLY SO

49.

Dexter stands over me. He's jostling my arms and lightly slapping my face. His whiskey-colored eyes are filled with worry. The locket around his neck dangles and sways like a hypnotist's watch. The air around me is loose, and there's plenty of light. Elvis smiles down at me . . . from the concert poster taped to the ceiling.

I'm still in Beautiful Things.

I try to sit up. My abdomen hurts, and my hands burn and tingle. "Riley tried to—" I cough into my shoulder, and my lungs punch at my ribs. My stinging palms are strawberry colored. "Where is she?" I scan the room.

Riley stands near the staircase banister.

I point at her as I struggle to my feet. "You were trying to kill me."

Dexter says, "Whoa. Hold up."

My limbs burn as I launch myself across the basement. "You tried to kill me!"

Dexter grabs me by the waist and swings me around. "Stop! Just wait a minute."

I buck in Dexter's hold. "Call the police. She tried to kill me."

Riley rolls her eyes and folds her arms.

"Why isn't she tied up or something?" I demand, wild eyed. "You're working with her."

Dexter shakes his head. "You've completely lost it, and *you're* the one who's going to jail. *You* can't steal from me and expect me to look the other way."

"What?" I screech.

He holds up Nadia's ruby pendant necklace. "I found it in the trunk of your car."

Millions of invisible ants are now marching across my skin. "What are you talking about? I've seen that necklace exactly one time—"

"See?" Riley says. "Told you she'd say that."

"I didn't know where it was," I explain. "I wasn't here to take it when she died. I didn't see it around the store; nor did I see it upstairs in her apartment."

Dexter folds his arms. "What were you doing in my mother's apartment?"

"We *know* what she was doing in Nadia's apartment," Riley says, chin high.

"Ohmigod, to use the bathroom." I chuckle. This is a joke. Has to be.

Dexter slips the necklace into his pocket. "Keep laughing. I'm glad Riley stopped your ass. I didn't believe her when she told me that you were a thief. And here we are."

I gape at him, and then I gape at Riley. "You're serious?"

"Am I laughing?"

"Dexter," I say, "you *know* me."

He pushes up the sleeves of his black Henley. "Why? Because we slept together?"

"I'm not a thief," I say. "I don't need to steal. I don't need any of this shit. I came down to the basement because Sarah Park—"

"Do *not* change the subject." The vein in the middle of his forehead throbs. "I won't press charges against you for stealing—"

"I didn't steal—"

"If you won't press charges against Riley for—"

"I didn't—"

"Assaulting you."

"But that's only because she stole from you, Dexter," Riley says.

I point at her. "You told me that you told Nadia hiring me was a bad idea."

She waggles a finger at Dexter. "And I was right."

Still pointing, I take a step in her direction. "You said I'd destroy everything."

"Again," she says to Dexter, arms out. "I knew something was up. She's always on her phone, always disappearing to her car. And now we know why—she's stealing *your* stuff. *Destroying* everything, just like I said."

I shake my head so fast that I make myself dizzy. "You said that you were gonna keep me down here—"

"Why are we listening to her?" Riley shouts. "I change my mind. I'm pressing charges."

Dexter is staring at me now.

"She said that she was gonna keep me down there with the other one."

He asks, "What other one?"

"Sarah Park." My gut lifts—the nausea is gone now that I've said her name. I point to the trunk and to the bike. "She said it when I was trapped over there and—"

A smile plays at the edges of his lips.

I blink at him. "What?"

"You're looking for Sarah Park."

I nod.

"You find her?"

"Riley stopped me before I . . ."

"So *now* you're accusing my mother of killing someone she loved?" Any humor he had is gone.

"Dexter," I say, hands up. "I . . . I . . ."

"Admit that you stole Mom's necklace, and I'll drop it," he says. "You will then get out of my shop."

I square my shoulders. "I didn't steal anything."

"Why was her necklace in your car?" he asks.

"Because Riley put it there. She probably stole my keys when I was at Anna's. Ask her why she had a bungee cord and a plastic—"

"I'm shipping a few things," Riley says, "and really, it's none of your business."

"Your mother," I whisper. "*She* had a plastic bag just like the one—"

"And she stole our collector's edition of *Anna Karenina*," Riley blurts. "It's in her bag up in the office."

"Why the hell are you going through my purse?" I demand.

"You stole a book, *too*?" Dexter screams.

"Your mother sold it to me."

How did the book get in my purse? I saw it last . . . last . . . I don't remember.

"For how much?" Dexter asks.

"I only had a five-dollar bill—"

"She sold you a book worth a cool grand for five dollars?" Riley asks.

"Yes," I shout. "On my first day here."

Dexter holds out his hand. "Receipt?"

My face warms. "She didn't give me a receipt."

"See?" Riley says to him. "Once again . . ."

I open my mouth to protest, but Dexter holds up a hand. "Leave. Now."

The edges of my vision dim, and I stay put because I cannot see.

"If you aren't out of my store by the time I count to twenty—"

I stand there, defiant. "You asked me to come here."

"And now I'm telling you to leave. You're trespassing. And I'm sure your boss wouldn't want me blasting to the world that his *ex-girlfriend* tried to steal from a dead client."

His mention of Christopher loosens my feet. I rush up the stairs to the office.

Dexter follows me.

I grab my jacket and the power cords from the back counter. "Your mother died with a plastic bag and bungee cord over her head. Just like the bag that Riley—"

"Six . . . seven . . ."

"Is this a joke?" I whisper to him. "Are you doing this for show? You know what's going on, don't you? You know I wouldn't—"

"Fifteen, sixteen—"

I throw one last look into the office. The hedgehog key chain, the crocheted baby shoes, the map with pushpins on the edges of North America . . . "Ask Detective Winchester about the fingerprints he found on your mother's bag."

"Nineteen," he says.

I hurry back through the shop and rush out into the cool air and the dying light. It's my second time in twenty-four hours to be thrown out and into the tired-looking breezeway of this decrepit shopping plaza.

Dexter skulks in the doorway.

"I didn't steal the necklace," I shout. "And your mother sold me the book."

His face is petrified oak.

"Riley tried to kill me," I tell him. "Because I'm finding things out. Because she knows that your mom knew the Dashing Devil—"

His eyebrow lifts. Is he listening? Is he weighing my words against Riley's? But then the veil drops back over his eyes, and he steps into the store. The door slams behind him. The plaza settles into fitful silence, and I am glad to be outside in the cold. I am glad to be standing beneath a sky that swirls with crows and a police helicopter, and my heart is clanging, and those crows are swooping lower, and I press my fingers against my eyelids to think . . .

Wait . . .

The recording.

50.

Silver fog rolls in from the west and hides the golds of the sun. Fog tries to disappear the bulldozers and crane, but the yellow refuses to completely vanish. Music drifts from the RV community. Men talk bullshit, but I can no longer see their faces. I've slathered Vaseline from an ancient tub left in the glove compartment on my injured hands. They're now protected in the pair of archiving gloves I keep in my bag. I sit in my car with my digital recorder and ignore the dull thuds booming in my head, my chest, and my shoulders. I cannot delay.

Nadia's strong voice fills the quiet of the Benz's cabin. I close my eyes and see myself following her through Beautiful Things.

The store's very first collectible. I didn't acquire it. The original owner of the shop found it back in the late seventies.

The few cars that park here pull out of their spaces and leave the plaza. The sun's light is a mere glow, a hint that a single fiery ball sustains life here.

Well, here it is. And now, it's yours. From me to you.

My eyes snap open. Here's the recorded transaction between Nadia and me during our one and only meeting.

You have a dollar? she'd asked me. I'd had only a five. *Sold!* And she took my money. Here was my proof!

In some ways, she never left. In every way, she's still here. That's what Nadia said, too.

My heart races in my chest. I knew that she sold it to me, but there's something perplexing about gaslighting. I will share this recording with Dexter—

He leaves the store and jumps into his Jeep parked at the curb. Lights still shine in the shop, and the sandwich board remains in the breezeway.

Riley is a liar. But there's something worse than her lies. Why did she set me up? What has she told Dexter?

If Riley leaves, I will follow her. If she stays, then I will return to the store, this time with my Taser in one coat pocket and the can of Mace in the other. Most importantly, I will have the recorder, the one I paid too much money for but that picks up the most delicate sounds and saves those sounds in the Memory Bank cloud. Because something is happening here, and whatever it is, it's bad and I will find out.

At six o'clock, I am still sitting in the Santa Barbara Plaza parking lot.

Mr. Kim has left his shop. Anna's Place is empty. My stomach growls at the thought of eating one of Anna's grilled cheese sandwiches, chomping french fries coated in seasoned salt, and slurping Diet Cokes strong enough to resurrect the dead.

I send two last text messages and then leave my car. My legs are strong, but I want to vomit. Before I step into the store, I press "Record" on the device in one pocket and touch the trigger of the Taser in the other. I slowly open the door to keep the bell above it from ringing. No one stands at the register. Riley's canned energy drink sits near the register and her laptop.

Websleuths's Dashing Devil forum blinks on the screen.

On Thursday, November 21, the Dashing Devil left this earth. After leaving twenty bodies over almost fifty years across the country—

Upstairs in Nadia's apartment, someone flushes a toilet.

I sneak over to hide behind the journals table.

The lights in the store pop off.

I am dunked in darkness. There isn't much light shining from the laptop. There isn't much light reaching past those thick cranberry curtains.

Riley eases down the stairs, humming as she limps back to the register. I can hear her glugging and the can clinking against the counter. Her face glows blue as her fingers fly across the keyboard.

I stand, not speaking, just watching her. Once she's done typing, I say, "Great trick."

She hops off the stool and spins around to find me in the gloom. Her eyes bulge in the laptop's glow.

I smile. "Accusing me of stealing that book and the ruby necklace. Great trick."

"You should go." She closes the computer—no light at all now. There's a slight quaver in her voice. I've caught her off guard.

"Nope," I say. "I wanna stay and visit." I slip away from my spot, my own hands out to feel through the shadows.

"I'm warning you . . . You don't know who you're fucking with."

"Then tell me: Who am I fucking with? Use lots of adjectives."

She doesn't speak.

"I'm waiting," I say. "Tell me. Now's your big moment. Who are you? Another keyboard gladiator? Another internet geek? Are you gonna cast a spell? Do some special melee attack? Or do you only *follow* monsters like the Dashing Devil, who actually, you know, *kill* people?"

Her jeans' pocket lights up—her phone has just alerted. She steps around the counter.

I take one step back and bump against a cabinet. The crap inside it rattles.

"And how do you know I haven't killed people?" She takes a step in my direction.

"You have delicate-looking wrists." I watch the light in her pocket until it blinks off.

Riley snorts. "The Dashing Devil trained me to take her place and to collect more beautiful things." Another step toward me. She grabs something that scrapes across the wood. A knife? A letter opener? It could be *anything* in this store.

I say, "Winchester is on his way. I texted him and I texted Dexter before I walked back into this hellhole. He's gonna hear Nadia selling me the book because I recorded her just like I'm recording you right now. Sarah Park is down in that basement. I know it and you know it."

Riley doesn't speak.

Where did she go?

A silhouette moves against the curtains. A shadow lurks near the register.

Which shape is true?

"Nadia killed Sarah," I say.

"*Nadia* didn't kill her." She's on the left side of the room, still near the register.

Hand out, I creep in the opposite direction. Belts . . . books . . .

"Riley," I say, "is Norma Diefenbacher related to Nadia?"

"How do you know her name?" Riley's close now, but her voice is coming from the other side of where I'm standing.

I grip the Taser.

"You said you're recording me right now?" she asks. "Where's the camera?"

I bump against a stand, and it wobbles and sends whatever it holds clanking to the floor.

"Show me," she says.

"You'll go to jail. You'll get the death penalty."

"I hope so," she says, closer. "I'm the only one she told. I wish she hadn't. Too late."

"What did she tell you? Who is 'she'? Norma?"

"I'd had a similar idea as you," she says, "and I told her, blurted it just so that I got to live, and she said that we could make so much money. She promised that we'd be just like the Zodiac, but even better because we were women. No one would know if the Dashing Devil was dead or alive. Take more women, and then everyone would see the 'DD' and it would be just like old times. But then, she forgot all that. She forgot that and she chose you instead."

"Where is she?" My mind screams and I can barely hear myself.

"She left me out. Replaced me with you, and she wanted to get right with God before . . ."

"Before what?" The floorboards beneath my feet creak and give away my position. I stop walking. Sweep my hand before me. Glass. Round. Cold. What *is* that? Where am I?

"No one cares about the whores and Blacks and the women men kill," she says. "Name one dead woman."

My mind whirls—none of the names of Ted Bundy's victims come to me. None of Gacy's, Rader's, Dahmer's . . . I know the name "Steffanie Minsky" only because she was a job to me. I wouldn't have known about her floral-decal Beetle. I wouldn't have known about her smoking habit or that she'd dropped out of high school.

"No one knows my mother's name," Riley says, sounding broken. "No one cares that she made incredible art and that she liked root beer candy. No one knows she made kaleidoscope necklaces and that she promised to give me the one she used to wear. Norma took my mother

393

from me, and she took that necklace from her, but she kept me and called me a new name, and she called me 'daughter,' and she tried to make it up to me even though she's the one . . ."

The mini kaleidoscope—artifact number three in Nadia's memory bank.

"Shawn Eckert," I whisper. "I know her name. Riley, what's your real name?"

"I didn't want to," she whimpers. "Not at first, but she threatened me, told me that she would kill me like she killed my mom, and I had to, and now . . . now people are gonna remember me. And I forgive you."

"Forgive me? For what?"

"For stealing Norma away from me."

"I didn't steal—"

"You can work with me. Say yes." Riley sounds closer now. "I can make you say yes. I didn't want to, but I had to . . . to survive. I just wanted her to love me. Like she was starting to love you. So say yes. Say yes to survive, too."

I move away from her voice. "You lied about me stealing that necklace. You lied about me stealing the book. And I know you're lying about being a killer—" I step on something that splinters, and I lose my balance. I catch myself before falling.

"I tried to scare you away," she says. "I sent you text messages and you kept blocking me. I watched you from the park sometimes, but then I went inside . . .

"You drink vanilla lattes," she whispers. "There's a Magic 8 Ball by your bed. You sometimes forget to lock the door to your apartment above your parents' garage. Your bedroom window screen is now laying in the yard."

I gasp. The wind didn't rip the screen off the window. Michael Anthony didn't leave the iced coffee on the countertop. He didn't leave the refrigerator door open. He didn't text me, either. I shudder again in the silence.

Too much silence.

I am listening for her—no heavy breathing, no creaking shoes . . .

"Allison Cagle. Chloe Kurtz." Riley's voice crumples, but she shakes it off to say, "And Nadia Denham. Those are mine." She sounds . . . low. Her voice feels like it's hitting my knees. "My name is Cheyenne. My mother called me—"

My phone vibrates from my coat pocket.

She lunges at me.

I scramble to the other side of a table and smack into another table. Pain zings through my hip and stops me for a second.

She pushes over that table. The old journals spill across the floor.

I back into something hard—a big glass case.

She tramples over the books to reach me.

Close enough.

I shriek as I whip the Taser from my pocket and press the trigger.

Electricity shoots through the air, and fifty thousand volts pulse through Riley's body. For five seconds, her body jerks like a fish on land as she falls to the floor. I smell urine as her bladder releases. I use my phone's flashlight. She's as still as the butterflies pinned in their glass case.

Shaking, I stand over her, Taser out, ready to shoot again if she reaches for me. My own pulse bangs around my body, and I stand like that for hours, days, as the darkness outside turns bleaker, waiting . . . waiting . . .

51.

I don't move, even as the wails of sirens speed closer, scream louder. I don't move, even as people crowd me and a pair of strong hands wrap around mine to pry the Taser from my gloved grip.

Detective Winchester snaps his fingers in front of my face. His lips are moving but . . .

"Who called?" I ask, my voice far-flung, my gaze trapped in the space between his head and his shoulder.

"You did," he says. "You don't remember?"

I blink. I'm sitting in the front seat of a squad car. I glare at the police radio, willing it to stop squawking. It doesn't. I stare at my injured hands still hidden in those white gloves, willing them to stop shaking. They don't. Even out in the open, the world feels like a looking glass. Another me, at another plaza, in another world. In both worlds, lightning flashes across the sky and brightens the heavens. Or hell.

Detective Winchester convinces me that Riley is alive and on her way to jail.

Ice forms in my belly. I can't believe him.

"Trust me," he says.

"Why?" I ask.

He's listened to my recording.

That's another thing I don't remember, giving him my digital recorder.

Beams of light skip all around the insides of Beautiful Things.

Sarah Park is in that steamer trunk.

There's no other place she can be.

52.

Over three days, Riley Eckert is booked and indicted for trying to kill me, and for the murders of Allison Cagle, Chloe Kurtz, and Nadia Denham. Every time I think about my life ending because of that curiosities shop at 111 Marlton Road, my entire body shakes. I'm a smoothie on the inside because I think about Beautiful Things a lot.

Riley's taped confession may not be admissible in court. But then, her fingerprints are all over that bag found over Nadia's head. The district attorney knows about her account at Websleuths and the Dashing Devil forum. The district attorney tells me that Riley wrote posts about Allison and Chloe—and Allison's emerald nose stud and Chloe's *Storms Don't Last Forever* key chain were found on the project table in Nadia's office. The fountain pen remains a mystery. Who is the poor woman who loved that pen?

Though Riley won't solve those mysteries, she's admitted that she forced Nadia to write the suicide note, but only after Nadia told her that she wanted to die. Riley didn't know that Nadia had already written an earlier note and hidden it beneath that blue pinafore she wore as she lay dying.

If only Riley had waited . . .

Over those three days, my phone battery cannot keep a charge because of the constant calls and text messages.

Will you talk to us?

Could you tell us what happened at that store?

We will pay you if you share your story

When the time is right, I will talk. Now, though, it's time to sleep, to drink Hemingways with Imani and Sasha as we coo over Sasha's new Egyptian towel sets and the espresso maker. It's time to eat takeout Thai food with my parents and stream strange German sci-fi TV series.

I'm in New York, Christopher texts. What the hell happened?

I'll tell you in person

I'll be here all week

Then you'll just have to wait

Dexter has also texted, but I haven't responded more than I'm fine. He didn't believe me. He accused me of lying and stealing. And I was right about Sarah Park being killed and left in that steamer trunk. For almost forty years, his mother moved around a shop she'd stolen and pretended that Sarah had actually returned to her family and friends.

"Riley is pleading insanity," Uncle Bryan tells me over the phone. "Norma Diefenbacher kidnapped her after killing Riley's mother. What little girl *wouldn't* snap?"

It is five in the evening by the time I pull into the Santa Barbara Plaza parking lot. After this stop, I will start my Christmas shopping at the mall across the street. The heavy rain has lightened to a sprinkle. The lights are still on in Pepper's salon and Mr. Kim's key shop. Beautiful Things is closed and so is Anna's Place. I came to also check in on Anna, but serial murders and bodies in basements haven't helped her already-fragile state of mind.

The news vans with their live feeds and coiffed field reporters have all gone. Almost all the RVs have shambled to some new location in the city, and construction equipment inches closer to the last two campers that remain. Shadows move behind those dirty glass windows and tattered curtains. People are still living inside those mobile homes. Someone is still riding the scruffy orange bicycle latched to the mini-Winnie's bumper. Someone is still resting in that ripped leather recliner.

My phone vibrates with a text from Dexter.

Almost there

Thanks for agreeing to see me

He wants to apologize in person. He also wants to return *Anna Karenina*. I may have paid only five dollars for it, but the book belongs to me.

An old station wagon is parked near the bulldozers. I know this car. Nadia's best friend was driving it on my first visit here. Esther Little-Linton-Lyden. Or was that another alias used by Norma Diefenbacher?

I climb out of my car. The denim in Mom's jeans and the wool of her sweater are thick and bulky and protect me from the cold. The city's night-song plays loud tonight—hundreds of car tires splashing through rain puddles, the faraway cries and whirs of ambulance and fire truck sirens, the squawk of the order box at the Taco Bell across the street.

Does Detective Winchester know about this station wagon? That it's parked here? Where has it been all this time? It may hold some very important clues.

I hurry over to the station wagon. Inside, I see an open box of black trash bags, a flashlight, and a black jacket. The carpet and windows are spotless. I drift to the rear of the wagon and spot near the RVs . . .

That Buick!

This is the car that chased me through the streets of LA that night.

This is the car that prowled my street and parked near my house.

This car belongs to the man who left notes at my door and accosted me at the coffee . . .

This Buick belongs to—

The air is knocked from my back and explodes from my mouth.

Someone grabs me around the waist.

I try to fight and spin around, but I can't.

A hard, calloused hand clamps across my mouth.

I twist my neck and see some of his face.

Tawny. Scarred . . .

His hard eyes bore into mine. The whites of his eyes are bloodshot. His irises are . . . blue.

He says, "You Angie."

He's here. Michael Anthony is here. It is happening. The worst is happening.

My face burns from his hand, but my arm burns more.

"Why are you—" I try to push away from him. "Let me go!"

I smell beer . . . and must . . . and damp hair . . . My perfume, my fear—I smell that, too. My shoulder . . . Something is happening . . . I see . . . Can't understand . . . I look down . . .

"I never wanted you," he mutters. "You took my Angie away from me."

His right hand is moving against me . . . Not punching me but . . . pinching me with . . . There is silver, and then silver turns red . . .

A knife. He has a knife.

The red is . . . blood. My blood. I scream.

"You took her, you took her." He's stabbing me and whispering, "Angie. Angie. Angie."

I scream until my cries become rasps. My heart booms in my chest. It will stop any minute . . . I feel burning.

"I made you, I made you, you mine." He keeps stabbing me.

I bite down on the hand clamped against my mouth and rock against him. I do not know—am I standing? Are we on the ground?

He killed my mother. He will kill me.

No, no, no.

He keeps saying, *Angie. Angie. Angie.* Then he cries, "She ain't here cuz of you. I'm dead already cuz of you, and you gotta die, too, cuz we family."

I cannot die.

I bite down on his hand again as hard as I can.

He jerks away from me.

I scramble backward, crab-walking on asphalt slick with blood. "No, stop!"

He lunges to grab my ankle. "You belong to me."

"No!" I kick him in the face with my free foot.

The knife clatters to the ground.

I scramble forward and grab it.

He falls on top of me. His hand wraps around my neck. "Ain't nobody coming for you. Where that bitch now? She look like Angie— she ain't." His hands tighten around my neck.

With my left hand, I push against his face. With my right hand, the one gripping the slippery knife, I plunge the blade into his temple.

He screams.

I pull out the knife and aim toward his temple again.

The knife sinks into his eye.

His screams sharpen, and he rolls off me and onto the asphalt. He is clutching his face and he is saying her name.

Angie. Angie. Angie. A prayer. A mantra. A curse.

I have been fighting forever.

So quiet out here even as he's trying to kill me and screaming *Angie* and . . .

He is quiet now. Her name no longer trips off his tongue.

Flames burn all around my body.

Michael Anthony lies on the asphalt slick with blood—his blood, my blood. He never said my name, not once. I am no one to him—just a possession, just a ghost of the woman he needed to kill again.

Are my eyes open or closed?

I don't know.

The sun has come out, though. The sky is lighter. Brightness surrounds me.

I can hear music . . . "Claire de Lune" . . .

I have been fighting forever.

The music has stopped now.

All is quiet.

I will . . . close my eyes . . . just for a minute . . . rest . . . but just for . . .

Forever.

53.

Tubes.
    Beeping machines.
    A television high on a wall.
    Mom.
    Dad.
    A vase of pink roses.
    A vase of white lilies.
    A vase of . . .

◆ ◆ ◆

Mom has not left my hospital bedside.

Though I was not awake, I know for a fact that she stood beside the surgeon as he stitched me up. That afterward, she visited God and demanded that he let me live. And then, after he agreed, she took her place beside me in the ICU.

Every time my hundred-pound eyelids open, she is there. Sometimes with Daddy, sometimes with Uncle Bryan, sometimes alone.

She holds my hand. Pats my hand. Squeezes my hand.

When fire crackles across my body, she does a magic trick and fills my veins with ice.

She is that ice queen from *Frozen*. What's her name?

My eyes are open.

Mom is not here.

My pulse jumps.

I squirm in bed.

"It's okay." Dad stands over me now and strokes my forehead. "It's okay."

"Mom . . . ," I croak.

"She's sleeping—she needed to rest. But I'm here, Mouse."

I try to nod but my neck aches. "How did he know I was there?"

"Guess he saw you once. He had friends living in those RVs over at the plaza."

Terror creeps past my meds. How long was he watching and waiting?

"You're not alone," Dad says. "I'm here. Just rest."

The world goes soft again. But my father is holding my hand. He will not let me slip away. He holds my hand like he did as we swam in the Pacific off Kauai. He holds my hand like he did as we snorkeled with manta rays in Cancun. He holds my hand like he has all my life.

He will never let me slip away . . .

Christopher stands at the foot of my bed. Pebbles of water shine on his jacket.

Mom sits in the chair beside me.

I turn my head. I have a window. This room is quieter. On the television, an episode of *The Golden Girls* plays. Blanche is going through menopause. Back at the window, silver streams down the glass. Rain.

Down at my feet, Christopher says, "Hey, Mickie." He smiles, but his eyes are sad.

I turn to Mom. "Don't leave me." I suck in air—there's fire still burning in my body. My hand holds a pump. My thumb presses . . . Ice, ice, baby . . .

◆　◆　◆

I've been here now for ten days.

Christopher's lilies are now Christopher's violet roses. Dexter stands near the window. He doesn't speak as the orderly removes my lunch tray. Turkey and mashed potatoes. Fa la la la la. Mom sits right outside my room even though I am fully awake, even though I am closer to life now than death, even though Michael Anthony died by my hand in that parking lot. He left me behind with a broken rib, a punctured lung, and twenty stab wounds. Bandages cover everything except for those injuries no one can see.

Detective Winchester has already visited. Official police business. He sat beside me and asked, "What happened?"

Words poured from my mouth, and I cried as I talked. He offered to stop, but I didn't want to. Before he left my room, I blurted, "The station wagon."

"What about it?"

"That's the car Nadia's friend Esther drove. I was looking at it before I saw the Buick."

He pulled a picture from his coat pocket. "Is this the woman you saw?"

Old woman with long red hair and a jaunty fedora . . . "That's her."

He offers me another photograph, this one a tattoo.

"Nadia had that tattoo," I told him. A heart. A pair of dice. *Good Luck.*

Detective Winchester jotted something on his notepad, then said, "Get some rest."

Moments ago, I opened my eyes to see Dexter sitting in that chair.

"You were gonna tell me something," I remind him.

He pales and his head hangs. "Other than how sorry I am?"

"Yes." I want to feel alarm, but the drugs keep me smooth and glassy.

He bites the inside of his cheek. "Josh Kirby: that's my real name. I didn't know that . . ."

My eyebrows crumple, but I'm not surprised. But I don't know why I'm not surprised.

Dexter notices my subdued reaction. "You know that name," he says, nodding.

I say, "Yes," but I can't . . . The memory is there, hummingbird quick, though. It will not stay still long enough . . .

"Patricia Kirby," he says.

"The locket," I remember.

"That was one half. I'm wearing . . ." He lifts the locket from the chain around his neck. "The DNA test I took . . . Nadia is not my biological mother. Patricia Kirby is."

Fear pushes past that anti-anxiety medication, and I sit up in bed. "But Patricia . . . She left Hartford to go live with Norma."

He nods. "And then Norma Diefenbacher killed her. I didn't know that I'd been kidnapped. I was a baby then. Nadia renamed me 'Dexter,' the only name I knew. And Nadia was the only mother I knew. But Patricia . . . That's *her* blood on that knife."

Joshua Kirby—Nadia never said it, but *he* is the most beautiful thing in her collection.

And Norma Diefenbacher's. Her DNA is on the knife, too.

Dexter squeezes the bridge of his nose with a hand that hasn't stopped trembling.

I bite my dry bottom lip and ask, "Did . . . have you . . . do you . . . ?"

"Have I met Norma? Once, a very long time ago—and we didn't meet formally. I was five or six, and I was sleeping in my mom's—in *Nadia's*—room." He blinks and a tear tumbles down his cheek. "I remember waking up. She thought I was asleep, and she undressed . . . Took off her trench coat. Took off her hat . . . and a long, red wig . . . She turned to make sure that I was still asleep, and so I closed my eyes again and . . .

"You saw her once," Dexter continues. "You called her 'Esther Little.' Riley told me that she came around only in the evening, when she thought no one was around. The night you saw her . . . You weren't supposed to see her. She'd been hiding all this time."

"So Esther . . . ?"

"Michaela . . . Esther *is* Norma. Norma's wanted for murders across the country, remember? For killing Patricia—my mother. For kidnapping me. But taking another name, another alias, wasn't enough."

"So?" I asked.

"So . . . when I was old enough to really start paying attention, Norma decided to become someone totally different. Since no one knew her in LA, she didn't have to do much. She didn't need surgery. Didn't even need makeup. Plain smock dresses and clogs and that ruby pendant—that's all she needed to vanish."

"Who told you this?"

"She did," Dexter says. "In that second suicide note that Detective Winchester kept from me, the one I didn't know about." He finds the note on his phone and reads: *I've now lost my mind. I don't want this. Nadia Denham helped me disappear because the entire world ignores plain women. I'm sorry for the pain I caused little Joshua and sweet Cheyenne. I couldn't help myself. They were all so beautiful.*

Dexter swallows, shakes his head "And so, just like that, Norma became someone new. She became my mother. She became Nadia Denham."

April 1, 2020

I cannot finish Mom's memory bank.

In random moments, my vision dims; I cry . . .

Sometimes, my daily dosage of Zoloft helps calm my nerves.

Also, we are all quarantined in California and throughout the world. A new coronavirus has killed more than three hundred people in this state alone. I've had plenty of quiet moments between my tele- medicine visits with my psychiatrist, between pushing through panic attacks, between baking quarantine cookies with my mother. Before we were all ordered by the governor of California and mayor of Los Angeles to stay home, before the courts closed, I gave a deposition in the case of *People of California v. Riley Eckert.*

I want to recover and return to normal, but that is impossible with- out hugs from my girls. Without sharing drinks on a restaurant patio with Sasha and Imani. Virtually, they remain my tonics, but it's not the same.

Christopher reaches out to me every week, and I send courteous responses. But we're done. I remain an employee of the Memory Bank, out on disability.

Michael Anthony's family has tried to reach out to me. They are angry, regretful, snide, warm. From *Why did you have to kill him* and *He'd been through enough* to *I am so sorry* and *He deserves to burn in hell.*

I didn't want to kill him, but what was I supposed to do? Let him kill me?

Mom has asked the Anthonys that question. No one has said yes, but no one has said no, either. Their lack of an answer only adds to my sadness. More than six feet will continue to separate us.

And Michael Anthony—I think of him every time I look at my reflection. I've duct-taped towels to my bathroom and vanity mirrors. When I'm strong enough, when the wounds he gave me pale, I will remove the towels. As for the internal scars? I turn to telemedicine, Zoloft, Anna's peach cobbler, and gumbo on Fridays.

Norma Diefenbacher had several aliases: Dale Forrester (which Riley had adopted), Esther Little, and the one I knew, Nadia Denham. In 1979, she was almost caught. She'd been driving drunk in New Orleans, and police entered her fingerprints into the statewide database. Of course, she never showed up for that hearing. Instead, she fled to California. There, she met Sarah Park—first as Norma, and then, after killing Joaquín Reyes, as Nadia. Then she murdered Sarah and took ownership of Beautiful Things.

Riley, as Dale, murdered Allison Cagle and Chloe Kurtz and planned to kill me, too.

Late at night, after Dexter was asleep or when she was away on her "collecting trips," Norma would ditch those smock dresses and clogs for jaunty hats and designer clothes she found in thrift and consignment shops. She would roam the desert diners or the forest roads wearing Halston to find vulnerable women who figured that a woman dressed to kill would never . . . *kill*. In fact, these trips were her time to do just that.

DNA links Norma Diefenbacher to the murders of:

- Katrinka McLaren, owner of the teakwood music box, hitchhiker across Texas;
- Darla Schoelerman, owner of the hair circle, stranded motorist in Taos;
- Donnamarie Queneau, owner of the cashmere scarf found in Nadia's bag and not included in the memory bank, from New Orleans;
- Shawn Eckert, owner of the mini kaleidoscope, Good Samaritan, and Riley's mom in Oregon;
- Renee and Christina Spiro, owners of the checkbook cover and gray felt mouse, residents of that crummy apartment in Syracuse;
- Joaquín Reyes, the original handyman of Beautiful Things;
- Bonnie Hargreaves, owner of the hedgehog key chain, magazine salesgirl from Fresno;
- Lucia Montez, owner of those dangle earrings and Norma's roommate from Fresno;
- Sarah Park, owner of Beautiful Things;
- Brenda "BB" Barton, owner of the pearlescent pocket pipe in Sky Valley;
- Steffanie "Steffie" Minsky, owner of the Zippo lighter, displaced teen in Vermont;
- Sharleen Bosler, owner of the crocheted baby clothes, in Palm Springs;
- Ernest Macklemore, con and Sharleen's brother, in Palm Springs;
- Patricia Kirby, owner of the gold locket and mother of Joshua in Hartford; and
- Beverly Prescott, owner of the swollen-paged *Recipes* journal, from Galveston.

Left in deserts, steel barrels, dumpsters, channels, burned-out cars, and steamer trunks. "DD" carved into each of their backs.

So I created a memory bank filled with pictures and stories for a serial killer. I fell in love with a music box stolen from a dead woman named Katrinka. I thought of Nadia as a savior and rescuer of desperate women simply because of the stories left for me. These thoughts always threaten to send me into a spiral.

I'm getting better now.

Riley thought by having Norma's body cremated and cleaning the apartment above the store, all DNA would be destroyed. She didn't know that Dexter had already collected spit from Norma's mouth as she slept.

Dexter has reclaimed his true name. Right now, he's driving across the country, returning each item that Norma Diefenbacher stole. He also wants to meet his mother's family in Hartford. Have they moved past their bigotry surrounding Patricia's decision to have the baby of a Black man? Dexter wants to find out. With this pandemic, though, I wonder how far he's gotten.

Once the stay-at-home orders lift, Peter Weller wants me to be his guest at the chef's table at Vista Malibu. Last week, he texted, You helped to make progress possible!

Sasha wants me to go out with her husband's fraternity brother. His name is Justin, and he practices environmental law, has a credit score of 798, and drives a Tesla. He enjoys Christopher Guest movies, hates avocado, and plays the piano. *No drama,* Sasha's promised.

Justin and I have texted. He wanted to video-chat, but I'm not ready for that. Once I can look at myself without wincing, then I'll be ready for a stranger's eyes. For now, I'm cool with us streaming movies at the same time.

Detective Winchester has read my entries in Nadia's memory bank for clues about Norma's movements. He works out of the Dashing Devil task force office and stares at that map of pushpins. Some pins remain and belong to mysterious victims. He knows, though, that each victim most likely died on the third of each month. For Norma Diefenbacher, there was something about that time. What, though?

And how many women did the Dashing Devil kill?

Alzheimer's disease. Norma didn't want to forget all the beautiful things she'd stolen after the murders, and so she came to us at the Memory Bank.

As I now warm up another bowl of Anna's peach cobbler, I remember how I looked forward to curating the collection of a shop owner named Nadia Denham . . .

An elegant name that evokes lovers and dances, spiced teas in fragile cups, and secrets, lots of secrets.

Old ladies keep the best secrets.

And the most horrible ones.

ACKNOWLEDGMENTS

This novel is unlike the others I've written, and it took a village to make it happen. Jill Marsal, as my agent, you've helped me make hard decisions throughout my writing career, and you were the first to champion this story. Thank you for your advice and friendship.

Thank you to Jessica Tribble, my editor at Thomas & Mercer. You "got it" and never thought it was too weird, too twisty, too different to publish. I'm grateful for your trust and enthusiasm. Thank you to my developmental editor, Clarence Haynes. Dude, you have all the words and knew exactly how to help shape mine. Mike Corley, your illustrations transformed my dreams into art, and I thank you. Megha Parekh, Laura Barrett, and everyone at Thomas & Mercer, thank you for your care and excitement. I'm thrilled to be a part of the family.

Kristin Sevick, you may not have edited this one, but its existence came out of working with you over the last eight years. You strengthened my confidence to dare write a story that featured freakin' vignettes. I will always be grateful to you.

Jess Lourey, your support and attagirls mean so much to me. I'm inspired by your journey and encouraged by your success. You deserve all your roses, girl. Kellye Garrett, Naomi Hirahara, Wendy Walker, Alex Segura, and Hank Phillippi Ryan: I've confided in you, raged at the sun and stars with you, and listened to something you told me that changed the course of my career. Thank you for your friendship.

To my readers: your hoorays, buys, and social media posts uplift me, especially over this last year. I'll keep writin' 'em if you keep reading 'em.

To my family: Mom, Dad, Terry, Gretchen, and Jason. Our DNA is sprinkled throughout this book—from the most beautiful memories to the not-so-beautiful. Thank you for letting me write it all down. I love you.

David, this is number nine, and throughout our twenty-six years together, you've helped these stories of mine get twistier and weirder. Thank you for crying, "More! More!" I love you.

Maya Grace, thanks for being you—Mickie is the older Meatz in many ways, and like her, you are my beautiful dolphin. You helped transcribe edits into this manuscript during a pandemic, and I am so proud and thrilled to share this creation process. I love you more than any story ever told.

ABOUT THE AUTHOR

Photo © 2019 Andre Ellis

Rachel Howzell Hall is the author of the *Los Angeles Times* Book Prize–and Lefty Award–nominated *And Now She's Gone*; and the Anthony Award–, Lefty Award–, and International Thriller Writers Award–nominated *They All Fall Down*. She also writes the acclaimed Detective Elouise Norton series, including *Land of Shadows*, *Skies of Ash*, *Trail of Echoes*, and *City of Saviors*. Rachel is also the coauthor of *The Good Sister* with James Patterson, which was included in the *New York Times* bestseller *The Family Lawyer*. She lives in Los Angeles. You can find her at www.rachelhowzell.com and on Twitter @RachelHowzell.